THE MISSING
MARK

THE MISSING MARK

A JOSHUA WALKER NOVEL

AMANU ENSIS

ASHLEY HOUSE PUBLISHERS, LLC

Ashley House Publishers, LLC
A Virginia LLC

Requests for information should be addressed to:
Ashley House Publishers, LLC
2400 Carolina Road
Chesapeake, VA 23322
www.themissingmark.com

The Missing Mark
© 2012 by The Leviticus Trust

ISBN-13: 978-0-9889994-0-4
LCCN: 2013941735

Printed in the United States of America

Trouble creates a capacity to handle it. Meet it as
a friend, for you'll see a lot of it and you had
better be on speaking terms with it.

Oliver Wendell Holmes

And He said to them, "Assuredly, I say to you that
there are some standing here who will not taste death
till they see the kingdom of God present with power."

John Mark for Simon Peter

Dad,

I miss you. I lost you. But I will find you. And once we are reunited, I will never let you go again. It's been a long time, but I still remember you coming all the way to Grand Rapids. And, as I grew up, every time I passed a Burger King.... All those wasted years. I cried every time. Thinking about all the time we've spent apart still makes me cry.

So, in my attempts to find what we've lost all these years, I've learned a lot. About you. About me. About the world we lived in. About the past. And about our future.

And it all started with the extraordinary things that happened to friends of mine. What happened that week changed my life. Forever.

You think you know somebody and then you learn you have no clue.

You think you know a lot about the world around you, and then you learn you know nothing of what is true.

You think you've finally found love, and just then, like that, it gets taken away from you.

Your loving daughter

1

THE FIRST BODY crumpled quickly. A figure covered in black silently appeared where the guard had stood. Just as quietly, it vanished back into the shadows. Eight ghosts moved in concert, an orchestra of precision and skill throughout the heavily protected building. Darkness shrouded the fortified complex as the second and third members of the security force dropped to the marble floors.

The phantoms had breached the granite structure from above. A silent helicopter allowed the team to appear from nowhere, on the rooftop, one by one. The building's head of security had recently been forced to curtail the manned contingent at the top of the six-storied ancient structure in favor of high-tech surveillance and alarms. He had complained about the budget cuts. And he'd warned the owner that even the best electronic security systems can be disabled.

He was right.

It had only taken a few seconds. A highly sophisticated computer was attached to a camera wire. The virus did the rest, traveling through the cable to the monitoring station and shutting down the entire system with a program that mimicked a pod of killer whales after a stranded seal. A moment later a line of professionals snaked through the broken steel door at the roof access. Its heavy deadbolt was now hanging useless from its carriage.

Winding their way down each floor, the team of heavily armed men and women quietly dispatched seven more guards. From the central lobby on the first floor, their leader motioned to the unit to fan out. Their intelligence sources hadn't been able to pinpoint the access to the basement level. Time was running out. They had to find it fast or leave empty handed and fail in their objective.

IT WAS A VIBRATION on everyone's utility belt that told them to stop looking ... then a location, transmitted silently into their comms, spoken by a computer-generated voice heard through subdermal receivers. Eight black-clad figures converged at a small insignificant-looking door in the eastern wall that ran north to south at the end of the building. It was already open, and a sliver of light from a street lamp outside briefly illuminated each soldier disappearing into the aperture. Worn stones, bowed by centuries of foot traffic, led down a tight stairwell. A huge iron gate blocked the entrance into the bottom level.

A wiry man with long, thin fingers moved to the front of the dammed up force. His lanky body folded into a neatly compressed package as he pulled a small cylinder from a holster on his calf. With a few quick motions he assembled other parts from a pack on his thigh, and the blue flame of a powerful blowtorch cut into the darkness.

The leader was watching the numbers count down all too quickly in the middle of the eerie green face of a digital Suunto. The operation was running behind schedule. In less than twelve minutes they needed to be back up in the overcast, early-morning sky. A single bead of sweat streamed down her blackened forehead, falling to the dusty concrete floor. Determination overcame anxiety and her eyes were back on the oxyacetylene flame, willing it to cut faster.

It took two long minutes to take the rustic barrier down. But strong arms heaved it out of the way as soon as the torch finished its work.

The line of bodies sliced into the dampness of a long subterranean hall. Every door was opened as they passed through, every room checked. Powerful flashlights now lit the corridor that connected the windowless rooms. They all had instinctively checked their compass readings on their wrists. The tunnel led back to the center of the building.

Their leader motioned ahead, marking the spot with a white beam of bright halogen light. There was no need to keep checking rooms. A brushed silver glint reflected back the narrow shaft of light. They covered the remaining distance in no time. Two ordnance specialists approached the flanks of the massive vault that sat heavily on granite flagstones like a great beast poised to swallow them all whole. Packs of C4, reliable and easy to carry, were strategically placed. As soon as they finished setting the explosives, the closest room was filled with soldiers all wondering what such a mammoth and modern safe was doing in the basement of a nine-hundred year old building. And how did it get down here anyway?

The blasting caps detonated the plastic explosives and the circular, 18-inch-thick steel door creaked and fell outward into the corridor. Its tonnage cracked the thick granite as it crashed to the floor. Piercing a dark cloud of white dust, a solitary figure darted into the vault and retrieved the prize, handing it off to a Mongol-Dravidian giant of a soldier.

The big black metal case weighed down the bulky soldier. His thick arms hung from substantial shoulders that helped to keep the burden away from his body. Three of the others led the way out, their leader now at the rear. The column moved quickly, almost effortlessly, back up seven flights of stairs.

As they burst out into the warm night air, lines dropped from the strange silence above. Each soldier grabbed a cable and slipped the toe of a combat boot into the metal foothold at the bottom of its length. Rising into the darkness, they disappeared from the rooftop as the sound of sirens filled the streets below.

ABOARD THE SUPER-QUIET Bell Jet Ranger crew-carrier, the leader congratulated the team for a successful mission. She glanced back at her watch: thirty-five seconds to spare.

At that very moment, armed men were flooding into the building below. The crime scene quickly garnered local law enforcement, national police, and even high-ranking members of the military. The scrambled signals of a dozen secure calls started bouncing off a private satellite 22,000 miles overhead.

No one saw the small figure that crept out from his hiding place among the mechanicals atop the violated building. He rolled off the edge of the roof and deftly landed on a narrow cantilever underneath the cornice work. The slightly built man swung himself to a copper down spout and descended it hand by hand to the cobblestone alley that smelled of heavy garlic. Still unnoticed, he slipped into a service entrance carved into the adjacent hotel and paused to catch his breath. He looked at his camera bag and patted the Nikon D3X inside. Certain he had captured the identity of the woman that led the heist, he smiled and hurried away. He had a long trip ahead of him, but with this kind of success to report to his superiors, he wouldn't mind the tedious flight home half a world away.

IN THE BASEMENT of the ancient behemoth, the special investigator was the first to step into the broken vault. The dust from the explosion was still settling as he surveyed the inside of the formidable safe that had failed to protect such a priceless, irreplaceable object.

Alone in the center of the steel floor inside the vault, amidst the white powder from the blast, he noticed a single rectangular parchment. He pulled a rubber glove over his right hand and picked up the ancient vellum. His other hand held his heavy flashlight so that he could read the neat handwriting on the brittle skin. Unmistakably, he was looking at a letter written by a hand long since buried. He knew the vault had contained only one item. The thieves had taken it. But in its place they'd obviously left the antiquated document intentionally. It was a cryptic message: one he knew he'd never personally solve. He put the parchment back where he'd found it. Biting his lip, he spun on his heels and left the burglarized vault.

"Secure the area. Don't let anyone in there." He motioned to the broken door on the floor and beyond to the gaping maw of the huge safe. His command lingered in the air as he marched back down the corridor. He hit the first speed-dial on his phone.

"He needs to get down here," he said. He listened impatiently to the objection he knew would come.

"No. *Personally!*" he was emphatic.

Behind him, alone in the empty vault behind the destroyed door, the vellum parchment begged an answer. It fluttered slightly and turned in the shadows.

ב

HIS FACE WOULD draw you in. His warm smile would win you over. With dark brown eyes he could captivate you. He knew how to look into your soul. But it was his insightful wisdom that made the professor seem much older than he looked. Students at the university made a game of guessing his age. His colleagues didn't know. Dr. Joshua Walker had quickly earned the respect of his peers and students alike. But no one really knew anything about him. Even the administration was unable to verify his *curriculum vitae*. The college of arts and letters in *El Iskandarîya*, Egypt no longer existed. The graduate school in China's Anhui province had been impossible to reach. The dean of U of O's graduate school of history had tried to no avail to contact the first six of an impressive list of highly credentialed references. He'd given up, and in his haste to secure such a well-regarded educator, he'd processed the approval against policy. It was only a visiting professorship, he'd reasoned. By the time the Oregon State Board of Higher Education noticed anything, the issue would be moot.

The dean suffered a few sleepless nights recently though. It had been two years since the hiring was finalized. Sure, the students were thrilled. Professor Walker enjoyed unanimous support from his peers. The administration was very pleased. The University President was the dean's new best friend. Alumni donations were way up, and applications for teaching positions were coming in from all over the world. As for extraordinarily qualified student applications?

Stratospheric.

But it was all the attention his department was getting lately in the press that was worrying the dean. It was Walker's newest project. So unprecedented. CNN. The BBC. Fox News. Reuters. Even *Al Jazeera* had picked up the story and splashed it on screens all across the planet. Just this morning, Atlanta's morning anchor-man reported that Oregon's visiting professor of antiquities was leaving in a week for Europe with five of his graduate students in tow. Now the world waited with nervous anticipation. The dean was sweating. His desk was cluttered with requests from journalists for more information. They were desperate to feed their ratings-hungry, round-the-clock, cable news machine. A couple of aggressive reporters were already on campus asking around. Too much attention was on his visiting professor. There were already too many unanswered questions. Just one more week, he begged God. All of the attention would then shift away from the university and he would be safe. He could stop praying to the God he didn't believe in anyway.

Surely the events in Rome would overshadow the enigmatic background of his superstar professor. Hopefully, no one would find out that there was nothing but a single résumé in his employment file.

Professor Walker quietly surveyed the grounds of the campus he now called home. He enjoyed the Maple trees. He felt at home among the Douglas Fir that dotted the campus. He loved walking the thoroughfares that crisscrossed the university grounds. The old section of the campus that began with Deady Hall in the late 1800's was his favorite. But he also had an affinity for the ugly cement buildings that were strikingly modern decades ago. Joshua enjoyed the charged atmosphere where the most liberal politician in the country was never far-left enough. It made him smile that he was flourishing at such a radical institution despite his antithetical world view. He started considering again the unique nature of his on-going research and its implications to mankind. Would they find what they were looking for in Rome? If they did, how would it change the world? For he was certain that the world would change.

"There you are!" A lithe blonde woman bounded up to him. Sarah Byrd was his head GA. And she deserved the position. She had fought long and hard for it. In a way, she was just as responsible for their invitation to Vatican City as he was.

Joshua smiled. "I'm out here hiding."

The autumn leaves in Eugene were a vivid orange mixed with striking yellows and reds still glistening from the morning rain.

"Tell me what you think we will find," Sarah imposed.

"You've asked that of me several times already."

"I've been taught to ask until I get an answer," she responded, grinning.

Joshua loved her energy.

Sarah continued, "My PhD sponsor always says…."

The chairman of her PhD committee finished the remark, "Keep asking and you shall receive." He smiled and added, "Yes, I know."

"Keep seeking and you will find what you seek," she added.

"But we are knocking on a very old door," he warned. "We may not find anything at all."

"Don't they know what they have?"

"Does the Library of Congress?"

"Everything is catalogued," she persisted.

"Everything?"

"Well, I'd assume so."

"What did your professor teach you about making assumptions?" He laughed.

"Okay," Sarah conceded, "then just tell me what we *might* find."

Joshua motioned for her to follow him and he stepped into a brisk trot back to his office. The tall brick box, that housed his small desk in a closet of a room, watched them as they approached.

"This place is so ugly," she mourned.

"I like it," he said as he held open the glass door for her.

"I know. I don't understand what you see in this place." Her chagrin was transparent.

"You chose it," he countered. "You could've gone to Harvard."

"My father liked Harvard. But I don't know how he could have ever left the Pacific Northwest."

"You grew up here. That must've been wonderful."

"Sisters, in the Cascade Mountains." She smiled and replied, "I could never leave Oregon. And my folks just love Ashland … retired to a golf course in the mountains."

"Lots of rain here though."

"The Willamette Valley is heaven."

"Kind of like Eden?"

They'd been climbing the stairs at the end of Prince Campbell Hall. His fourth floor office was clustered among those filled with assistant professors and other non-tenured educators. He was content though, stuffed inside the dull red brick tower.

"Better." She smiled.

He gave her a curious look that made her wonder.

"Have you been to Hills Creek?"

"Not yet." But he'd heard plenty from her about it over the past year or so. Sarah still frequented the Cascades. Hills Creek's best rainbow trout were less than an hour drive from campus.

"Did you make it to the coast yet?" she prodded.

"Next year," he responded, thinking it would be too cold by now.

"At this rate you'll never pull two dozen mussels from the rocks and cook 'em over a campfire on the beach."

"I'll put it on my calendar." He grinned as he stepped over the threshold of his tiny office.

"You are missing out on unspoiled wilderness in your own back yard," she whined. Sarah kept her dad's old fly rod permanently in the back of her truck.

"I don't do tents," he joked as he sat behind his desk.

She shut the door and slid into the single worn wooden chair that was squeezed into the corner on the other side of the old metal desk.

"When are you getting a decent office?" Sarah twisted her face as she surveyed the sagging wooden shelves overlooking the desk and two chairs, crowded as if languishing in a self-storage unit.

"I like the view," he said with a smirk.

Looking off in thought, "Another university?" She didn't want him to leave.

"Eventually."

She sighed and then leaned over the desktop to brush lint from his shoulder. "You were going to answer my question." Persistence.

The professor looked down as her graceful hand withdrew. His disheveled jacket helped hide a wrinkled white oxford. "Yes. I was." He paused and then answered, "You've heard of The True Cross?"

"Fragments of wood that are scattered all over the world ... believed to be remnants of the *original* cross Jesus was crucified on."

"That's right. And there are records that were kept."

"For each sliver of wood?"

"We will see."

"How far do they go back?"

"To Antioch," he said with some confidence. "Perhaps further back."

"In Latin?"

"And Syriac."

Sarah pondered that for a while.

Joshua absently looked over her head at an antique clock keeping poor time.

"We're late," he said.

Without another word, each picked up several old books and hurried out the door.

Sarah's '82 Bronco was waiting for them in the parking lot. It rode high on top of the 4-inch lift she'd installed. Half SUV, half full-sized pick-up truck, her white Bronco's fully convertible hard-top was weathered by the rain and bleached by the sun. They piled the books into the back, stacking them precariously, cozied up to a Coleman lantern that used to be a deep forest green. Climbing up into the vehicle wasn't easy with the frame raised up over axles that turned 34″ off-road, snow-studded tires.

The metal studs clicked steadily over the asphalt parking lot as Sarah rolled forward toward the narrow street.

"Didn't O.J. have one of these?" Joshua chided.

The tight look on her face told him she'd heard that one too many times.

"Starbucks?" he asked with a feeble smile.

"No. Bear's hooked on some new place," she said, grinning. "He says their Double Chocolate Mocha is his new girlfriend."

Only five blocks from the edge of campus, Sarah slowed the 351 V8 and pulled into a small parking lot with vehicles forming two lines that snaked around the back. The string of cars and trucks then ran adjacent to either side of a diminutive but brightly painted blue and white structure. The Bronco barely squeezed into a parking space in the rear, and they slid down from their seats to the gravel lot below.

"Dutch Brothers?" Joshua read the sign. "They're packed!" he said with surprise.

Sarah pointed toward their "old haunt" across the street. It looked deserted. Joshua just shook his head in amazement. From pretentious and erudite to … he regarded the simple, fast-food drive-through design along with its garish blue … Pennsylvania Dutch Dairy Redneck, he decided. Like the student body all of a sudden had tossed aside American Eagle and started buying their clothes at discount stores.

Sarah grabbed two of the volumes that had managed to stay atop their stack. Joshua retrieved a couple of books that had slid onto a North Face sleeping bag. Leaving the rest of the books in the vehicle, they worked their way in between and around the continuous stream of caffeine-starved customers all anxiously sitting behind steering wheels and glued to their cell phones.

He held the door open for her, and as she entered she gave him a look that made him a little nervous. Following her into a small room in the back of the coffee shop, he counted all of six small tables. Barry Logan and Charlie Farris were seated at one in the corner. They were in the middle of a heated exchange.

Sarah joined their table, sitting down to enjoy the show. Her shoulder length blonde hair was tucked neatly behind her into an orange scrunchy at the nape of her neck. Joshua stood for a minute taking in the dramatically understated blue-collar décor, mixed with the aroma of gourmet coffee.

"How'd you hear about our grand opening?"

The voice came from behind the professor. Joshua turned and looked. The first thing he noticed was the open door to a small office. The narrow wooden door bore a small placard announcing, "Office." A tall man in his early thirties smiled at him from behind silver-rimmed spectacles. He was neatly buttoned into a blue dress shirt that was tucked firmly into pressed navy slacks.

Joshua detected a self-assured idealism. "I didn't," he answered.

"The one in Grants Pass shut down." The man buoyantly poked his thumb out the window to the round, green logo seeking solace on the other side of the battlefield.

"You're the owner." Not quite a question. Joshua was still trying to figure out how a Dairy Queen styled coffee shop was successfully waging war against the giant of the ubiquitous siren and her pastel-plastered chic hangouts.

"That's what the sign says." The man's dark hair was slicked back above deep set eyes that darted to the wall beside them. His hands twitched nervously. He made the professor think of the successful drug-dealers who owed their survival to refusing to touch their own product.

The simple colorless frame on the wall displayed a business license less than six months old. It had been issued to "My Coffee Shops, LLC." Joshua passed on the obvious incongruity of the man's claim and asked instead, "How many stores?"

"This is my first," he boasted. Joshua's forehead wrinkled up as his mouth slightly gaped. The man felt compelled to continue, "Of many, they'll be everywhere, on every corner. Like 7-11."

"Like Starbucks," Joshua suggested.

"Yeah." The man's grin was annoying.

Joshua skeptically looked around for a wide variety of convenience items in stock. There was no retail inventory to be seen.

"Hold on." The proprietor of the "unstoppable chain" rushed up front to the kitchen screaming with hissing steam, fast hidden behind large metal canisters of thick, creamy whole milk and half-and-half.

Over at the table, the two students were still sparring. Sarah had stopped enjoying the banter and now looked up at the professor with a pleading look.

"What do you think, Doc?" Charlie caught Joshua as he was sitting down.

"I...." He was interrupted by a very large, hot paper cup that was set before him with gusto.

"I thought I'd lost you!" Mr. Shops intoned, as if Joshua had hidden himself amongst a hundred patrons in a mall food court.

"That was fast." The professor was being pedantic.

"Try it," he urged. Or commanded, Joshua couldn't tell which. "It's on the house!" The wide grin of a pusher.

It had better be, Joshua thought as he opened the plastic lid to look at the contents.

"Our best seller!"

"If you don't like it, *I'll* drink it," Bear interrupted.

"Double Chocolate Mocha?" Joshua guessed.

"So you've already heard. World Famous. It's made with chocolate milk, chocolate syrup, and extra espresso," frenetically spoken.

He sipped the drink, pleasantly hot, but drinkable and super sweet, a strong taste of rich milk chocolate, the powerful flavor of dark-roasted coffee beans. "Good." He smiled, starting into a second long pull. "Very good."

The owner looked on his prey proudly and then headed for the door to pounce on other unsuspecting victims. Charlie and Bear watched their professor suck down half of the drink before coming up for air.

Sarah was amused. "Like it?" She colored her question with good-natured sarcasm.

"It's like Pepsi and Coke," he said, "except that Pepsi will never win."

"You don't like Pepsi," Sarah said.

"It's too sweet," he agreed.

"But this?" She pointed at the cup.

"Is very sweet, but I really like it. Maybe I like it too much." And he pushed it over to Sarah. "You drink it."

"It's got a kick, huh Doc?" Bear leaned into the table eager to add another addict to his group.

"No." The professor started, but then it hit him. He stopped and held onto the table with both hands.

"You okay?" Charlie looked worried, and sporting a surfer's deep tan, he looked out of place among the others.

"Are you okay?" Sarah stopped sipping the mocha and set it back down.

It took a minute, but Joshua was finally able to respond. "Yeah, I'm okay. I've never felt so ... *alive*."

"Euphoric," Bear offered.

Sarah snatched the document that sat between Bear and Charlie. "*This* is what they were arguing about."

"Taking sides?" Charlie protested, as Sarah handed the paper to their professor.

"As a matter of fact, I am." Sarah used a proper, almost formal tone. It drew a cheer from Bear.

"Charlie?" Joshua asked.

"It's an inventory that may help us establish provenance."

Joshua smiled at Charlie, noticing the coral chain that kissed his neck at the top of his Volcom tee. The faded yellow of the shirt almost matched the color of his sun-bleached hair.

"It's in Syriac," Joshua said.

"I've got it translated." Charlie pulled another piece of paper from a folder under his chair. "Here," handing the page to Joshua, he added, "I think the cross was fully intact. At least it was until 1021 AD in Edessa."

"Barry?" Joshua looked at the bookish kid with dark hair that covered the top of his eyeglass frames. What was he? Nineteen? He was already working on his PhD.

"He's a myth," said with confidence. Bear pushed his spectacles up the bridge of his nose.

"Really?" the professor goaded.

"Prester John is an invention of the Roman Catholic church." Bear was smug.

Charlie vigorously shook his head back and forth but kept silent.

"And you?" Joshua turned to Sarah. She immediately blushed, prompting knowing looks between Bear and Charlie.

"I agree with Bear," she recovered and replied.

"Why?" The professor's tone was hardly inquisitive.

She felt like she was in the middle of a Platonic dialogue. "Simply that this inventory is dated in the 11th century. The Legend of Prester John didn't appear in Western Europe until the 12th century."

"It sounds convincing." The professor raised the photocopy of the original ancient Syriac script. He examined it closely. "Where did you find this?" he asked Charlie.

"The Orthodox Church still keeps its Byzantine records in Istanbul." Charlie didn't talk like someone who grew up on the beach. "I sent an email to a Greek bishop who's been there forever. I asked him about Edessa's archives."

"I thought the church in Edessa was completely destroyed," Joshua challenged as he continued to stare at the document in his hand.

"It was, but some of the clergy in the metropolis left early. When they left Edessa they took much of the church's property with them ... manuscripts mostly, some icons."

"Metropolis?" Bear asked.

"Like a diocese or presbytery," Charlie explained. He felt like he was making some headway. "Edessa was a Holy See."

"The Church was destroyed?" Sarah didn't look very happy.

"It was part of the widespread genocide from the 8th century until the 20th: religious, ethnic, political. It really doesn't make a difference what's behind it. Innocent men, women, and children murdered by the tens of thousands ... by the millions." Charlie had done his homework.

But Joshua wasn't finished. He volleyed back at Charlie, "When were the documents taken to Constantinople?"

"In the 1140's," Charlie maintained. "That's when the Turks sacked Edessa. Almost fifty thousand people vanished. Most were killed. The city became a ghost town for the rest of the century. My source in Istanbul says the monks got out in the nick of time."

"Why go to the capital of Orthodoxy? I thought the church in Edessa was at odds with the Orthodox Church?"

"They were. Most of the Eastern churches had been written off by Rome and Constantinople for centuries. They called them heretics, or worse. But by the mid 12th century the Arabs and Turks had destroyed almost every church within their Muslim Caliphates. The Jacobites were practically annihilated and the Nestorians were hanging on by a thread. By the 15th century the Christians were all either dead or scattered into Europe. Some ran off to the Far East." Charlie paused.

But Joshua just raised his eyebrows to ask for the conclusion.

"Oh yes," Charlie continued, "so the monks went to the only safe place they could think of. The Byzantines were still powerful and expanding their influence into Eastern Europe and Russia. So it makes sense that this inventory of Edessa's valuables would have some bearing on what was still there when they moved everything. And if Prester John's inventory is correct, the true cross may have been part of what was taken to Constantinople."

Joshua leaned back in his chair and read the Syriac inventory out loud. He read it with ease. He spoke it as if it were his own native tongue. Then, looking over the top of the document, he regarded his students with curiosity. Perhaps they would understand. Perhaps not. Best not tell them he recognized the handwriting. Not yet, at least. He settled on a final question to Sarah.

"When did you say this bogus letter was circulating in Western Europe – the one signed by a 'Prester John'?"

"The 12th Centur...." She halted. Her pause came as she put it together for herself. She then turned to Charlie with an apologetic look and clarified the date for everyone. "In the 1140's."

THE EMERGENCY COUNCIL had lasted for two days already. Everyone was exhausted. Only short breaks were allowed. They shared sleepless nights in makeshift quarters on the floor in the room. Otherwise, they worked non-stop. Food was brought in. Heavy bags pulled on their eyes as they watched the sun come up – for the third day in a row – from inside the large conference room.

The sounds of the *muezzin's* call to prayer pierced the patriarchate's vigil. The *Phanar's* heavy air of failure filled the room. It was the Patriarch himself who finally stood to acknowledge defeat.

"We have to tell Rome," he said.

A murmur rose. It was sustained. Then it grew louder. Another *Azan* outside their compound depressed the gathering even more.

The white-haired Greek Orthodox *Patrig* raised hands from under his flowing robe. Into the ensuing silence he said, "We haven't survived under this Turkish pall all these centuries to give up now. We've never given up. We never will. There's only four thousand Christians left here in Constantinople, but…."

"Father!" The bishop couldn't resist interrupting. "We have been the guardians. We've kept it safe for all these years. And, more importantly, we've kept the *secret* safe. We don't owe Rome anything."

The old man sat back down wearily. "They keep their own secrets just as well, my son. We have to be honest with our brothers." That drew protesting groans. "*Even,*" he stressed, "when they haven't always been honest with us."

"What about the parchment?" It was the same bishop.

"Our lab here in Istanbul is the best in the world." The Patriarch rose again from his seat and stepped to the large, ten-pane window to gaze into the faintly sunlit gardens at the edge of the courtyard outside. On its other side, in the morning shadows, loomed the defeated fortress that had guarded the greatest treasure and the greatest secret the Christian world had ever been known to possess. Still shuddering from the violation three nights ago, the old building looked sad. Standing there on the other side of the courtyard where it had stood proudly for centuries, now it was mournful, seeking solace as it gazed on the same garden of tulips, crocus, and cyclamen that its Patriarch stared at now.

"Our technicians and their scalpels, probes, and microscopes have compared vellum samples, analyzed the ink, and even conducted carbon-dating over the past 48 hours. They say it's genuine."

Another cacophony of murmurs ... a tiny minority of distraught believers, surrounded by millions presently bowing in *salat* and reciting *Fatima*. A remnant. Heartbroken.

He turned back from the glass. His kind features had aged significantly since the heist. "We don't know the significance of the letter yet. We don't even know why the burglars would intentionally leave it behind. But we are hopeful that it will lead us to the perpetrators. We must...." His voice faded into silence.

The bishop broke the quiet. "But what could we possibly deduce from a thousand-year-old letter written by a presbyter in Edessa?"

It was with this question that the Patriarch of the Orthodox Church of Constantinople was to solve the riddle. It was as if the enthroned Gospel, on the dais over his empty throne, spoke to him. From Jerusalem. From Antioch. From Alexander and Rome. From Jundishapur, Nisibis, and Edessa. Bartholomew the First heard a thousand voices.

He knew what he must do.

*   *   *

BEAR'S WORN LEATHER jacket hung loosely over his short frame as he lugged his heavy carry-on down the impossibly narrow aisle. Surely Boeing had fewer passengers in mind when they designed the 767, he thought.

Charlie was already seated. He had his small duffle in the overhead bin. The big commercial jet was parked up against the terminal.

"What's in *that?*" Sarah laughed at Bear's overstuffed bag. She was seated next to her best friend, Arkesha and her fiancé, José, who was recently engaged to the South African. He was storing their bags overhead while talking to Joshua. They were already on the second leg of a long series of flights from Eugene to Rome.

"Stuff I couldn't check," he defended himself.

No one had talked during the short flight on the puddle jumper to Portland's International Airport. They were just now all waking up.

"I'm surprised they let you on the plane with it," Charlie teased.

Bear glared at him. But he didn't say anything. He just sat next to his friend, clutching his bag on his lap.

"Honey, they won't let you fly like that," Sarah cautioned, pointing at Bear's bag.

Bear's glare hardened. "What? Now you're gonna side with *him* on everything?"

"Bear!" Sarah gave him a hurt look.

"Well, I'll have you both know that I've been researching this Christian missionary-king of yours." He gave Charlie and Sarah alternating looks of mild derision. "And the only source who actually believed that Prester John was even real was that fabricator, Marco Polo."

"Bear!" Sarah protested.

"Prester John is a fiction. A fantasy. Pure and simple. Where was this New Jerusalem of his anyway?" He didn't wait even a second for an answer, "See? No one knows, because no one ever saw it. How can you rule over a Christian utopian kingdom if you have no subjects? If he had subjects, surely they could have attested to his regal existence. But no, they didn't exist. Just like he never...."

"Sir!" the stewardess addressed Bear for the third time. This time she yelled.

Bear looked up at her ... startled.

"Sir, you'll have to check your bag."

He withdrew and his eyes turned down with pouting.

"Dude," Charlie counseled, "she's not your mom. I don't think that's gonna work with her." He suppressed his smile. To the flight attendant he said, "I'll help him get it stored."

But she ignored Charlie's offer. Her short black hair framed an angular face. She must have been practicing her stern look in front of the mirror for the past thirty-five years. "Sir," she said as she placed a firm hand on Bear's bag, "you'll *have* to check your bag."

The ensuing tug-of-war would have gotten out of hand quickly if a calm voice wouldn't have intervened.

Sarah watched Joshua diffuse the fight. Her professor even managed to wrest a small smile out of the wiry enforcer after she finally released her hold on the wheeled case.

Bear seemed confused. Joshua was unzipping his bag. The stewardess had been correct. His case was stuffed. It was too large to fit in the overhead bin, much less under the seat. The professor quickly removed an assortment of books, papers and a cigar box full of thumb drives. He had all of the items piled high on Bear's lap as he closed up the lightened luggage and swung it up overhead. In seconds he was back with his own carry-on. All the items fit nicely inside. Bear got a sly smile as Joshua returned to his own seat.

Charlie offered enthusiastic applause.

The attendant gave a final glare at Bear before she traipsed back up the aisle.

As soon as the coast was clear, Sarah pulled out her iPad and slipped it across the narrow walkway. "Bear, check out this Venetian icon."

A skeptical look preceded his curiosity. But as Charlie looked over his shoulder, Bear clicked the little photo of St. Mark's and started reading from the Retina screen.

"Sarah." It was José, sitting two seats over. Her back was turned to him and Arkesha as she was twisted, leaning half-way across the aisle towards Bear and Charlie.

"Don't you think Arkesha looks especially beautiful today?" he continued.

"You say that *every* day," Sarah spoke as she spun around. She gave a short smile to the man who stole her friend's heart. "Trying to make me sick?" She stuck her finger into her mouth over an outstretched tongue.

"We've set a date." Arkesha beamed from behind elated Ngoni eyes.

"Already?" Sarah didn't try to hide her shock. "What's it been? A month?"

"Hey, that's not fair!" her friend responded, with pleading infused into her thick Afrikaans accent. "We met two and a half months ago."

"And you've already set a date." Disapproval. Disbelief. A measure of sarcasm mixed in.

José smiled warmly. He leaned over the top of Arkesha's lap as far as he could. His face drew up close to Sarah's own. "Sarah?" His voice was sincere. "Have you ever been in love? Really, truly in love?"

Her eyes darted to the row behind them. But she quickly looked back at the love-struck couple and replied with a simple, "No."

Arkesha smiled wide. "Who knows, Sarah, maybe your school-girl crush will turn into the real thing."

"I don't...." Sarah started to retort, but Charlie was yelling excitedly on their crowded airplane bound for JFK airport.

The militant stewardess had been demonstrating how to buckle an ordinary seatbelt to a cabin full of adults, over forty years after it had been government mandated equipment on all new vehicles sold, in a nation with more cars and trucks than people.

Charlie's thick mop of unruly, sun-streaked hair contrasted nicely with his reddening skin. He mouthed, "I'm sorry," to the rigid flight attendant who had stopped her show with clenched teeth.

"We'll be lucky to make it to Rome," José quipped. "If they don't kick us off *here*, they'll certainly deposit us on the tarmac at Kennedy."

"See that guy over there? He's one of those sky marshals. I saw him reach for cuffs," Arkesha giggled.

"It's not funny," Sarah said.

Charlie was whispering now, although his voice was still loud enough to interfere with the safety presentation. The stern lady was now in the middle of her demonstration of how to vomit into a paper bag.

Charlie's excitement was still very evident. "Sarah! How'd you find him?"

Sarah motioned for her iPad. As Bear passed it back across the thin divide he earned another piercing look from the stewardess. "I feel like I'm in third grade again," Sarah muttered. Using the stylus, she wrote a quick note and converted it to typed text with a click.

Giving the flight attendant a defiant smile, Sarah gave the computer back to Bear.

"You guys take this religion stuff too seriously." José was addressing his Xhosa bride and Sarah, who had settled back into her seat. Then he stole a kiss from Arkesha. The 767 finally started taking off.

Sarah rolled her eyes. "Maybe you guys *should* get married already." Her resignation was tentative.

"We don't believe in long engagements," Arkesha said, while gently squeezing José's hand.

"At least you believe in something."

"We believe in God."

"You believe in *a* god. Even atheists have their own version of a Supreme Being," Sarah said gently.

"My mother's a good Catholic," José boasted.

"If you grew up in South Africa, you'd not be such a big fan of Christianity either," Arkesha moaned.

"We're headed to *The Vatican* to establish the point of origin of shards of wood that may be part of the cross that suspended Jesus over Golgatha." Sarah's tone was spiritual.

"I love history," Arkesha answered the implied question, "but José's right. You guys are far too into religion."

"History means nothing to you?"

"I don't know. How can anyone, really…?" Arkesha gave Sarah her best sheepish look. "Anyway, the professor is on my thesis committee and he asked us to go."

"I was *raised* Catholic," José added.

Sarah gave him a frustrated look.

"I know, I know," José held up his hands in mock surrender, "this is not about Catholicism, it's all about Christianity. You told us that six times already."

"You met Arkesha in Tanzania, right?" Sarah asked.

"Yeah." Drawn out. He had no idea where this was going.

"Climbing Mt. Kilimanjaro?"

"Yeah." He drew it out again.

"Fell in love at the top, looking out over the Serengeti?"

"Yeah," he said dreamily, and he and Arkesha shared a loving look. Her eyes reflected the sparkle of Lake Malawi.

"While you guys were up there you didn't think about God even once?

Why He made what He made? Why are you part of it? What does He want from you?"

"Well...." José swallowed hard and a stupid grin crossed his face. He looked at Arkesha.

She looked back at him while she finished what he was trying to say. "We were a little too busy getting to know each other. You know. Talking and kissing. Kissing and talking."

And they started kissing again.

"You missed the view entirely? Highest peak in all of Africa! No wonder people miss God when He's right in front of them," Sarah mumbled.

"I heard that!" Arkesha stopped kissing just long enough to blurt it out.

The jet was roaring into the sky. Sarah looked around her. Joshua was already buried in a book. *Sons of God, Old Testament Angels?* Interesting title. Bear and Charlie were still arguing. Both of them were pointing at the iPad's screen as if the same image supported one point of view over the other. Her best friend was in her own world, deep in conversation with her man.

SARAH HAD MET Arkesha on her first day in Eugene. The foreign student was trying to register for her graduate studies classes. Becoming fast friends a couple years ago, the two had been inseparable since. That is, until Arkesha had traveled back home this last summer and took that trip to her ancestral homeland, Nyasaland. Sarah had never heard of it. Not even by its new name, Malawi. Arkesha had told her it was near Tanzania. That didn't help much.

When Arkesha came back to Eugene, José was with her. He had promptly enrolled in the University of Oregon's PhD program instead of studying at Cornerstone. José had grown up in Brownsville, Texas, the eldest son of Saul Gonzales. His folks were both illegal immigrants. It was hard for him to adjust after his parents were naturalized. But he'd started working hard when he was in high school. He'd graduated with honors from Northwestern and then earned his MA from Notre Dame. But then he'd headed to New Zealand for a year of canyon shelling. He'd come from Christchurch on his trip to Mt. Kilimanjaro. Sarah still felt like she didn't know him. It worried her.

SARAH HAD SPENT the last several days deep in her research. Soon after Joshua had indicated that he thought it a mistake to dismiss Prester John out-of-hand, she'd read everything she could on the subject. Much of the secondary and tertiary sources were skeptical or worse. But then she'd run across some amazing primary sources that discussed the priest-king … credible sources. Most of them were within documents from the 12th century that had been housed in the university in Nisibis in Asia Minor.

That's when she'd come across a blog. Sarah had googled "Nusaybin," the Turkish town that used to house the largest Christian university in the world. When a daily blog returned in her search results she was more than curious.

The blog was untitled and anonymous. It appeared to be attached to a public server in Ankara, Turkey. She posted a comment. It was promptly answered by email. So she used a little trick she'd learned from Bear and tracked the IP address to Istanbul. Why the subterfuge? Her simple question about Sanliurfa received a curious response. He knew about the city that used to bear the name "Edessa." The response was signed "Cyril." Wasn't that the same name as the Greek monk that created the Church's Slavonic language with his brother? The Cyrillic Alphabet was created originally for the Russian Orthodox Church in the 9th century, in Istanbul – called Constantinople back then. Sarah shut her eyes as she thought about it.

Why the anonymity? She'd wondered. But the blogger clearly knew his history. Sanliurfa was formerly known as Urfa, one of the two powerhouses of Islamic faith in Turkey. It was built on the remains of one of the greatest evangelistic cities in early Christendom: Edessa. But it was something else in his email that had got her thinking. So she read his blog again.

There it was.

He was asking about a letter penned in the 12th century in Nisibis. But he was being cryptic. So she'd sent him a second email.

"HOW'D YOU FIND HIM?" Charlie was in the aisle crouching between Sarah and Bear.

"I already told you. It says how in my white paper." She pointed to her iPad still clutched tightly between Bear's small padded hands.

"He's *my* source," Charlie said in a hushed tone.

"What are you talking about?" Sarah was staring into his eyes.

"Cyril," he whispered. "Bishop Cyril is the Greek Orthodox in Istanbul who sent me the inventory."

Sarah showed surprise. "It does make some sense," she said. Cyril had responded to her second email, although belatedly. His answer was in her white paper. Bear was still dumbfounded after reading it. Charlie was acting like he'd just been appointed as an international spy.

The blog was reaching out to the world's academic community. Cyril was looking for information, any information, about a letter written in Edessa in 1138 AD. He'd included the entire text of the missive, except the name of the author. In his final email he'd revealed the name. He'd acted embarrassed but told her his hope that it might help her answer his questions. He was asking her to help him shed some light on the letter. And she was able to. It surprised her.

Now Sarah recalled the text of the email Cyril had sent. It was just yesterday. But it felt like years ago already. He'd said, "I know you are not going to believe this, but it is signed, 'Prester John.'"

While she continued to consider this enigma, her mind flashed a picture of Joshua. When she'd looked back at him earlier, he'd been reading. Now, she could clearly see the full-color image that had etched itself into her mind: the way he held the book, the rich colors of the hardback's glossy jacket, the face just beyond its golden-leafed edges.

A face? It hadn't registered before. She had only noticed the interesting book title. But she'd seen it, a woman's face, her dark brown hair. Her eyes were boring into the back of Joshua's head. Her face, with perfect features and flawless skin, had been hovering over an expensive camel turtleneck bearing a large floral diamond brooch. The woman had been smiling. What kind of smile? Sarah wasn't sure. It was just a quick glance. The face hadn't even registered before, but it was bothering her now. She didn't like it. Not one bit.

As the memory stuck with her, she disliked it even more. Who was this woman? The image wouldn't fade. Increasingly bothered, Sarah was compelled to take another look. Surely at least some of her recollection was imagined. Embellished. A fabrication of her own insecurities. Fears. Worries. Surely.

Feeling like a jealous wife, she found herself twisting around in her seat to look down the aisle.

Joshua was still reading his book. Sarah's gaze lingered a moment or two. Then she focused behind him, one seat back, across the far aisle. There it was. That face. The woman. She was still staring at Joshua. Her smile was a knowing smile. A satisfied smile. A dangerous smile.

Sarah blinked in confusion. She had been certain of the woman's attire. The image was still in her head. Full color. Camel turtleneck. Diamond brooch. She must have had it wrong, however, because the woman was clearly wearing an emerald-green cashmere top. The neck was deeply scooped. And there was a brooch balanced near the side of the neckline. But it was not the diamond she'd first seen. Now it was a huge ruby with a circle of silver dolphins wrapped around the stone.

Sarah shook her head as if to clear cobwebs of clouded memory. She wasn't sick. She didn't take any kind of drugs, even over-the-counter. She hadn't been drinking alcohol. The image was still there, the live one – this strange woman, reveling in an absent stare – at Joshua. Her professor. Her…. And the woman was smiling like the cat that just ate the proverbial canary. Sarah's face must have shown every bit of her confusion at that moment. Should she tell Joshua? Did he know her? Did he know she was there? Couldn't he feel her eyes on the back of his neck?

Still hanging onto the top of her seat, fixed on the unchanged scene, she froze. A primitive fear made her shiver.

For now the woman's eyes were staring right at Sarah.

The smile turned sinister while still painted in the same satisfied curve.

§

CARDINAL ACAMAYO sat in his office overlooking *La Plazá de Armas*.
He was waiting with the rest of the world, wondering who would be chosen.
It had been a busy week. Rome was preparing to fill the vacant office of the
Prince of the Apostles. The Church needed a new Pope.

Acamayo had to get to Rome. He was required to be there. He would
participate in the vote.

But he had another concern on his mind: not just his vote, his nomination.
For he was among those chosen for consideration. His supporters told him
he was favored. One of his closest friends in Vatican City said that the vote
would just be a formality. How could that be? There had never been a Pontiff
selected from the *Archidioecesis Limanus*. The nomination itself had made
him nervous. The thought of actually being chosen had made him feel sick.
Now, it appeared certain to happen. He found it overwhelming and quite
unbelievable.

Lima's heavy coastal mist was just starting to lift when a knock at the
heavy rosewood door interrupted his reflections.

"Come in," he responded.

It was Stauffenberg.

"Heinrich," Miguel welcomed his friend, "sit please." He motioned to
the group of plush, wingback leather chairs and love seats. The furniture
occupied the alcove at the northern end of his expansive office. The frail
figure of an old man plodded slowly to the nearest chair. He folded into it,
almost disappearing from view behind its high bracketed back.

The Cardinal quickly moved to the matching armchair that sat beside the one cradling the gaffer's bones. Despite his active involvement in the *Front der anständiger Leute,* the geriatric German had fled Europe. He blamed Versailles. Over time he'd had plenty of opportunity to return, but his native Gotha had still been suffering behind the iron curtain. Most of his family and friends had died in the war. Over the years, the rest eventually passed. By the time the iron curtain lifted, none of them were left in Germany, or anywhere else in Europe. Lima was his home.

Heinrich had never been summoned to Nuremberg, not as a witness, or otherwise. But he still felt shame. For himself. For his countrymen.

It was a simple question, delivered with a kindly tone, but the old man's lugubrious response was puzzling. "It's the *Chinchorros.* They inhabited the *Atacama Desert.* You may remember the find in *Arica* in the early 80's. The Chileans didn't really know what to think at the time. Almost a hundred mummies … can you imagine?" He didn't wait for a response. "Like being in Memphis or Thebes, but it was in the opposite hemispheric quadrant. Then scientists started extracting DNA from the cadavers, better preserved than King Tut himself. But now? Now they unearth even more mummified bodies: this time right here in the *Norte Chico* pyramids – the first in *Huaricango,* then *Caral* – two of the twenty-five cities that once rivaled the ancient Mesopotamian city of Sumer, collectively, in size. Of course, they wasted no time extracting DNA from the mummies they found here."

Heinrich's voice was tired and somewhat distraught as he digressed, "*Caral* covers seventy hectares. One mound is 18 meters tall with a 152 meter base. To put that in perspective, the Pyramid of the Sun in Mexico is the third largest in the world at 61 meters tall with a 213 meter base." Of course, Miguel already knew.

Heinrich paused and took a deep breath as if he was headed under water. His heavy German accent still strained against the smooth language of Peru. "And the DNA was conclusive enough to spring a convicted man from death row." Watery eyes now looked up at the Cardinal as if just now realizing he had an audience. "They were, of course, quite surprised to find *Chinchorros* in *Norte Chico*."

Miguel scratched his greying head of hair and allowed his dark features to relax before responding as gently as he could. "*Mi amigo,*" he said, "but what does any of this have to do with pre-Columbian Christian missionaries to the Americas?" The Cardinal's initial question remained unaddressed.

"Ah yes," said like a man just awakened in the middle of the night. "*Con permiso, no soy yo mismo*. As you might say, get to the point. Under the mound in *Caral* they found *this*." He reached under the lapel of his jacket with his liver-spotted hand and brought forth a thick scroll. Tightly wound, it appeared to be quite lengthy. Thick. But not as such, compared to one of the larger Dead Sea Scrolls of Isaiah. Miguel's mind was buzzing.

Heinrich didn't seem concerned that his bare skin was in contact with the ancient parchment. Sure, his hands were cold and dry, like the discarded skin of a molted snake, but it made Miguel nervous.

"Put it there." The Cardinal motioned to the coffee table at their feet.

"You think I'm *imprudente*." The old man's words were sour but not angry. "I have no oils left in my skin, *mi amigo*. Here, I brought these for you, my only pair." He handed Miguel lifeless latex gloves that surely were designed for a child.

"*Gracias, Dios te bendiga*." Miguel nodded humble thanks. He stretched the protective gloves over large hands and gingerly lifted the scroll off the polished mahogany surface. As he carefully unrolled the skin, his dark eyes spread wide in amazement. He stopped unrolling with only a couple of lines of exposed manuscript.

"You see?" Heinrich reacted.

"*Ciertamente*." That was all the Cardinal could muster … and in barely a whisper.

They were interrupted by the ringing of the office phone. It sat on the huge desk in the middle of a bank of windows on the other side of the office. Beyond the phone a pair of French doors opened up to the iron-rail enclosed balcony and the clearing day.

Miguel ignored the intercom page. He was lost in thought, captivated by the consequence of what he held between his fingers. "Has this been dated yet?"

The phone continued to ring, begging for attention.

Heinrich responded with mild skepticism, "Yes, 7th century … penned by an early Maronite scribe in *Sūr*. Tyre, that is."

The phone stopped complaining only to be replaced by an insistent knock at the door.

"I don't believe any of it," Heinrich continued plaintively. "The *conquistadors* brought their aberrant version of Christianity to Peru in 1532, forty years after Columbus first landed in the Caribbean. Pizarro's priest presented the Inca Emperor, *Atawallpa*, a Christian breviary as part of the deceptive trap that allowed his 168 soldiers to massacre six thousand unarmed Incan troops in *Cajamarca*. Over the next three hundred years the Spanish found no evidence of Christian influence prior to their arrival. When they finally left in 1826…."

Miguel interrupted by finishing the sentence with his own perspective, "They had destroyed most of the evidence of the history of the Incaic Empire and the Quechuan people. They had never allowed any archeological work during those three centuries."

Both of them let those words sink in.

The weary-eyed German nodded in agreement and offered the obvious curiosity, "Then how did a 7th century Christian scroll end up buried in Peru with 4000 year old mummies?"

"The better question is, *when*?" Miguel's voice was now slightly agitated. It was the rapping on the door that had not ceased since the phone stopped ringing.

"You'd better get that." Heinrich allowed himself a rare smile. Then he paused and added, "There is one thing we can be absolutely sure of."

"What is that?" Miguel asked as he reluctantly stood. He started for the door, still clutching the precious scroll.

"That your scroll was inserted into the tomb before Pizarro's arrival. Therefore, your theory is proven. Whether or not the manuscript ends up being a copy created much later than the 7th century, we are still looking at pre-Spanish Christian missionary work in the Americas."

"I agree." Miguel paused and turned back to his friend. "But that is not the only issue raised by this find. Don't you realize? This scroll will shed more light on the running controversy." The impatient knocking caused the Cardinal to turn back toward the door.

"Ah yes," a knowing German agreed, "Peter's gospel." The former Abwehr junior officer had worked as a historian now for many decades. He was adjunct to the prestigious *Universidad Catolica* in *Parque de las Leyendas* and had been essentially working directly for Miguel the entire time. "Young John Mark penned it from his own notes. Interviewing the stubborn fisherman took much effort. The only synoptic gospel that was by one of the inner circle."

Miguel knew that fact but still paused to consider its importance once again. The rapping on his office door was competing for his attention.

"Matthew," Heinrich continued, "was an eyewitness too, but he wasn't on the mountain of transfiguration. He wasn't allowed to see Jesus raise Darius' daughter from the dead. He was left behind in the Garden of Gethsemane. Luke? Of course he relied entirely upon interviewing eyewitnesses. John was part of the inner circle as well, but he focused on orations more than events."

Miguel knew how significant Mark's gospel was. Hearing Heinrich lay it out like that was inspiring. He smiled. "I've never heard it put quite like that before." Then a thought occurred to him. "You've read it?" He pointed at the scroll in his hand.

"How could I resist?" the old man responded. "You know I read Greek."

Miguel turned back to the incessant knocking. He strode quickly for the impatient door. But then he stopped again. He had no patience. Never did. "How does it end?" He had to ask.

Heinrich grinned. He knew Miguel would be thrilled to know. "It's the longer ending." His eyes dropped to rest on the scroll. He smiled once again, but briefly.

Miguel's face carried a broad smile as he finally answered the door. A red-faced young prefect with red knuckles showed a huge expression of relief. Tears were streaming down his face. It took a few seconds for the man to realize that the Cardinal was now standing before him. Looking up, the exhausted priest looked into Miguel's face and blurted out a string of words in a high-pitched chirp.

"Father! I'm so sorry. I was told I *had* to interrupt you. Oh, I'm sorry, Father, you already took the call? Goodness! They said they've already secured the two-thirds plus one. Do you realize what this means? You know already don't you? You took the call? You look pleased. Oh my! Father!" And with that, the prefect wilted towards the floor.

Miguel reacted quickly. He reached out for the fainting cleric and caught him without risking harm to the scroll. The priest slowly revived in the Cardinal's arms. His eyes focused and a look of embarrassment followed.

"I've not been on the phone," Miguel said, as the young man struggled free and stood. He straightened his cassock and cleared his throat with an air of regained formality. Then the young man spoke.

"Then, Father … I must implore you … to answer the line. I placed it on hold." His halting sentences made Miguel want to laugh.

"Pedro my son. Calm yourself. It's okay. I'll get the call. But who is it?"

"*Oh Padre, lo siento!* I should have said at first! Oh no! They've secured sufficient commitments in advance of the voting! It's the Dean. He's on the line for you. Rome. He says you're going to be the…." With that the priest crumpled down to the floor, slipping through Miguel's hands.

*　　　*　　　*

ONLY THREE HEAVILY armed soldiers followed Via Bonzon. Each was goggled to keep the wind-driven sand from blinding them. They moved fast through the dry storm as it tore into the barren landscape west of Baghdad. The four mercenaries blended into the dull beige blast with their desert-camouflage wrapped bodies and weapons. Immediately to Via's right and behind her, the burly form of Tran, obscured in the same shroud of particulates, towered above the others despite his Vietnamese blood. Although his Southeast Asian features were pronounced, his bulk and height likely came from a Dravidian genetic strain that reached back beyond his Tartarian heritage. He ran swiftly with the others while bearing easily a large black metal case.

Flanking Tran on his other side, the slight figure of Mandy James raced over the hot sand as if floating on the base of the storm itself. The young, former MI6 agent was braced as if they would be intercepted at any moment. Her Russian-made AK-74 assault rifle was equipped with a grenade launcher that strained against its leash. The smallest of the lives at risk as they approached the nondescript compound, Mandy didn't show any signs of anxiety. She knew Via had selected her for this mission precisely because of the significance of their success to her grandfather's oeuvre. Now, here she was on the outskirts of the ancient Chaldean city about to storm a stronghold and recover a piece of history.

On Bonzon's blind side the squared shoulders of a body-builder moved effortlessly through the violent cloud of sand. Her thick muscular thighs propelled her heavy frame with a grim and unstoppable determination.

AN EXPATRIATE WHO had been raised on South Boston's violence, Nena Bencini had fled to Europe at sixteen. She'd been drawn to explore her roots that beckoned back to the Alpine foothills north of Torino. But it was in Lyon, near Via's Chambéry estate in France, where she was recruited. Nena had easily won the female ultimate fighting championship, pinning her final opponent in the first minute of Round One. Via had found her in the locker room after the match. It had not been a pleasant exchange.

"How did you get in here?" Nena had growled in broken French.

"I'm Via," speaking in English as she extended her hand. "I'm here to offer you a job."

"Get out." She'd zipped up her sweat-jacket, pulled a knit toboggan over her long, mocha-streaked hair, and turned her back to the unwanted intrusion.

"If you change your mind, I'm prepared to pay you twice what you're making now." Via had been calm, delivering her even tone to a pair of deaf ears that were now bending over a blue Nike duffle.

Even those who can't hear can sense the sound of money. But the stubborn anger inside of her responded instead, "You know nothing about me. Get lost!"

But the command had lacked conviction. Whether intentionally or not, she didn't know why and didn't care.

However, a year later she was still glad Via had picked up on it. Via had known everything about her, including her father's release date from the alcohol rehab place in Kingsbridge. Via had already known about Nena's long rap sheet that served as a résumé. It accentuated her extensive expertise with assorted firearms. Nena figured she was lucky that the Feds routinely ignore the juveniles, hoping they grow into bigger fish.

Nena often thought about Via's only mistake back in Lyon. The amount she'd offered had turned out to be almost three times what she'd been making. She was happy.

THE DRAB CEMENT walls of the Mesopotamian compound looked deserted as they swept into the shadow of the razor-wire topped bulwark. The once bone-hued stockade of steel bars, threaded through molded cinder blocks twelve meters high, had weathered down to the rare patch of white pigment recessed inside mortared seams. The coiled teeth atop the cemented barrier would efficiently shred both flesh and bone.

It was Nena who carried the pack that Via opened, as the fighter bent to one knee at the base of the towering wall. Quick movements lightened her load significantly and the mule breathed a sigh of temporary relief. As Via pulled the metal frames from the large backpack strapped to Nena, she handed the frames off to the auburn-haired Brit.

Mandy's proficient dexterity assembled the custom-built aluminum sections. Fitting first the two wide poles of squared hollow tiers, she then telescoped each end from the center to over forty feet of weight-bearing strength. Via positioned herself to raise the modern siege work. It was a slim tower that once raised allowed gravity to drop, at appropriate intervals, horizontal steps that winged off of either side. Mandy mused that it resembled a vertical formation of gliders affixed to the pole.

Via slid underneath the monopod stairway to keep it braced securely against the aged block impediment. Nena was already pulling a Kevlar *heaume* over her head and to the base of her neck. Still carrying more weight than even Tran, Nena now scurried up the ladder as it yielded to her every step, bending generously in a wave of tension that shook in relief as she disappeared into the sandy cloud at the top of the wall.

Mandy followed quickly on Nena's heels. Her steps barely curved the extended aluminum, and when she reached the top, she disappeared as well. Tran, lugging his black case on his back, scrabbled up the pole as gracefully as one could with the unwieldy burden banging against the back of his body. A rappelling line for their leader was dropped flush with the cement rampart. Via let the monopodium scaffold down as she negotiated the earthen-colored nylon hand-over-hand quickly upwards.

A tripod of strong light metal at the top of the bulwark suspended a dual belay point. It was raised about a meter over the top of the narrow ledge on the wall's apex, amidst the curved menace of razor-tipped barbs. Lying underneath the nylon ropes now slung over either side of the wall, Via was pleased to see Nena's body depressing the collapsed coils beneath her Kevlar shell of full-body armor. She was smiling from inside her protective helmet. The others were already safely on the ground, having breached the compound in silence, undetected. Via now repeated her forerunner's method of navigation and stepped onto the thick thigh-guards on Nena's legs. She grabbed the rope on the other side of the triadic belay post and rappelled swiftly downward, landing within a perimeter guarded by Mandy and Tran.

Nena knew the next couple of seconds were crucial as she deftly transfigured the tripod into a horseshoe grappling hook and threaded the rope inside its narrow protective gutter. As she lay face up, she moved the device above her head and slid it between the top of her helmet and the hungry metal teeth trying to devour her. And then, in one nimble motion, she rolled off the ledge with her Kevlar and leather gloves firmly clenching the nylon strand that would lower her into the modern Babylonian fortress. The rope held as her weight swung her body like a pendulum scraping the bowels of a broken clock. The motion had barely subsided when she loosened her grip and started sliding down the line. She was racing to the dirt below. For a moment, she feared, too fast. The landing may injure ankles or knees. But Nena's worry left her as quickly as lead tore into the side of the parapet just above her hands. She reacted by letting go. She free-fell the rest of the way down. Stinging pain shot up from strained metatarsals through sciatic nerves and into her entire frame. She had hit the ground hard and rolled.

Three angry assault rifles were already returning fire as Nena rolled back up to her feet. Strong thighs over bent knees had absorbed most of the impact. She would ache a lot like one who suffers after a car accident, but she knew she'd sustained no more than soft tissue injuries. And as soon as she'd completed the somersault over her right shoulder, her AK-74's butt was pressed firmly against it with the barrel spitting round after round past Via's left flank. The sand still swirled wildly, like a trapped animal inside the compound. It made visibility sporadic and poor. But as Via swept 45 degrees from the right of the team, the others moved with her like wolves rushing after their Alpha male. Despite the lack of clear sight, they felled combative targets quickly as they skirted the fusillade that was still focused on where they'd vaulted the stockade. Quickly reaching a long, two-storied structure only ten meters inside the wall of the compound, they found the door where it was supposed to be. Nena took the lead and crashed into the door without breaking her stride. Not built with significant strength anyway, the wooden door splintered at the knob's latch and madly swung into a dimly lit room.

Occupying the small space inside, a young man dressed in camel fatigues jumped from behind a communications console. He immediately lifted his arms in surrender. Mandy bound his wrists and ankles efficiently with plastic ties as Via addressed the man in Árabic.

Tran strung a trip-wire to the door as he shut what was left of it. The explosive charges at either end of the wire would be lethal to anyone who followed them. Finished, he anxiously adjusted the black case still perched on his back and looked expectantly at Via. "We gotta move," he said.

Via was still interrogating their prisoner as Nena picked up the man like he was a sack of feed. Mandy led them into a long, narrow hall. Tran closed the door behind them just as it shuddered from a blast. He hoped the trip-wire had eliminated at least four of the enemy. They were going to need all of the help they could get.

The end of the hall was a significant distance away. Nena estimated it was a hundred feet, slightly longer than the blueprint showed in the stratagem they'd studied back in Chambéry. She knew they had to make it about half-way down this hall, to the stairwell. It was supposed to be on the left.

As they moved down the confining corridor, a large figure dove out of an open doorway well down the length of the hall. The man was spraying bullets from his carbine. Mandy squeezed off one short volley to cut him down. She did, but not before one of his bullets hit her leg. She stumbled, but immediately she stood back up and regained her position. The team kept advancing toward the stairs.

Tran was taking up the rear. He had stayed behind to wire the door behind them.

"Okay," Via signaled.

Nena set the hostage in the open room to their right and shut the door.

"He said it's still there." Via sounded tense but pleased. "Urfinjad keeps it under his bed, of all places." Via was already running for the stairwell. Her three soldiers rushed after her, with Tran moving closer to the injured Mandy.

Via disappeared into the alcove at the bottom of the flight of steps. Nena was just behind her. Mandy was dragging behind, limping. She was the first to see it. Tran's eyes widened a split second later.

The door that faced them at the far end of the hall had just opened to reveal the tip of a hand-held grenade launcher already in position.

It was pointed straight at them.

Nena dove headlong into the stairwell. Mandy almost tripped and fell, but Tran pushed her hard, hurling her into the protection of the alcove. Tran was still a leap away from the stairway's landing. He kept his eyes glued on the tip of the weapon that was going to release the incendiary device. The RPG fired.

"Ahhhhh!" Tran's feral yell echoed his extreme effort. His primal scream, a forceful determination, joined his dive to the floor just as the missile careened over his ducking head – successfully lunging underneath the grenade as it passed down the middle of the hall. He was still carrying the bulky black case on his back as he scooted on his stomach into the stairwell alcove, without a second to spare.

Tran's first trip-wire survivors were in the radio room trying to disable his second trap. The room was full of enemy soldiers anxious to pursue the intruders. They were waiting for their ordnance specialist to cut the right wire, reaching through the access hole he had made in the door. The figure hunched over, reaching Tran's intricate handiwork fast, his fingers moving smoothly and expertly over the circuits. The squat man grinned widely from beneath a scraggly beard and proudly swung the door into the room to announce his success.

But as the door swept open, his smug smile became a frightened frown of helplessness. The group of soldiers, in that instant, all found themselves aware of the flash of the RPG thrusting itself through the open doorway.

Via was still rushing up the stairs with the others close on her heels when the building shook with the explosion.

The radio room went up in flames.

Via knew that they were quickly running out of time. Again.

At the top of the stairwell, Via pulled a small electronic device from a pocket in her sleeve. After a brief glance, she tucked it back into its spot and rushed into the hall, heading for the second room on the left, going back towards the destroyed radio room a floor below. She dove and slid along the tiled surface, spraying as many bullets from her automatic rifle as she could. A shower of lead left her weapon's muzzle as she moved across the slick surface on her side. The wooden door shredded near the bottom and a cry broke out in protest.

Nena was quick to follow up with a concentrated barrage through the shattered door to ensure that their would-be assailant was unable to hinder their mission.

Tran ran ahead to the room after making sure Mandy was still mobile. The prize may still be within the walls of the bedroom as their ephemeral hostage claimed. Tran's empty case ached to cradle such a precious piece of history. Lost for so long. Now almost found. Almost recovered. Almost rescued. Almost.

It had to still be here. And, they had to get out of this alive.

Mandy's limp had become aggravated. She bent to tighten the crimson stained cloth that she'd tied around her wound. The loss of blood was weakening her. She was already feeling light-headed. Her bleeding now curtailed again, she focused on her need for strength to go on. A syringe was tucked into a mesh compartment below her chest. She injected a cocktail into her thigh, thrusting the large needle through her clothing to pierce her skin. She then sheathed the empty antibiotic cylinder and moved quickly to catch up. Mandy was the last one to enter the apartment, half-way down the northern side of the floor.

Via's electronic surveillance device had only shown one heat signature on the entire level. They didn't bother to sweep the rooms. Tran reached the small apartment's bedroom and swung open the door. With one quick motion he pushed the bed aside. As the queen-sized sleeper slid from its berth in the center of Urfinjad's quarters, a large wooden crate was revealed. It was now alone and exposed in the middle of the floor.

The small group crowded around the pine box that smelled of stale straw and dust. Tran lifted the hinged lid, and a collective gasp filled the room.

Tran lost no time opening his large black case. The inside was filled with egg-crate foam dyed a creamy grey. Carefully lifting from the pine crate's interior the fragile piece of antiquity, Tran gently placed it in the center of the metal case's protective lining.

There were twenty-two windows lining each side of the second story. They were evenly spaced by drab brick that tenuously clung to the cinder block frame. As Tran rose to his feet with the carrier in hand, all of the windows shattered on their side of the building. The glass yielded to steel tipped boots as a small army invaded, having rappelled from the roof. Tran and the others were immediately faced with two men bursting through the windows into the bedroom. Their carbines were already blazing.

Mandy turned her attention to the pair of soldiers who simultaneously breached the living area of the two-room apartment.

Via and Nena quickly dispatched the armed figures in the bedroom. Tran rushed to help Mandy. Only seconds later, four bodies lay lifeless across the white-tiled floor.

They didn't have the time to take a breath. They could hear the pounding of eighteen sets of boots echoing from the hall.

Tran slid a silver hockey-puck-size disc underneath the door. It slid into the hallway as he ran for the farthest shattered space where glass used to stand. Mandy stumbled for her own window exit. Black ropes still dangled down to the center of the open frames. Tran re-strapped the case to his back as he scrambled up onto the sill and reached for the length of cord coming down from the roof. The sand storm had stopped and the scrubbed air was clearing.

Nena was already out one of the bedroom windows and climbing to the rooftop as Via paused to carefully lay a frayed parchment scroll inside the straw-filled crate. She reverently closed the pine lid and ran for the last hanging rope just as a brilliant flash of light penetrated the apartment's living areas through the crack under its front door. There was no explosion, but the brightness was so extreme in the hallway that the pulse of light was its own destructive force, burning all biological matter into instant ash.

Tran was pulling Mandy over the edge of the roof as Via came to help. She gave Tran a nod and he ran towards the far north end of the long structure's rooftop. Nena pivoted, circling rapidly, the point of her weapon drawing a wide circle. Her gloved finger twitching against the trigger, she was daring the enemy to pursue them any further.

Mandy sank to the gravel-covered tar of the flat roof. "Leave me," she said, resigned to her situation. Her bloody leg was soaked in red.

Via just smiled and tucked her shoulder into Mandy's desperate torso. Bending Mandy's midriff, Via lifted with a strength that surprised them both. And then, the older woman started running, a brisk trot opposite from Tran's end of the building. The big man was scurrying around the edges of the northern end of the rooftop, planting black carbonado spikes into the metal flashing between the roofing's rubber sheath and the bricked outer rim that jutted up like an ill-conceived earthwork.

Nena caught up with Via and snatched the now limp figure off Via's shoulder as if Mandy was weightless. Picking up speed, they rushed for the south end of the rooftop. Behind them, Tran, his supersonic ordnances in place, sprinted to catch up – his bulky figure accentuated by the oblong shape of the case strapped to his back so that it rose up over his head like a mountaineer's pack.

Tran was still several paces from catching up to the women when the building shook. The violent tremor started like a seiche wave behind them and a rippling mass of rubble roared fast, now chasing them. As the building recoiled from Tran's planned quake, the team finally reached the other end of the building.

They made it to the southern edge just in time to greet life-threatening rounds that were slamming into the top of the cornice bricks and upwards into the air. They backed away from the edge in quick defensive strides. Now out of the line of fire, they couldn't see two more trucks pulling up next to the Light Armored Vehicle that bore the mounted cannon.

"This had better work!" Nena yelled, looking over her shoulder at the wave of debris rolling fast towards them.

"Get ready!" Tran yelled, looking delighted with the challenge. He braced himself with his back to the tar and gravel seiche. The three of them looked poised to ride the wave … if it could be ridden.

The rooftop in front of them was quickly disintegrating into its own unique demise as the shelling continued to thrash it from below. Dozens of soldiers poured out of the back of the transports and grenades started flying up into the air, aimed right for the perpetrators of the desert heist.

In moments, their position on the crumbling rooftop would be littered with exploding grenades … if the seiche didn't get them first.

Nena breathed in deeply. It could be her last.

THEY STARED AT each other, stubbornly willing the other to back down first. The feelings that welled up inside of Sarah were powerfully uncontrollable. She took on the role of protector and defender and all the while wondered where it came from. By nature she was sweet, gentle, kind-hearted, and had a soft spot for both the down-trodden as well as their oppressors. It was new to her to want to fight someone. But it suddenly hit her. She realized what it was. She saw the woman as a threat. To Joshua. And to her.

Behind that woman's pretty face was a malevolent desire that the richly woven fabrics of expensively tailored clothing couldn't mask. Even the brooch seemed poised to draw attention away from the face of one who would lure you in, an unsuspecting victim. All she could think about were the insects and spiders that spawn females who devour their mates.

She must have been lost in her thoughts during the stare down, because it took Sarah a minute to realize she was now staring at an empty seat. The woman must have gotten up to use the restroom. Perhaps, she thought, I was successful. The woman will stop. It's a long flight to New York. What if he's in real danger? I mean, what do I really know about him? He has aroused in me so many strange feelings over the past couple of years, but I don't even know where he's from. But then, knowing where one is from is so overrated. Does that really tell us anything about a person? Really? He's from Philly. She's from LA. He's from London. Can a city, or even a culture, define one's character? Let's say I meet his folks, his brothers and sisters, his childhood friends, every biography I've read tells me these things don't define you. There are hints sometimes, but maybe they only *become* endowed with supposed meaning in perfect hindsight. And once you know someone's true character, what about when they then act *out* of character?

Exhausted from the mental gymnastics, she slumped into her seat and waited for the woman to return.

"SARAH . . . SARAH." Arkesha was gently touching Sarah on the shoulder to let her know that they were getting ready to land.

She finally moved, a feeble effort to respond.

Arkesha touched her shoulder again. "Put your seatbelt on, sweetie. We're landing." Arkesha's Nyasa vocal tones were getting closer, less surreal.

Finally, still drowned in sleep, Sarah managed to reply. "Rome?" she asked.

"We can't land at JFK, young lady, until *you* are buckled up and your seat is in its upright position!" It was the formality of the abrasive flight attendant.

"New York?" she responded groggily, wiping her mouth on her sleeve.

The stewardess glared and pointed at the still unbuckled belt.

It got fastened, but not before Sarah swiveled to look behind her.

The woman's seat was still empty. Perhaps she moved seats, Sarah thought. She felt a bit victorious.

"Move your seat to its…."

"Okay, okay already!" Sarah's tone was uncharacteristic.

"You were smiling," Arkesha said.

"Huh?"

"Before you yelled at that drill instructor."

"Oh."

Sarah was about to tell Arkesha about the strange woman, but Bear's voice abruptly interfered.

"It's a fake!" he gasped.

Sarah turned to look. Bear and Charlie were both glued to a streaming video on Bear's iPhone.

The landing gear rumbled. Its vibrations signaled the lowering of the massive wheels under the wings.

"Don't let Miss Strict catch you with your phone on," Sarah quipped as she turned from Bear and looked up the aisle at the back of the militant attendant marching off to enforce more rules.

"Didn't you hear me?" Bear was oblivious to Sarah's warning. "It's a fake!"

"What's a fake?" She felt like she was in an argument with her little brother when they were both in grade school.

"The Shroud!" Bear announced. "The Shroud of Turin!"

"Bear," Sarah started in a slightly condescending tone, "that debate has been raging for a long time. What makes you think that they've learned anything new about Jesus' burial cloth?"

Bear gave her a smug look and passed his phone to Sarah. Charlie gave her an empathetic scowl as Sarah puzzled up and focused her gaze on the illuminated screen's moving picture. An anchor was in the middle of some repetitive monologue, while sitting rigid at an ABC News Special Report desk. The graphic tag read, "Shroud of Turin proved a Fake."

She turned up the volume.

Amidst the muddy river of nonsensical words that modern news organizations use to fill the space in their round-the-clock broadcast cycles, Sarah heard only three words. They became etched in her mind. The anchor repeated them. The force of the story, the one that the media was trying to stress, was the fact that now there was conclusive proof the age-old relic that the Roman Catholic Church had so proudly displayed for centuries was not, in fact, genuine. The "Breaking News" story was replete with content that reiterated the tag line's big bold statement. But the proof itself was the bigger story, and the media was missing the entire point, as they so often do. Most of the time the news organizations just hide the information they don't like. It's easy for them to choose what to report and what to ignore. After all, that's their prerogative. But it's actually amusing when they find themselves in a quandary, like this one, thought Sarah. So badly they wanted the world to know that a Christian artifact is not authentic, anything to discredit Christianity, that in this case, they were forced to report information they would never otherwise have published. For the real story was *how* it was now known that the Shroud of Turin was not the true burial cloth of Jesus Christ, and that proof, those three words, were now indelibly carved into her memory.

It became part of her permanent record.

It became part of who she is.

Sarah said them to herself over and over again as Arkesha leaned over her shoulder, listening to the same webcast.

Then she said them aloud.

Perhaps Sarah was trying them on to appreciate the full import of it all. The implications were enormous. Her questions were numerous.

"Real Shroud Stolen."

Sarah spoke them again, almost reverently.

But her musing was abruptly cut short as the iPhone was roughly snatched out of her hand.

As the flight attendant headed to her jump-seat at the front of the plane, Bear gave Sarah a sour look.

"Better get my phone back," he said accusingly, ignoring the fact that it was he who had turned it on prematurely in the first place.

"I will. I will," her now conciliatory tone preceding her apology. "I'm sorry I misunderstood you."

"We have two hours between flights," Bear hinted.

"What do you want?" Sarah resigned.

"What do you think he wants?" Charlie laughed.

"Okay, I'll find you a double chocolate mocha. But Starbucks or Peet's will have to do. JFK doesn't have any Dutch Brothers yet."

"We have a lot to talk about." Charlie changed the subject.

"I'd say," José piped up. "I always knew that Shroud was a fake."

"Right, you *always* knew." Arkesha poked him in the ribs.

"But that's not the point is it?" Charlie queried Sarah.

"No," Sarah answered from a distance, already lost in thought again. "That's not the point."

"Yeah," Arkesha added. "Where was the *real* Shroud stolen from?"

"Why was it hidden?" Bear chipped in.

"Who had it?" Charlie asked.

"Who *stole* it?" Sarah added.

"And why?" Arkesha's question made them all pause.

Then, after a shared silent pause, "And how do they know this one's the real one?" José offered.

"Yeah," Sarah concluded as the plane touched down. "We have a lot to talk about. Do you think the professor knows?"

"He's asleep," José said.

"All right. We'll tell him as soon as we get off the plane." Sarah sighed and looked up front at the stewardess. She was dreading her task of retrieving Bear's phone. She added with relief, "At least *she* won't be on our next flight."

*　　　*　　　*

NENA'S MUSCULAR LEGS tensed even as she bent her knees to absorb the shock of the building moving beneath her. The weight of Mandy's body on her shoulder suddenly became heavier. The rooftop's wave was now waist high, only a few meters away from surely knocking them down and crashing over them. She looked at Tran for assurance. He turned to her and smiled again. He nodded his head to indicate that she should follow his lead.

As Tran leaned forward, feet positioned with toes pointing sideways, his right foot slightly to the front, he stretched out his arms like he was about to take flight. Via ducked under Mandy's limp frame and took half the burden from Nena. She put her arm around Nena's waist. Nena wrapped her left wing around Via and they both spread out their free arms to steady themselves.

A seismic boom rumbled suddenly underneath them. It flattened out the wave of gravel and tar as quickly as it had started. The surface under the standing trio moved on a level plane. Shifting forward and slightly downward, the entire building began to travel. The roof line started moving southward dramatically, staying relatively parallel to the ground two stories down.

The .30 caliber gun that had been tearing into the building immediately lost its triggerman and the assault from the cannon ceased. The men that had been swarming into the building were now stampeding back out as fast as they could.

From below, the building looked like a folding animal cage being collapsed for storage. Each corner a pivot point, its foundation stayed in place, but the roof was being propelled forward toward the three newly unattended trucks at its south end of the moving building.

Via's team was silhouetted against a slate-grey sky. As the sandstorm's veil continued to subside, the figures on the roof were visible from the ground, surfing the falling structure as it raced toward the compound's wire-topped front wall.

The air was almost cleared of sand, that is, until a huge cloud of dust rose up from underneath the launching roof line. As the billows of particulates engulfed the soldiers on the ground, the structure's leading wall crashed into the trucks and collided with the compound's outer wall. The building pancaked both the trucks and the wall beneath its weight. The roof itself, however, rode on long steel girders and slid right over the top of the collapsing rubble. Still intact, the huge longboard skidded over the pile of bricks, tile, twisted steel, and glass. It continued moving past the ruined wall, outside the compound into the desert, until it lost momentum and slowed to a stop in the sand.

Via let Nena take Mandy and she leapt off the expelled rooftop to the ground only two feet below them. Timing was still critical. Via checked her Suunto. It'll be better if he is early, she thought.

She ran forward out into the desolate wasteland north of *Al Fallujah*. With Nena and Tran flanking her, Via put as much distance as she could between them and the compound. She knew that in only minutes they would be pursued. And their hunters would not be on foot as they were. Tran stopped and knelt to the ground as the women pressed on.

He was running to catch up when he heard the vibration of vehicle tires grinding into the dirt behind him. He turned to look back.

A jeep led a convoy of three: a converted Mitsubishi truck in the middle and another jeep bringing up the rear of the single file column. The line of vehicles was loaded with gun-waving fury.

Tran knew they had only seconds. Surely they were in plain view except for the cloud of dust where the building once stood. But the trio of trucks was already emerging from its silty covering. Tran's group was well within the range of even the poorest marksman. So he flipped a bright blue marble onto the sand and distanced himself as fast as he could. The land mine he'd set seconds earlier wouldn't be enough.

As he kept running, Tran depressed a trigger on the control assembly wrapped around his wrist. Behind him, the catalytic response shot a geyser of orange flame high above the ground. It glowed brighter and turned white in its center as it fanned out from the base.

Tran smiled as the pillar of fire cloaked their retreat. It would only give them five minutes, far short of the forty years Moses enjoyed, he thought, but plenty of time for their needs at this moment.

He was right.

Just as Tran caught up with Via and Nena, the horizon revealed a sixties-era Land Rover racing towards them. Plenty of time, Tran decided. He stopped briefly to grab a breath and spit out the mortar grit that had accumulated around his teeth.

Nena was denuded of strength. She doubled over, laying Mandy's unconscious body on the sand that was spread thinly over the hard earth. Via was suddenly garrulous, obviously communicating with the approaching driver through her subdermal radio.

"*Tikrit?*" Via asked.

"The road to *Al Mawsil* had road blocks."

"Keyontay. We're going to the river."

"I can get us to *Dahuk*. We can cross the border north of *Zakhu*."

"I trust your driving skills, Keyontay. That's not what concerns me. Just get us to the Euphrates as soon as possible." Via's English was colored with a heavy French accent, more than normal. From inside the old truck, Keyontay smiled, having grown up in Richmond, Virginia, he loved working with Europeans. He found it exotic.

"Via. How will we make it to *Silopi* in time if we go down river?"

"Leave that to me. You know the back-up route."

"Yes. You had us studying maps and memorizing our time-tables three weeks ago. I trust you. I just like knowing how it's actually going to pan out."

"You could have arrived a couple of minutes earlier," Via chided the young man, as the susurrus of tires over ancient desert bedrock grew closer.

"You're the one who keeps drilling us about precision," Keyontay retorted.

Via looked at her watch again. He was right. He'd arrived within ten seconds of his designated rendezvous time.

The soldiers readied themselves as the '66 Land Rover, outfitted with a safari roof rack and brush guard, tore through the remaining stretch of barren ground. As it pulled up, it turned and braked simultaneously, skidding sideways, stopping on a dime. The rear bumper came within an inch of Via's unmoving, erect form. Unflinching, Via motioned for Nena to put Mandy into the rear hold as she opened the back tailgate with a single, fluid movement. Tran slipped into the seat behind the driver, an African-American with shoulder-length skinny dreads. His thin strands of knotted hair moved like they were dancing with excitement. The native son of Myanmar had set the black case upright in the middle of the rear's bench seat. As Via closed the cargo door, Nena melted into her seat opposite Tran.

"Hey kiddo!" Nena addressed their driver.

Keyontay smiled. "Looks like you guys really tore up the place."

Just then, as if to underscore the observation, an explosion ripped through the air on the far side of the pillar of flame. Tran's land mine had done its job.

"Yeah." Tran turned back around from looking at the cloud of smoke, barely visible beyond the white flame. "I get to do the fun part," said with a wide grin.

"I like the fireworks trick. How much time we got, my man?" Keyontay asked.

Tran consulted the Wenger on his wrist. "Sixty-eight seconds."

Three anxious faces brightened as Via jumped into the empty front seat and their driver hit the accelerator with aggressive resolve.

The old Rover lurched off its mark – like a Bengal tiger with fire on his tail.

"What'd you do to my jeep?" Via challenged.

"I didn't think you'd mind." Keyontay's tone was slightly apprehensive, but playful. "I've had some time on my hands waiting around while you guys were goofing off here in the Assyrian outback." He laughed.

"What'd you do to my jeep?" she persistently demanded.

"Nitro," he said sheepishly.

Via wasn't smiling.

"I thought this was the Babylonian outback," Tran quipped.

"Depends what part of history you want to reference," Keyontay remarked, cocky.

Via sighed. "Okay."

"Huh?" Keyontay turned to his boss.

"It's okay. It's fine. We're going to need it."

"Oh, so you like what I've done with your jeep."

"No, I will fire you as soon as we get back home alive."

Keyontay was about to object when Via's thumb jutted behind her. Everyone looked back to see Tran's cloaking inferno sputter and die.

"We're going to need it," Via repeated.

There were now a dozen vehicles poised behind the retreating flames. The ruins of only one jeep were visible in the foreground over the top of the small crater with Tran's prints on it. The rest were aching to resume the chase. As soon as the fiery barrier fell into the ground, the drivers all gunned it. The scene reminded Tran of clips of a Mogadishu video he'd watched: a stew of haphazardly equipped trucks, mostly converted civilian pickups and a riotous gang of assault rifle waving men. The only difference was the clothes. "Bedouins," he murmured under his breath, "haven't changed in three thousand years."

Bullets started cutting through the air, whizzing past the Rover at first. Two Audi commercial trucks, custom-styled flatbeds bearing .30 caliber cannons, appeared out of nowhere to Keyontay's left, moving quickly to try to cut off the fleeing crew.

"Are we at top speed?" Tran asked nervously as he stared out the window at the rapidly approaching former produce trucks.

"Not yet." Keyontay smiled as the needle passed 120 km/h. He veered right and dropped his hand to the center console. The top lifted up to reveal a titanium tank, shining bright red underneath the console. He lifted a lever and the suspension lowered the Rover's center of gravity, and its axles extended out a full half-meter on either side.

He was about to make everyone buckle up, but he didn't have to. He smiled as he saw his passengers strapping into the three-point belts.

"Ready?" he asked instead.

Three nodding heads responded. Keyontay's dark chocolate complexion contrasted sharply against a full set of gleaming white teeth. His wide smile opened slightly to allow his bright pink tongue to just barely protrude out between his teeth.

He hit the green button on the fire-engine red tank. The speed unloaded like a Maverick dropped from an F16.

The man, behind one of the cannons strapped to the back of one of the converted vegetable transports, became bug-eyed. He'd just sent off a fusillade of rounds slightly ahead of the Land Rover, calculated to make violent contact within seconds. But what would have cut Via's jeep in two now hit empty air.

The colonial British safari truck was gone.

Despite the force crushing her into the back of her seat, the Gs starting to distort the skin on her face, Via managed to thank Keyontay for his initiative.

"*Merci*," she struggled, pushing the word out from between flattened lips.

"*Il n'y pas de quoi, de rien, Mademoiselle*," he replied with Parisian flair, impervious to the tempest of physics on his frame. Then, as they raced off toward the ancient Babylonian river, approaching two hundred kilometers per hour, "Are you still going to fire me?"

*   *   *

MIGUEL LOOKED OVER his shoulder at the still blinking light on his phone sitting on his desk. He placed the scroll on a table just inside his office and bent down to pick up the pale prefect, carrying the young man to the sofa across from where Heinrich was seated. The German's frail body balanced precariously on the edge of the chair's seat cushion.

"Oh my!" the elderly scholar started.

"He'll be fine. He fainted." The Cardinal paused for just a second or two. "Twice." He grinned. Then, "I have to get the phone."

Miguel hurried to grab the impatient handset on the top of his massive desktop. He was thankful it was still showing a line on hold. He was sure the Dean was anxious on the other end, but not as nervous as he.

Maybe the Dean was calling to inform him that the Cardinal from Barcelona was now favored, or perhaps the Cardinal from Vienna. The informal polling prior to their convening was proscribed, but it happened behind closed doors for as long as he could remember.

Or was the passed-out priest correct? Did they really have a solid vote already locked up in his favor? He couldn't believe it. It just didn't seem possible. As he positioned himself behind his desk, he gulped for air and reached for the phone. But just then, another priest rushed through his still open door

"Father!" he yelled unbridled, rushing up to the far side of the wooden desk. His face was flushed and he was almost completely out of breath.

Miguel's hand was on the phone but he stopped to ask, "What is it, my son?" Calm, smooth, collected … on the outside.

The Cardinal, in truth, was not used to juggling so much simultaneously.

His well-ordered life had always … well, for a while at least … been serene: often, he thought, too much so. But he had never craved excitement. He was content with long, quiet days. He enjoyed meditating on the Holy Scriptures. He loved spending hours in prayer, uninterrupted, in the cathedral. His favorite spot at the church was tucked up in the nave near the quire where he could bask in the colored light that filtered through St. John's westward facing stained-glass windows. The sun always reflected a deep orange glow as it dipped into the Pacific at the end of the day. Miguel would otherwise prefer the mornings, but the heavy fogs in Lima obscured the early sun's light for hours almost every day. If he did go to St. John's Basilica before noon, he would often walk the cloisters alone, singing the latest Hillsong chorus. He worked hard to refrain from dancing.

"The tv!" the middle-aged cleric finally managed to blurt out.

Miguel nodded in consent. The robed messenger fumbled his way to the small set near the window.

Soon Peru's 24/7 *Canal N* was glowing from the screen.

"Hello," Miguel answered into the phone he had been holding.

"Yes, I'm sorry I was detained.

"No. Thank you.

"Okay.

"Really?" A tone of disbelief unmasked.

"Wow!" he exclaimed. "I would have thought that they'd end up picking another … more *traditional* member.

"Yes.

"Okay," Miguel replied.

The talking head was still vying for the Cardinal's attention, and now Miguel was being asked if he had seen the tv news.

"I'm watching it now," he said into the phone.

"No. It's okay.

"Sure. Forty minutes? I think I can get everyone together that quickly.

"Certainly. Thank you.

"God bless you too."

Miguel hung up the handset. A flood of emotions buried him.

"Father?" The priest standing by the television looked at the Cardinal for some direction.

"Assemble everyone in the chapel," he said.

A quick nod and the prefect was gone.

The other priest was now sitting up on the couch. His eyes were fixed on the news anchor still spewing rapid Spanish over the banner "*La mortaja de Torino es una falsificación.*"

Miguel rose and turned off the bluish glow. He hated tv. Everything about it bothered him, including the high pitched whine that filled a room even when the volume was muted. He turned to address the revived priest.

"You okay, Pedro?"

He stood up in response. "Yes, Father. I'm sorry."

Miguel regarded the young man with concern for his safety. He appeared in no danger of passing out again. "Are you okay to walk to the chapel?"

"Yes, Father."

"If you feel lightheaded, stop and sit down."

"Yes, Father." The priest tried to suppress a smile.

"Like your mother, aren't I?" Miguel returned with a warm curve of his lips.

It was obvious the young prefect didn't know how to respond. Cardinal Acamayo was so different. So kind-hearted. So informal at times. Always happy. Most of the archdiocese didn't really know how to act around him. It had been sixteen years since he'd been appointed Cardinal of the *Archidioecesis Limanu del Plazá de Armas*, and only a few, like Heinrich, had allowed themselves to become close enough to realize that Miguel was simply content to be himself. He never put on airs.

"I may go?" the priest finally asked.

"Yes, of course," Miguel said, nodding.

As Pedro hurried from the room, Miguel took his seat next to his friend.

Stauffenberg spoke first, "They picked you, didn't they?" A parched smile cracked the grizzled face.

"So it would seem." Miguel paused in thought. "But the decision is hardly final. Anything can happen during the voting. And if I am ultimately chosen, it looks like I'll have quite a mess on my hands."

"The Shroud?"

"Yes."

"But you knew." Heinrich's tone was only slightly querulous. "You knew there was another."

"Yes," Miguel admitted. "Many of us were told." He confirmed what the old man evidently had learned himself at some point.

"The Byzantines?" This time it was obviously a guess. "They had the real one."

"Why would you say that?" Miguel asked. The information hadn't yet hit the news.

"I have spent many years doing a very particular type of research, my friend. I have read many things. I don't know if there is a secret left for me." Eyes still sharp, they peered out at the Cardinal from a body that looked verdigrised with age.

"But you *are* guessing."

"Yes, but only because the last record was in 1784. I've found nothing more recent than that. But clearly the true shroud was in Istanbul – that is, Constantinople – until then. It is very likely that it stayed there up until the First World War. The Ottomans finally lost power in the 1920s, so it is possible it was moved after that. Or perhaps it was moved in more recent times now that the Islamization of Asia Minor has been completed.

"The secular government in Ankara," he continued, "has already lost control of the more radical *jihad*-minded groups. Christian missionaries are being kidnaped and killed. Indigenous Christians are almost non-existent outside of Istanbul itself. But for the government's protection, they'd be gone by now, as would the shroud, sooner than it was. But the secularists are on their way out of power. Like Iran, just slower. You see Damascus changing hands the same way, as the Ba'ath loses ground to the clerics at an ever-increasing pace. Then, of course, there's Egypt, Libya, Yemen, Bahrain, Saudi Arabia…. Which direction are they headed? The continuing unrest won't stop any time soon."

"The Shroud was stolen from Istanbul," Miguel confirmed.

"Ahhhh." It was almost a moan that seeped from deep down inside the thin man's hollow chest. "So it's been there all this time," Heinrich said after a lengthy pause, "since it left Edessa in 1140."

"I believe so. It's unlikely that it's been moved from Constantinople and back again during all this time." Miguel nodded. "We left it there intentionally. It follows that the Orthodox Patriarchate wouldn't have moved it either. They've controlled the Holy See on the Bosporus, more or less, since the Shroud arrived from Edessa. When Rome sacked Constantine's New Rome in 1204 they were after the Shroud, among other items. But cooler heads prevailed during the half-century of Latin control of the city. So they decided to continue to utilize the counterfeit shroud extensively. The Vatican has always been worried about the true Shroud being stolen."

"And now it has been swiped."

"Yes. When the Phanariotes in Constantinople's Greek quarter were allowed to keep the real thing, many in the Vatican remained nervous. But our Orthodox brothers have done a wonderful job over the years. Rome, of course, kicked itself in 1453 when the Ottomans took the ancient city and converted Hagia Sophia into a mosque. But to their surprise, the Turks allowed much of the ancient Orthodox tradition, started in 330 AD in Phanar, to continue. Ankara tolerates the Patriarchate; although, they still maintain an official position that the metropolitan has ecclesiastical authority over only the Greek minority inside Turkey's borders."

Heinrich couldn't help but interrupt. "But Bartholomew the First is the spiritual leader of over 300 million Orthodox Christians worldwide: Greece, Ukraine, Russia, Albania, and the huge numbers of Eastern Orthodox believers scattered all over the globe."

"That's right," Miguel agreed. "It's only been recently that the heretofore stubbornly secular Turkish government has allowed bishops who are from foreign soils on the Standing Synod of the Patriarchate."

The old man squinted as he studied the Cardinal's face, taking in the history that he didn't already know, assimilating it with his vast body of knowledge. Wondering. Thinking. Heinrich weighed his next question carefully.

Miguel seemed to be able to read his thoughts.

"Go ahead and ask me," the Cardinal said.

The German grinned and said, "Who stole it?"

ך

JOSHUA HAD THEIR full attention. He'd just finished giving his students a historical overview of the Shroud of Turin as well as the Byzantium Shroud, including the fact that the fake shroud had been in Chambéry, France in the possession of the Savoie family for about 400 years. Each student sat in deep thought while tucked into the recesses of Peet's aroma-filled café. Bear was already on his second double mocha and Charlie was leafing furiously through a binder of other documents he had gathered from Istanbul and his source in Armenia.

"I have one from *Bardaa* and two from *Tabriz*," he said. "Translations from early Nestorian tablets."

"From Cyril?" Sarah prodded.

"No. Oddly enough, the Syriac tablets were translated into Arabic in the 11ᵗʰ century. I got copies of both from a collector in *Vedi*."

"Where in the world is *Vedi?*" Bear asked. He prided himself in his knowledge of world geography, but always asked if he didn't know. He'd rather learn more and slight his rep than pass up the opportunity of adding to his mental library.

"Near Ararat, in Armenia."

"I thought Mt. Ararat was in Turkey. That's where they found Noah's Ark, right?" José chipped in.

"Found and lost again," Joshua bemoaned. "The Turkish government won't let anyone near the mountain now."

"*Vedi* is across the border from the mountain's peak," said Charlie, "but Ararat is also the name of a town in Armenia, just south of *Vedi*. Some historians claim Noah and his family actually first settled in what is now Armenia before moving farther south to the Mesopotamian valley."

"The tablets?" Sarah reminded everyone.

"Yes." Charlie already had his thumb on the first page of the set. He started passing his three-ring binder around. "Six pages altogether," he began. "The first three are just black-and-whites of the tablets themselves. Ibn says he has the original tablets in his collection."

"Ibn?" Sarah queried.

"Just Ibn," Charlie said. "He wouldn't give me another name."

"But he gave you *these*." Sarah was holding the notebook while flipping through the pages.

"I had a few things of interest to him," Charlie responded, looking pleased. "It was a fair trade."

"So? What do they say?" Sarah kept flipping pages. "Everything's in Syriac and Arabic."

"The English translation is not yet in my notebook. I just got it completed right before we left. It's in my email, though."

"Let me see." Sarah reached for Charlie's phone.

He pulled it back away from her grasping hand. "Sorry, I have an old T-Mobile Blackberry. You can open the attachment but it's too small to read. But I can tell you generally what the documents say. Basically, all three of the tablets are the same type of writing. They are each a charge, of sorts – like a detailed job description, or a commission."

"May I?" Joshua was across from Sarah, holding out his hand.

She slid the notebook from her side of the table. She kept her eyes on Charlie. "To whom?"

"A missionary from Nisibis. That's how Ibn and I found each other. He responded to a post on my Facebook while I was digging for stuff on Prester John. Evidently, while St. Elias was in Samarkand on one of his many missionary trips from Merv, St. Yuhanna took off to convert Yemen to Christianity." Charlie's summary was well-grounded.

"That makes sense," Joshua stated matter-of-factly as he studied the notebook.

"Yemen?" Bear reacted with disbelief.

Ignoring Bear, Charlie continued. "But I was a bit confused," he admitted. "These guys were early 11th century."

"What about that concerns you?" Sarah asked.

"The missionary to Yemen is referred to a bit curiously for a Nestorian saint. He evidently made it as far as Socotra Island, off Yemen's southern coast. He founded metropolitan sees in what are now *Al Adan, Ibb*, and *Al Mukalla*."

"Christians in Yemen?" José asked with disbelief.

"Hello?" Bear inserted. "That's *my* question!" Everyone had been ignoring him.

"Absolutely," Charlie addressed José. "Bahrain too. And Syria. And the Arab State of Lakhmid, which is now part of Iraq. All of them were *Christian* nations."

"Impossible!" Bear protested.

"What do you mean by that?" José stayed focused on Charlie.

"I mean that most of their citizens were practicing Christians and their governments controlled by those who claimed to be Christians – like Constantine."

"Or *Charlemagne*," Bear added with a scornful tone. But no one reacted to his comment.

"Wait a sec!" Sarah said excitedly. "Didn't Prester John claim to *rule* a Christian kingdom *outside* of Europe?"

"That's just the thing that bothers me," Charlie said. It would fit that Prester John was referring to Lakhmid or...."

"The Ghassanids," Joshua interrupted.

"The who?" Charlie gave the professor a puzzled look.

"The Syrian Ghassanids were one of the Arab Christian kingdoms. But could Prester John have been boasting about Ethiopia, Nubia, or even Georgia? Osrhoene, Armenia, or Adiabene? All were Christian nations at the time his infamous letter was circulating in Western Europe."

"All beyond the reach of Rome," José gasped. "I always thought that the Middle East, Asia and North Africa were Muslim."

"Muhammad didn't originate the religion that bears his name until the early 7th century," Joshua counseled. "Six hundred years is a long time. Christian missionaries had evangelized most of the civilized world, from Jesus' resurrection until 610 AD, when Muhammad claimed to have had his first Joseph Smith type of epiphany. At that time, there were hundreds of millions of Christians throughout Africa and all of Asia, even Japan and beyond. Abyssinia, that is, Ethiopia, was sending out *armies* to protect Christian communities on the Arabian peninsula. India had a string of Christian communities up and down both coasts. Sri Lanka had numerous churches. Even *the Americas* were being Christianized in the first millennium AD." Joshua's tone turned mysterious.

"What happened? Christianity only survived in Europe?" Sarah bemoaned, missing the implications of the professor's last comment.

"That's a long story," he responded, "but remember that the Coptic Christian community in Egypt traces continuous roots back to the first century. And the fact that Lebanon was founded as a Christian nation following World War II tells you that Middle Eastern Christians never completely left the Middle East." Their professor pointed at the last page of Charlie's research. "But this does seem to indicate that Lakhmid may have been Prester John's realm."

"See!" Charlie burst out. He was glad to get back to the subject.

"But you said it didn't make sense," Sarah reminded Charlie.

"Yeah, the timing is off," said Charlie, "but otherwise I think this missionary, St. Yuhanna, *is* the enigmatic Prester John."

"Possibly." The professor hedged a concession. "And this charge," he explained as he pointed to the last page, "instructs Yuhanna to evangelize Yemen and then head to *Al Hirah*."

"Where's that?" Bear decided to join back in with a mouth full of apple and sour cream pastry.

"*Al Hirah* was in what is now Iraq, on the Euphrates," Joshua explained. "But more importantly, it served as the capital of the Arab Christian kingdom of Lakhmid."

"Okay. Yuhanna is Middle Eastern for John. I get it. But I'm still having a hard time saying the words *Arab Christian*." Bear smiled with a mouthful of wafer-thin enriched dough.

"So Prester John was the *king* of Lakhmid?" Sarah queried.

"But that *can't* be! That's the problem," Charlie whined. "This charge has him in Yemen a hundred years or so *before* his letter was circulating Europe in the 1140s."

Didn't Marco Polo say he *met* Prester John?" Sarah asked. "Polo was around in the late *13th* and early *14th* centuries. So that makes the stretch even more unbelievable, doesn't it?"

"Marco Polo said a lot of things," Bear mumbled, reminding them of his position on the Venetian.

"Like Kublai Khan's ships that went around the world?" Charlie offered.

"Yeah," Bear said, taking a long drink of his lukewarm mocha. "Zheng's treasure fleet didn't sail until the 15th century. Kublai's fleet drowned in the sea of Japan in the 13th."

"But Zheng He traded with Yemen and Calicut, Baghdad and Baharain. Wouldn't he have written a record of Prester John's kingdom?" Sarah asked.

"There is a record, but it's from Kublai's fleet. They didn't sink until 1281. Some years earlier, they sailed up the Euphrates," Joshua added, "and guess who was on board when they docked in Lakhmid's capital?"

"Marco Polo?" Sarah guessed.

She was right.

Bear held up his hands. "Okay, okay. I give in. Prester John, the missionary priest-king, *did* exist." Then he added a sly smile. "So what was he, 150 years old when he met Marco Polo? His letter circulated Europe in the 1140s. Remember?" With a smug smile.

Arkesha had been silent for a while, but now she summed up her own thoughts about the evidence so far. "*Al Hirah*, the capital of the Arab Christian kingdom of Lakhmid was *on* the Euphrates. Yuhanna likely was based in the capital. So it stands to reason that Prester John was in *Al Hirah* when Marco Polo arrived. They could have met then."

"Quite the mystery." Joshua's admission was intended to answer everyone's comments as his eyes moved from one to the other of each of his students. "It is also possible that this St. Yuhanna isn't Prester John after all."

"But," Arkesha began, looking at Bear and wanting to address his hypothetical alogism, "the inventory from Edessa is dated in 1021 AD and signed by Prester John. St. Yuhanna was in Edessa in the 1020s, over a hundred years *before* the letter circulated in Europe boasting a Christian kingdom beyond the reach of Rome." Then her eyes surveyed the entire group and came to rest back on Bear with a look of alliance. "Polo's claim was surely over a hundred years *after* the controversial letter – probably 150!"

Arkesha let that one sink in. She watched Bear cross his arms over his puffed out chest. He painted an arrogant smile before she volleyed her own challenge his way. "But what if Prester John was a young man in the early

11th century? Who's to say he didn't live until late in the 13th? How long did Moses live? 120 years. Abraham? 175. Abram's father lived for 205 years. His great grandfather for 230. Go back another three generations and you'll find Eber. He lived to be 464 years old before he finally died. Middle Eastern dudes got some longevity in 'em." The South African tried on her best American soul-sister tinge. She flared out her hands in emulation of Queen Latifah.

Sarah laughed along with the rest of the group, sans Bear. "And you don't even go to church!" she ribbed her best friend. "But you sure have the Biblical ages down pat. However, that was during the second millennium BC. People were lucky to make it to sixty in the Middle Ages."

"In *Europe*," Joshua clarified.

"The Chinese have plenty of genealogical records from the Middle Ages showing ages up to 150 years," Arkesha offered. "Japan still boasts that one of their women reached 183 in the 14th century." Arkesha smiled at Bear.

"I have a question." José took over. "What's all this got to do with the true cross? Isn't that what we are headed to Rome to research?"

"And what about the stolen Shroud?" Bear squinted.

"It's here in the charge," Joshua answered, "near the end."

Charlie couldn't let the professor steal his thunder. "It makes mention of them both."

"The Nestorian tablets?" Sarah asked in disbelief.

"Yes," Charlie eagerly offered, "the final tablet mentions the cross as well as the Shroud. He talked like he was out of breath.

"So they were both in Edessa?" Sarah asked.

"It doesn't necessarily say that," Joshua cautioned, "but it implies they were kept in either Edessa or Nisibis. The language implies a contemporary, not historical context."

"My translator didn't tell me that part," Charlie said. "I used Global Visions. They do a great job with translations and interpreting."

"I've used them too," Joshua added. "You have to request a conference call with the translator to discuss possible nuances and inferences in the text, especially with Arabic, Syriac, and Farsi. They are very colorful languages used by an extremely expressive people."

"Emotional," Arkesha claimed.

"Why do you say that?" Charlie asked, turning to her. Arkesha was sitting between him and José, and like Charlie, she didn't look like an academic. Her dark chocolate skin and high forehead only accentuated her athletic build. She was a born Olympian. But she'd also earned her Master's Degree in Eastern Religious Philosophy from the University of Witwatersrand in Johannesburg in less than the normal two years. Now, she was well along in U of O's PhD program. She worked directly with Professor Walker on the impact of Christianity on the Japanese Shinto tradition.

"Just my experience." Arkesha downplayed her own comment. "You meet a lot of people when you compete internationally. I always found the Arabs, Berbers and Persians very sentimental."

"*Fanatical*, is more like it," Bear blurted.

Joshua gave Bear a disapproving look. "Look who's talking," he said.

"Hey! I don't blow up people," the student sneered.

"Neither do most Muslims," the professor retorted. "Just remember that we all live in glass houses. How many accusers were left to stone the woman caught in adultery after Jesus finished writing in the sand?"

"None." Bear's voice suddenly dropped along with his chin.

"It's not a bad thing to be passionate, Bear, but we need to understand better why the Islamic religion inspires so much violence along with its rapture. Muhammad died a mere two decades after he authored the Quran based on his knowledge of the Jewish, Christian and apocryphal texts; drawing from a Syro-Aramaic liturgical book, some from the Infancy Gospel of Thomas, some from the Protevangelium of James. He also borrowed heavily from the Old Testament. Joseph Smith wrote the Book of Mormon much the same way. But the important issue is why *so many* would choose to believe it. And, more so, why some become so fervent – to the point of homicidal rage."

"So, is there any clue in these translations where to look for the cross?" Sarah refocused the discussion. "And have we heard yet who stole the Shroud?"

"No, on both counts," the professor replied, shaking his head and pointing, "but these Nestorian tablets do mention another item of interest."

"John Mark's gospel!" Charlie interjected with excitement.

"That's right," said Joshua, "its reference to Simon's testimony is very likely a mention of the Gospel According to St. Mark, the Apostle Peter's account of Jesus' ministry."

"It appears they'd lost the original manuscript by that date," Charlie added.

"I agree, the language hints that a copy with the shorter ending of the gospel was being used in Edessa's metropolitan at that time," Joshua said.

"I've seen that in my Bible before, what's that all about?" Sarah was on the edge of her seat.

"There remains some question which ending was in the original manuscript. Mark 16 has three possible endings accepted by the church today," Joshua said with confidence. "Of course, there are other endings in lesser manuscripts too, but most are dismissed out of hand."

"Three?" Sarah was confused. "My Bible says there are only two."

The professor replied, "There's the longer ending, the shorter ending and the theory that chapter 16 ends at verse 8. It's the context and style of the manuscript *prior* to Mark 16:9 that has many theologians suggesting the gospel actually *ends* at verse 8."

"But then it would sound like Mark never finished it," she suggested.

"Exactly." Joshua pointed at her with approval. "Maybe he didn't."

The ensuing silence was deafening.

"The original is *missing?*" Bear must've been in his own world.

Joshua responded professorially, "*All* of the source documents for the scriptures have long since been lost or destroyed. We have numerous copies though, most of which are vastly consistent with each other – attesting to their authenticity. Also, there is plenty of provenance for the vast majority of the manuscripts."

"If the originals are missing, how do we know the Bible is accurate?" Bear persisted.

"Besides the fact, historically speaking, that it contains one of the most substantiated records from antiquity, it's a matter of philosophical logic," the professor answered.

"Like Anselm's argument for the existence of God?" Sarah posed.

"Somewhat ... yes," Joshua agreed. "Communicating in writing is the best way to ensure uniformity of the message. The Supreme Being that obviously created the universe is perfectly capable of protecting the authenticity of his rule book. He has preserved the Inventor's Owner's Manual quite well."

"Wouldn't it be so much easier if God just lived among us?" Bear offered.

"He did," Sarah said. "But look how we treated him."

"Both times," added the professor.

"Both?" the group said in unison.

"Oh look." Joshua tapped his watch. "We need to get to the gate for boarding." Smiling wide, he got up and wheeled his carry-on out of the coffee shop.

V

KEYONTAY MADE record time to the river's edge, about ten kilometers east of *Al Fallujah*. The Euphrates was placid, its languid currents hidden beneath the dark surface of the ancient channel.

"I don't see anyone," Keyontay said, as he slowed and started running parallel to the shore.

"That's a good thing. How far is my baby going from here?" Via was patting her Rover goodbye.

"You'd wanted at least two kilometers, right?"

She nodded.

"How's twenty sound?"

"Really." You know the tone she used. Not at all like a question.

"Really, really." He smiled and produced his remote driving device for her.

She turned the paper thin computer over in her hands. "I don't pay you enough."

"I don't do it for the money." He grinned and stopped the truck. They all piled out. Nena took Mandy in her arms. Tran grabbed his case.

"I'm going to introduce you to my friend, Naomi." Via patted her driver on his shoulder.

"Please don't," Keyontay said, holding up a palm, "I enjoy flying solo."

"But you don't even have a girlfriend," she protested.

"It's better that way. When I do meet the right woman, it'll be all over for me. Marriage. Kids. A *day* job." He laughed. "I've a world to see first."

"You have no idea. Wait 'til you meet her," Via predicted.

The four walked to the river's sandy beach and waded out into the blackness of its antiquated waters. They were surrounded by inky swirls of heaven's tears up to their waists when a slate-grey dome broke the surface. As a strange submarine rose to its full height off its waterline, it took the unique shape of a huge flounder. The giant flat fish was only six feet out of the water when it came to rest, awing them all. It had a streamlined deck that started at a bio-mechanical looking fin that ran down both sides of the craft, curving up bulbously to an apex with a hatch that lifted up on smooth hydraulics. As the porthole opened it made Keyontay think of how the top of his metal kitchen trash can popped up when he stepped on the floor lever.

No one came out to receive them as they stepped up onto the fin and climbed to the rounded metal surface which covered most of the unique sub. Keyontay disappeared down the hatchway first, and Nena passed Mandy's still unconscious form to him. The rest quickly followed, and the port-lid closed behind them.

The ship silently vanished back beneath the pall of the Euphrates' oily film.

Inside the submersible the faint light was a lime hue, giving the interior a modern, ethereal feel. Small pinpricks of red and yellow lights pulsated from control panels on sleek walls implanted with flat screen monitors and recessed keyboards. They were in a narrow hall, and they had the distinct feeling of being alone, like they just boarded a ghost ship.

"Come on," Via announced as she disappeared down the narrow corridor. Down the length of the hall, one of several ensconced berths carved into the side of the passageway was appropriated for Mandy. Via told Nena where to find the medic's closet.

"She's lost a lot of blood," Via said. "You'll find a supply of universal Type and NS, and an 18-gauge large-bore needle in the locker's refrigerated compartment. Bottom left. I'll be back shortly to see if you need any help."

With that, Nena stayed behind to strap in her patient while the others continued down the passage to the bridge. It was a short distance, the entire ship being only 27 meters from bow to stern. As they entered a cramped command center, Via stood at the front of the tiny entourage with Tran at the rear, clutching his heavy cargo case.

The bridge was shaped like a small apse, rounded in front at the pilot's seat, and rectangular through the balance of the tight space. A small periscope station occupied its center. The walls were lined with consoles facing empty seats. The captain's chair faced a series of angular windows shaped somewhat like those in a commercial jet, or perhaps a stealth bomber, its seat occupied.

"Hello, Admiral," Via announced. "Nice of you to pick us up," she said, smiling.

The finely accomplished older gentleman didn't turn around. But he answered her in a good-natured, salty tone. "USN *Captain*, retired. My dear, you remember that. But thank you for the compliment."

"You commanded your own aircraft carrier, my friend," Via responded. "You'll always be an admiral to me and a lot of others."

"It was a small aircraft carrier, my dear. I'm just a washed-up, old sea dog." His warmth saturated his words as he remained focused on the instrument panel before him. "Welcome aboard *Jonah's Ark*."

"*Jonah's Ark?*" Keyontay blurted.

"It's a long story." Via put her hand up to hush him. To the Captain she said, "I'm nervous about traveling north, Admiral."

"I can take you to the Gulf," the genial man responded, "but I'm confident we can cross into Turkey using the river."

"But the Tigris isn't deep enough through the Dahuk region."

"Yes, as well as a few other areas north of Tikrit, we will have to surface," he said, using pelagic tones.

"That's too dangerous."

"My dear." His white locks topped an affable set of eyes that twinkled as he spoke, like it was all a big game for him. "We will cross the shallows tonight. It is supposed to be quite dark after twilight, not much of a moon and a cloudy sky. We will be fine. I had my friends in Stuttgart engineer a completely silent propulsion system along with a few other neat tricks. Anyway, our displacement is only .68 meter with the air cushion deployed. We can get through some pretty shallow waters." He grinned.

"All right," Via seemed pleased. "North it is."

As Via led her people out they whispered to each other, "Do they not realize we are on the *wrong* river?"

Mandy was awake when Via came to help Nena. Tran and Keyontay had retired to their bunks, since they had first watch during the night. Mandy held out her hand and Via grasped it. "How do you feel soldier?" Via asked.

"Like I've been carried all over Iraq on someone's back." Mandy cracked a smile.

"Bruised up a bit?" Nena teased.

"I'd say. I've a feeling I know who slung me around like a training bag."

"Not I," Nena protested. "But I do need you healed up by the time we reach Silopi. We're on foot for 12 hours into the mountains eastward from there. Our ride will meet us in the forest. We have a tight schedule, but at least we'll get the manuscripts we need from *Vedi* before we get to Bariloche."

"We're not flying out of Dubai?" Mandy asked.

"No. It looks like Ibn will get what he wants after all." Via pulled out her Blackberry Curve and reviewed a list of cryptic lines, each with precise dates and times. "We had better be in Silopi by 0445, earlier if we can."

"I'll be ready." Mandy seemed confident.

"You have the option of staying aboard. Our man in Dubai can get you on a commercial flight to Lyon. You can wait for us in Chambéry."

In front of both Via and Nena she spoke her resolve, "And miss meeting the legendary Stauffenberg?"

"I can't imagine he'll be in Bariloche *personally*," Via cautioned.

"How old is he now, anyway?" Nena asked.

"I really don't know, in his 90s, or perhaps he's passed into his centenary. He was a young man during the war, but not *that* young." Via thought about it for a minute. "He's been in the basement of that cathedral in Lima since '47. I'm surprised those damp archives didn't kill him a long time ago."

"Isn't Pizarro's crypt in the chapel there at St. John's?" Nena screwed up her face as if smelling the decay of the corpse.

"No, actually, they found his bones underneath the basilica's main altar," Via answered.

"Inside the sanctuary?" Nena's face contorted further.

"Yes. Unceremoniously packed away in two separate metal boxes as if by obligation, knowing he had no right to be buried on holy ground." Returning to the subject, Via added, "Heinrich's been digging in the basement archives for decades: The records go all the way back to November 16, 1532."

"The Cajamarca massacre." Mandy dipped back into the conversation.

"Yes," Via said. "And a steady stream of documents from Europe have been stashed in Lima ever since. First the Spanish, then the Portugese, and most recently the Germans and Italians. It seems that the Church has been using Lima as a safe haven for storage outside of Europe for quite some time now."

"Quite the treasure trove, huh?" Mandy feebly added.

Via heard the weakness in her voice. "We're headed to the bridge. Get some sleep, sweetie. We'll be back to check on you in a bit. Hit the call button if you need anything. You'll be able to eat after another hour, so let us know when you wake up, we'll bring you some food."

"But I'm hooked up to a gourmet meal already." Mandy managed a small laugh.

Nena turned to Via. "I gave her four pints of O negative along with 240ccs of Normal Saline and a piggyback of Cefazolin. Her bp was 70/40 and her pulse was 120. She lost a lot of blood back there. She'll be out again in a minute or two. It'll keep her under for a while."

Then Nena turned to Mandy. "We love you, girl. Get well soon. We're going to need your help." She stepped away to hide teared up eyes and headed for the bridge.

Via stayed behind. "How long has it been since you've seen him?"

"I was just a child when we moved to London." She was starting to get groggy. "My mother married an Anglican missionary. Put on top of that strain…." She faded away into a drug-induced sleep. Via stayed for a minute and then finally let go of Mandy's hand. "It's going to be okay, sweetie. I believe in redemption."

Λ

THEIR UNITED AIRLINES international flight was full, and the student's seats were spread out from the wing to the back of the tail. Sarah ended up by herself. She looked around her at the sea of people stuffed inside the coach section of the 777. The only set of paired seats for their little group went to José and Arkesha. Bear and Charlie's seats were nearest the exit.

Sarah Byrd settled into her seat. It was to be another long flight. They were set to stop at De Gaulle, but they wouldn't switch planes. She didn't even know if they would be allowed to disembark at the terminal. With over an hour on the ground, she sure hoped so. Her eyes kept searching for Joshua, but she couldn't find him in the flood of bodies, packed like sardines inside the fuselage.

"You need to put that away and fasten your seat belt." Sarah recognized the voice to her chagrin. She refused to look up. That voice was supposed to be part of her past. A forgotten bump in the road. A bad dream you never have to remember.

She quickly tucked her iPad into her purse and put the purse under the seat in front of her. She buckled up.

She could sense the strict flight attendant from their last flight leaving so she looked up. She saw the back of the enforcer as she marched up the aisle. This is gonna be a long flight, she thought.

Charlie had given her his three-ring binder. Sarah smiled at the opportunity to examine its contents. She pulled it out of the pocket in front of her where she'd stowed it earlier. Without the distractions of the still ongoing Prester John debate between Bear and Charlie, Sarah started examining each document carefully along with Charlie's copious notes.

There were copies of papers he had gathered from all over the world. Most were sourced from Istanbul and *Vedi*, but he had a few from Lima, one from a church in Brisbane, of all places, several from churches in Europe, and a couple from libraries in New England. She started by reading through a thick set of letters in Spanish. There was no translation and Sarah struggled to read the contents. She was fluent in the romance languages, but quickly recognized the need for a specialist. It's like one who speaks modern English trying to read the same language as it was written only a few hundred years before. Really not the same language any more. It's like that with a lot of things.

She'd worked with an epigrapher before. So she was going to give it some effort. The linguist had walked her through a few Spanish inquisition era documents last year: Catalonian. They'd been written in a cornucopia of medieval Castilian and Catalan Provençal. Funny, she thought, English is a conglomeration of German, French and Italian – Greek too.

Armed with this limited exposure to Iberian medieval languages, she began to pick over the first document as the flight took off. JFK dropped away below her and the nose of the big Boeing pointed towards Paris.

Soon Sarah was full of amazement. Her eyes flitted back up to the top of the first letter in the section. She flipped back through each page, looking. She had picked up on something. What was it? What is it? Just a feeling?

The dates of the letters ranged from 987 AD to 1716 AD. Where had they originated from? Where had they been stored?

Two of the letters contained maps showing coastal details. One had a long list of figures that she couldn't interpret, but the references appeared to have something to do with a lunar eclipse viewed at different meridians. Charlie's notes were buried at the bottom of the stack. From the almost illegible handwriting, Sarah was able to deduce that Charlie had indeed not had the documents translated at the time he assembled the binder. However, he did have a few interesting facts about them listed. His notations looked like he was jotting down a list from a spouse before going to the grocery store. Perhaps his translator was on the phone? He'd said he'd gotten an email without the nuances. Joshua must be able to read these. He already seemed to know what they meant when he was looking at the notebook earlier. Not just the Syriac either.

Sarah examined the papers for another hour trying to figure out what her thoughts were telling her. Exhausted, she stopped thinking. She just stared at the name of one of his sources. Part of this group of letters came from Lima, from a German archivist. The link was there. But what was it?

Her mind still spinning, Sarah turned back to the letter in the front. She tried to clear her mind and start fresh. It was dated in 1092 – written by a monk. Who else knew how to write back then? He'd been in a monastery in Tarragona. He'd written to a monk. Who else knew how to read in the 11th century? She was glad to be born in the 20th. The recipient lived in his monastic cell in Kenneshre, on the Euphrates. The letter looked like, from its context, the last in a long series of correspondence between the two. Two scribes deeply immersed in their work. Modern Christianity owes so much to these dedicated souls. And we complain if we have to touch an electric typewriter, even one with a memory card. She smiled. She was married to the Internet ... to her iPad ... to her phone. What would she have done with a candle and a quill?

The letter referenced *convivencia* and the recapture of Toledo from the Moors. But it was the mention of the cross that drew most of her attention. A mention of the artifact, if one could call it that, being moved from Jerusalem to Antioch. Then to Edessa. Was it common knowledge back then?

Hermano Narvaez was informing his Middle Eastern Christian brother that Constantinople was vying for the transfer of all of the church property in Edessa and Nisibis as early as 1089. He wrote that the Orthodox Church was passionate about gaining possession of it all. They were incessant.

She started thinking it through. If the cross really was in Edessa right before the city was destroyed in the 1140s, and if it did get moved to the Orthodox See prior to the Turk's decimation of the center of Syriac Christianity, then would its presence in Constantinople have prompted Rome's sacking of the city in 1204? There was no name mentioned in the letter other than "*mi hermano,*" so she had nothing to go on other than where the recipient lived: Kenneshre. Iraq. Still a strange anomaly to her. The modern world just doesn't get it – the Middle East was thoroughly Christian for 1000 years following Christ's crucifixion.

Not being able to decipher much more from the letter, she turned to the next one that drew her interest. It was a 13th century Spanish translation of a letter between an Egyptian monk and a monk on Mount Athos, Greece. The missive was penned in 1220 AD. The author had claimed that copying the Codex Sinaiticus was his life's work. She thought about that for a few minutes. What if her job, day in and day out, was to hand copy a long manuscript with perfect accuracy. Every word. Every bit of punctuation. The Bible. And then, once done with a complete copy, to start over and do it again. And again. And again. Every day. Every year. From the beginning of your life with the Church, until the day you were too weak to write. Or too blind to see.

But millions of Christians did just that over the course of time. From Noah until the printing press. Maybe in the 1500 years before The Flood, too, unless they had copy machines back then. Who knows?

The Egyptian monk was based in Alexandria. A dedicated scrivener, he had been taken in by the monastery as an orphan, a child of only six when his Coptic parents had been killed by Berber raiders to the west of the city. Their farm was burned. He'd been found huddled in a ball on the floor of a ravine. The dry river-bed had saved his life. God had preserved him for a reason, he wrote to the Greek. It was a letter of introduction to the Orthodox monk stationed at St. Peter's, on the small outcropping of rock in the Aegean, part of the Patriarchate based in Constantinople. After the lengthy introduction, the Coptic dove into a treatise on the mystical powers prevalent in the first century church. He spent a lot of time on oral history and St. Paul's first letter to the church in Corinth.

Sarah found the letter quite strange. She didn't understand the references to Jesus' blood. The sentences that discussed the power of the cross seemed out of place, more like she was reading a Buddhist musing instead of a Christian text. There was no mention of the location of the cross.

Confused, she moved on. Perhaps she was misreading certain words – the meanings of which have changed significantly since the 13th century. There were several words in the letter that she couldn't figure out. She thought, perhaps, it had been an imperfect translation into medieval Spanish from the original Greek as well. Greek, of course, would have been used by the Coptic in writing to the monk on Mt. Athos. She tried to put all of her questions out of her mind again. Thus, she moved to the next letter she'd earmarked.

Again, she was looking at a strange mixture of medieval Iberian script. Like a recipe that resulted from a bachelor's boredom. Disorganized. Haphazard.

But this letter was mostly Castilian, so she found it easier to read.

The translation was from Syriac correspondence written in China in the year 1269 AD. A monk, calling himself *Bar Sauma*, was writing what appeared to be a letter to a dear friend. And his friend wasn't a monk. Interesting. Someone besides a monk who knew how to read? Even more curious, the letter's recipient was a stonemason who'd risen to become a Master Builder in Lalibela, the New Jerusalem in Ethiopia. He'd been placed over the construction of one of the many incredible rock-hewn Christian churches built in the huge city during that period.

Sarah read the two-page translation, only getting stuck on a couple of words. She had a pretty good guess, using presumed Latin roots, how to interpret the few words she didn't already know. Thus solving the puzzle of the missive's contents, she paused. Squinted her eyes. Smiled big.

She was awestruck. She read the letter again.

Bar Sauma claimed to have *seen* the cross. Jesus' cross. Intact. On public display. In Constantinople. Inside none other than the Hagia Sophia.

If that was true, wouldn't such an event be part of the history books? Could it be true? The Hagia Sophia was still controlled by the Orthodox Church at that time. It would make sense, if the cross had been taken from Edessa to the Bosporus, that they would put it on display. But why would all formal records of the event be erased from history?

Curious, she turned her attention to a section of the letter that really freaked her out. The writer in China made a quick reference to vials of blood being stored in Jundishapur, as if it were common knowledge. Apostles' blood. She'd never heard anything like it before. What was a 13th century Nestorian missionary in China doing talking to a friend in Africa about stored blood? She'd heard of *Bar Sauma* before. He was a well-known member of the church during his lifetime. Why would members of Jesus' original twelve disciples even have their blood taken for preservation? How would they have preserved it? Why would it be in Persia? Vials? Did they even have vials back then? Certainly they didn't have refrigeration. In Siberia, maybe, but not in Persia. Well, in the mountains, maybe, but Jundishapur was in the valley. Well, it was at the foot of the.... No, it just didn't make any sense. She must be misreading something again.

She wondered what the people of Tehran would think if the world found out that such a New Testament stash was resting in the cold heights of one of their peaks.

"Sarah."

"Yeah," she answered without looking up. She was lost in the foothills, walking over the ruins of a Persian Christian monastery, looking up at the snow-covered mountain on the edge of the fertile crescent.

It was Arkesha. "Come with me." Urgency.

"Huh?" Still lost in Iran's hinterland east of the Tigris.

Arkesha grabbed Sarah's wrist and pulled. Hard.

"Hey!" Sarah was yanked out of her reverie.

"Come on!" a harsh whisper. Sarah slipped the notebook into the back pocket of the seat in front of her. She was still buckled in. It was a struggle to get unfastened as her body was being pulled to leave the seat prematurely.

Then she looked at Arkesha's face. It was enough to make her speed up. Her mind was back in gear.

"What is it?" Women's worse fears flooded her thoughts.

Arkesha just pulled. "Come on."

Sarah was dragged along, past row after row of sleeping passengers, until Arkesha abruptly stopped and pointed.

They both saw the same thing. Their professor engaged in animated conversation. But for Sarah, it sent chills up her spine. Because the individual gesticulating maniacally opposite Joshua was *that woman!* The dark short hair. Yet another tight top. Yet another gaudy brooch. Unmistakable. It was her, the woman from the last plane!

But Sarah had looked for the interloper while disembarking in New York. She'd watched for the woman at the gate while boarding for this flight. She'd stood at the gate and waited until she was the last passenger to give up her boarding pass at the top of the ramp.

Sarah was positive. That woman didn't get on this plane – yet here she was.

The mystery deepened as Sarah watched the two argue back and forth.

The woman had been staring at Joshua silently before. But now they acted like they knew each other. Then it hit her … she had told no one. Arkesha hadn't known about the stare down on the flight from Portland. How then did Arkesha know Joshua was in danger? He was, wasn't he?

"What's going on?" That was all Sarah could muster.

9

"WHAT A GOD-FORSAKEN place!"

Roland Enson was puffing on a thick Montecristo, standing in front of the stone clock tower in *San Carlos de Bariloche*.

"If I wanted the Swiss Alps, I'd go to *Grindelwald*. Whose idea was this!?"

Pure derision.

The broad-shouldered man wore a silk Canali that reflected the sun almost as much as the Andean white-capped points behind him.

Mt. Tronador, comparable in height to much of the range that dominates Switzerland's landscape, towered over the western horizon. The small town nestled at the top of the Patagonian foothills in Argentina served as the center of South America's European Alpine transplants of architecture and culture.

The mighty Andes range straddles the Argentine-Chilean border all the way from far north of their common boundary to Tierra Del Fuego in the south. The CEO had always imagined a world without national boundaries. He turned to stare at the imposing teeth cutting into the sky. His lust for power made the peaks look small. Just one more hurdle to gaining more of it. Addiction. He would never have enough.

Enson had been using English, but he switched. He chose Dutch to offer up a string of curses like some bloody sacrifice to an ancient god. His steam expended, he turned to his companion.

"We've still got the boat close?" he barked.

"We're still anchored in *San Matías*." The untidy stick of a man was resisting his urge to grovel before the world's wealthiest man. "It's a short ride to *Puerto Lobos*. We can take the launch and be...."

The black-tressed executive cut him off. "The helicopter's too slow!" Roland's steel-grey eyes grew colder.

"But only *Puerto Madryn's* airport has sufficient runway length to accommodate the Hawker." Enson had been insistent on using his highly customized Hawker 900-XP private jet.

"Then we should be anchored in *Golfo Nuevo*, shouldn't we." Not toned as a question. The scoff flew out of Roland's mouth along with just enough spittle so that Porfiry had to wipe it off his cheek.

"*He* ... suggested *Lobos*. 'It has nice cafes,' he said," reported Porfiry as he drew himself up to his full height, notwithstanding his bloodshot eyes and his sore feet. He wasn't sure how much longer he could bear to work for this man. But it was better than Kiev, he thought ... for now.

"*He suggested Lobos*," Enson mocked. "That decrepit old Nazi. He's worthless. He'd better be on time."

"But he's not able to make it ... in person." Porfiry cowered as he spoke. His greasy hair fell from his forehead into his eyes as he rushed to explain. "He's sending the papers with a trusted courier. He said...."

The big man cut him off, slapping him across the face with enough force to jerk the Russian's head to the side.

"Imbecile!" Enson yelled. "You know you should have told me before now!"

Now he wished he'd stayed in the Ukraine.

"Now we will be lucky if we get anything from that old crook!" Enson glared.

"He wouldn't meet us in Lima. He said...." The spindly frame shook as his teeth clattered. He was already backing away from another impending blow.

A young French couple nearby became frightened and rushed away from the scene.

"*He* said. *He* said." Roland threw his Cuban at the assistant's chest. "Is that all you can say?" His face turned fire red. "I'll tell you something. If we don't get those papers ... *all of them* ... you won't be working for me by the end of the day."

"But I can't afford to lose this job!" Porfiry whined.

That's not all you'll lose, Enson decided.

*　　　*　　　*

"HOW ARE WE GETTING to the Tigris?" It had been bothering them.

Keyontay's tone was one of curiosity that dipped into disbelief.

Tran was nodding in agreement.

They were sitting across from Via and Nena in the tiny galley aboard *Jonah's Ark*. The men hadn't been able to sleep, especially after smelling what the Admiral had cooked up.

"This ship is amazing!" Nena ignored them. "Can you believe that it's designed to be run by a crew of one?"

They sat at a nice table, showcasing a huge platter of braised scallops over an Alaskan Halibut. The big plate was a replica of a Ming porcelain platter. It sat atop a polished teak surface in the center of sautéed vegetable sides. Keyontay was staring at the fish while he addressed Via, thinking all along that the strange submersible carrying them looked a lot like what they were about to eat.

"We *are* under the surface of the *Euphrates* right now, right?" Keyontay underscored his original question. "We *are* traveling *north*, right?"

"Smells good." Nena dug in and filled her plate. The meaty fish was stuffed with spinach, mushrooms, and melted goat cheese.

Via answered, "We're taking the canal between the two rivers. It's just a few kilometers north of here."

"I was wondering," Keyontay responded, looking concerned. "Here we are in the middle of Iraq, and as I remember my geography, to get from here to the Tigris by water we'd have to pass through Kuwait. I wasn't privy to this part of your planning."

"Need to know. Need to know." Via teased.

"I didn't know about the canal."

"*Canals*. They were dug by Nebuchadnezzar in the 6th century BC."

"Doesn't the Euphrates start in Turkey just like the Tigris?"

"It does. But far from the Armenian border. We must take the Tigris to get anywhere close to Ararat."

Nena was devouring one of the sides: candied yams.

"Where'd you get those?" Tran reached for one of the tubers on Nena's plate.

She slapped his hand. "Get your own! They're in the warmer." She pointed to a large metal drawer under the convection oven. Tran slipped out of his chair and pulled out the stainless steel drawer. It was divided into three sections. He found the yams and then peeked into the other compartments. One held freshly baked cornbread with sweet corn kernels, steaming from the sweet, grainy dough – the other an assortment of wheat and white homemade rolls. The swirl of fresh bread aromas hit the room and every mouth watered.

He smiled and grabbed a platter from the counter, filled it up, brought it to the table … everyone's hands reached for the breads.

"Where's my jeep now?" Via turned to Keyontay and asked with a mouth stuffed with cornbread.

"Let's see," he offered and pulled out his remote. A small LCD screen gave him a view out the front windshield of the Rover, showing a barren wasteland where Abraham once grazed a thousand fat-tailed sheep.

He tapped the bar on the bottom of the screen. It pulled up a command menu. His fingers moved quickly over the surface as the device responded, giving him several different readings.

"They haven't found it yet," he boasted.

"So it's safe?"

"For now."

Just then, they were startled by the sound of a pulsing alarm.

Lights appeared along the ceiling in the galley. They blinked from the corridor just outside the open hatch. Via jumped up from her seat and disappeared into the hallway, running for the bridge. Only Tran stayed in his seat for a couple more seconds. He took another bite before rushing to catch up, still chewing a wad of scallop.

"What is it Admiral?" Via asked with urgency as soon as she'd entered the bridge.

"I'm going to need all hands, dear. This ship can navigate with only a one-man crew, but when we're under attack it's best if I have a team on my side."

"Tell me what to do," she offered.

"Look at the screen on your right. Then just dole out the assignments for me, would you?" A tone of a man of leisure.

Via didn't have to ask any more questions. She turned to the screen. The computer was amazing. It showed her everything anyone would want to know about the threat and the submarine's capabilities. Both offensive and defensive.

Nena was at her shoulder looking on with awe. "Trouble?"

"Yes. It would seem that *The Ark* is under attack."

"Who?"

"The Americans."

"They're still here?"

"You thought they'd *ever* leave?"

"Campaign promise."

"But they eventually *did* leave."

"Pentagon promise."

That drew a laugh.

Nena counted off in her head the post-war bases Uncle Sam still had all over the world. Germany. The Philippines. South Korea. Japan. Italy. She kept counting.

"You take this station." Via pointed at the screen. Nena understood. She vanished before Via could say another word.

"Keyontay?"

"Here." He had slipped into Nena's spot right at Via's left.

"You stay here with the Admiral. Learn to drive this thing. If he gets hurt, we'll all be in your hands."

"No pressure." He gave her a broad smile though her back was to him. She could feel the warmth, but moved on.

"Tran?" Via's command started with a tentative tone as Keyontay stepped to the side and took a seat at one of the empty consoles.

The man was still swallowing scallop, a bulge squeezing down his throat like a rodent traveling the length of a snake. "Yes ma'am," he managed.

"Your position is up here." She pointed. "See how you get in this spot?" She drew a line on the screen from the bridge to a weapons station in the back of the craft. The path was highlighted through the see-through 3D image.

Tran was gone.

"Admiral?"

"We're surfacing, Via, brace yourself." The voice came from under the Admiral's strikingly handsome, thick head of hair.

The vessel lurched dramatically as it angled sharply to the surface.

"Strap in!" His voice rose with triumphant excitement. A kid in a candy store. "Hold on!" Jubilant.

Via knew she was in the hands of a man having fun. Grown-up toys. The Captain was chuckling with glee as the piscine sub shot out of the water. It jetted out of the murky river just underneath a triumvirate of Blackhawks. The jet-powered rotors stirred the Euphrates' dark surface like some angry witch over her iron pot. The swirl of waves broke free behind them as the sleek water craft quickly sped out from under the hovering birds. Chopper pilots were dazed. Their crews confused. The video feed back at the FOB had soldiers wondering how to classify the odd looking craft that raced away now on top of the river's surface.

The Captain typed another command. His right hand's fingers tickled the keypad as his left pulled back on the yoke.

At that moment, Tran was climbing into a small compartment that sat slightly above and behind the back of the hall that traversed the length of the keel. As he positioned himself in the swiveling seat, he noticed how little room he had. He couldn't see any controls. There were no windows. No screens. But he strapped himself in and buckled up.

The walls rose.

Slowly the controls appeared along with video screens … even a slit of window that wrapped around him 180 degrees. He could see the river falling behind them at break-neck speed. It reminded him of the jet-boat races he'd watched off the coast of India last year.

Tran looked to his right, then to his left, facing out of the rear of *The Ark*. The river's banks were a blur. The sides of their sub were sprouting wings. They were shaped like a humpback whale's long fins. Corrugated flippers.

He turned his attention back to the screens. There were five liquid crystal displays that followed the circular line underneath the window. He locked his eyes on the armed trinity that dipped their noses and accelerated in hot pursuit. The Blackhawk helicopters leaned hard into the desert air and started to gain.

As *Jonah's Ark* morphed from a flounder-shaped submersible into a winged, metal-clad flying fish, Tran's monitors brightened. Warnings flooded each screen. He didn't know which to address first. There – the most immediate threat – the iron-locust in the lead bore armor-piercing missiles. A radar-controlled projectile was locking on to them. He knew that as soon as the bird's pitch lever leveled it out, the Blackhawk would send an

AMRAAM Sparrow towards the fleeing anomaly. His throat tightened and he had difficulty swallowing.

A heads-up display jumped out into the center of his world. Tran gaped but reacted with decisiveness. It gave him a choice. He liked choices.

Via was going to have a hard time getting him off this boat, he thought. More alarms. Two more Sparrows locked on. All three of the US helicopters were about to destroy their target. How was he going to stop three missiles coming at them at the same time?

Below, the Captain was daring the chasing choppers to fire. A good-natured, vocal challenge came from his smiling mouth. He leaned hard to the right of his seat, bending the yoke into a joystick of one huge video game control.

Via stifled a scream as she saw the river's shoreline rushing to crash into their bow.

Tran was equally startled by the sudden turn to the bank. The canal was still a bit farther north. Here the sand and rocks of a wild desert would greet them with a simple crush of finality.

We are going to crash! What else would Tran have thought?

A consummate soldier, he blinked and focused on the job at hand. In the remaining second or two he enjoyed before a violent death, he made his choice.

The heads-up display had made it fairly simple. Just pick one of a few graphics that depicted some defensive options. He chose the coolest one.

"Drone."

١ ٠

UNITED'S INTERNATIONAL flight 259 touched down on one of *Roma Leonardo Da Vinci Liumicino's* runways southwest of the city on seven hills. Sarah languished in her seat. Her thoughts were muddled. They raced uncontrollably. The mysterious vixen's sudden reappearance out of nowhere was perplexing her to no end. The contents of Charlie's notebook confused her. Then there was the cross, the Shroud, the vials of blood ... her own research fit into the maze somewhere, but it was like a forgotten puzzle piece that never made it into the box. And her growing feelings for Joshua clouded it all. After Arkesha had dragged her down the aisle and she'd seen the argument, Sarah had felt a huge weight and trudged back to her seat. How did that woman get on the plane?

But her professor hadn't seemed stressed. He'd been at ease during the intense conversation, like he knew the woman. Of course he knew the woman. She certainly knew him. Who was she? And what's with the new outfit each time she shows up?

Sarah looked down at her own simple attire. Basic. Comfortable. It's what she'd selected to put on this morning ... 4am in Eugene. Long day. They were traveling back in time, toward tomorrow. It made her head hurt just thinking about it. No wonder people suffer jet lag when they arrive in Europe from the States.

The enigmatic siren had changed clothes three times since Portland: once, for sure, while on the plane. But now that they were finally in Rome, Sarah didn't even bother to look for the woman. She got off the plane glad she'd slept through the Paris layover, glad she could get into a bed soon.

Their hotel was near the Vatican. Their meetings didn't start until tomorrow. Was it tomorrow already? I hope not, she thought.

Sarah focused back on the research they were conducting. They had a lot to be excited about, and a bunch of questions that needed answers. They had a huge amount of work in front of them.

"Are you okay?"

Bear put a small, soft hand on her shoulder.

"Bear!" she exclaimed, more than glad to see him.

She almost knocked him down. They were standing at the front of the empty 777. The concourse stood gaping at them, the rest of the passengers having already disembarked.

"Come on!" She started pushing him backwards with both hands on his chest. He dropped his carry-on's handle to the carpet.

He looked down … started to bend over to get it.

"Leave it!" Sarah demanded. "We'll be right back." She spun him around and now pushed on his back, again with both hands, straight back down the aisle and towards the back of the plane.

"What are we doing?" Bear protested, while allowing the slight figure to direct him back into the depths of the fuselage.

"I have to show you something." Now she was whispering. It echoed off the empty rows.

"Why are you whispering?" He wasn't.

"We're supposed to be off the plane." Quietly.

"Oh." His tone joined hers.

"Okay – here." She stopped pushing. "Stand right here. Look this way. No. Like this." She used her hands to manipulate the position of Bear's chin.

He was amused. This was more attention than he'd ever had from such a pretty girl. Sarah was a natural beauty. She didn't wear much make-up and wore her blond hair in a simple ponytail most of the time. Her face and body were perfectly proportioned and her constant outdoor recreational activities kept her in great shape. But it was her genuine warmth and amazing smile that captivated people. Everyone wanted to be her friend. A constant stream of would-be suitors tried in vain to get a date. Bear just let himself get pushed around and a big goofy smile spread on his face.

"Pay attention!" she whispered hoarsely.

He wiped off the smile and looked as directed. "I see a bathroom." Demurely.

"Right. Okay. So if you are standing here, on your way to use that bathroom, and you notice it is occupied, and then you see someone come out of it and close the door behind them, and then you walk from here...."

He was thinking Sarah needed to slow down, already.

"Walk!" she commanded.

He obeyed.

"Okay, so you head to the bathroom and...." She stopped. "Hey! Keep your eyes on the door." She pushed against his jawbone again.

He did as she said.

"Okay. So you walk from here to ... that's right. Okay. Right. Now we're here. So you open the door. No wait!" She grabbed his extending hand and pulled it back. "You don't open the door. You were going to open the door. But you can't."

"I can't." He didn't whisper.

"Whisper!"

He pressed his lips firmly together as if to recapture the sound.

"You can't."

"I can't."

"Right." She continued with a mystical hue, "You can't because the door is locked."

"But someone just left the bathroom. How'd the door get...."

"Shush!"

He shushed.

"The sign says it's *occupied*." Her whisper was now conspiratorial.

"But it's not."

"But it is."

"No. It's not." Bear wasn't being quiet again. "'Cause I just saw the last passenger to use it leave and shut the door. So the bathroom is empty."

"Yes. So it would seem." Her tone was now deep cover. A covert op. Cloak and dagger. "Nevertheless, it *is* indeed occupied."

He twisted up his mouth.

"So," Sarah continued, "you stand here and shake the door."

"Because it must be broken," he was whispering again.

He shook the door. "The lock must have slipped. I'll just jiggle it free."

"Right," Sarah confirmed, "but as you are jiggling – the door suddenly opens!" Drama.

"I jiggled it free?"

"No!" Sarah scolded, "Pay attention."

He did.

"The door opens and a woman steps out." Sarah tried on her most foreboding sound.

"There were two people stuffed in here?" Bear now opened the door and peered into the tiny space. "It's not big enough for two."

Sarah stood by his side and waited … impatiently.

"But I guess they both squeezed in here. That's why you dragged me back here to the toilet? Some riddle." Disgusted, he turned to leave.

"Wait!" Sarah held up both hands.

"The others are surely wondering where we are. We need to go."

"I know there weren't two people in the bathroom."

"How do you know?" Reluctant.

"Because Arkesha saw the whole thing."

"O-kay." An inflection that said, "You are wasting my time."

"She was the one waiting out here, watching the door, jiggling the lock."

He gave his best *I'm not impressed* look.

"And *you* were the one who'd just left the bathroom."

Bear opened the door again and looked in. "I did see Arkesha when I left here." He looked in the closet-sized bathroom again. "But I was the only one in here." He said it like he was stating the obvious.

"That's my point."

"Oh." And then, "Oh, it is." Realization.

"So I want you to tell me how the woman got in here after you left, without Arkesha seeing her go in."

"What did she look like?"

"Short, dark hair, big ugly brooch … what does that matter?!" Exasperation.

Bear paused and was obviously thinking. Sarah was actually hoping for a solution to the riddle. Bear had a practical mind. Logical. Analytical. She must have overlooked something. The woman couldn't have just appeared inside the bathroom out of thin air!

"Arkesha was mistaken," he finally said what seemed to be the simple explanation.

"That's it?" Sarah shouted. Not happy.

"Every other conclusion is impossible," Bear said firmly. "Unless you think I was packed into this phone booth with a lady."

Sarah didn't even consider the possibility.

Perhaps he was right. Maybe Arkesha was just too tired to remember clearly. Okay. Puzzle solved.

"You two again!" exclaimed the brash stewardess, hands on her hips, only a few steps away.

*   *   *

"I'M AT THE AIRPORT now, just about to get my boarding pass." Miguel was on the phone.

He was both nervous and excited. He'd known for some time now that the progressive factions in the Church would likely be choosing the next Pope, but he'd really not pictured himself as being the one they'd select. He figured they'd pick a moderate.

A moderate, he wasn't.

In fact, he was so liberal in some areas that he'd been accused by some of being a Protestant. Yet, he always sided with the conservatives on the Deity of Jesus and issues of moral purity. However, he believed priests should not only marry, but most of them should be required to do so. First Corinthians 7 was used to argue both sides of that one.

Despite angering every faction at one time or another in doctrinal discussions, he worked hard to foster unity in the Church. For that he was lauded, even by his detractors.

"You just landed?" He spoke into the phone again. "Good. We'll get together when I arrive. You should already have all the necessary passes. The permissions were processed last month." Miguel checked his watch. He was dressed unassumingly, almost clandestinely considering he was practically guaranteed the most powerful church office in the world. It was a miracle the press hadn't figured it out yet. Usually the pre-vote polling was less obviously conducted.

He was glad to be just another face in the crowd, at least for a little while longer. His camel cords fell over white K-Swiss tennis shoes. A comfortable cotton long-sleeved t-shirt kept his vicuna woolen sweater off his skin. He smiled as he stood at the ticket counter. He was still waiting for his boarding pass.

"Hold on a minute." He took the phone off his ear and peered over the barrier. A small man with fustic-colored eyes stared back at him. Miguel was traveling alone. He was getting onto a commercial flight for the last time in his life. From now on he would be imprisoned by security concerns. He wasn't relishing the thought of waving out at crowds from inside a bullet-proof Plexiglass box.

After receiving the boarding pass, Miguel put his phone back to his ear and started walking toward his gate.

"You still there?" he asked.

"Good." Miguel's smile was warm.

"Thank you. I had to wrestle with the best *Jorge Chavez* has to offer. I'd rather fly out of *Chimbote*, but, alas … *satietas vitae.*

"No. I'm doing fine," he continued as he walked past a kiosk renting Hollywood DVDs: in English of all things. He shook his head from side to side.

"Did you get the package?

"Yes?

"Good. Your assistant was very thorough."

Miguel stopped to purchase a newspaper. He chose *El Peruana*. "Heinrich said there's more that may help you here in Lima. We have an amazing collection in our archives.

"Yes.

"No. You'd have to come here, it's far too much to send copies. Some of the papers are too brittle to handle.

"Yes. A restoration specialist could….

"Yes. I think so.

"Okay."

He walked from the newsstand and found a crowd waiting at his gate. The laughter of children playing. The cry of a baby with a soiled diaper. Anxious looks. Faces of worried travelers and exhausted parents.

The phone's signal told him he had an incoming call. He looked at the screen. "I need to take this call. I'll see you tomorrow.

"Okay. Thank you.

"Bye, Joshua."

１ １

AN EXTREMELY SHORT *Sirionó* seemed to appear out of nowhere.

Enson ignored him.

A wide set of crumbling teeth opened beneath a pockarred nose that resembled a shriveled pear.

"*Se llama usted Señor Enson?*" The voice was wanton, empty, and as Neolithic as the strange clothing that hung loosely over an emaciated frame.

"Is this a joke?" The large man squared his shoulders and scoffed at the small figure in front of him.

"What's *that* for?" Enson pointed at the cane long-bow slung across the native's back.

"*Si. Señor Enson.*" The man seemed satisfied that he'd found his man.

"What do you want?"

"*Por usted.*" A briefcase materialized in the diminutive dark-skinned hand. He extended his arm and the briefcase floated toward the CEO. His face seemed to completely ignore the rude reception. He focused on his mission. It was simple. The indigenous man's eyes stayed focused on the task he must complete.

Porfiry cringed. "From Stauffenberg," he concluded. He reached for the leather case.

The aboriginal Bolivian pulled it back. "*Solo Señor Enson,*" he insisted.

Roland Enson reluctantly thrust forward his thick paw. "It had *better* all be in there," he threatened.

The warning went unheeded. A weathered set of stubby fingers pressed the briefcase into the clutches of Enson's large hands.

Enson snatched the case and stared into the scarred face of the small man that stood there defiantly. The black coarse hair that sat atop a flat forehead looked unkempt. His skin appeared ravaged by years of malnutrition and unprotected sunlight exposure. His bare arms were muddy and covered with so many scars that he looked like he'd wrestled wild animals daily and slept among brambles each night.

Enson shooed him away.

The man vanished as quickly as he'd appeared.

*   *   *

THE COLORFUL CHORTLE of laughter emanated from the pilot's seat as *Jonah's Ark* crashed onto the sandy shoreline of the Euphrates, immediately *rising up* over the banks of the ancient Mesopotamian River on a cushion of air.

"Ho!" the Captain rejoiced. His free hand rose up above his head in triumph.

"Do your grandkids know?" Via asked from behind her whitened face.

She didn't get an answer. The craft was racing up the slope, leaving the murky waters behind. They started creating some distance between them and their pursuers.

Tran watched in amazement from his seat at the back of the sub. The Blackhawks continued to race upriver, chasing an image of what looked like the winged halibut water craft. If someone had been able to see his face, they would have seen it cast in disbelief. Tran was looking out the window as he shook his head at the sight of the holographic drone running up the river. He saw the dusty desert passing directly beneath *The Ark*, but he couldn't see their tail or the whale wings. The slate grey exoskeleton of their ship had disappeared.

The interior of his compartment was still visible. But outside, he was sure that their hover-crafted submersible was now invisibly cloaked.

In the bridge, the Captain congratulated Via, "Your man Tran did well."

She started to ask.

He clarified quickly, "Tran selected my favorite. Not to mention, the safest defensive deployment. I wouldn't want to hurt my boys." The retired US military man's loyalty ran deep.

Via's eyes locked onto the flat screen, above the Captain, that now displayed the scene outside. She smiled a gentle curve on her normally stern face. "I like your toy, Admiral. I'm going to have to get one of my own."

"Interesting you'd say that." The twinkling eyes were still hidden from her. "I've an order being filled for Great Britain now, but there'll be a couple of extras if you want 'em." An entrepreneur's smile.

"*Nice*," Via said with youthful inflection.

"I sold my first game years ago," the Captain continued, "and I've been inventing games and toys ever since."

As he was speaking, a three-dimensional image of an F-15C American fighter jet popped up on the main flat screen.

Keyontay reacted first, "Can it see us?" He'd been watching the simulated image of the action that showed when *The Ark* had disappeared.

"I have a SHRIKE system that jams their radar. So, no. Not with the naked eye, and not with their standard radar systems. But we have only limited protection from heat-seeking sidewinders and … yep, looks like they picked us up. Those defense contractors – they have some cool toys too."

Keyontay read the warning blinking on his screen and looked at the back of the Captain's head. Their pilot didn't seem to be the least bit concerned.

All screens now blazed in unison showing two F-15C jets. The red-lettered warning read "missiles launched – 4 incoming."

"Hmmm." The Captain scratched his chin as if considering a menu item at his favorite Mexican restaurant. "I wonder how our Burmese soldier will handle these fighters."

Tran was sweating. He saw the Blackhawks abandon their chase as their Sparrow and AGM warheads shot through the holographic image mimicking *The Ark*. The missiles detonated under the slow-moving currents of the river. He read his own warning screen showing the two approaching fighters. A new menu of defensive selections begged a decision. Again, he went with the most outrageous choice. He touched the screen over the box bearing the word "Freeze." But just as he did, the Captain had made his own decision as well, and the entire crew felt a sudden burst of speed that pressed them back into their seats.

The ground underneath them fell out of view as the nose of *Jonah's Ark* pointed upwards. The sub rushed toward a large cloud bank that hung over the distant Kurdish mountains.

"Your little submersible converts into a neat little hovercraft," Via needled the Captain, "and now a mini-stealth aircraft?"

"I don't usually use the term myself," the Captain responded, while still pulling back hard on the yoke. They were shooting upwards approaching MACH 1.

"You've outdone yourself, Admiral," Via grinned, "but I have a few questions for later."

Tran, meanwhile, was watching his screen. A simulated picture of his defensive weapon was on display. It showed a flurry of liquid-hydrogen filled capsules pouring out behind the ship as they flew off high into the sky. The sub-zero liquid swarmed out of the back of *The Ark* like squid ink, clouding the air. Each dose of the lethal freezing agent was riding inside its own little leaded glass bead.

As the missiles passed through the mist of super-cooled gel-caps, they broke open the million tiny vessels of fluid and became instantly doused in a shower of the -259C hydrogen solution. The chemical wash instantly froze the metal alloys of the warhead as well as its transport. Each sidewinder shattered into a billion bits of harmless matter that dropped like winter hail onto humid desert.

For her part, Nena had been in a communications cocoon trying to reach their headquarters in the foothills of the French Alps. She'd also radioed the US Command Center trying to get them to back off. Having made no progress on either front, she was texting their contact in Armenia that they may not make their rendezvous, when she paused. She noticed the ship had leveled off. She checked a monitor and gasped as her stomach hit her throat.

At that moment, Mandy woke to find herself strapped into her bunk. Her IV bag was a shriveled plastic membrane hanging lifeless beside her. She managed to unstrap herself and unhook the catheter line and its lumen terminus. All she could think about was eating.

They can't follow," Keyontay spoke with confidence, his back leaning into his seat in the bridge.

Via gave him a curious look.

He answered her stare from gleaming eyes. "The F-15C can climb higher than the Pentagon is willing to admit. Its full capabilities are classified. But I have a friend at Xeton. They design the cockpit pressure systems for the 15C and the 117. I happen to know that our flying fluke is already beyond their reach."

"But not yet beyond the reach of their missiles. Via's grim reminder fell heavily into the G-forced air.

"Perhaps. But it looks like Tran's well-supplied to keep any at bay if they do find us *up here*." Keyontay gave Via a sly smile.

"How far up are we?" Via had been busy on her comms, trying to reach her contact in Vedi.

It was the Captain who answered with a chuckle. "As I was saying, my dear, I don't usually use the term 'aircraft' when describing my baby." He lovingly patted the console in front of him.

Jonah's Ark had reached an altitude at an astonishing two hundred *miles* above the Earth's surface as he finished his statement.

"Properly, she is nothing short of a nimble little *spacecraft*."

*   *   *

JOSHUA WAS WAITING for them at the top of the ramp. The brash flight attendant may as well have been dragging Sarah and Bear by their earlobes.

Sarah was embarrassed, her face flushed and her eyes downcast.

Bear didn't seem the least bit disturbed. He seemed to relish getting in trouble.

The stewardess gruffly spun back around after depositing the two trespassers and slammed the door behind her. A tirade of unkind words vibrated the metal closure as she descended the mobile hall.

"She's *cute*." Bear was looking at the shut door to the gangway.

"She is too old for you," Joshua said.

Sarah found herself uncontrollably looking at her professor. "Age isn't important." She caught herself and abruptly cut off her gaze. She turned quickly to join the others who were standing in the walkway off of the waiting area.

"What's with *her?*" Bear shrugged and stepped out to follow.

Joshua hadn't really heard the response. He was preoccupied. Miguel had lobbied hard for permission for the professor and his students to be given access to most of the Vatican's archives. It was unprecedented. Joshua had known all along that there was a chance that Cardinal Acamayo would be elected Pope, but he'd seen it as a long shot as opposed to a real possibility.

Now that Miguel was being promised control of the Vatican, perhaps they could negotiate even greater access. Joshua figured at least twenty centuries of records lay beneath the Holy See in Rome. So much had been buried over the years, hidden from the public for one reason or another – much as the Bible itself, until the printing press and then the Protestant Reformation. Between those two events, a surge in general knowledge of what the Scriptures actually said started to transform the world. Joshua walked after Bear, but he was in another state of mind. He was thinking back to another period of time.

As the group assembled in the passageway to the main portion of the terminal, it was Arkesha who remembered their professor had left them hanging back in New York. "Dr. Walker?" she started. After a short pause, as they walked in a tight group towards the baggage claim, she continued, "What did you mean earlier about Christ having come *twice?*"

"Yeah." Bear remembered now too. "Wouldn't that make his return at the end of the world Jesus' *Third* Coming?" He was the only one laughing.

"He has a point." Joshua had come back to reality slowly and put his thoughts of ancient history behind him for the moment. "Perhaps I was a bit misleading."

Everyone stepped in closer as they walked.

"See!" Bear blurted.

"He's been here more than twice," the professor smiled as he casually made the statement, "in physical form." He paused to catch the reaction on everyone's face. "Of course, outside of human form, Jesus never left. He's been here from before the creation of the world," he added.

"John's gospel starts with the assertion that Jesus is The Creator," Sarah said, nodding with some understanding of what Joshua was saying.

"That's a given," stated in a professorial tone, "if you properly understand God's omnipresence, it makes it easier to fathom how the Son of God can simultaneously be the Everlasting Father."

Professor Walker's reference to Isaiah 9 made the students' heads swim.

The group arrived at baggage claim amid a cacophonous foray of questions and argumentative statements. The volley was entertaining to say the least. When they stopped, they took their places in the crowd already staring at the empty conveyor going round and round. It teased the weary passengers with every pass.

Joshua gave them a minute of silence before offering a few simple observations. "When I referred to two visits in human form, I was talking about Jesus of Nazareth and the King of Salem, Melchizedek. Of course, he also appeared in human form to Abraham, Jacob, Moses, Joshua, Ezekiel, and Daniel, to name a few. Following his ascension, in the form of Jesus, he appeared to Paul and later to The Presbyter in Patmos."

"That many?" Sarah asked.

"More. And those are just the ones recorded in the Bible. There have been many more that have not been recorded as part of our scriptures." The professor was exuding confidence and knowledge like he was an eyewitness.

"So why did you single out God's appearance as Melchizedek?" Sarah asked.

The others were all still bunched together listening intently.

"Because it's his most visible appearance mentioned in the Bible. In Genesis, Psalms, and Hebrews, we get a clear picture of God in the form of the High Priest-King. It was a very physical, very public appearance." Here he hesitated, then continued with caution, "Some believe he actually reigned as King in Salem for a lengthy period."

Silence … just the murmur of unhappy passengers waiting for their elusive bags.

Walker's students were trying to process the information.

As if on cue, the luggage started appearing from behind the vinyl strips that veiled the wizard manipulating the controls. The man behind the curtain was busy rolling dice to see which bags would become lost.

Sarah pulled on Joshua's arm. He had always been careful to keep his distance from the pretty student, keeping his interest in check, or at least deeply internalized. But now his guard was down, and he unintentionally allowed himself to notice how beautiful her flaxen locks framed her delicate face. He watched her magnetic mannerisms as she dragged him to the side for a private talk.

"I need to ask you about Charlie's notebook." With urgency.

He blinked.

"Are you okay?" Sarah saw he looked dazed. She hadn't realized her hand was still on his arm. She quickly withdrew it.

"Yes. I'm sorry," he said. "I've not read everything yet. It looks like he's got some good stuff. Some of it most certainly came from the papers Spain sent to the New World sometime between 1808 and 1814. Virtually all the monasteries and cathedrals emptied their archives onto ships bound for Peru.

From what we can tell, all the vessels made it except one. All the records in trunks aboard a frigate captured by Napoleon's *Iphigenie* were taken by the French and subsequently by the British. Those have not been traced yet, but I would hope they are somewhere in London. Many believe that the Algeciras papers will be quite revealing."

"The ship left out of Algerciras' port?"

"Yes, with papers from three monasteries and one cathedral. We think the documents were more valuable than others because the ship's manifest shows a Cardinal from Madrid aboard."

"What happened to him?"

"Napoleon hanged him as a traitor."

"Oh." Sarah recoiled.

"Bonaparte had tight controls on the Vatican during much of his reign as Emperor of France, but it started as far back as 1796 when he commanded the French Army in Italy and sacked the Vatican's treasure trove. They carried priceless artifacts and art back to Paris. That's when Cardinal Francisco Antonio de Lorenzana smuggled a bunch of stuff out of Rome to Toledo. The Church in Spain eventually did the same thing, but by then it appeared Napoleon would rule all of Europe, so they chose Lima."

"Did everything stay in Lima?"

"We're not sure, but it's likely. José de San Martín invaded Peru in 1820 and by 1826 Spain surrendered the colony. Spain's navy had been decimated at Trafalgar in 1805, and it's doubtful the Church in Spain could do anything. France was at war with Spain again by 1823. The Papal Territories in Italy could have sent ships to retrieve the papers between 1814 and 1826, but I seriously doubt that they did."

"Spain *was* the world's superpower in the 16th century."

"Right. During the height of their political power they accumulated just as much religious power. When they invaded African kingdoms, they even gutted the Nestorian and Jacobite treasuries of artifacts, books, letters, and likely everything else of value. So in the 1800s Spain's wealth was still very attractive."

"That makes sense. Charlie's notebook also contains a letter from a Nestorian monk in China to an Ethiopian Master Builder." Sarah's excitement was building.

"Isn't that your bag?" He pointed at a large tattered hiking backpack, The

Northface logo faded along with the sun-bleached fabric. It inconveniently interrupted their conversation.

"Yeah. Thanks." She picked it up like it was weightless. Joshua figured it for 60-70 pounds. He felt old and allowed himself a slight smile.

José was beside them. He already had two large suitcases. One was black and the other was a bright pink Samsonite. As he stood over his wards, he took the opportunity to butt into Sarah and Joshua's conversation. "I think one of my ancestors was on that ship."

They both looked at him tongue-tied. Neither of them knew he had been listening.

"The frigate," he explained.

He got the same look. So he continued. "My grandmother loved telling the story. Her mother's name was *Isabella*, named after the Queen."

The area started clearing out. The noise level dropped considerably. The entire group had their bags and crowded around as José laid out the story.

"She was born in Aragon. At sixteen, she was sold to slave traders in Algerciras. Her parents were the ones who sold her. If they hadn't, their creditors would have. Algerciras' port routinely harbored pirates and slave ships from the 15th until the 19th century. *Isabella's* ship was captured. The French warship *Iphigenie* took their captives aboard in 1810, and *Isabella* ended up in the hold of the warship. Her cell happened to be right next to a Cardinal who had been a passenger on the frigate. She never got his name. Over the course of the next week, the Cardinal gave all of his meager rations to the girl. As he passed each day's crust of bread through the rusted iron bars, he would assure her that he was going to die anyway. She needed to live, he told her. He gave her a charge. A blessing. A challenge. '*Tú honrarás Dios.*'"

Joshua just then noticed that everyone was accounted for, bags and all. He motioned to José to grab his load and spun his hand over his own head with a lassoing motion. His invisible lariat roped the troops, and everyone bunched up in quick step to follow.

"Don't stop," he prodded José as the group began to move for the exit.

He continued the story with every ear pasted to the words as he breathed out the family saga. "After a week the Cardinal was taken away in chains. But *Isabella* never forgot him. She had been starving aboard the French ship until he had given her something to eat. Only three days passed after they left the port where her benefactor had been taken to the gallows in Paris. Only three days and she was awakened from her fetal position on the wet splintered boards by the sound of cannons. The sound was deafening. *Isabella* screamed with her hands pushed to the sides of her head, but nothing could stop the booming terror, the crashing of iron balls ripping through planking and beams, the blasting of gunpowder, the shaking of the wooden sailing ship as it was ripped apart.

"A tremendous crush of weight thrust itself through the hull of her ship right next to her. A cannon ball broke through the *Iphigenie's* shell and pushed all the way into her cell. She was almost killed by the impact, but Providence spared her any serious injury. Another inch and her small frame would have been torn apart. As it was, the sound and tremor of the intrusion sent her reeling. She felt the wet air of the sea blowing on her tattered dress. She opened her eyes to discover that the near death assault had breached the barrier to her freedom."

The group made it to the taxi stand and Charlie asked the dispatcher for a van. In moments a VW minivan was double parked on the other side of a cabbie's Fiat sedan. The driver of the van was already opening the sliding doors and the rear hatch. It didn't look large enough to carry everyone as well as their bags, but such is the case in Europe.

As they were piling into the Volkswagen, their driver explained in thickly accented English, "We do not regard luggage racks as fashion accessories." With that and an unshaven Italian smile, the gangly driver stuffed the back of the van and strapped the balance of their bags on the roof of the vehicle.

"*Trionfale*," Joshua said to their cabbie.

"Marriott?" the Roman asked.

"*De Russie*," he responded.

"Ah." The native approved with recognition.

The van was already moving when José started up where he had left off. "*Isabella* couldn't swim, but she remembered the words the Cardinal had left with her, *"You will honor God." Isabella* felt it was a prophesy and it gave her hope for a future. She climbed out of the *Iphigenie's* damaged hull and slipped into the water, taking hold of a floating timber. She held on for dear life as the battle raged on around her. The current quickly took her away from the danger of man and into the danger of the open sea. It was four against one, and the British won the skirmish. The victors promptly combed the ocean for survivors, spotting *Isabella* still hanging onto her flotsam.

"She ended up aboard *The HMS Africaine*, locked in a cupboard in the wardroom."

"They locked her in a cupboard?" Sarah was aghast.

"Evidently they had nowhere else to put her. The cell was more of a small pantry, allowing her to stand or sit with her knees bent up to her chest. They regarded her as a slave. She was. Now she was their property. She was eventually turned over to a captain on his way to New Orleans." José had a grim look on his face.

"Another slave ship?" Sarah protested.

"No. A merchant sailing vessel." The captain arranged for her to work in the galley posing as a boy. Once in the American port city, reality returned, and the captain sold her. The buyer was a wealthy plantation owner, a Mexican. His holdings were all in what is now the State of Texas. During the war, though, the Mexican land baron was forced to move south. He had been kind to *Isabella* over the years, and she had faithfully worked as a domestic on his ranch. After they resettled in what is now the Tamaulipas region of Mexico in 1847, her owner asked for her hand in marriage." José now beamed.

"Amazing," Sarah mused. "Did she ever say anything else about the Cardinal?" She focused her point. "Did she mention his trunks?"

"No. I don't think she knew anything about them. But the Cardinal did give her a keepsake. On her deathbed, she gave it to my grandmother. When my *abuelita* died...." José pulled out the chain that hung around his neck. From underneath his silk shirt, a shiny gold ring appeared.

The collective gasp filled the interior of the van.

"May I?" Joshua held out his hand.

José pulled the chain up over his head and handed the jeweled ring to the professor. Joshua held it between his thumb and forefinger. He let the light shine on its highly polished surface. He figured the large gem on its face for a very valuable ruby. "A pigeon's blood red from Myanmar," he guessed out loud. The intricate designs on each side of the bulky ring included a family escutcheon on one side and an insignia on the other. He showed it to Bear, the master symbol guru in the group.

Charlie whistled. "That's one expensive-looking ring!"

Bear recognized the insignia right away. "He was a Donatist."

Sarah took it out of his hand. As she looked at the odd insignia she described it. "A four pointed star or stylized cross. A wooden challis. A loaf of peasant bread." The symbols were set within a Moorish dome.

The family crest on the other side of the ring was a standing pard in profiled pose. The leopard stood in front of a shield. It was simple, but in brilliant, wealthy colors underneath the star-cut corundum stone.

Bear started up again as the ring made it around the group and back to him. "The Donatists were a Christian sect during the time of Emperor Constantine." He hesitated and looked at José with some skepticism. A slight color of worry entered José's expectant eyes. "The Cardinal was from 19th century Spain?"

"Yes," he responded, emphatic but worried.

"The Donatists," Bear continued hesitantly, "had been excommunicated by the Catholic Church and then systematically exterminated by the Roman Army. The few survivors were killed by the Muslims when they took over the region."

"Oh," all José could manage.

"By the 9th century they were gone," Bear concluded, adding with great chagrin, "all of them." He continued, "As for the escutcheon, I have no idea. But I can find out." He was already on his iPhone's browser.

"I've seen this before." Sarah's voice was a whisper as she ended up with the ring again and stared at the family crest.

"Me too," added Charlie.

"Your notebook," Sarah breathed. A light had turned on in her mind and she came alive, twisting around and reaching into the back of the van from the rear-most seat.

"My notebook's in my carry-on."

"Which one is it?" Sarah was already digging through the floor-to-ceiling rectangular jam of luggage behind the seat.

"Joshua?" she asked as she moved bags around, loading Bear's lap with a few.

"I don't remember seeing either of those symbols in the notebook," the professor answered.

"The family crest. I know I saw it in there." Sarah's voice was frenetic.

"I saw it," Charlie again confirmed her suspicion.

"I'm pretty sure it's not in the group of papers you got from Lima,"

Sarah said, doubt creeping into her voice as she realized she was really not that sure after all. "Augh! It's gonna kill me!" She mocked pulling out her hair and smiled a little deliriously. "Charlie, where's your bag?"

"It's the jet lag." Arkesha defended Sarah as everyone stared at her like she was an attraction at the local zoo.

"We have been traveling for twenty hours," Joshua reminded them. It may be daylight here, but we need to get some rest. He turned to Sarah. "Do you think the mystery will wait until we're all rested? We've an important appointment tomorrow morning, we need to be ready."

"Really? Why?" Sarah asked.

"Because we're meeting with the new Pope."

١٢

"YOUNG MAN." The Captain's cheery voice roused Keyontay from a dream-like state. Via's driver was watching the blue sky turn to the black of space out the front portals. Off to their right, the slivered moon shone brightly in space, the shadowed portion of the ball clearly visible against the emptiness of their new realm. "How'd you like to take over for a spell?"

Not waiting for an answer, the sturdy sailor rose from the pilot's seat revealing a robust frame that moved easily towards Via. He extended his arm to the lady as if at a cotillion, leading her with formality out of the bridge. "Don't crash into any satellites!" he warned over his shoulder to Keyontay. The young man smiled as he scurried into the seat in front of the controls.

The Captain's study was only a few steps from the bridge. It was here that they ran into Mandy wandering down the center corridor.

"Mandy! You're up!" Via said with surprise.

"Feeling great too, but I'm…." Mandy showed a weak smile.

"You must be hungry," the Captain anticipated. He asked Via to excuse him for a moment and left her in the hall as he led Mandy into the galley. There Mandy joined the others who were back to devouring the gourmet seafood.

Seeing that all was well, the Captain rejoined Via at the entrance of the study. He smiled from behind a square jaw, bowed slightly and swept his left hand wide towards the study's open hatch, the gesture of a gentleman allowing the lady to proceed first.

As they entered, he shut the door behind them. They took seats across from each other, a rosewood tabletop reflecting the soft yellow light between them. A small box of worn maple craftsmanship accented the surface. He noticed Via staring at it inquisitively. "It's a pelorus," he said, "an old mariner's compass." He unclasped the bracket that held it in place and handed the boxy device to her.

"I don't see a needle," Via said with curiosity.

"No magnetized needles. See those sight vanes?" He smiled.

"These two upright pieces with slots?" Via turned the device slightly in her hands to get a better view.

"Yes, quite the precision navigational instrument in its day. Did you know the Chinese were the first to map the globe?" The Captain's eyes twinkled as he poured them each a drink from a crystal cordial.

"No."

"Turns out you don't need GPS," he chortled. "The Chinese used the North Star when they were above the equator, the Southern Cross and Canopus when they were below it. From those stars they were able to determine their latitude anywhere on the earth. They used lunar eclipses to figure longitude from fixed locations on land. A Cantino planisphere and a water clock helped them estimate their longitude at sea. With those tools, and one of these babies," he pointed to the pelorus, "you can find your way around the world without a chronometer. Of course, a gnomon pole helps clean it up a bit once you find some land." He laughed.

"Admiral," Via hesitated with her request. "I know you are supposed to just get us across the border, but we are concerned about Mandy. Would you be free to take us to Bariloche after our meeting in Armenia?"

His smile vanished. He poured her another drink, frowned and said, "On one condition."

"Admiral, I…," Via started.

"I get to come to your meetings." The big smile was back.

"You're too easy." Via offered a pleased smile.

"Actually, I've some information that may be helpful to you." Now his tone turned to the serious.

He had her attention.

"I once employed a Russian national. He had been connected with the embassy in Istanbul. Seems Moscow pays a lot of money to know what's going on around the Black Sea." He poured them both another drink.

Via pursed her lips and sat up straight as a board.

"So my Russian tells me yesterday that the recent … *event*," he continued, raising his eyebrows and boring his eyes into Via's own, "has created some interesting problems for the Orthodox See ... and for Mother Russia."

Via cleared her throat and tried to relax her poise.

"I assume you know the history of the Russian Orthodox Church?"

"Yes," responded Via.

"Then you know it was founded by the Constantinople Metropolitan."

"Yes." She was still trying to relax herself.

"Anyway," his tone became suddenly nonchalant, "I don't have a horse in that race, but Serge says that Ambassador Pavlavich is already in Rome lodging a formal complaint."

"The Russian ambassador to Turkey is in Italy complaining about the missing shroud?" Via shifted uncomfortably in her seat.

"Evidently, they care about it even more than the Patriarchate. Ankara couldn't care less. I think Turkey would just as soon deport every Orthodox Christian from Istanbul."

"So they think the Vatican is behind the burglary?"

"Whether they are or not *this time*," he winked at her knowingly, "is quite irrelevant. But considering what they took back to Rome when they first sacked Constantine's stash...." He fiddled with his fingers as he became lost in thought.

Via nodded. His point was well taken.

"Remember, the Western Roman Empire only lasted until the 5th century. The Byzantine's lasted another 1000 years. A lot happened during that period, a lot of turmoil between the Roman Catholic Church and the Patriarchate in Constantinople. More than we will ever know."

"What used to be in Constantinople," Via paused, "has likely found a home in Rome."

"If you...." He caught himself quickly. "If *one* were to seek anything else that may have been in the holds of the great city on the Bosporus, I'd start my search in Rome." The Captain smiled. "But what I couldn't find in Vatican City, I'd look for," he drew a long breath and squinted his eyes as he poured them one last shallow drink, "in *Moscow*."

*　　　*　　　*

THEY HAD ARRIVED in Rome at 5:29pm local time. Sarah had looked back over their itinerary. Seven and a half hours from Eugene to New York.

Another seven and a half to Paris. Then, two more to Rome. With layovers, it was almost a full twenty-four hours. It had been more than that since she'd showered in her apartment near the U of O campus. She'd thrown on jeans and a sweatshirt, jumped in her truck and picked up Bear and Charlie to make it to the airport in Eugene on time. She'd had some sleep on the plane, but sleeping sitting up isn't the kind of rest her body needed.

The *Hotel de Russie* was exquisite. Sarah had never seen anything like it. It was about 7pm when they had finally checked in, but she'd managed to check out the gym, the spa, the hydropool and the ornate Turkish baths – and found herself most mesmerized by the Secret Garden. The terraced garden's lights were softly warming the view over *Via del Babuino* as dusk fell slowly over Rome's ancient vistas. By the time she'd returned to her room, Arkesha was getting into bed .

After an impossible hour-long wait, ensuring that Arkesha was fast asleep, Sarah quietly slipped out of her bed. She was exhausted, but it was too hard to fall asleep with the questions still streaming through her mind. She wouldn't be able to get the rest she needed until she'd looked in Charlie's notebook again. Arkesha was breathing deeply from the other bed as Sarah tiptoed to the door and snuck out.

Walking up the hall barefoot with her Oregon-duck printed pajama pants and golden-yellow trimmed, forest green t-shirt a comfortable reminder that she should really be in bed, she crept to the door of José and Charlie's room. Her mind was racing with ideas, and the burning questions needed to be answered. The boys would just have to wake up and let her in. Charlie was a light sleeper, perhaps she wouldn't disturb anyone else. Surely, Charlie would understand her need to wake him.

Sarah knocked lightly.

The door opened quickly.

José stood in front of her grinning, from a fully lit room.

Startled, she asked, "You're up?"

"Up? What took you so long?" He laughed.

"Is that Sarah?" Charlie's voice yelled from the back of the small suite.

She rolled her eyes.

José held his side and laughed louder.

"Bear! You owe me $20," Charlie again amidst more howling laughter.

"Ha. Ha." Sarah pushed past José, almost knocking him to the floor.

"Give me that notebook," she said as she walked up to Charlie. He already had the research binder in his hand for her. She snatched it from him and promptly sat down on the floor with it.

"Go ahead and look," Bear teased. "We've already figured out the riddle anyway. It's time for us to go to bed while you now try to solve it."

Charlie joined in. He faked a gaping yawn and climbed up onto his bed.

Bear stood up from his spot on the carpet. "Really. I am going to bed now. See you guys." He reached into his front jeans pocket and pulled out the wadded bill of unbacked currency.

Charlie got his twenty.

José was still laughing.

Sarah tried to ignore them all. "José," she added, "let me see your ring again."

As José handed *Isabella's* ring to Sarah, Bear shut the door behind him and headed back to his room.

"What did he find out about the family crest?" Sarah asked as her eyes followed the shutting door.

"Nothing," José answered. "It's in none of the online databases."

"Perhaps it's not Spanish, after all," she posed.

"He looked at Castilian, Catalan, and Portuguese as well," José said.

Charlie joined in, "I told him to look at French, Norman, and Italian."

"What if he is a Moor?" Sarah suggested.

"A Cardinal? In Spain?" José was shocked. "How could a Roman Catholic be a Moor?"

"Why is that so far-fetched? In the 19th century, Spain was full of *conversos*, many of whom were *moriscos*. Not to mention that Rome had quite an influence in all of North Africa prior to the Muslim conquests," Sarah reasoned. "Here," she said, handing the ring back to José, "look at the escutcheon. See the leopard?"

"I thought it was a mountain lion," José said as he turned it over between his fingers and held it up to the bedside lamp. "*Tú honrarás Dios*," he spoke the words with reverence. "You know I signed up for this project in honor of *Isabella*."

"Is that all?" Sarah guessed.

"No, the whole thing … actually … it's why I'm in Walker's PhD program, partly … at least … you know Arkesha had a lot to do with it."

Sarah had a look on her face that second-guessed his veracity.

He ignored it. "I was already registered at Cornerstone U in Grand Rapids. Dr. Carroll had already looked at my dissertation outline. Of course, Carroll's in Texas now."

"I've worked with some of the professor's former students. Cornerstone's Center for the Study of Antiquity produces some of the best research in the world. Michigan's really cold, though. I never considered moving there." Sarah was talking, but her mind was buried in a document in the open notebook.

"I know you don't believe me. You think it's just Arkesha. But once I found out what Dr. Walker was up to, I had to do it. I mean, I wanted to be with Arkesha, but I had to do this. For *Isabella*. I had to. It wasn't a choice anymore. And I'm doing this for my grandmother, too. She was just a child when *Isabella* gave her the ring, but with it the charge was passed on: '*You will honor God.*'"

"So now I will," José's voice became ethereal, "for her."

"And?" Sarah prodded.

"Well, for one, I'm going to find those trunks. Who knows what we will find in them?"

"Here!" Sarah interrupted his reverie. "Look at this!"

Unwilling to part with the entire notebook, Sarah opened the metal rings and pulled out the plastic covered page and handed it over. "Second paragraph from the bottom. Third line down."

"I can't make it out." José struggled as he stared at the antiquated language, with Charlie peering curiously over his shoulder.

"Silly," Sarah said, half teasing, "you're a native Spanish-speaker."

"I grew up in Texas."

"My point exactly."

Charlie laughed.

Sarah continued, "Is Brownsville even still part of the US? Do they even speak any English there anymore?" she needled.

"Funny," he said sardonically. He handed the paper back to her. "Just tell me what it says."

"It's a reference to the *original* manuscript that John Mark penned, as Peter related his own eyewitness account of Jesus's ministry."

"You mean the oldest copy?" Charlie interjected.

"No."

They both stared at her in awe.

She continued somberly, "It says it's the *first* draft of the manuscript. The *original*."

"The Missing Mark," José mused.

There was frantic banging on the door.

Charlie broke away to get it.

Arkesha burst through as soon as the latch was released.

"Oh God! Thank you! Thank you!" She ran for José and buried her face into his chest as his arms wrapped around her. Then she broke free and fell down on the floor next to Sarah. On her knees, she held Sarah's face in her hands. "You are okay. I'm so glad you are okay."

"What are you talking about?" she asked her friend.

"I thought they took you!"

"Took me? Who?" Sarah's brow wrinkled.

"The men! There were two of them."

"Where?"

"In our room!"

Everyone gasped.

She continued to tell them what happened. "I played like I was asleep. I had been. But something woke me and I opened my eyes and saw them with their flashlights. I just froze. But I watched. I thought they had kidnapped you before I woke." She let her hands drop from Sarah's cheeks. And she sat back onto the floor, leaning against the side of José's bed. Her breathing was still heavy. "I tensed. I was ready for the fight of my life. But I think they found what they had come for because they took your backpack and left."

"My backpack?"

"Yeah. As soon as it was safe, I ran here." Her breathing was finally starting to slow.

"Why would they take your backpack?" Charlie asked Sarah.

"Who are *they?*" As Sarah's eyes teared up, instantly her question became much more important.

"I don't know. It was dark. I didn't really even get a good look at either face in the shadows." Arkesha looked scared now. "I'm sorry, Sarah."

"I'm just glad you are okay," Sarah said. "I'm not worried about what they took."

Silence.

Then Sarah had an after-thought. "Which backpack?"

"Oh, that's right." Arkesha put her hand to her head as she took a seat next to José on the bed. She allowed herself a slight smile as she remembered. "The small one."

"My carry-on. The only things in my carry-on were my iPad, Chromebook, and my signed copy of *969*. My purse was on the floor next to my bed."

"You lost all of your research!" Arkesha moaned.

"Not unless they took my purse too. I back up everything religiously. My flash drive is in my handbag. It has a copy of all of it."

Sarah looked at Arkesha for the answer without asking the question.

"I don't think so. I don't know. I didn't see them take it though."

"Well, it's either there or it isn't," Sarah resigned. "Charlie?"

He was already on the phone to the lobby. As he hung up he told them, "Security is on the way."

"Who would steal your research?" José asked her.

"Who besides us even knows about it?" she said, bewildered.

"We need to tell the professor," Charlie decided.

"No!" Sarah blurted. "It can wait until morning. We all need to get some rest." She was suddenly overwhelmed with exhaustion.

"Not in *that* room, we're not!" Arkesha demanded.

"Yeah. We need to get another room." Then Sarah blinked. "How did they know what room we were in? And how did they get in?"

*　　　*　　　*

THE CAPTAIN WAS back at the controls as *Jonah's Ark* passed over the resting place of Noah's Ark. He'd taken his ship down to only 10,000 feet before dipping to earth just over the Armenian border.

"This is the safest location I can find. I'm sorry it's so far from Ibn's place." He said this as if it was a bother or terrible inconvenience. "Did Nena reach him with the coordinates?" He wrinkled his nose.

"She never got through. But I did get a text back from Ibn that said he would be there. We are now ahead of schedule, thanks to you, Admiral." Via smiled. "But I don't know if Ibn will arrive on time or not."

"He's *this* side of Vedi?"

"Yes. So I hope he will be there when we land. Are you sure you want to join us? I'm concerned about leaving your submarine unattended." She said it with a grin as she thought about their entire trip.

The Captain smiled too, but the twinkle in his eyes didn't have anything to do with her mischaracterization of his ship.

"Admiral, tell me how your ship," she paused, looking into his eyes, "can do all of this!"

Switching to auto-pilot, he swiveled his chair around and leaned back. "Well, my dear, we have a new alloy we experimented with for several years. Once processed, it has a fantastic microstructure. It is extremely light weight as well as extremely strong; it withstands both fantastically high temperatures from rocket fuels or sun rays as well as being able to handle extremely low temperatures. We built a double wall with it. Between the two layers we have adjustable pressure, sufficient to withstand being under water as well as being at high altitudes. We use nuclear power to activate a catalyst which in turn creates gases that fill the space between the walls with pressure. Holding the two walls together is the same alloy in a honeycomb design. I had a Lego set as a boy that got me thinking and excited about creative possibilities. Of course, the same nuclear power is used in different systems – designed to keep us under water – or up in the higher altitudes – or even skimming the ground. The air pressure system is all computerized to respond to both the exterior environment as well as the interior needs."

"Amazing!" Via tried to see behind his bright eyes.

The Captain chuckled and proceeded to bring the ship down.

The landing was accomplished much like the vertical touchdown of a Harrier jet. But this bird of prey landed much softer, quieter and with more control. As the ship finally settled just above the tall grasses in the clearing, *The Ark* pushed out a strong cushion of air and the hovercraft slowly pillowed the last couple of feet to the hard earth. As it did, the whale-fin wings tucked themselves back in under the sides and the engines started shutting down. Everyone grabbed their gear and headed for the already opening hatch.

The entire ship emptied into a small meadow encircled by a ring of trees in the Ararat foothills. As they were still scrabbling over the mid-back of the pelagic spacecraft, a battered old Moskvich four-door sedan, with an extended trunk that made it look like a truck, rattled up over the uneven field.

Tran and Nena hit the ground and drew their weapons in one fluid motion.

"No!" Via held up her hands as she jumped to the ground behind them. She ran in between their crouching bodies with both arms pushing down against the dusk's air, her command to lower their arms.

"It's Ibn!" she said.

They both gave her stern looks.

"I forgot to tell you," she had a shocked look on her face as she just now realized it. "I got through to him."

Nena's glare remained. Tran's face relaxed. They both lowered their assault rifles.

From the disheveled farm truck stepped a tall man in traditional Arab dress. His head was uncovered, revealing a mess of matted grey hair.

"*Tu es là?*" he asked Via as she led the group's approach. His voice had a warm, expressive tone and a syncopated rhythm that matched his broad smile.

Via answered in English, "Ibn, so gracious of you to come early."

"But the pleasure is mine." The man bowed slightly as he drew to a stop in the dry grass. "You saved me a long drive into Turkey. Even in Ararat no one likes Armenians there. Only Georgia even lets us freely move through their borders. It is in honor of Queen Tamara, I think. She was one of the first Christian monarchs."

Ibn was rail-thin and talked in an animated fashion. He used wild gesticulations with his skinny arms and long, spindly fingers. His demeanor was congenial, disarming. But Nena's eyes never left the holstered Makarov 9mm pistol on Ibn's right hip. Tran was looking at the man's waist as well, but he was fascinated with the short Turkish *yataghan* sword sheathed opposite the sidearm. Via noticed their stares and grunted an admonishment.

"Our transportation was surprisingly efficient." Via stepped up to their host and extended her hand. "Thank you for your courtesy."

But Ibn didn't shake her hand. Instead, he took it in his own and raised both hands up to a set of very dry lips. His thin kiss felt rough on the back of her hand. He held her hand up near his mouth as he looked into her eyes from behind deep-set puffy orbs surrounded by eggplant looking skin. His thick, bristly eyebrows were divided by a large, hawkish nose. "Yes. I *see*." With a slightly vinolent inflection to his words leaping out over brittle teeth, "You have a fine *submarine*."

He gently released her hand and bowed once again, a bit deeper. But this time to hide his untamed face. It was etched in hilarity.

"Did I say that?" Via blushed. *"Excusez-moi.* I wasn't thinking clearly. You see, when we boarded, it was a...." Via dropped it. It was much too difficult to explain.

"Don't be concerned." Ibn raised his head and straightened his smile. "When I received your sat-text that you were arriving here early, at these coordinates, *here*, in the foothills of Ararat in a *submarine*.... Well, I just had to jump in my truck and come see for myself. I even broke an engagement so I wouldn't miss your landing." He allowed his lips to curve up generously.

"I'm so sorry," Via continued, "I didn't mean for you to have to change your plans."

"If I were a younger man," he said sweetly, "you could make it up to me over a romantic dinner." He abruptly stepped back. "Alas, however," he began as his long arms reached skyward, "I am much too old for you. Why, I was here when the last strange water craft moored itself in these mountains."

With that, he wheeled around and started opening the doors to his truck. His sweeping arms welcomed the group and with grandiose charm he greeted each as they boarded.

Mandy was the last one of Via's group to enter the Moskvich. As she slipped into her seat next to Via she couldn't help ask, "He has lived here since Noah's Ark?"

She was whispering, but the others all heard her and the old Russian cab filled with giggles. The laughter was suppressed as Ibn rounded the front of the vehicle and made for the driver's door.

"Don't let him hear you say that," Keyontay cautioned.

"You aren't concerned about leaving the ship here unguarded?" Via asked the Captain.

"Ahhh." The Captain smiled. "Thank you for the reminder." He dug into the pocket of his slacks and pulled out a key-fob. The fob bore a Mercedes emblem of brass sewn onto leather that wrapped itself around the hard plastic shell.

Ibn was just settling behind the large steering wheel when the Captain pointed his remote at *Jonah's Ark* and depressed his thumb.

The familiar sound of a car-alarm sound beeped in response.

The ship vanished.

"I want one of *those*." The Arab pointed at the space where *The Ark* hid under a nano-tech cloak. He grinned, revealing a mouth full of cracked and broken teeth.

The truck ground into gear, Ibn rolled it back and around and headed for the gap in the trees. They started bumping over the field towards the thick stand of birch that separated them from the main road.

The group rode in silence, cramped inside the Moskvich cab. Everyone was tired. The road was barely still hanging onto old pavement as it wound around the sides of steep hills in the heavily-wooded terrain. Thankfully the drive only took a little over half-an-hour. Ibn slowed, and turned off of the broken macadam and asphalt onto hard-packed dirt. The drive was badly in need of re-grading, and it dipped sharply downward. They headed deep into a mossy ghyll stuffed with weathered stones.

It finally leveled out at the bottom of the ravine next to a fast-moving creek. Two black spires of smoke drifted upwards into the dark of the now fully starlit sky.

"It looks different from down here." Mandy stared into space as she spoke to no one in particular. The group was already piling out of the vehicle and moving toward the front of the house that spewed the smoke. But Mandy just stood next to the old converted sedan and gazed heavenward.

Everyone else was walking up a narrow path to the front porch of the small dacha that Ibn called home. Mandy rushed, limping to catch up.

The tiny assembly filed into the cottage, following their host, but Mandy stopped again. She just stared at the billions of stars and the thread of the crescent moon rising from behind the tree-tops. She was thinking about how the work she was doing with Via would inevitably cause her to cross paths with her grandfather, after all of these years. What would she say? How would he respond? Would he have any clue as to what she now knows about him? A bitter tear fell down one side of her face, and she quickly gathered herself and wiped it away.

She walked up the steps.

Through the door.

And into another world.

Inside the wooden structure, a cozy display of modest furnishings and bare pine-planked walls, black with aged tongue oil, whispered of a difficult history. Families torn apart. Zealots. Bigots. Religious. Political. Wealth. Exploitation. She looked from the sad walls to the large wood-burning stove that was the centerpiece of the room.

Mandy noticed that she could see a small kitchen through an open doorway in the back. She was immediately reminded of her childhood, her grandfather's home in the Andes north of Lima. She finally closed the front door behind her.

As she did, she felt the heavy wood in her hands and it brought back more memories. Sundays, those were the best days of her life.

Everyone was still standing despite the availability of what looked like comfortable seating. Mandy was confused. "What's going on?" She touched Nena's shoulder.

"I don't know. Ibn just asked us to wait for a minute."

The old Arab was bent over at the base of the big black stove, reaching under its iron belly. His hand searched the rough red brick hearth, and his dry mouth kept muttering something unintelligible. "*Et!*" he said, pulling back his hand and smiling.

"Okay," he announced, "if you will all just follow me." He unfolded his spider-like frame and stood erect, dusting himself off.

Everyone just stared. Dumbfounded.

But as he finished his invitation, the dacha groaned and the pot-bellied stove slowly rose toward the ceiling. The Captain was the first to react.

"Bravo!" he called out, clapping his hands. "Bravo!"

Underneath the hearth's bricks a spiral stair started to appear. There was just enough space to duck into the opening once the stove had reached near the ceiling. Ibn spun into the passage and started down the metal wedges.

Mandy took up the rear again. With some regret, she finally made her way into the dark stairwell. She paused and took another look at the alpine feel of the wooden-encased home. She imagined her grandfather at the front door calling for a visit. He would always bring a bouquet of fresh flowers for her mother, a pint of Beck's for her father, and a huge Belgium bitter dark chocolate bar for her – always with raspberry filling, her favorite. But as the pleasant images faded into the pain of reality and it stabbed at her heart, she hurried down the spiraled stairs.

Above her, the brick hearth was already dropping back down as if it knew who was the last to descend. The center newel pole retracted silently, stacking the pie-shaped steps on top of each other as it compacted. Mandy completely forgot her hurt once she stood at the bottom of the coiled stair. Some twelve meters below the dacha's foundation, a huge concrete bunker spread out before her. She looked overhead at the bridged ceiling and imagined the rocky stream running over the top of the reinforced cement. Brilliant, she thought. The running water would shield the existence of the underground bunker from the electric eyes that Uncle Sam continuously flies over the planet. She stepped out of the shadow of the stairwell into a warmly lit space that looked more like the Courtauld in London than an underground shelter in the Armenian mountains south of the Black Sea.

To her left was a computer screen next to a huge bank of blinking lights. The screen was streaming with an endless march of characters: a data-mining program, she surmised – several of them running simultaneously.

Beyond the computer, she looked at a long wall that stretched for a good distance. It was cluttered with books. From floor to ceiling, a huge bookcase reached from one end of the wall to the far side. It looked as if the volumes themselves held up each shelf and even served to hold one end of the steel supports that traversed the ceiling. She was close enough to the bookcase to pick out a few titles. Dostoevsky's *Crime and Punishment* was nestled beside Jack London's *Call of the Wild*. Above them, a large worn leather spine bearing the name Nestorius. A thick-bound Bible. A Qur'an. A Hadith. And a brand-new monstrous tome that looked out of place among the antiques gathering dust. It declared itself, "*A Treatise on Origenism,* by Jundishapur."

Mandy saw that the others were now scattered along the opposing wall, staring at old framed maps and pictures and glass cases below them filled with various parchments, books, and artifacts. Ibn was in the center of the room working feverishly to dispense coffee from a silver samovar into seven gold-rimmed finjan cups with arabesque designs in lavender glazes. The cups were neatly arranged on a tray that sat at the end of an antique sideboard that braced the foot of the central seating. In the middle of the buffet was a plate of *ras el abed*. The crème-filled chocolate shells were stamped with a Damascus confectionary's logo and produced a strong and inviting smell. The old Arab carried the tray of hot coffees to the low-slung table that served as a footstool for a neat arrangement of IKEA furniture.

Mandy took up one of the Arabic porcelain cups and sipped the heavily sweetened Turkish coffee. She moved to the displays, making her rounds behind the rest. Ibn joined her while she was stopped, admiring a strange map framed above one of the glass display cases.

"*Piri Reis*," the Arab collector said.

"But I don't remember…." She seemed puzzled.

"That's right. This is the 1515 cartographic masterpiece. The first map he assembled is still in Istanbul's *Topkapi Serai* museum." Ibn smiled.

"There's a *second Piri Reis?*"

"You're looking at it." No hint of humility.

"You can't be serious," she said.

"You think the Ottomans only made one map?" Ibn's wrinkled face stretched into a wide smile.

Mandy was staring at the entire globe. It was colorful, and flattened out into a two-dimensional pattern with incredible accuracy. The artistic renderings of flora and fauna were just as ostentatious as those that adorned the earlier drawing that showcased South America and Antarctica.

"This is amazing," the only words she could find.

"Look in the case." His narrow, crusty forefinger poked at the glass below.

Beneath the clear cover she found herself staring at another copy of the same map, but without the drawings of indigenous plants and animals. It was covered with vertical lines full of Chinese characters.

"Alas, I do not have the original," Ibn moaned. "But this one is a good copy of the Chinese handiwork. The original map was completed in Nanjing in 1424. As you can see, it is quite good. The Turks likely obtained a copy of Zheng He's brilliant achievement in 1514. They had already obtained a part of one of Hong Bao's maps a year or two earlier. That's how the first *Piri Reis* was created. Getting these maps from the Chinese is what spawned their fanatical quest to get more of China's technology and to build fleets to sail the world." Ibn scratched his head.

"Where's the original now?" Mandy was mesmerized, and her question had a distracting effect on Ibn. He had been thinking of the Iberian peninsula.

"Destroyed. By Zhu Zhanji, most likely. If not, surely it was destroyed after 1644 when the Qing dynasty tried to obliterate every trace of Zheng He's work." Ibn's smile re-appeared. "We are lucky the black market has always thrived, eh?"

Mandy didn't know how to respond.

"The Turks," he continued, "got their maps through the black market. The Portugese got them from the Turks the same way. Then the Spaniards.

If it weren't for the black market in China, Asia Minor and then Europe, perhaps America would still be…."

Mandy had moved on. She was now standing in front of a large framed poster of Olga Korbut on a balance beam. Strange, she thought. The display case beneath the poster of the Russian gymnast contained a silver-jeweled chalice and a stone that was covered with glyphs.

"Early *Rus*, from when Kiev was just a fortified village. There was no Cyrillic alphabet yet." Ibn didn't mention the poster. Mandy moved on.

The next frame hanging from the whitewashed cement wall was an etching of what looked like a monastery. The legend beneath the detailed drawing was a beautiful calligraphic name plate in Roman lettering, "*Mor Gabriel*."

"In Turkey," Ibn said proudly, "it is still standing." He grinned like a father of a newborn.

In the case beneath the framed etching, a small book sat alone. Mandy thought it looked so old and fragile that it would disintegrate into dust if she were to touch it … too worn to read. A square linen label read, "Psaltery of Isho'dad of Merv."

Despite her extensive knowledge of church history, Mandy was puzzled. She'd grown up reading everything she could in her father's extensive library in their flat off Gray's Inn Road. Of course, her proximity to Dickens' house encouraged her to read enough British literature to become a philologist. She regretted not being able to learn what her grandfather knew. Picking up some of his books back in Lima when she was a child simply showed her how many words she didn't yet know.

Next, she admired a sketch of a Nestorian Metropolis in Kanbalik, China. She thought the compound small and the buildings too simple, almost nondescript for China. The space beneath the picture held a few articles of jewelry surrounding a Soghdian parchment. A pair of earrings, a wedding band, and a simple silver chain kept the vellum company and indicated a personal connection between the items displayed.

Everyone else was already seated in the center of the room. They were all either sipping sweet coffee or eating chocolates. Keyontay had just stuffed one of the huge truffles into his mouth as Mandy made her way to the group and took her place next to Via on a white leather sofa.

Ibn sat down in his chair near the sideboard and faced the rest of the group. The wide, red velvet covered chair atop conical, chromed legs supported his thin, robed frame. The Captain was to his immediate left, Nena was directly to his right, sharing a love seat with Keyontay.

"You feeling okay?" Via whispered to Mandy as she settled into her seat.

"Just a bit light-headed," Mandy replied. "I probably just need to get some rest. My leg is starting to throb a bit. But mostly I'm just in shock that such a private collection exists, and *here*, of all places."

Tran was sitting on the other side of her. "Did you see the Oromo pseudepigrapha?" Coming from a muscle-bound Burmese soldier.

"The what?" Mandy twisted around in her seat to face him.

"An Ethiopian manuscript. It purports to be written by the Apostle Peter. In the corner display." He pointed.

"Peter couldn't read or write," Mandy said confidently.

"Similar gospels are universally accepted as obviously not written by the named author." Tran defended. "But," he conceded, "I've never heard of this one before."

"John Mark could have written it for him," Via offered.

Mandy dropped it. She just kept looking around the room as the Captain chatted up their host. "I just had no idea any of this stuff even existed." She was flabbergasted. "How could it be that all this has remained hidden for so long?"

But Ibn was ready to begin his presentation.

"I've spent a lifetime," he started, gathering the attention of his guests, "collecting." He gestured slightly with his arms towards the vast collection. "My primary interest has always been Christian history. Unfortunately, much of it has been destroyed, as is the case with most historical artifacts and records. What hasn't been destroyed has been lost over the centuries. But I've managed to recover some of those items that had been misplaced or hidden away and forgotten. Most of my work is assembled in this room." He now spread his draped arms wide, exposing a dark olive skin that covered bony arms up to knobby elbows. "Some of this comes from archeological digs. Others were in private hands for generations. Still others I have found in the oddest hiding places imaginable."

He had everyone on the edge of their seats.

"For example, I have obtained a 1st century Syriac Codex that had been in a used bookstore's storage bin in Tehran since at least the 17th century, long forgotten, waiting – just waiting for me to rescue it." He paused and his dark eyes surveyed his audience before he continued. "I will supply you with copies of *anything* within these walls."

Via brightened.

"But I want two things from you in exchange." He glared with purpose.

Via shifted nervously in her seat.

١٣

"IS YOUR NEW room okay?"

They'd been in Rome since the evening before, and while not on a normal sleeping schedule for the local time zone, everyone was somewhat rested. Joshua and Sarah were drinking coffee, sitting at a small table on a stone-paved terrace inside Vatican City. Their view, past a planter full of violets, stretched across the wide plaza in front of the Basilica of Saint Peter. It was already crowded with pilgrims awaiting the outcome of the Cardinal vote.

Sarah was excited about their upcoming meeting with the Pope. It was all she could think about. "We didn't have to move out of the hotel," she said with disassociation.

"We're safer, housed here inside of Vatican City," Joshua said. "Are you nervous about meeting the Pope?"

"Yes," she admitted. "Can you imagine *me,* a small-town girl from Oregon … meeting *him?*"

He smiled. "Yes. I guess that *is* something." He stopped to take a sip of coffee. "He's very popular, you know, with many in the Sacred College of Cardinals. I'm actually not at all surprised that they chose him."

"But it's not official yet."

"Well…." Joshua pointed.

Sarah looked up. She saw a thin spiral of white smoke rising up above the city. "The signal," she said.

A wave of chatter arose and then fell abruptly out over the crowd packed in the square. The people were quieting as the Dean stepped out onto the balcony.

"It looks like it is official now." Joshua smiled. "He had better win. He promised us unlimited access to the archives."

Sarah almost dropped her china. As it was, some of the rich dark liquid spilled over onto the shaking saucer she was holding in the other hand. She was speechless.

"It's great news," Joshua beamed. "I know … but because of the theft of your pack last night, I am gravely concerned."

"It's just a backpack, Chromebook and an iPad. They can be replaced, but my signed copy of *969*…." She laughed.

"I think I've placed you all in danger."

Sarah wasn't taking him seriously.

"And with Miguel's *carte blanche* permissions, our danger is greatly increased."

Sarah put her cup and saucer down on the round mosaic-topped table. "You really mean it?"

"Yes." He gave her a solemn look. "I do. There are many people who don't want those archives touched. They would rather have them destroyed."

"What kind of danger are we talking about?" Sarah squirmed in her seat.

"The worst kind."

Sarah didn't like his tone.

Joshua stood. "Let's go. We don't want to be late."

She ran alongside him as his long stride quickly moved over the length of the covered walkway. She followed him up a long flight of marble stairs. Their meeting was scheduled to be a small, personal affair. It was planned to take place in one of the common buildings in the vast compound, if you can call any of the structures in Vatican City common.

They reached a closed door and were able to hear voices inside the conference room that had been chosen for their audience with the Pope. Joshua stopped at the door and placed his hand against the large, solid oak surface. "I think I know who took your bag." His hand left the door and reached for her shoulder. "If I'm right, we may have to call this whole thing off."

Sarah frowned and her eyes darkened.

The door swung open to reveal a beautifully sunlit room with high

Palladian windows facing east. A faint pink hue colored the walls. They were neatly trimmed in wide, white, wooden baseboard and crown. Long sheer curtains hung from golden rods bearing floral end caps. The only furnishings consisted of a long cherry wood conference table surrounded by comfortable black leather chairs. José and Arkesha were sitting with their backs to the windows. Charlie and Bear were facing them. Three seats, the head of the table and its two nearest chairs on either side were empty, as well as seven others at the far end. The dark reddish surface of the table was bare except for Charlie's notebook and Bear's laptop – which appeared to be battling each other. Their owners were matching the stand-off, deep into one of their many discussions.

José and Arkesha were talking about wedding plans.

But they all became quiet as their professor took his seat. Sarah took the chair across from Joshua, next to the head of the table.

"I'm booking us a return flight immediately," their professor declared.

He received a collective moan.

Bear objected, "But we are supposed to be here for two weeks!"

"We'll go ahead and have a look at the archives today. But we must leave tonight. We'll just have to continue our research from home."

More moans. Bear was the loudest complaining, but everyone was verbalizing their disagreement with the change of plans.

He continued, "I'm going to ask the Pope to supply us a prefect here who will serve as our resident RA after we leave."

More negative reactions filled the room. It went on for awhile, everyone talking over each other. When the din finally faded, Sarah spoke resolutely, squaring off with the professor on behalf of all of the students. "I'm not afraid of staying. We shouldn't let some simple thugs scare us off. This is an opportunity of a lifetime. It's worth the risk."

The beginnings of a cheer started but the room suddenly stilled.

"Well said, young lady."

The voice came from behind her, from under the lintel of the open door.

Sarah spun around in her chair. She found herself looking at the formal white raiment and unique Roman Catholic headdress of the Vicar of Jesus Christ. The newly elected Pope had just finished addressing the crowd in St. Peter's plaza.

"The Pope!" Bear blurted.

He spoke again. Using a calming tone, he said, *"Paucis verbis."* His smile filled the room. "Welcome, my friends." Miguel spoke to them in the plain, unaccented English used by American newscasters. He stepped towards the window as everyone rose from their seats. He embraced the professor. "Good to see you again, Joshua. Please introduce me to these bright young people."

Their professor was starting the introductions when Arkesha noticed the well-armed security just outside the still open door. She caught Sarah's eyes and used her own to signal her friend, coupled with a pointing finger hidden at the table's edge to prompt Sarah to turn around and look.

As Sarah got the hint and turned, the guards at either side of the doorway stepped aside. They lowered their HK416 assault rifles and nodded a salute to their commander as she passed through them.

Shutting the door behind her, the uniformed head of security, carrying her own HK on her back, slid into place against the wall behind the Pope's chair as the introductions continued.

Sarah couldn't help but stare at the face of the pretty woman. Her short, dark hair barely hid the comms gear attached to one ear. Her throat mike was visibly taped to one side of her neck, and black combat attire was perfectly contoured to her attractive figure. But as the Pope took his seat, Sarah turned her attention back to the meeting. This, she thought, is the most important day of my life!

SARAH HAD GROWN up in Sisters – the small, quaint, and friendly resort town in the Cascade mountain range that divides Oregon east from west: dry highland to the east and the Willamette Valley and coastal mountain range to the west. Sarah enjoyed the entire state as a child traveling with her parents, mostly camping and fishing as they traversed the Pacific Northwest. Among her favorite parts of Oregon was the coast. Much like Maine's coastline, Oregon's coastal range drops right down into the ocean at places, creating a picturesque, rocky coast with small, sheltered beaches and great imposing cliffs.

She attended a Brethren church in Sisters. It was small. The best thing about it though was that it was organized like first century congregations with preaching elders, but no head pastor. When she moved to Eugene to go to college, she joined the Willamette Christian Center, an Assembly of God ministry with an active young adult program and dynamic praise and worship. Sarah was amazed to see so many people all together in one church. It felt like the whole town of Sisters could fit under that one roof.

SHE'D NEVER BEEN inside a Catholic church.

Yet here she was. Face to face with the Pope!

Sarah knew a lot about the Roman Catholics. It was part of her field of study. As much of church history deals with the Europe-based metropolitan, she learned the good, the bad and the ugly about the Vatican and its cathedrals throughout the world. However, increasingly, she had learned of its huge counterpart in the east: the Orthodox, Nestorian, Jacobite, Coptic, and other Christian churches that had thrived in Africa, Asia and the Middle East for as long as the Church in Rome. Each had a spotted history. But Sarah loved learning about all of the good men and women who over the past two thousand years gave their lives for the gospel in all of the branches of the church of Jesus Christ.

She knew the history of the Protestant churches as well as the others. It was a much shorter history. The first modern Protestant church had grown directly out of the defiance of a Roman Catholic priest; Martin Luther had famously posted his "Ninety-five Theses" on the church door in Wittenberg, Germany in 1517.

Sarah disagreed with many of the practices prevalent in the Catholic church today. Considering much of what Protestants say about their brethren on the other side of the aisle, she was surprised with how many things that Rome taught that she agreed with. In matters of important doctrine, for example, like that which is expressed in the Nicaean Creed, she was in complete agreement. It was the Catholic's Marion Adoration, prayers to saints, confession to priests, and the doctrine of transubstantiation of the all too venerated wafer and wine that got her twisted. But she wholeheartedly recognized her responsibility to pray for them, along with all of God's children. She wanted to be prepared to share the truth of the Holy Scriptures with anyone willing to hear. She had to trust God to lead others to the truth.

As all of this spun around in her head, Miguel, having been introduced to everyone, began addressing the group. "As I said, Sarah spoke well."

She blushed.

"I know you have been targeted, and you may be again, because of your work." The Pope's tone was somber. "But what you are doing is too valuable to curtail. It is unprecedented – what you have accomplished so far. And that, without access to the 2000 years of evidence buried in our vaults."

The Pope took off his mitre to reveal the common man beneath the crown. "I'm prepared to give you all the support and protection you need. And I would hope that you would choose to stay longer than the two weeks, of course. It would take you years to even scratch the surface."

"But Roland…." Joshua started to interject.

Miguel cut him off, "Roland?" His eyebrows raised only slightly. "So you suspect that Roland Enson was behind the burglary at *Russie?*" He blinked and held up his hand. "Oh, that reminds me. Michelle?" The Pope lifted his index finger in a slight motion behind him.

The commander produced two packages from behind her back. She stepped forward and handed the small parcels to the Pope. As she did, Sarah noticed the woman looking at Joshua. Sarah's eyes flitted to her professor. To her dismay, he was looking back at the soldier, slightly nodding and smiling. Recognition.

"He knows her?" She worried. Then she remembered the strange woman on the planes. But her anxiety was interrupted by the Pope. He was speaking her name.

"Me?" It just came out.

"No," Miguel smiled as he spoke, clearly joking, "the *other* Sarah."

Bear laughed and everyone stared at him. He abruptly got quiet.

The Pope handed Sarah the packages. "Please," he said, indicating that she should go ahead and unwrap them now.

As the Pope adjusted his simar, Sarah got the strange feeling of being a little kid on Christmas morning. But this time Santa Claus was physically present to watch her open her gifts: a new iPad and a new Chromebook!

She could feel the heat of the blood that rushed to her face. Without thinking, she leaned over and kissed Miguel on his cheek.

"Thank you!" Sarah exclaimed as she reached into her purse, pulled out her thumb drive triumphantly and inserted it into one of the USB ports on the Chromebook. She was now focused on the screen. For a few minutes she forgot where she was, lost until her subconscious scolded her.

"You just kissed the Pope!" it said.

"I just kissed the Pope!" she heard herself saying. Thankfully, she had said it under her breath. Did anyone else hear her?

She looked up from her Chromebook. It looked like no one had heard. Maybe.

Miguel had started talking again. "So I've asked Michelle," he said, motioning behind him, "to provide protection for you while you work here. I want you to safely conduct research in Vatican City for as long as it takes."

Michelle approached the Pope's side. She was now standing at the edge of the highly polished table. Conspicuously, Sarah thought, in between her and the Pontiff as if she, Sarah, was some kind of threat. Joshua took the opportunity to address both Miguel and Michelle. "Indefinitely?" he asked.

"Permanently!" the Pope proposed.

The whole room gasped. Michelle followed Miguel's words in a string of fast German, directed solely at Joshua. Sarah felt fire in her belly. Her mouth filled with warm saliva. What was this woman saying to her man? Ah, her professor.

"As *guests* of the Bishop of Rome," the Pope continued, "you will have unfettered access to all of our archives, the treasury vaults, the libraries. All of our resources will be at your disposal." The tone turned to one of presumed acceptance of his plan. "The Holy See, our monasteries, every archdiocese, and of course all of our universities would be pledged to support your work."

Jaws were … on the floor.

"I'm prepared to grant *each of you* university appointments here in Rome. Joshua, you would have an endowed chair and serve as Dean and full Professor of our Antiquities of Faith Department. And each of you," he added, waving his hand from one side of the table to the other, "would be appointed assistant professors."

Bear practically fell out of his seat.

"However, once each of you has been awarded your PhD, we are prepared to offer each of you full tenure."

The words were still sinking in as the electrifying opportunity created so much excitement and energy that everyone, including Joshua, was speechless.

José was the first to speak after a long period of utter silence. His words were directed to his fiancée. "We could afford to move up the wedding date."

Sarah laughed. Nervous, but the release was welcomed.

Everyone laughed.

Michelle worked to subdue it. She gave Sarah a curt look and motioned for silence. "We are scheduled to begin in twenty minutes." The formality was hardened and cold. "My people will lead you from here to the main archives. Be ready to leave in ten minutes. We are moving your bags to a more secure location now. When the day is over, we will escort you to your new lodging beneath the city." Abruptly, "I need your phones." She held out her hand expectantly.

No one moved.

The Pope explained, "It's for your own safety. We have new phones for each of you. You will have an opportunity to transfer your data from your old phones after we scan them for tracking devices. Each of you will have new phone numbers, new email addresses, and we are going to have to kill your Facebook pages within the next week. I will make sure you have a central Facebook access through our own secure connection within a month."

Bear withdrew his iPhone from inside his leather jacket and slid it across the table as if it had suddenly become radioactive.

"Wait!" Sarah was always an independent thinker with a stubborn streak. "They came in *my* room, not *yours*." Her finger pointed at Bear.

"That stewardess had my phone!" Bear retorted. "And I loaned it to Arkesha so she could bluetooth a song. It was in your room last night."

"Isn't that illegal?" Charlie grinned at Arkesha and then Bear, as he passed his Blackberry to Michelle with a smiling wink. "Michelle, you should report them." He looked at her for a reaction. He got none.

Arkesha blushed visibly from behind her dark mocha complexion and passed her phone across the table in resignation. José did the same without comment.

Joshua held out in solidarity with Sarah and gently addressed Michelle. "I want to be present when you scan the phones." He followed it with a short sentence in German that made Michelle turn a slight shade of embarrassed red.

Sarah watched the entire exchange aghast.

Michelle didn't respond verbally to Joshua but she silently nodded her assent.

"And, *anyone else* who desires to be present." Joshua looked directly at Sarah.

Michelle was slow to respond this time, but eventually indicated her consent.

Joshua slid his phone across the table. Only then did Sarah turn hers over with a statement of bravado, "I want the same brand." She glared at Michelle.

Miguel responded, "Each of you can select any phone you wish. Upgrade if you want. We will preload anything you want. Music. Numbers. Data. Apps. Anything. Please don't worry. We will take care of everything."

A swarm of questions headed his way.

The Pope lifted a cautious hand. "If it was Enson who took your research, he won't stop until he finds what he is looking for. If he wants to stop your work, he will relentlessly pursue you. He is a *very* dangerous man."

"What is he looking for?" Sarah asked.

"Perhaps he has already found it, and now he will leave us alone," José suggested. "Sarah," he turned to her, "what all was loaded on your Chromebook and iPad?"

She wrinkled her forehead. "So much – where would I start?"

Joshua offered, "Roland Enson runs several multinational enterprises. He is into shipping, oil refinery, mining, electronics, and pharmaceuticals – just to name a few." His voice dropped with a tinge of desperation.

"But it's his pharmaceutical empire that is driving his interest in our research."

*   *   *

"FIRST, I WANT copies of everything you get from Stauffenberg."

Via responded with a look of shock. "How do you know…?" she started, and then she bit her tongue. The old Arab's voice was pleasant, but Via found herself staring at the weapons still fastened to the wide leather belt around his waist.

"And I need your help." Ibn drew himself up to the edge of his seat. His humble tone made Via relax. He looked at each of his guests, in turn, with pleading eyes, finally resting his gaze on Via. "I need you to stop Roland Enson."

"Who?" Via was now thoroughly confused.

"Enson is in league with Stauffenberg. Well, perhaps I should say it 'topsy-turvy.' Is that how you say it?"

"I think he means that Enson is calling the shots," the Captain quietly clarified for Via. "What are they doing that needs to be stopped?" The Captain was leaning towards Ibn with cutting eyes.

"Destruction." A cabalistic tone. The Arab's eyes grew wide and slightly maniacal. His long fingers splayed, separated by large bulbous knuckles. He became apocalyptical. "Destroy everything. They will. If they knew what I had here, they would blow up this entire ridge just to make sure it was turned to dust! Do you know this bookcase contains *second century* copies of sermonry from Stephen, Phillip and even the Apostle Paul himself? Once Enson finds what he is looking for, he will destroy it all."

"What is he looking for?" Again, the Captain spoke for the group. The rest of them all appeared to be in apoplectic shock.

"*The Missing Mark*." He was now wild-eyed. "Since the original manuscript was lost, we think Enson's been obsessed with finding it."

"He's been looking for it for two-thousand years?" The Captains brows were arched high.

Ibn left the question unaddressed.

"Isn't Enson that industrialist who's always on tv?" Keyontay spoke.

Ibn nodded.

"He's easily the world's richest dude, the CEO and majority shareholder of umpteen transnational corporations, right?" Keyontay talked with the ease of one who grew up on the streets, but Ibn recognized his highly developed intellect.

The Arab was slow to explain. "Enson's after something that he believes will make him even wealthier. Evidently, his laboratories in Heidelberg are developing a super drug that will," he coughed nervously as he spoke, "that will … extend life … uh … indefinitely."

"What a crock." Via rejoined the conversation. "What would one of the gospel manuscripts have to do with pharmaceuticals? Especially one of that nature! Did Jesus tell his disciples a recipe for a wonder drug? *Je ne sais quoi!*" She threw up her hands.

"Ah, but Enson is a fanatic. A crazy man." Ibn looked the part as he used gestures that looked uncontrolled, as if a puppeteer was distracted while controlling his marionette. "Enson is convinced that the missing Mark was stolen because it contains … uh, a treasure map."

Via exploded in a tirade of French that pushed her up out of her seat. The imprecation in a foreign tongue looked to precede her imminent exit from the room. "*Mal vu!*" she barked at Ibn as she teetered there on her feet, trying to decide which way to go.

The Arab remained calm. He held up his hands as if to say, "Don't kill the messenger." He waited. Via finally decided to sit back down. Then, Ibn continued as gently as his raspy voice could manage, "It gets worse. This man is delusional. He actually believes that this drug of his will give the user *eternal life* and supernatural powers."

The Captain laughed a deep bellow of a laugh.

Ibn continued, "It is evidently based on using Jesus Christ's DNA ... uh ... the blood of the Son of God."

Looks of utter disbelief became mixed with giggles and derisive laughs. In the case of the Captain, it was a guttural laugh as he slapped his hand on his knee over and over.

For her part, Via's words were bursting out from between her pursed lips, "*S'ouvrir les veines!*"

"But even though he is off the deep end with his thinking," Ibn continued as soon as it had quieted, "he's very dangerous. He's a true believer. That is more dangerous than all of his wealth and power combined."

Via had finally regained her control. "How does Stauffenberg fit into all of this?"

"He refuses to cooperate with me. Instead of delivering documents to me, he is turning them over to Enson. Heinrich will lead Enson straight to the missing Mark!"

"You think the original manuscript of Mark's gospel still exists?"

"Yes. I do."

"Why is Stauffenberg refusing to work with you?" Via pushed.

"I believe that there are several reasons." Ibn hung his head slightly. "But primarily, he has told me that he disagrees with my plan."

Via didn't have to ask. Her face told the Arab that he'd better get to the point quickly. She was ready to leave without a deal.

"I've been scanning my library, years of work, digitally photocopying the entire lot of it: everything you see here." He spread his thin arms wide like a barren tree in the dead of winter reaching for the sun. "Loading the digital images over there," he said, motioning toward the computer still running vertical lines of code down its face as it hummed, "I will launch the website with a video live from this location." He spread out his gangly arms once again, his fingers resembling a bat's pinions.

"I have gathered 1.4 billion email addresses as of this morning."

He got wide-eyed looks from everyone.

A bony finger was pointing at the screen streaming data behind where Mandy was sitting.

They all turned to look at the computer that was poised to inform the entire world of the evidence that Ibn had been carefully gathering.

Ibn was the first to notice. "Mandy, dear, are you okay?"

Mandy was white as a sheet.

١٤

"THAT'S JUST WEIRD," Sarah responded after Joshua finally finished attempting to explain Enson's quest.

"Is he like a vampire or something?" Bear suggested.

"What kind of treasure map?" Charlie asked. "Like a drawing, or just written instructions? Did Peter have the directions memorized?"

"I think it is disgusting," Arkesha added.

"Sacrilegious," José agreed. "Jesus' blood shouldn't be experimented with."

"Why did one of the gospels contain a treasure map anyway?" Sarah posed.

Miguel and Joshua let the questions keep coming. Finally, the Pope said, "Look, we are out of time. We will get together again within the next several days and I will have answers for you. Just tell me one more thing before we part. I have so many meetings, I won't see you for a few days, at least." He had their attention. "Have you been able to track down the family crest on José's ring?"

Sarah grinned, realizing that Joshua had found the time to tell the Pope about *Isabella's* ring. She was the first to answer. "It doesn't exist," she said with blatant finality.

Joshua gave her a concerned look. The Pope allowed a slight smile, almost a look of relief.

The other students shifted in their seats. Sarah continued with unbridled confidence. "The reason we can't find it is because the Cardinal was a *converso*, taking the Castilian name of *Aviles* after his conversion to Christianity."

The Pope looked stunned.

"Where did you find that?" Joshua asked.

"I didn't." Sarah was still smiling proudly. "*Isabella* was imprisoned next to Cardinal Martín de Aviles, a Franciscan priest before his ascension to Bishop and then to Cardinal. Aviles simply adopted the family crest of Avila that was widely used throughout the Iberian Peninsula during that time. In honor of his Mauretanian heritage, he replaced the maned lion with a red leopard. Other than that, the escutcheon on *Isabella's* ring matches the Avila family crest perfectly."

José had the ring out, looking at the crimson feline standing upright, as if boxing against a blue and gold background. "Mauretanian?" he whispered.

"May I see it?" asked the Pope.

"The Cardinal was a Moor?" Bear blurted.

"Of course," José answered the Pope, handing the ring down the line through Arkesha and then Joshua to Miguel. "*Isabella* would be so amazed, as would my grandmother, if she were still alive. When I tell my mom, she's gonna flip that the Pope held *Isabella's* ring."

Miguel held the ring out in front of his eyes and turned it in the morning sun that streamed through the open curtains. "Beautiful!" A mystical tone of admiration laced with recognition. And then he said the most curious thing. "The pugilist reminds me of a cartoon."

"Alex," Sarah quickly agreed.

"Alex?" the rest repeated, with blinking eyes.

"Alex, the lion!" Sarah exclaimed. "Madagascar! You know, '… like a fish out of water, like a lion out of the jungle….'" She was singing.

All but Miguel gave her a bunch of blank stares.

"They escape from the New York City Zoo and end up with the lemurs and the fossa?" Sarah's tone was struggling to get others to remember.

More of the continuing lack of recognition stared at her.

"Am I the only one with nieces and nephews in the room?" she pleaded.

The Pope stood and picked up his headdress. He bent down to Sarah's ear and whispered, "I saw all three movies. Alex is my favorite." He put his hand on her shoulder, "Perhaps we will visit an orphanage together soon. I'm scheduled to visit the Lillian Trasher Orphanage in Asyût, Egypt next month. Would you consider joining me?"

Bear couldn't resist interrupting Sarah's response with a final question to the Pope, "What papal name did you choose?"

Miguel smiled.

He looked at Bear for a minute and then slowly began his answer. "The first Pope was St. Peter. No other pontiff has taken the name since. I wanted to, but there would have been an uproar. So I chose to take it, but to add another name with it to soften the blow. Innocent. Innocent III ushered in the Inquisition, and I want to redeem the name in honor of all the good things he did before he set up that tribunal that mistreated and killed so many. It was Innocent III who set up the Dominican and Franciscan orders. I plan on highlighting St. Dominic's and St. Francis of Assisi's work with orphans. That's one reason why I've already planned a visit to Lillian Trasher's. It will be the first step on a world-wide tour of orphanages, convalescent homes and institutions that house the severely disabled and the insane. From Egypt, we'll go to Uganda. The Watoto Orphanage in Kampala is amazing. The Skinners have poured their lives into those kids. You've not been truly blessed until you've heard the Watoto Children's Choir. They tour the world now, a bunch of kids who've lost their parents to AIDS as it continues to ravage Africa."

The Pope now turned back to Sarah. "Perhaps you will come with me to Watoto too?"

"Yes, of course. I would love it!" Sarah beamed.

Pope Innocent Peter stepped towards the door with a small wave of goodbye to the group. His pallium reflected the mid-morning sunlight as he prepared to step back over the threshold.

Sarah suddenly remembered that she hadn't finished. "Wait!" she almost yelled. "One more thing," she said in a much quieter voice and with a much redder face.

The Pope stopped and turned to Sarah. She was already out of her chair and facing the man who was still holding his mitre at his side, his pate still capped only with his white zucchetto.

"Yes?" he said.

"He didn't die," she said.

The Pope's face drained until it matched the color of his cassock.

The sound of air escaping came out of everyone's mouth.

Sarah turned to face both the Pope and the rest of the group. She made her announcement. "Cardinal Aviles wasn't hanged."

José was the first to form the words audibly. But the same question was on the mind of everyone in the room.

"How do you know?" José asked.

"Charlie's notebook." She pointed at the research binder still in its place on the table in front of the surfer. "The letter I had read earlier didn't have the crest or the insignia on it as I'd thought. I'd just imagined it. But my mind had latched onto something. After José told us the story about *Isabella*, it jogged something in my memory. So I read the letter again this morning and I found the answer."

Everyone waited silently as she took a deep breath.

"It's a letter from a priory in England. It's signed by a Dominican monk named James. It is addressed to a Franciscan monk outside of Seville." Sarah grinned. "And I quote, 'The trunks are safely back to you, sailed from Dover a fortnight ago with the Cardinal. He boarded *The Plymouth* bound for *Puerto Real* in the good hands of Cpt. Bauren. Thank you for confirming his identity. A touching story about his ring.'" She had grabbed Charlie's notebook and was still reading from the medieval script. "It's in Castilian, but I'm confident that my translation is accurate. And the letter is dated *18 de Octubre, 1815*."

"After Waterloo," Joshua noted as the Pope edged for the door.

"I looked it up," Sarah said. "Napoleon was exiled to St. Helena in the South Pacific where he died. He'd arrived there on October 16, 1815. So the Cardinal wasn't hanged by Napoleon after all!"

*   *   *

ENSON STEPPED OFF the plane in Lima. He had left Bariloche by helicopter and flew over the mountains to the closest airport with a runway long enough to accommodate his jet. Chile's *Puerto Montt* was a relatively short hop, and his Hawker 900XP was waiting for him outside the executive hangar – with the flight plan already approved.

As he disembarked at Lima's Jorge Chavez international business terminal, he walked with Tobin Legg, a tall, smartly dressed American. She wore a navy skirt and a navy jacket over a white silk blouse. Her heels drew her up to Roland's own six foot frame. She was carrying the case that Roland had been given in Bariloche and they both disappeared into the back of a silver Maybach Landaulet limousine.

The driver made the mistake of asking, "Porfiry?"

Roland said in a curt response, "He couldn't make it."

A grim look on the chauffeur's face acknowledged the news with sadness. He secretly wondered how long Tobin would last. The sedan pulled off the tarmac onto a drive where customs officers stopped the vehicle at a red and white road-guard.

"Mr. Enson." The customs official, wearing a silk suit and tie, leaned into the open window with syrup in his voice. "Welcome to Peru, sir. If there is anything you need...." But the gate was already rising and Roland waved his driver to move along. The electric tinted window rose quickly – only the black reflection was left for the government official. Embarrassed, he straightened and dusted imaginary lint from his sleeve.

The Maybach was gone.

As they proceeded south on *Callao's Avenida Elmer Faucett*, Roland was seething. "I'll teach that double-crossing Nazi."

Tobin's phone rang. "Strange," she said, looking at the "unknown caller" displayed. "No one has this number. This is my first day as your new PA. I just got this number assigned to me this morning."

Roland Enson ignored his new employee. He was reading through the papers in the briefcase, again planning his revenge. Heinrich would be hidden behind stacks of old books containing records of every birth and death the Church in Lima had posted for the last 450 years. The old man will be as musty as the annuals he immerses himself in, Roland thought. It's a wonder the mildew in that Cathedral basement hadn't killed him years ago. "How long will it take before they find him buried under all those papers?" he asked himself aloud.

"What?" Tobin asked, still staring at her phone as it continued to prompt her to answer.

"Nothing." He hadn't realized he'd said it audibly. Then he noticed the ringing of Legg's phone. It was unnerving. "Doesn't that have a voicemail?"

Tobin cringed. Top honors MBA from Yale, she thought, and I forgot to set up my voicemail. "I'll get it," she said.

Enson started planning for another PA already. Perhaps that spunky blonde that works out of his Singapore shipping firm.

"Hello?" Tobin finally said into the phone.

"Yes. He's here." She gave Enson a confused look.

"It's for you." She handed the phone to her red-faced boss, not realizing how lucky she was that today would be her last day employed by Enson Enterprises.

Roland took the phone and put his hand over the mouthpiece. "Who is it?" he hissed.

"Oh yes. Sorry sir." She tried to look apologetic without appearing incompetent. "He said his name is Joshua Walker."

*   *   *

THE CAPTAIN WAS already at the controls of *The Ark*. Nena was sequestered in the women's berthing area with Mandy. They were deep in conversation, Mandy in tears. Keyontay hadn't boarded yet. He was still outside the ship, standing in the field next to Tran and Via. Ibn was facing Via, shaking her hand vigorously.

"I'm so pleased with our deal," he said.

She didn't flinch, but the Arab detected something.

"I hope you are equally as pleased," he added, searching for a response.

"I had authority to agree, but whether or not the principal will be pleased, *that* remains to be seen," Via cautioned. "However, the deal will be honored. Rest assured."

"As a token of trust, I've already loaded the entire collection for you." He handed her an external hard-drive. "So your client receives my life's work well before it goes online. You will supplement my library? Yes?"

"Everything we are able to obtain from Stauffenberg," Via promised again.

"And, if you find it in your heart to send me digital video of the items you picked up in Istanbul and Iraq," Ibn cordially stated, "I'd be eternally grateful."

She looked at him and narrowed her eyelids to a mere cut. How did he know anything about their exploits? "Okay, Ibn," she smiled, "I'll ask my client if we can send you the video files." But she had no intention of complying with his request.

"I'll make my own stills," he interjected anxiously.

"Okay." Via abruptly changed her mind. "I will send you raw video. You can do with it what you want … on one condition."

Ibn looked nervous. He wrung his hands. "Yes. Your condition?"

"You tell me your full name."

The Arab froze. It took several minutes for him to open his mouth. Via shifted from one foot to the other. Keyontay felt bad for the old man. He was feeling uncomfortable just standing there in silence. He looked over at Tran. It appeared that the soldier from Southeast Asia found the exchange amusing.

As the thin lips parted, Ibn's voice was cracking. "Ah. *Mademoiselle.* Ah. Any other request. Ah." Each word took effort.

"Ibn means *son* or *son of.* You don't want us to know who your father was?" Via asked, playing on traditional cultural pride.

"Ah…." He looked at Keyontay and Tran pleadingly.

Via caught the cue and motioned for the two to board the ovaloid craft. It only took a moment.

She and Ibn stood alone. The night air chilled them.

"What's the big secret?" she prodded.

"You do not tell me who your client is," Ibn stammered.

"That is not my decision," she retorted.

Out of ideas, Ibn traced his foot in the dry grass still hanging onto the loose dirt. His head dipped as he asked quietly, "You will keep this between us only?"

"*Oui Monsieur,*" she promised.

"Okay…." A long pause, and then he reported, "It's Zebedaeus Jundishapur."

"You are called *Ibn Zebedaeus Jundishapur?*"

"Yes." He dragged his foot back across the dirt. "Or Ibn Zeyedi."

"You are Persian? But…." The mixed names suddenly confused her.

"On my father's side, half Persian, half Turk."

"Your mother was Arabian?" she guessed.

"Half Arab, half Egyptian."

"But Zebedaeus is…." Via was stumped. For some reason though she dropped it and asked instead, "Why do you hide your name?"

"I share the name of a very great man. My parents had high hopes for me. They named me after our most venerable ancestor. He founded a monastery, a university, a city that became a metropolitan … the first in Persia. It was a huge burden to put on a child."

Via raised her eyebrows.

"But what have I done to be worthy of the name?" He spread out his twig-like fingers. "I tried the Mt. Athos monasteries when I was young. Two of them kicked me out before I moved to Paris. There is where I failed seminary. So I moved to Damascus and started trading in antiquities. I was an embarrassment to my parents. But I did well in Syria. I excelled at being a merchant. So I moved to Beirut and expanded into international trade."

Via blinked. He was losing her.

"But Ibn is still not fulfilling *their* dream. He is not a monk like his brother. He is not a priest like his father. Ibn is a failure."

"Stop it!" Via stepped closer to him to wipe tears streaming down his face. She felt awkward, but she leaned in and gave him a hug. Then she quickly decided that was a bad idea. His clothing smelled like freshly sheared, fat-tailed sheep. She winced and withdrew. She looked up into his crenulated face and saw the sad dark eyes continuing to spill large tears. They each drew a rivulet inside the deep-purple crevices along his high cheek bones.

"I will *personally* return," she promised, "with Heinrich's *entire* library if there is anything I can do about it, I will find a way." She took his long skinny hands in hers and squeezed her assurance.

"Too kind," he said. "You are too kind," he repeated and started sobbing.

"I've got to go, my friend." Via suddenly realized she was holding up the Captain. "*Au revoir!*" She stood on tiptoes to kiss one of his wet cheeks.

"*À bientôt*," he said, holding back his tears. He waved goodbye and watched as she climbed up the back of the sub and slipped into its hatch. The hatch closed and the ship rose in perfect silence on its cushion of air. Ibn stood still, admiring the strange craft that appeared bio-mechanical and lifted up into the air vertically as if on a string from Heaven itself.

He remained standing in his spot where some of his tears had dropped to the parched earth. He continued to follow the ship as it flew back over Ararat's peaks and its lights disappeared into the midnight sky.

Once *The Ark* was out of sight, he wheeled around and walked to his vehicle. As he stepped to the Moskvich, he took out his false teeth. Before reaching the driver's door, he removed his wig. Opening the door, he placed these items on the seat and pulled off the latex mask, the gloves, and the rest of his disguise. A much younger man stretched and then rubbed his face and hands, then the skin on his arms, all red from the material that so perfectly made him appear to be an old man. He removed his belt with its weapons still attached and lay it on the floorboard, then pulled the robe up over his head. The man that emerged from under the robe wore blue jeans and a plain green t-shirt. He bundled up the robe and climbed behind the wheel of the old converted sedan.

Ibn backed up, turned around and headed back to his *dacha* hidden in the ravine.

١ ๑

"I'VE GOTTA LEARN medieval Spanish."

Charlie was keeping up with Sarah as the group walked along a granite flagstone walk between tall ecclesiastical structures housing the Vatican's finest scholars.

"Bear's been promised a cache of 8th century Nestorian prayer journals. Can you believe he is getting them from Beijing? Maybe you could learn how to translate medieval Mandarin or Cantonese." Sarah laughed.

Charlie gave her a grunt in response.

"His contact," she continued, "is a paleographer named Wang Pei-chin. She says that none of the journals have been translated into any modern language yet."

Charlie didn't show any interest. Sarah just smiled.

They both looked ahead. "Looks like we need to hurry up; keeping up with that Austrian is a job in and of itself," Charlie offered.

Michelle had the group flanked with heavily armed men and women, all dressed in the same black fatigues as their commander. Sarah thought it a bit much. "Why the automatic rifles?" she asked.

"Please move along," a polite word from the stocky Slovak who had been introduced to them earlier as Benko. He was in charge of protecting the rear. Sarah and Charlie were responsible for the group being a bit strung out instead of tightly bunched up. They rushed to catch up with the rest and then moved into the middle of the pack.

Sarah now noticed that Joshua was walking quickly alongside of Michelle, deep in conversation. She slipped up closer, anxious to hear what was being said. But it was all in German. Spanish, French, or English, she could have listened in, but she knew very little German. She wrinkled her nose.

José and Arkesha were now in the rear, in front of Benko. José was admiring the architecture, his eyes following the ornate lines up to the elaborate cornice work above them. He could see the patches of blue sky above as clouds moved quickly overhead, passing from their hiding places behind one rooftop to another, as if eluding a pursuer. He thought of the many centuries of history surrounding him and how proud his mother would be once he had a chance to fill her in. She had been the first to hear about his upcoming trip to Rome. He couldn't wait to tell her about the assistant professorship. She will faint, he thought. Her eldest son working for the Vatican? He would call her tonight.

He was still looking at the sky when he saw the flash of light. It wasn't much, just a bit of sunlight that reflected off a metal surface high above them on a rooftop. But it was ephemeral, and the glint was off a dull finish. His mind started buzzing.

His curiosity was piqued, so he focused on the section of the roof line where he thought the source of light had come from.

The flash didn't reappear but he saw movement. Then suddenly, it was gone.

Something was there.

It had withdrawn from view.

His senses were heightened. Years of participating in extreme sports will do that to you.

"Keesh," he said.

"Yeah?" she answered as they hurried along.

"Did Michelle say anything about security on the rooftops?"

"No." She was a step ahead of him on the ancient path. "But I would assume that she's got people crawling all over this place. After all, the Pope is here." She smiled.

"I don't know. The formal coronation is next week. The announcement was this morning … our own mission going on here."

"Why do you ask?" She was breathing hard as they hurried along.

"I think I saw something. Up there." He pointed to a section of the roof line that was now slightly behind them. "It's probably nothing, but I have that feeling."

"The same feeling as K2?"

"Yeah." José immediately was flooded with emotion. He could never forget the last time he'd felt like this. It was a feeling that came from nowhere. He had no logic for it. That's why he hadn't said anything. He'd tried to assuage his guilt. What could he have done about it anyway? They were half-way up K2 when that guy's carabiner broke. Had he said something, he would have just been a wild-eyed Hispanic with an intuitive harbinger. He didn't even know the guy. They'd met briefly at base camp a few days before, but there was no relationship, no trust, no bond. He'd have been the laughing stock of the Karakorum Range if he had been wrong. He had not dealt with it, not before the accident, not after, not at all ... not until he shared his pain with Arkesha their second day in Africa. He'd had nightmares. He'd wake up in a cold sweat.

Arkesha was no longer beside him. He'd already raced to the front of the column. He was already in Michelle's ear, "Do you have men on the roofs?" His half-whisper was pushed out between deep breaths.

"Yes," a curt but polite response.

"Last contact?" He tried not to sound disrespectful.

"Why?" spoken with genuine interest and only a slight hue of annoyance.

"Strange movement above us."

She didn't answer.

Five seconds.

Only five seconds later she made her decision. She didn't even make a call. "Go!" She commanded. It was just loud enough for the man to her left and slightly behind her to hear.

He took off, running up about twenty paces before darting 90° to the left. He disappeared into an arched opening near the north side of an adjacent building. "Clear!" José could hear the announcement blare from Michelle's earpiece.

"Follow!" Michelle directed her command to José as she pushed against his shoulder. She was simultaneously looking at Joshua on her other side. Her intent gaze told him to run as fast as he could.

Joshua darted after the soldier into the archway, and the entire group followed at break-neck pace. Six guests, eight armed guards ... they sprinted as one. José held back just long enough for Arkesha to catch up. Benko brought up the rear. It had been a matter of seconds, Michelle had quietly cleared the walk and brought the entire group over the threshold into an old library off their charted route.

The arch above them boasted a perfect half-circle of hand-hewn stone wedges that spanned the entry in beautiful ancient handiwork. The large blocks of granite on either side, stacked up twenty feet, served as the posts for the engineered lintel and the shiny black slate paving stones below. A long row of tall windows had been added centuries later to enclose the alcove. What used to be open to the weather now brought in the light, but kept out the rain. Michelle quickly turned to face the group and started....

She didn't have a chance.

Just as Benko was crossing into the alcove, a huge explosion tore up the walk just outside their shelter. It ripped into the opening and burned black the ancient blocks of stone. Every window shattered. Glass bits flew like tiny missiles. Had they still been out on the flagstones, the blast would surely have killed them all. The device was incendiary. The concussion and the power of it grabbed Benko just as he was diving into the alcove.

He died instantly.

The rest had the protection of the granite wall. In between the archway and the long line of windows was a space of about twelve feet where Michelle had stopped to address the group. Now they were all on the floor, having dropped down with the blast – shielding their heads with their hands and arms, huddling close to each other. The fire didn't reach them. The blast didn't get to them through the rock. However, they had plenty of glass fragments to pick out of their hair, their clothing, and for some, their skin.

But they were alive.

Michelle offered a brief look towards Benko's fallen form, made a fast sign of the cross and barked another command to the survivors.

"Come on!" she yelled.

Everyone was up off the floor in a fluid movement of arms and legs, backs straightening and heads lifting. The group was unified, acting in concert like a huge creature determined to escape the danger. Michelle quickly took them deeper into the building as they chased after her in a tight formation.

She had them zigzag. Right. Then left. Then left again. Then right again. Two more left turns. Three more right turns. Down a flight of sway-backed stones worn by centuries of movement by those who had dedicated their lives to the Church. Traversing a short hall, at the end of which Michelle opened a small wooden door with large iron hinges. The opening was so narrow it looked like it could be nothing more than a broom closet.

But it wasn't. It led them down a subterranean stairway. It was a long, straight path, steep and damp, dark and cold. They finally made it to the landing that opened up at the bottom. It opened up into a large space that looked very much like a basement underneath an old schoolhouse in England. One wall stood behind a collection of white plastic, five-gallon buckets with large faded labels. Another wall bore a skeleton of metal shelving that reached from the floor to about ten feet up. It held only a little from a left-over life: an old pile of paintbrushes with stiffened, dusty bristles; a rusty old toolbox on a bottom shelf; and, incongruously, a sizeable collection of ping pong paddles, lonely in their gathering on an otherwise bare shelf half-way up.

Michelle whizzed through the center of the giant room, her path lit only by the light that now shone from her weapon. No one else had turned on their lamps, they just followed the thin beam that stretched out in front of their leader. At the far end of the basement, Michelle flung open a large metal door and started down yet another set of stairs. Sarah felt the barely flexible steps underneath her feet. She heard the soles of boots on metal as the group took the steps downward two by two. Everyone was racing down, flight after flight, turning 180° at each landing interval. At least it wasn't as dark. Michelle now had each of her soldiers using the lights fixed to their assault rifles.

When Sarah had reached the first landing, she'd glanced back to the top. She'd seen their new rear guard closing the metal door and barring it from the inside. When she had reached the second landing, amidst the confusion of crisscrossing lights in the dark well, she had begun to wonder how many similar escape routes were bored into the earth underneath the many buildings that made up Vatican City.

The third landing.... She was already breathing heavily.

A fourth landing.... Then a fifth.... Sarah was getting really tired.

She wasn't the only one. Everyone was taking the steps one at a time now. They were all still hurrying, but it was more of a jog than a sprint at this point.

At the sixth landing, looking down at her feet, she saw the most curious thing. It was a small square of light below her. It looked about the size of a Rubik's Cube. She could see it through the metal mesh that served as a floor. Below her, now a flight or two ahead, she could see Michelle's beam of light cutting through the darkness in the deep tunnel they were vertically descending. They continued to spiral around the white square of light underneath them, buried in the darkness below.

Sarah's adrenaline pushed her to keep moving. Her shock kept her from crying. And she was counting.

Each flight had twenty-four steps. It made her think of the twenty-four elders in the book of Revelation … likely not a coincidence. After all, she thought, we *are* in the Vatican. She had been keeping track of landings too. She'd counted from six to ten, from ten to twenty. They kept going.

Twenty to thirty. Now thirty two. They had slowed down considerably. Sarah was amazed that they were able to descend so deeply into the earth. She peered through the grated metal floor again. The square of light was slightly bigger now, about an inch bigger on each side.

Off in the distance, like perhaps in a dream, Sarah distinctly heard the sound of gunfire. Not the sporadic shots of a pistol, but the merciless, messy barrage of automatic fire. It wasn't small caliber either. To her, it sounded like the heavy shelling represented by Hollywood to mimic the noises made by the big machine guns – the kind that are so heavy no one can carry them around without mounting them on a truck.

But there was another sound coupled with it that rose above the constant pounding of the still slowing rubber soles against the steel stair treads. It was the sound of tearing metal, wood, and stone. She didn't know it at the time, but the basement's barrier that kept out the danger, the door that had barred the enemy from pursuing them down the stairwell, was just now shredding into little bits.

"Breach!" the yell came from just above her.

Impossibly, everyone's pace quickened.

‏‏‫ ‎١٦

SITTING NEXT TO the pastor of Pee Dee Baptist Church in Florence, South Carolina, Naomi was enduring an introduction being delivered from behind the weary, old pulpit. She'd grown up in Maryland, earned her bachelor's and master's at Rice University in Texas, and worked in Washington now. She lived *inside* the beltway, on Capitol Hill, nonetheless.

The culture in the South was different. Sure, it had its similarities, but African-Americans from DC didn't get along with South Carolina's blacks. Or so her brother told her. And he still ran the streets in B-more. Not Naomi. She was the youngest of seven that her ma had raised single-handedly. Her aggressive initiative drove her to excel.

Baltimore was a rough place to grow up. The public schools barely recognized her intellectual talents and abilities. They weren't programmed to encourage it. She'd worked hard every year, and every so often she'd run across a teacher who had cared. But caring alone didn't cut it. The best teachers usually transferred out – or just quit. The good ones who did stay were so busy policing an increasingly crowded classroom of unruly kids that the few children who had the desire to do well were ignored.

Naomi was self-taught. When her twenty-three year old cousin showed up at her home deep inside the projects one weekend, things began to change for Naomi. Her cousin was there to study for her GED test. A twelve year-old Naomi helped her cousin study for and pass the test. Two months later, Naomi took it herself. She passed. She immediately started applying to colleges.

It took her an entire year of applications. She did the paperwork and made the phone calls and even visited the schools in person. Morgan State.

University of Maryland, Baltimore. Goucher College. Same with the other five colleges in the metropolitan area. Finally, the little girl stepped off the big steps of a city bus in front of Baltimore Community College. She smiled now as she thought back on the day. A thirteen year-old, skinny girl from the 'hood sitting in the admissions office with braided, beaded hair. A little black girl demanding to speak to "whoever's in charge here." But Naomi had been enrolled as a full-time student the following day. They'd given her a full schedule of classes, even though the quarter was three weeks in session already. She finally got the grants and student loans approved mid-way through her second quarter, but not without lots of help from the school and her ma's reluctant signatures. One year of perfect scores on every quiz. Every test. Every paper. Every project. And Rice University accepted their first fourteen year-old transfer student into its sophomore class.

The old lady at the Baptist lectern droned on. She was apparently reading from Naomi's promotional *vitae* that the NAACP always sent ahead of her when they lined up speaking engagements. Naomi tried to glance at her watch but didn't dare move lest someone notice. Another smile graced her smooth, milk-chocolate skin, drawing attention to her almond-shaped, dark brown eyes and her full lips. She wore her hair straightened now. It fell just past her shoulders. She was thinking back to the day the Greyhound finally stopped in Houston. Back then, her hair was puffed up proudly into a large afro. Her black poser doo was only a few decades behind the times, but the young lady had worn the hair style well. It fit her old soul. As she had stepped off the long ride into a cloud of diesel fumes, she had been greeted by the President of the school himself. He'd arranged for everything, even finding a family to take her into their home for the first two years. The President did promise that she could live on campus her senior year.

"But I want to live in the dorm! Now!" she protested. "I want to be like everyone else."

"You are not like everyone else," he had said. "Don't worry, you will get to experience dorm life. Just be patient."

He'd only been half wrong.

She *wasn't* like the other students. But she never made it to a dormitory. Naomi graduated two years later.

The pastor now stood. He was clapping aggressively. It prompted the entire congregation of at least two thousand to precede her remarks with a thunderous standing ovation. This type of response to her speeches, first only at the conclusion, then at both ends of her remarks, had initially been embarrassing to her. She had not been comfortable with all of the attention; but gradually it grew on her, and now she fed off the energy of the crowds. She drank in the euphoria of their praise. It helped animate her speech.

Naomi breathed in deeply. She was still seated, smiling and nodding in appreciation. It was a practiced delay before standing, which she'd learned studying the best of the best. After graduating from Rice and delivering the valedictorian address from behind the rostrum, she'd continued to utilize libraries and the Internet to advance her education during her master's tenure. She was always learning. She couldn't even read a good novel without looking up every unfamiliar word and committing it to memory. She laughed to herself because her favorite reading chair was next to a small bookcase that held an unabridged dictionary, an extensive thesaurus, an almanac, a single-volume encyclopedia, and the most recent hardbound Oxford's World Atlas ... all necessary tools when reading Charles Dickens, Ralph Ellison, or Jane Austen.

When she did rise from her high-backed leather chair that guarded the stage with the pastor's matching seat, the standing crowd's applause rose with her. It was a significant change in both volume and pitch. The voices all joined in with their clapping palms. Perfect. The rousing ovation caused a surge within her and her 5′7″ figure towered over the gregarious welcome. Hands perfectly still, fingers wrapped just slightly over the edge of the lectern's sloping top, as if she might just carry it out the side door with her, Naomi smiled at the Pee Dee congregation.

Only after the ovation finally subsided, and nearly everyone sat back in their seat, did Naomi finally move. And then, it was only her lips. Perpetually cast into a warm smile the entire course of her address, her mouth was controlled, even and purposeful. Besides the constant curvature of her lips, she found it effective to project her heart into each person in her audience. Finding face after face, looking deeply into pair after pair of eager eyes, she offered hope. It was hope, after all, that wove its common thread through every group. From small assemblies of lawmakers to Joel Osteen's masses in her adopted home of Houston, everyone needed it. Everyone sought it. Hope.

Now in her mid-twenties, she'd already been courted by both major parties to run for Congress. More than a few power-brokers had pulled her aside to suggest grooming for the Presidency ... the first black female leader of the free world. She wasn't so sure about that. That is, her being a head of state, as well as the other part of that ignominious misconception. She had been able to candidly express her total disinterest in holding any public office. Unfortunately, that made her even more attractive to those whose lives revolve around the endless cycle of fielding, molding, running, and then managing the political figureheads. Naomi didn't wish to waste her life as a pawn in someone else's game. Her smile firmly fixed, eyes shining with enthusiasm, and the first few words of thanks now perfectly delivered, she gently released her hold on the podium. Her willowy fingers and graceful arms finally joined the powerful force behind her message.

"Do you like being used?" she asked.

Such a simple opener. Her ma had always told her, "Don't ever ask a question you don't already know the answer to." In this shortly worded query, she was unlocking generations of emotions – painful memories, anger, regret and at the same time inviting total engagement in her speech. She wanted to establish a deep, almost spiritual connection with the multitude of beating hearts that would alter their behavior. Not just tonight.

Permanently.

A resounding "No!" volleyed from every pew and sent shivers up her spine. This delivery would be another success.

NAOMI HAD HER shoes off sitting on the bed in her hotel room. She was going over the results of the night. The audience had expressed their total agreement with her. She'd collected complete contact information from everyone in attendance, bar none. The reply cards were filled in with all the boxes checked as designated. Comments overflowed the space provided for them.

"Yes! Add me to your mailing list."

"Yes! I will read all your emails." Funny, she mused, even the cards that were marked "none" beside the email address entry blank.

"Yes! I want to study your voting guide before I vote."

"Yes! I promise to vote in every election."

And the one she *really* liked: "Yes! I want to purchase an advance copy of your first book."

She turned over card after card and shrugged with eyebrows raised.

Every single card had all of the credit card information properly completed on the back. She was pleased. But she should have been thrilled.

She was too tired to be thrilled.

Her phone rang.

"Naomi," she said dryly.

"How'd it go?"

"Fine." She was so very tired she certainly didn't want to be talking on the phone.

"That's it? Don't leave me hangin'."

"The door count was 2291." Casual and short.

"And?"

"100 percent." Almost lackadaisical.

"Really?"

"Yes." Sounding like she was about to cry. Was she sad?

"Not *almost* all of them?"

"All 2291." She felt an antipodal tinge of regret.

The voice on the other end of the phone whooped and hollered. Naomi had to hold the phone away from her ear. She was smiling but didn't share his excitement. She was too exhausted to be exuberant about anything. And her antonymous emotions made her feel anemic.

"Do you know what this means?"

"Should I?" She was ready to get off this call.

"We're over a million! One million, Naomi! Can you imagine where we'll be this time next year? Eight months ago you were only getting 34 percent and I was ecstatic! It just gets better every time! And now? 100 percent? That's just amazing."

"I'm glad you are happy. Can I go now? I'm really tired."

"You should be *out*. Celebrating! No one has ever accomplished anything close to this. Naomi, we…."

"I just want to go to bed." She stood up and gathered up the loose cards. She was putting them back into the cardboard box the church had given her.

"All right. Okay. But can I ask you?"

Silence.

"What about your book?"

"You aren't involved with my book."

"Oh come on. How'd you do?"

Silence.

"For an old man?"

She smiled. "You're not old. In fact, you are the youngest President of the NAACP we've ever had."

"So you'll humor me?"

She paused and pursed her lips. She was turning out the lights.

"All of them," she finally admitted.

"100 percent?"

"Yeah," she said in an almost defeated voice.

"Renee! You've gotta hear this! Honey!"

Naomi had to hold the phone away from her ear again.

His voice quieted and she could hear his wife answering him from a distance.

"Warren. I'll call you tomorrow." So wearily spoken it was almost too faint to hear.

She hung up before he could reply. Her thumb moved until the display read "ringer off." She clicked it.

She cried.

It took a little over a minute for her to fall asleep. She was still wearing her light green business suit as she lay prone, on top of the hotel's floral comforter.

١٧

SARAH WAS STILL counting stair landings as they raced down the rectangular coil that dug deep into the ground. She'd passed seventy, and then eighty, descending flights when she realized the box of light below them was a brightly lit room. It must be huge, she thought.

Ten more landings, too sore to go on, she stopped to catch her breath, only to be pushed along by the soldier who came up behind her.

"Ma'am, they are gaining on us," he said.

His words spurred her on, but she had no idea how he would know that they were gaining. And why no elevator? Who's bright idea was it to design *this escape route* for a bunch of old priests, down a shaft over 90 stories deep?

The square of light was much larger now. Huge.

Ugh. This endless staircase!

"100."

She kept descending. She was keeping count while doing the math in her head. She figured a seven inch riser was fairly standard. The step size felt normal to her. Twenty-four times seven? 168. Quick when you break it down to seven times twelve times two, fourteen feet when you take out the twelve inches – fourteen hundred feet. Wow!

How tall was the Empire State Building?

Five more landings. She began to imagine the utter terror and helplessness that would have overwhelmed each and every one of the exhausted men and women fighting for their lives as New York's Twin Towers burned. So many almost made it down the stairwells only to…. She couldn't think about it. She still prayed for the families of those who died that day.

Five more. 110? Where's the bottom of this thing? Below her, all she could see was the now blinding light reflecting off the bright white expanse of floor.

Finally, delirious with her own exhaustion, along with her uncontrollable OCD math problems that dominated her thoughts, she stepped off the last metal tread. She stepped onto a highly polished floor of white cement. As she did, she already knew.

144 flights.

2016 feet.

Dubai … pretty close to the height of the world's tallest building, Burj Khalifa, previously named Burj Dubai. The Dubai Tower. Cool.

She couldn't identify the light source. That made her start wondering. New problems to solve. Likely more math. Perhaps physics equations. Maybe later.

Instead, Sarah was rushing to keep up again. Michelle was already halfway into the center of the vacant white space. A dark spot was rising up from the floor in the middle of the aircraft-hangar-size room. Moving slowly upwards from an aperture in the floor was an apparatus that reminded Sarah of the big merry-go-round of swings at the Lane County fairgrounds. The swings reached at least twenty feet into the air before they stopped.

Black cables snaked down from spokes that radiated from its crown. At the end of each cable was a harness similar to those used in rock climbing, but designed to be much more comfortable. Old priests, an amusing thought.

As they reached the harnesses, Michelle and her team started strapping in the professor and his students. The soldiers followed, strapping themselves in as well. The floor around them pulled away. Simultaneously, the center pole telescoped back into itself, dropping everyone beneath the level of the floor. Sarah looked back above her. The opening in the floor was closing in on itself. The large metal support in the center of their harness cables was retreating to the closing space until only five feet of the thick cylinder and its long top-side spokes remained above the floor level.

A heavy fusillade of bullets hit the metal over their heads. The opening above them was still a little over ten feet wide, plenty of space for pursuers to shoot through, or, Sarah shuttered, drop through! The lead rained heavily against the top of their belay post. It was a shower of sparking and clattering that harmonized with the echoes of the released rounds. Sarah assumed that the enemy chasing them had reached the bottom of the stairwell and were now rushing towards the closing escape route. Were they firing at the pole, hoping to disable it? Or, Sarah shivered again, were they trying to sever the cables?

That's when she first looked down.

Down.

Below her was pitch darkness. The light that streamed through from above was bright, but not bright enough to illuminate a bottom. The harsh white light washed her and the other twelve in her group. She could see the circle of faces clearly as they descended within their safety harnesses. But she couldn't see any bottom to the hole they were dropping into.

Everyone was holding onto their cables. They were securely strapped in the harnesses, but each instinctively grasped the lines very tightly. Sarah thought of the word "lifeline." How appropriate, she grimaced to herself.

The security detail that accompanied her group from the university were all physically and emotionally tense. Each wore grim, determined looks. José and Arkesha were conversely excited and full of energy. Likely enjoying themselves, Sarah thought. Perhaps it's their idea of a fun date.

Bear looked frightened but composed.

Charlie was actually smiling. Okay, Sarah thought, huge waves and sharks are comparable, maybe even worse.

But it was Joshua's face that stunned her. The only way she could think to describe it is to recall the description of Stephen's own when he was being sentenced to death by stoning. Where was that? Acts 7? Acts 8? Sarah wished her mind would give her a break every once in a while.

Sparks were still flying furiously from the apex of the pole as it dropped into the darkness and the floor completed its reuniting fuse. They were suddenly immersed into total black, complete absence of light.

And silence.

It was like being dropped into a pool of dense blackened ink.

Completely devoid of light and entirely denuded of sound.

The barrage of gunfire was immediately muffled to nothing. Already it became a distant memory.

Because they were in a different world.

Like flying through outer space.

Or falling into it.

A bluish-green rod glowed at Sarah's eye-level about ten feet away. It was translucent in Michelle's hand as she cracked the inner seal of the cylinder.

Unceremoniously, she dropped it.

Looking down, Sarah watched it fall.

It kept falling.

It continued to tumble into the darkness until it almost disappeared.

Sarah listened hard. She was trying to hear it hit the bottom. Irrational. And all she could hear was her own heartbeat inside her cochlear cavity.

Their bodies were falling as well, but it didn't feel like they were dropping fast. Instead, their descent was relatively slow. Controlled. Restrained. Regulated. Safe. But they *were* falling, and the glow stick was still fast disappearing into the blackness below them.

After another minute in the dense, suffocating stillness of the black hole, a faint white light shone from somewhere far below them.

And they were off!

Fast.

Sarah felt her stomach kiss the back of her throat, depositing enough acid to make her nauseous. She could have sworn that her heart stopped beating. She had to force herself to breathe. An oppressive wind, cold and harsh against her bare arms and face, rushed up from below as they fell. Simultaneously, turquoise rods shone all around their circle. Every other cable held a soldier bearing one. The glow sticks' other-worldly illumination created a fluorescent shadow over the group as they rushed into the abyss. Sarah looked for walls. Sides. Any point of reference. But she could see nothing. She looked straight down again. The faint white light was still there, but it was no bigger.

Falling.

Surely the cables weren't slowing them now in the least. They were in a free fall.

Gravity's domain.

Free falling into a bottomless pit.

They just so happened to be attached to cables.

And their carabiners? Supposedly they were safe.

The twisted metal ropes? They might still be attached to the acme's arms, way up above them … somewhere way up there. She strained her head back and peered into the blackness of where they'd come from but could see nothing.

How far had they fallen?

It had been at least a couple of minutes already. Sarah was actually glad she hadn't looked at her watch before they started their free-fall. Had she, her worry was that her mind would now be calculating the distance traveled using an estimated rate of descent multiplied by the amount of time passed. She tried to take a deep breath and relax. But she was still trying to settle her stomach. Well, she finally decided, if the Pope can do this, so can I.

The free-fall eventually started slowing, barely discernible at first, then more so. Sarah's breathing became easier. Her hair settled back to rest on the top of her head again. Her stomach finally released its choke-hold on her. She decided to look up again. The aquamarine glow emanating from the rods cast the cables in a sort of bioluminescent sheen. The weird light made them look like mythical serpents, dropped from the heavens by angry gods. She estimated that the strange glow lit the plaited metal thirty feet up above her, and then blackness swallowed the light. The cables above them were soon immersed in a vast expanse of an empire of blind space. They'd fallen into a monster's maw. No cavern was *this* huge. No hole was *this* deep.

Their descent slowed ever further. Sarah squinted in the faint light to regard the other's faces once again. They all kept their appearance like it was before the free-fall – all except Bear. He now seemed to be enjoying himself. Had he joined ranks with the extreme-sports couple? Was he morphing into the persona of his tsunami-surfer friend?

Was she the only one worrying? What about some unknown threat that lurked below them? They were leaving the frying pan for the....

Sarah gripped her green viper tighter and looked down. Again. The white light was still there. But it was no longer small. No longer faint. They'd almost reached the light's perch on the bottom. Now? Now it was a huge flame. No glow stick she'd ever picked up at a festival turned into a bonfire. Way beyond what a safety flare generates, the rod that Michelle had dropped was now a bright white flame that marked the base of the great pit. The faint white light Sarah had seen from far above was just a pinprick at first, and now it was a huge blaze. It had been a great sulfuric fire all along. That's how high up they'd been. That's how far they'd fallen. How deep into the earth had they raced? How far down were they now? Had the planet simply swallowed them whole?

Off to the side of the cavern's floor, about ten paces or so from where the group would land their circle of anxious pairs of feet, the fierce flare burned strong like a widow's cruse. It was impossibly large for the simple fact that the rod dropped by Michelle was barely four inches long. It was maybe half an inch in diameter. How could this huge fire come out of a standard-sized glow stick? But it did. And the bright light it created lit a huge area at the bottom of their fall. Sarah looked around her.

They were in a wide place. It had a smooth gun-metal floor. It was bigger than even the bright light could reveal. Michelle, controls in hand, gently set the entire group's soles down onto the surreal surface … a solid floor. Even bottomless pits, Sarah thought, eventually have a floor.

Sarah immediately understood the brilliance of their escape route. There had been no power supply that could have been cut off during their initial descent in the stairwell. There was only a simple metal door, impervious to small arms fire and barred from the inside – no lock that could be picked and imposing, lengthy stairs that followed. The delay in getting through the door would give the good guys a head start at least. The stairwell seemed to lead to nowhere. Perhaps it would confuse the enemy. They would keep slowing to watch out for an ambush. Elevators can be stopped, disabled, or even boarded externally after they depart. And elevators need power but stairs don't. Add to that, the belay tower was brilliantly conceived. It had some kind of power source, but likely it was independent from the surface grid. The floor in the white room had closed over their head, leaving nothing but a bare steel and cement room with that insane white light. Had the enemy managed to figure out how to get the floor back open, how would they then descend into this pit, into the center of the earth? Surely no rope was long enough. The only empty harnesses had dropped along with them. Even if their pursuers had been able to descend the shaft, they would have had to have dropped relatively slowly, since they'd have been unable to see the bottom once Michelle's flare had burned out. Any normal flare wouldn't be visible from such a great distance, and one would run out of two dozen standard flares just trying to make enough light to mark the bottom, not to mention the fact that the enemy would be sitting ducks on their way down. Any decent marksman would have picked them all off by the time they reached the bottom.

But while Sarah's mind fussed with all of this, she was also plagued with other thoughts. How far down were they? An additional 2,000 feet? At least. For as long as they were free-falling she figured they could be another 5,000 or even 10,000 feet down.

But that would be impossible.

What was this hole that they'd dropped down into? The floor was obviously man-made. She assumed they'd be at the bottom of a large cave network with a rock floor … maybe at the shores of some underground lake or subterranean river. This far down? Maybe they'd come upon a prehistoric ocean.

As far as she could see, all Sarah saw was a smooth metal floor. As far as the light reached, that was all there was to be seen.

At least they weren't running.

Michelle and her security people unfastened themselves and helped most of the others. José and Arkesha were already free of their harnesses, walking towards Sarah with big grins plastered on their risk-addicted faces.

"New honeymoon idea?" Sarah greeted them.

"Hey, there's a thought," José quipped back. Arkesha nodded in agreement.

"Actually, I'm thinking business," Arkesha said.

"Business?"

"Yeah. Listen. You use a helicopter and you rig a huge wench in its cabin that can unreel a five thousand foot long nylon rope. The customer…."

"Whoa!"

Arkesha paused.

"Stop right there, girl."

Arkesha grinned.

"I've heard enough." Sarah was released from her harness and stepped away from the snaking cable with relief.

"No. Hear us out. You could *free-fall* over *any* location … places where skydivers can't go because of the terrain at the bottom," Arkesha argued.

"Like North Korea?" Sarah posed, with a shallow smile.

"Ha. Ha." José joined in. "No," he persisted, "like oceans and remote deserts and mountain peaks." He smiled and turned to his partner in the hair-brained scheme. "And Keesh had the best one. Tell her sweethea…."

"Antarctica," Arkesha said excitedly.

"Can you imagine a drop into the middle of the Gobi or the Sahara? Or up in the barren nothingness of the Andes? You get to touch ground, and then you get pulled up … right back up!" José grinned.

"With the rope accidentally looped around your neck? What a gust of wind would do. Helicopters aren't the most stable fliers, buddy."

He just looked at her. His smile waned.

"Or how 'bout this?" Sarah mocked. "Your customer pays you to be immersed in a simulated life and death chase with explosions and machine guns. Maybe you create a life-like hostage kidnaping drama complete with a videotaped beheading."

José and Arkesha just stared in confusion at their friend. They then exchanged glances with each other.

"That'd work." Arkesha smiled wide, accepting the idea.

"I like it. How would we simulate a beheading?" José faced his fiancée but kept Sarah in the corner of his eye.

"Cut it out!" Sarah turned and walked away. She could hear their laughter but she feared they were actually serious about all of it.

۱۸

THE PHONE RANG.

Naomi had been dreaming. Of what? It had already slipped out of her mind as most dreams do. You often remember them as you are waking up and start thinking about them as you get out of bed. But then, seconds later, in the middle of the recollection, the entire dream disappears. Forever. Like you never really dreamt it. No memory of it is left. She shrugged. It had been a good dream. Maybe. But it had vanished.

She kept her eyelids shut as she reached for the phone. It still lay where she'd left it the night before. It was on the unmade bed beside her. She groaned. She hit the green button. Her eyes were still shut. Eyes weren't necessary to know where the right button was on her mobile.

"Hello?"

The phone kept ringing.

Another groan. It was the hotel's room phone. It was sitting atop the ugly night table. Of course, it had to be. Her cell phone was off. She'd turned it off the night before.

Another groan.

The phone kept ringing.

She sat up. She was alone in a dark hotel room. Pee Dee Baptist. 100% on the cards. It was all coming back now.

For some reason she modestly straightened her light green skirt before leaning over and picking up the phone.

"Hello?"

"Naomi?"

She looked between the heavy curtains that were almost fully drawn. It was still night time. A crack of light came from underneath her closed bathroom door.

"What time is it?"

"Actually, I don't really know. My watch says a time. But it reads an hour that is relative. Relative to a place I used to be. But I can't remember if I'd set it for France or Iraq." Looking at her Suunto she could see three different time zones displayed. "Maybe one of these is France. Probably."

"And where are you now? Considering you woke me up at...." With sleepy eyes she looked at the large digital numbers of the clock next to the phone on the nightstand, "At 3:30am!"

"Central Africa ... 200 miles up. Just passing over the Congo."

Naomi rubbed her eyes and looked at the clock again. She yawned and stretched one arm over her head. She arched her back and slid off the edge of the bed. Standing up, her head started to clear. She instinctively walked straight for the coffee-maker on the counter over the mini-fridge. "I'm still asleep, Via. I thought you said 200 miles above Africa." She fumbled for a small laugh.

"*Oui.*"

"Really?" Naomi managed to get the four-cup pot brewing. "Isn't that normal for the International Space Station?"

"Pretty cool, huh?"

"Don't tell me you smuggled yourself aboard a satellite?"

"Close."

"Via?"

"Yeah?"

"How did you get this number?"

"It's listed, honey. All hotels do that. The hospitality industry doesn't do the whole unlisted number thing."

Naomi was rolling her eyeballs underneath the morning crust. She was trying to be patient while allowing Via to finish her joke. "You know what I mean," she finally managed, "how did you find me?"

Via cleared her throat.

"Warren?" Naomi guessed.

"He told me not to say," she quickly replied ... with a thick French accent.

"Well, let's see, since he and my ma are the only ones who know where I'm staying."

"He didn't tell me that part. Just the city. I called two other hotels until I found you." Via defended the man. "Your cell phone was going straight to voice mail."

"Warren was up?"

"I woke him up. It's nice when you have the cell number of the head of the NAACP."

"There is a good reason for my cell to be turned off." Naomi's voice cracked as the coffee dripped onto the burner while she poured the first cup, half emptying the glass decanter.

"Yeah, well … it's quite urgent."

"All this chitchat at three in the morning, but now it's urgent?" Naomi's tone carried a sardonic smile all the way to *The Ark*.

"It is," Via's voice turned down a notch. "I thought you said it was 3:30."

"Spit," Naomi demanded.

The coffee was too hot but Naomi took a long pull anyway. It seemed that the skin on her tongue was getting tougher. It didn't burn like it used to, but the insides of her cheeks still peeled. The roof of her mouth numbed up a bit. Bad habit. I need to add this one to my list of things to stop doing, she decided.

"Spit?" The heavy French accent was back. "*Je ne sais quoi.*"

"Spit it out. On with it. Go ahead and tell me already." A little frustrated.

"Oh." A short pause. Then, all business. "I'm short-handed. I need help."

"What kind of help?" Another drag on the caffeine.

"One hacker. Five medics. Two ordnance specialists. Twelve expert-evasive drivers."

No response.

Via continued after a deep breath. "Twelve vehicles."

"Only twelve?" The tone was as one might expect in response to such a request at that hour.

Via ignored the question, "And twenty additional boots on the ground."

"Where?" Same sarcastic tone, but now almost angry despite the extremely profitable $52,000 per day order, as Naomi calculated her standard fees in her head.

"*San Carlos de Bariloche*, Argentina." Another $35,000 surcharge.

"When?"

Naomi's tone may have gotten a little worse. Maybe some menace stirred in. Via wasn't quite sure. But she continued anyway. "By tomorrow. 1400 local."

Naomi spit out her third mouthful of coffee. It splattered all over the carpet.

"Are you okay?" A thick French accent again.

"Is that all?" Naomi asked. Not as much menace now. Good sign. Maybe it left her along with the ejected coffee. "I'll need $125,000, in addition to my daily," Naomi added.

"One more thing." Via accepted the price-tag without blinking.

"What?" The menace was back.

"And I'll have the money wired to your account in an hour. Zurich is open."

"What else do you need?" Lots of menace now, mixed with the impatience of knowing Via had put a lot of additional work on top of her already very busy day.

"You."

"I can't."

"What do you mean, you can't?"

"I just can't." Naomi poured her second cup of coffee while trying to remember how far down the street the Starbucks lay. She'd seen the green and white circle yesterday.

"I need you."

"I'll send someone comparable."

"But I need *you*."

"I can't."

"Remember the last chapter of Mark?"

"Mark 16."

"Right. What's it say?"

"You want me to read it to you?"

"No," Via pressed on, "What's unique about it?"

She had to think about it. During the pause she took a long draught from her plain white porcelain mug. "It has two endings."

"At least ... do you know why?"

"I assume because the manuscripts differ."

"They lost the original."

"*All* the originals are missing."

"Really?" Via didn't ever consider the fact.

"Really."

"Oh. Wow. Okay. How many originals are missing?"

"All sixty-six."

"Really?"

"Really."

"Wow, okay." Via's accent got thicker, the French coming out. "Well, anyway, we have a line on the original."

"The original of what?"

"Gospel." Via decided she'd better clarify, "The Gospel of Mark."

"You think an *original* biblical manuscript still exists?"

"It may."

"And because of this, you need my help, where?" Naomi's voice was strained.

"Bariloche."

"Argentina." A negative tone. She knew good and well where she was sending the team.

"Right."

"South America." Slightly more negative.

"*Oui.*" A sign of Via's nervousness.

"Where is Bariloche? Near Buenos Aires?" Naomi played with her.

Via's hopes lifted. She answered, "Patagonia."

"Patagonia? That's the end of the world! Isn't that where Magellan almost died?"

Silence. Then, "He almost died lots of times."

Silence.

Via added, "Until he did."

"Die," Naomi confirmed.

Silence.

Via tried to recover. "He died in the Philippines. Besides, Bariloche is much farther north than the strait."

"I would hope so. The Strait of Magellan is practically in Antarctica." Naomi paused to let that sink in. "You know I don't like the cold."

"But it's nowhere near Tierra del Fuego." Via's nerves were fraying.

"Will it be warm?"

Silence. This time Via was pressing her lips together. Hard.

"It's in the mountains," she finally admitted.

"The *Andes*." A hostile tone.

"But we are to meet with a World War II veteran. He is an expert in Christian antiquities. He's been the archival curator for the Archdiocese in Lima for the last seventy years. Most of medieval Spain's Church documents are there. He has agreed to give us complete access."

"Argentina fought in World War II?"

"He's from Lima."

"Peru fought in World War II?"

"He's … German."

"A *Nazi*."

Via figured Naomi's hostility had reached a peak. Perhaps it was the way she'd said that last word. Like she was snarling. Maybe she'd been baring her teeth as she spoke. I need to convince her to come, Via thought, but how?

"No amount of money?" Via asked with a bit of a whine.

"*Please*." No drop in hostility level. You've heard the inflection plenty of times.

"A really cute, talented, *very available* man is part of my ground team."

Naomi wrinkled up her nose and blinked with surprise. She had half a mind to just hang up. But she could hear a male voice objecting on Via's end. "Hey!" he said, and then it became unintelligible. Via had muffled her mouthpiece with her hand.

Funny thing, though. The man's voice made Naomi curious. Just one word, but she already had a picture in her mind. And she liked what she saw. The fact that he worked for Via, of course, was a definite plus. Via only hired the most talented. Naomi had met some of the most amazing people over the years through Via.

"Do they have decent hotels in Baril…?"

"Bari – loche," Via helped. "Yes. Five star. Luxury. The best." She was quick to add, "Resembles the Swiss Alps."

"Why wouldn't one just go to Switzerland?" Not a dumb question.

Via had to admit, "Well, after World War II, there were a … good number of European expatriates who had … moved to Argentina, and they wanted a place that reminded them of the European Alps."

Naomi caught on quick. "So, naturally, they would go back to Europe?" Prodding.

"Well," Via hedged.

"But they couldn't," Naomi answered her own question, "because they *fled* Europe. Although some were Swiss, some Italian, others Austrian and German," she paused for effect, "they were all Nazis."

Via protested, "Many were not Nazis in any sense of the word. They were just afraid of what their countries would look like in a post-war environment. They remembered what happened after World War I."

"Because of Versailles."

"Because of Versailles."

"Okay."

"Anyway. Bariloche was founded way before the war."

"What about this German we are meeting? What's his story?"

"Stauffenberg was part of the resistance," Via said with confidence. "The Front."

"Stauffenberg? I've heard of him."

"Not *the* Stauffenberg. His nephew."

"Hmm." A positive tone.

Via was encouraged. "I really need you."

A long pause. "I can't."

١٩

METHODICAL. ORGANIZED. Professional. Dead serious. The words that came to Charlie's mind as he watched Michelle. She was leading her people. They were herding their wards into a tight group to move again. The entire group walked at a moderate pace across the smooth slate-grey surface. He felt the weight of it under his feet. He could sense the mixture of iron and carbon that was at least ten feet thick. The soles of his feet could practically feel the molten steel, now hardened where it was poured on top of solid rock that stretched towards the Earth's core for another seven miles or more.

In the dim light, now finally fading, he could not make out the limits of the space they'd dropped into. The flare flickered and began to die. They walked for a good five minutes when the flare gave a final puff behind them. The small group was left with Michelle's bright halogen beam beneath the barrel of her HK416 assault rifle.

Charlie saw the shaft of white hit a vertical surface ahead. Ah, a wall. As they drew nearer he could tell it was made of the same grey steel as the floor. He immediately wondered if the wall was as thick. Michelle reached the wall. The group bunched around her. Charlie noticed a light switch ensconced into the thick metal. The outline of a large doorway paired with the switch reached at least thirty feet to its header. It was wide enough to squeeze a tractor-trailer between its jambs.

As Michelle flipped the switch, all eyes were immediately drawn to the enormity of the pit's interior. Bodies spun in circles as everyone scanned a huge circled floor braced between impossibly tall cliffs of the dull-grey metal. Even Michelle and her soldiers gaped despite having seen the sight before.

Charlie could see it all now, most of it, at least. The size of.... How would you even describe it? They were at the bottom of a huge metal cylinder, the entire bore of which could have been a mile deep and a quarter mile in diameter.

"We're almost two miles underground." Sarah whispered in his ear.

Charlie didn't respond. He couldn't. Beyond his wildest imagination, he could have never.... The largest wave he'd ever surfed was off Big Sur. Was it thirty-five feet? He'd gotten up early that morning, in a dive in Monterey. Drove in the dark. Headed south to one of California's best surf spots. First one on the beach. Like it was yesterday. He'd had to paddle furiously to get into position. He'd stood up on his shortie just as he pulled to the front edge of the wave. The drop? Incredible.

That was nothing compared to this.

The light switch not only lit the gargantuan shaft, but it activated the adjacent single-sectioned steel door that now slowly dropped into the adjoining floor. Beyond the heavy barrier, a huge garage appeared, dipped in a soft red light. A short, muscular woman's combat boots carried her inside the garage as soon as the door seemed to disappear as it leveled with the floor's surface. A diesel motor gurgled.

Then Charlie's eyes uncontrollably fell back on the soft features of Michelle's face. He reluctantly took his eyes off Michelle to reach for Sarah's shoulder.

"What do you think?" he asked.

"Huh?"

"Some bomb shelter. I'd guess nuclear war could burn the entire planet and all of Vatican City, heck, all of Rome could survive down here."

"Oh."

"So?"

"Huh?"

"What do you think?"

"Oh. I think she has her sights set on Joshua."

Now it was his turn. "Huh?"

"Michelle."

"Really?" He inadvertently revealed too much. Not only his inflection, but his eyes flicked back over to Michelle as he spoke.

"Oh." Sarah would have covered her mouth with her fingers. Despite her restraint, he picked up on it.

"Yeah. Wow." Charlie let himself stare with longing. "Do you think I have a chance with her?"

"Uh…." How to respond? She knew Charlie's reputation for getting any woman he wanted.

But then Charlie put his own conclusions together. "You're in love with him." It wasn't a question. They'd been kidding her about it for a while, but this was different.

"What?" Sarah feigned for a second. She knew he was being serious. "No," she said simply. She denied it without any emphasis, knowing he would see through it.

"All right," he said as if dropping it.

"What's that supposed to mean?" She took the bait.

He couldn't help but smile. "Okay. It means I'm good with it."

"You're good with what?"

A wider smile as he looked into Sarah's pretty blue eyes. "It means I'm good with you," his voice lowered, "hooking up with the professor."

She hit him.

The driver pulled a strange machine out of the cavernous garage. Still smarting from the ache of Sarah's fist against his arm, Charlie counted eight huge, off-road tires in the front of the beast of a machine moving out. The wheels in the front turned on two axles. Another set of huge tires hung onto two axles in the rear of the strange military-style vehicle. Charlie thought it looked like a giant Humvee that morphed into a naval personnel transport. It was hard for him to picture the Pope and a bunch of Cardinals and priests climbing up into the amphibious craft. He figured it had almost five feet of ground clearance and would carry up to 50 people.

Mounted near the center of a flat-bed on the rear of the carrier, Charlie's eye landed on a .50 caliber cannon. He let out a sound of amazement and respect.

As the diesel machine growled to a stop, it displayed an overhead door that pivoted out in a single, smooth motion. The barn-door sized hatch jutted out horizontally, partially inside and mostly outside the heavily armored vehicle. As the door swung up and out, a rigid grid made of a strong, light metal alloy lowered to the ground. Charlie looked at the strange mesh of steps tinged with metallic ochre and saw a spider's web of several ladders hanging side by side. Then it hit him – rat lines! Like the ropes sailors used to climb on the big wooden sailing ships.

"Let's go!" Michelle stood next to the opening, waving everyone inside.

José and Arkesha scrabbled up the ladder side by side. Bear and the professor followed. From where they were still standing, Sarah and Charlie received a few looks from Michelle's soldiers that let them know that they were expected to enter the vehicle. Now.

"Four at a time," Charlie mused. He and Sarah were climbing the metal rat lines in tandem with a pair of soldiers as the lights went out in the cavern.

"It carries 36, including the drivers." Michelle spoke as they climbed inside off the top rung. Charlie looked back down at her. "We have 144 of these down here," matter-of-factly stated.

Charlie's head started to swim.

Sarah couldn't help it. She did the math.

BEAR UNBUCKLED the three-point seatbelt that secured him inside the amphibious beast. He was along one side of the interior of the vehicle. It was already moving, but he moved deftly up to the cab. He crouched in the wide space between the two captain's chairs in the front and looked out the windshield. They were moving along at quite a clip inside the base of the giant well, now dark except for their headlamps.

An impressive array of controls and displays along the dash caught his attention. He surveyed them quickly, figuring out what each offered the two drivers. To his right, the primary driver had her hands on a small steering wheel. She was focused on guiding the huge machine forward along the smooth steel floor.

"Name's Zelfa," she said. "That there's Yusef." She pointed at the back-up driver without her hand leaving the controls.

"Bear," he said. "Good to meet you guys." He paused and looked around again. "Cool job."

"I'll say," she agreed. She had only a slight Greek accent tingeing her excellent English. "This is my third year here. I love it. I absolutely love it!"

"Where are we heading?"

"Out of the city."

"From here?" Bear couldn't believe it.

"Yes," she responded with a smile. "We'll hook up with a cave system that winds from here to the coast. There are a few man-made connections. But much of it is natural. A good part of it was first excavated in the 2nd century by Marcus Aurelius Antonius."

"Aren't we a ways from the coast?"

"Twenty-five kilometers – as the sparrow flies." She grinned. "Due to all the twists and turns down here, though, we'll travel almost forty."

"Will we come out underwater?" Dumb question.

"No." Zelfa laughed. "We will gradually move back toward the surface. We will come out near *Lido Di Ostia*." Then she added, "We're 2800 meters down."

"Over a mile and a half?" Bear blurted, "Hold on!" He jumped up and ran into the back.

"Charlie…," he started.

"I know. I know already." Charlie handed his friend back the crumpled twenty dollar bill.

"Ha!" Bear took the worthless piece of paper and stuffed it in his pocket. He looked at Sarah.

"Don't look at me," she said. "I didn't care *who* would win the bet."

"How'd he know you would figure it out?" Bear challenged.

"After you guys made that stupid bet?" Sarah shrugged.

"Oh."

"You really don't want to know how I calculated our depth." She smirked.

"No, I guess I don't."

Charlie interjected, "I don't understand it either, and that's after she explained it to me."

Sarah put her hands on her knees. "What I don't understand is why you *boys*," said with a bit of friendly spite, "insist on passing that poor, disgusting $20 bill back and forth."

Bear just smiled and hurried back to the cab with his winnings.

Looking out the front window again, he saw the same, monotonous color illuminated in front of them. Grey. Everything looked flat and smooth. Wait – there appeared to be a break in the floor up ahead. A narrow ramp cut into the floor. It was hard to see. Unless you knew where it was, Bear guessed, you'd miss it.

The amphibious carrier dropped onto the top of the ramp. Just as it did, the lights went out. The pit was plunged into total darkness. Startled he asked, "No head-lights?"

"We can't," Yusef answered. "If we use any light from this point forward, the exit won't open."

"Wow! Quite a trap," Bear said. "No one could ever get out of here."

"Not without the code." Zelfa's smile was crafty.

The heavy machine was barreling towards the thick steel wall in the midst of pitch black darkness.

"Code?" Bear asked.

"That I had to punch into this baby just to get it started." She pointed from her steady grip on the wheel. Bear followed her finger to the elaborate central display.

He found himself looking at a CGI of the ramp as they continued to descend. The virtual reality graphics moved in real time with their traverse along the length of the ramp that dug into the rock-hard floor. Bear stared at the image of a solid wall fast approaching. But then he saw the barrier seemingly melt away into an opening at the bottom of the ramp.

Zelfa didn't slow down.

"Aren't you going a little fast?" Bear asked nervously. "That opening looks a bit small for this huge contraption." He pointed.

"I have to keep my speed constant or we won't make it. The exit is barely big enough for us to squeeze through, and I had better be going 35 km/h when we push on out."

"The door would shut on us?"

"Worse."

Bear didn't want to know. He didn't ask.

The personnel carrier burst through the small aperture with little room to spare on either side. They shot into more pitch black space and then abruptly screeched to a stop. Immediately on stopping, blinding lights from a bank of halogen spots thundered on. The huge round lights were pointing right at them. Bear put up both hands to shield his eyes from the artificial sun.

"Now we wait," Zelfa said mystically.

"First the dark ... now the light ... now we sit?" Bear closed his eyes and put his tongue into the space between his upper lip and teeth.

"Five minutes twenty-nine seconds," she said, looking at her watch.

For some reason the time passed quickly for Bear. He had Zelfa and Yusef both explaining to him how this additional defensive mechanism worked. If a pursuer managed to escape the huge cylinder that now lay behind them, he would plunge into darkness, and then be blinded by light. It would be impossible to know what to do next. Zelfa demonstrated. "See?" she said, backing up the vehicle.

"What?"

She stopped the carrier and cut the engine. "What happens is...."

Her earpiece talked.

"She wants to let you see it."

"Who?" Bear was confused.

"Commander Galbrathur."

"Who?"

"Me." It was Michelle. She had crept up behind Bear and was now practically talking into his ear. "Come on. I'll show you."

"WELCOME TO ARGENTINA. Passport please?"

Naomi handed it over.

"Thank you, Ms. Young."

She forced a polite smile.

Via was waiting at the baggage claim.

"*Ezeiza* is nice, isn't it?"

"It's an airport."

"Oh, come on. Cheer up."

"I thought I was going to switch planes here."

"We'll make it in time. The rest are already there." Via smiled. "I thought you and I could explore Buenos Aires until our ride gets here."

That got a smile. Naomi hugged her. "I'll try not to be a wet blanket."

"I like you for who you are, kid." Via touched her cheek. "Thanks for coming."

"So you think I am a wet blanket?"

"Heavens no, honey. But I know you had to rearrange your busy schedule and…." Via's eyes were searching the bags coming out onto the conveyor.

"Mine's the light green one."

"Any angry Congressmen? Mad they won't be able to see their favorite lobbyist this week?"

"I'm *not* a lobbyist."

Via ignored that one. "How many speaking engagements did you have to cancel?"

"Only two. And I don't particularly care for the Distinguished Gentleman from the State of Pennsylvania, so I'm glad I had to cancel a lunch."

"The Senator can wait."

"Until…." Naomi bit her tongue.

Via found the bag, last out of the shoot – always.

"How is your book coming?"

"I'm self-publishing."

"Oh." Disappointment.

"Why do you say that?"

"Well, I figured you'd get a big advance from one of those New York publishers."

"It's not all it's cracked up to be."

"But *self-publish?* You're a well-known personality now. How many times have you been on CNN?"

Naomi just shrugged.

They made it to the cab line. "*Todo el dia, por favor,*" she told the driver in the front of the stacked up Scala wagons. Her words were pronounced with a stack of US dollar bills, enough to hire him and his old car for a week. The Pakistani *porteño* driver had been at the curb lounging against the front fender, now he was scurrying with utmost care. His polite gestures and kind words were ushering the two women into the vehicle as he gingerly put the single, large suitcase into the back.

"No carry-on?" Via hadn't asked at the baggage claim. For some reason she just now noticed.

"I catch up on my sleep when I fly."

"Hungry?"

"Starving."

"I know just the place."

THE PLACE WAS wonderful. Naomi sat on a comfortably upholstered antique dining chair, part of a Queen Anne dinette that overlooked *Parque Patricios.*

They ordered while admiring their second floor balcony view and took some time to catch up. Naomi breathed in deeply, savoring the sweet aromas and cascading colors of the Amazon's best orchids, in hanging pots clutching the outside rails.

"Emil's Rotisseri." She let the name roll off her tongue. "It's very nice. Have you been here before?"

The waiter, a tall Italian in his mid-forties, exquisitely presented their salads and vanished.

"No. It's brand new. A friend of mine suggested it." Via smiled and dug into her baby spinach, walnuts, and sprouts in raspberry oil and vinegar dressing. "After we eat, we're going shopping." She looked up for Naomi's reaction.

Naomi was praying over her food.

When she was done, Via blurted, "Sorry."

"Don't be." Naomi picked up her fork and played with her salad. "You still don't pray?"

"I'm not ready."

"But so much of your work…." She stopped, knowing that it was not a matter to argue over.

"My work stems from my family's history," Via said solemnly. She'd stopped eating and her face became slightly downcast.

"Didn't you tell me before? You changed your name over an ancient family secret?"

"A lie – deep, dark skeletons lurking in the Savoie ancestral closet."

"You are a Savoie? You never told me that."

"I was. And you were young, you wouldn't have known the name."

"I'm sorry." Naomi stopped eating too. "Weren't they the ones who…? Oh. I'm so sorry. Via, are you okay?"

Via had paled green.

"I'm fine," the Frenchwoman lied. "Better now, in fact, now that the truth is out."

"When did you learn the truth about your family's lies?"

"It was my grandfather. He told me on his death bed. I had been at the estate in Chambéry attending him during his last few months. He'd been suffering in very poor health for years. But it had gotten much worse. During those last few months he'd started making incoherent promises about leaving everything to me and gushing over the years when he was one of the most respected men in Europe."

"But he *did* leave you everything. Right? And he *was* one of the richest men in France."

"*Oui*. That much is true. He had actually changed his Last Will and Testament many years before. Well prior to the onset of his dementia. But it was that cold day in January, right before he died. It was the last time that I saw him alive. That's when he said what he said to me."

Naomi sat silently. She watched as the sunlight glistened off the tears forming in Via's dark eyes.

After some pause Via continued, "He was telling me that he regretted not being able to leave me the famous shroud."

Naomi had remembered correctly that the Savoie family had kept the Shroud of Turin in their care for many generations.

"He recounted the story I'd heard a million times since I was a little girl. I patiently listened, holding his trembling hand at the side of his bed. 'The shroud was kept in our family for over 400 years,' he'd said. 'We never should have let it go. I could be leaving it to you, *ma grand-fille*. Alas, all you will receive is the Savoie Family Trust.'"

"*Trust!*" Via shouted viciously. "I almost rejected it all. I almost signed the papers. I'd felt so betrayed."

Naomi watched Via take a deep breath and wipe away the tears that had escaped onto her cheeks.

"I should have signed the papers."

"But Via," Naomi objected, "you've done so much good for so many. Could you have been able to do it all without the inheritance?"

Via ignored her. "He confessed after his long sentimental story, after talking about family pride and passing the torch to me. He spoke of honor and integrity and the family name. But then, in a moment of weakness, or perhaps guilt, he said it. Or perhaps he was just overcome with his own regret that the shroud had been sent to Turin." Via's lips were quivering.

"He said...." She paused again. She bit her lip. It bled.

Then she started again with anger all over her face. "He told me, 'Thank God it was only a replica.'"

Via trembled with rage. "I immediately let go of his hand. All my strength left me. The blood drained out of me. His own tone had been one of relief and bitterness. Like he was blaming the Church for the loss of prestige that giving up the shroud had brought the family. I think, for some reason, he was finding comfort in the fact that the Church didn't have the real one."

Naomi reached across the table and took Via's quivering hands in her own.

"It's okay," Naomi said. "It's okay."

"No. It's *not* okay. That is why I've dedicated my life to the truth. I must redeem our family name. I must recompense our sin. We passed that cloth off as the real thing for centuries! Something so sacred. How could we be so reckless!" Tears were streaming from her face onto the white linen table cloth. "That's why I worked so hard to find it. And *expose* the fraud."

Naomi pulled her hands back as a shocked look of horror passed over her face. "That was you?" she gasped.

"*Oui,*" Via admitted. "By the time I'd located the real one, others had as well. Someone was going to take it, and I knew it had to be me."

"But why? How could you?" Naomi asked. "I mean … taking it … and then telling the world?" Naomi was calming down already but she didn't know why.

"If the Vatican had their way, they would have covered up the lie again. Probably just hide the true shroud again. They knew it was there. They've always known. At least since they sacked Constantinople, they've known. They conspired with the Greeks to keep it there … to hide it … forever."

Via shifted her tone. "Then, there's that maniac who wants it. He means to acquire it and take it to his lab. Thinks he can extract DNA from it. I wasn't going to let Enson get it. *Pour rien au monde,*" she growled.

"You said there were others. Who else knew?"

"I was asked to retrieve it. I had been preparing to leave soon to obtain it anyway. So I accepted the job."

"You got *paid* to steal the shroud?" Naomi's voice had been low and controlled until now. She didn't realize until it was too late. Her question was too easily overheard.

He stood at their table within a few seconds of Naomi's outburst. Clearing his throat in a manner to get their attention, "Ladies," their waiter looked uncomfortable but continued, "are you done with your salads?"

Naomi shooed him away. "I'm sorry," she said to Via.

"You don't have to apologize. I don't blame you for reacting the way you have." She wiped her face with her napkin and attempted another bite of her salad. "I should have told you before now."

Naomi was too hungry not to follow suit. With a mouthful of baby greens and red onions tossed in creamy Italian, she asked, "How long have you known?"

"For a year."

"Wow! You knew where the real one was for a whole year? That must have been something. How'd you find it?"

"I'd been tracking it for fifteen years."

"That long? Oh, honey!" Naomi reached over the table again. She was just now beginning to appreciate Via's intense desire to find redemption.

"I started in Jerusalem. Correspondence from Abyssinia to Jerusalem that had ended up in Caesarea. One letter indicated Joseph of Arimathea kept the burial cloths in Jerusalem until 69 AD."

"Wait a second! You are telling me there is a letter from ancient Ethiopia discussing the shroud?"

"Yeah. The real one. Get this. The letter purports to be from a Christian Eunuch in Queen Candace's Court in Aksum. He used the title, Viceroy of the Treasury, whatever that means. The man was writing to an apostle in Jerusalem. I didn't believe it at first. I figured it had to be a fake. I mean, there were no Christians in Ethiopia. And this apostle? I'd never heard of him before."

"Philip."

Via was dumbfounded. "How did you know?"

"If you'd read your Bible you'd know the answer to that question."

"It's in the Bible?"

*   *   *

MICHELLE OPENED the transport's heavy overhead door as if it was light as a feather. The hydraulics did all of the lifting and the rigid cover slid up into its place, offering a canopy above them as they exited the craft. She led them down the rat lines onto a smooth, but naturally formed, surface of hard stone. The rock was polished to a sheen that only countless trillions of gallons of water can produce. The landscape was nothing short of surreal.

The light that made it possible to see their immediate surroundings was incongruent with the natural cavern. The bright array of giant flood lights was about a hundred and fifty yards away from them. Fixed to the side of one of the cave's walls, they were stacked in a large rectangle of seven fixtures by twelve. Bear thought they looked like the banks of lights used over McKinley Field. Bear didn't care much for the Chicago White Sox but he loved their stadium.

His folks had sent him away to boarding school in upstate New York. He began to reflect on those unhappy days, first grade through twelfth at boarding school. What was wrong with the private schools in Chicago? They had good prep schools. Some of them were internationally renowned, scattered throughout northeast Illinois and southern Wisconsin.

"BUT YOUR FATHER went to school there. Honey, it's the best."
"Best for who?" coming from a six year old.
His folks flew him between Albany and Chicago constantly. At least his parents weren't the type who had no relationship with their kids but merely shared their last names and DNA, bragging about them – even to strangers. Or others who would only deal with the aggravation and expense if just to have an acceptable heir. *At least Bear's parents wanted him to be around them*. It was an effort they'd performed without skill, but they tried. Mostly it was the traditions of his parents that bothered him – the guilt and pride of societal expectations that controlled them, robbed them of their joy, kept them from truly knowing their son.
"Your traditions don't mean anything to me!" he'd say.
"They will someday, honey bear," his mother would reply.
"Don't call me that!"
"But your name is Barry, like your father's. Like his father's before him. Don't you think it's cute?"

"NO. I DON'T THINK it's cute," he now said out loud.
"What?" Michelle was right next to him, leading him towards the lights.
"Sorry," he mumbled.
They stopped abruptly and the group bunched up around them.
"Look!" she said. She pointed down only a few feet ahead of them.
Bear looked.
They had stopped at the very spot where Zelfa had stopped the big machine just a few minutes earlier.
His toes curled.
Shivers shot through his bones as he starkly stepped back.
Michelle offered a small laugh. "You won't fall."
"See where the bad guys will end up if they even manage to get this far?" she boasted. "They'll barrel out of the pillar and fall headlong over the cliff."

"Cliff?" He stretched his neck and looked down. Way down.

The lights prompted him to shade his eyes with his hand, but he could see what she meant. The bank of floods was mounted onto an opposing wall of sheer rock that rose from the bottom of the other side of a wide crevice. The rock face on the other side of the chasm dove deep into the cavern's strange landscape of hardened stone.

He couldn't even see the bottom.

For some strange reason it made him think of his father. Tradition. Reputation. Appearances. But the stony hardness of his father's pride is what led to his downfall. His perfectly tailored life had fallen into its own bottomless pit. All the money he had accumulated couldn't save him. His mother's tears couldn't stop it.

He put the thoughts out of his mind as he had so many times before.

"Where are we?" he asked.

Michelle leaned into his ear. "We're in a dry artesian basin."

He suddenly became even more uncomfortable on several different levels. Charlie was too.

Charlie was standing to the side of the crowd with his toes practically hanging off the rounded rim of the precipice. He had been enjoying the thrill. But the oblivion of the vertical drop wasn't a powerful enough draw to keep him from looking at the attention Bear was getting from Michelle. What's going on? Could the enigmatic sylph strapped into her combat boots be interested in Bear?

Bear thought for a minute about what Michelle had said. Then he responded, "Artesian wells are aquifers of highly compressed water in a liquid-bearing bed or stratum of rock, sand or gravel. They are *not* giant caves."

Michelle leaned back into his ear and put her hand on his shoulder as she spoke. "Slaves," she said. "Lots of Roman slaves."

"Huh?" Bear grunted.

"They *dug* the gravel out," she whispered in a way that stressed the enormity of the task.

The sound of a diesel engine rumbled in the distance. Its churning revolutions echoed off the water-worn walls of the enormous cavern. Sarah wouldn't stay near the edge of the cliff. She had enough sense to stand in the back of the assemblage. So it was that she was the first to notice the sound of the approaching vehicle. She turned to look.

Sarah saw a small strip of headlights stretching across the front of another amphibious transport. The craft was identical to their own and it was chugging towards their position. It was still off in the distance, buried in the darkness except for the beam of light coming from its nose. But as it rumbled closer, the shape of the craft became unmistakable. The truck came up behind where their own carrier had parked.

It stopped. A large group of people disembarked from the craft and began to stretch their limbs. Two figures broke from the pack and started walking through the dense shadows towards Sarah. It didn't take long for her to realize that one of the two men was the Pope.

And the other was her professor.

Joshua? How did he…?

Did the professor get out of the other carrier with the Pope?

No. That would be impossible. He was with her group.

Perhaps Joshua had heard the noise before she did and slipped into the darkness behind them.

Her lips curved into a dreamy smile as she watched Joshua walk her way.

Was she really in love with him? Sure, he was exciting! But wasn't that the extent of it? He didn't show the interest in her that she craved. There was something there though. He knew what kind of coffee she liked. He'd even brought her a caramel latte from time to time. What did that mean?

The Pope was wearing his long white robe and matching skull cap as he and Joshua came up to Sarah and stopped in front of her. Sarah twisted her mouth and squinted.

"What's wrong?" Joshua asked her.

"Huh?" She was lost in thought.

"You look disturbed. You okay?" He reached out and touched her arm.

Electric. Am I swooning? "Yes, I'm okay," she managed to reply.

The Pope smiled. "Sarah, my dear, I want you to look up." He pointed.

She kept her eyes on Joshua's face.

"This way." His finger finally got Sarah's attention and it led her eyes into the void of space that engulfed them all. He pointed about 45° from where they stood and back from where their own transport had emerged like a cannon ball out of the bottom of the shaft they'd descended.

Miguel pulled back the end of one of his sleeves, exposing a smartphone attached to his bare forearm. He manipulated the touchscreen with dexterous fingers and in seconds the app caused the intended result.

One after another, banks of flood lights like the first started popping on. More and more broke into the darkness, first near them and then farther and farther away. Sarah watched amazed as the huge rectangles of light burned three hundred yards apart, both horizontally and vertically in a huge grid pattern throughout what was now revealed to be miles of cavern walls. The inside of the artesian basin's empty space now lit up like a Christmas tree.

Artificial sunshine.

Sarah had been to Carlsbad Caverns in New Mexico. The largest cave open to the public is the Big Room, fourteen football fields. Utterly huge. But now she was trying to figure how many of Carlsbad's Big Rooms would fit in this mammoth of all caves. Too many to count.

Where countless trillions of gallons of water used to swirl against the ancient rock, smoothing the surfaces until they resembled the inside of a pewter cauldron, Sarah immediately focused on the fact that the huge space was not entirely empty.

An incredible sight.

She gawked at the outside of the steel shaft from which they'd traveled, looking at it now from a different perspective. The thick metal cylinder was huge, and it rose upwards as far as her eyes could see, a full mile high. It was so wide it blocked her vision on her left-hand side, perhaps a good ten percent or so of the panoramic spectacle before her. The straight dark shape of the pillar rose like a redwood trunk would appear to an ant. The endless tower stretched to a ceiling only barely discernible by the light of the last line of floods that marked the upper frontier of the emptied subterranean reservoir.

The rest of the sweep of her vision took in a sight even more incredible.

The smooth rock floor that supported their weight was also acting as a tabletop for a forest of other similar pillars. Each shaft dully reflected the light from the huge grid of floods. The other cylinders reached from one end to the other along the length and width of Vatican City high overhead.

Sarah could also tell that the rock she was standing on was no more than an island in an emptied sea that ran far past the outer limits of the tabletop.

As her eyes settled back on the polished granite of the surface, she noticed movement. More transports. There were dozens of them. They were streaming towards her from every pillar in the cavern. The Pope saw Sarah staring at the amphibious transports. "Lots of them, aren't there?" he asked.

"Incredible!" she responded, still fixated on the swarm of steel-clad creatures rolling their way.

"We had to evacuate the entire complex," Miguel mourned.

"Everyone is down here?" She was still watching the confluence of coming carriers.

"Not all. Most are actually in safe-house bunkers at higher levels. About twenty percent of us come down here in circumstances that warrant."

Miguel pulled at his woolen pallium. "I'm still concerned that we are not out of danger."

"What do you know about the attack?"

"Reports of at least three teams. It was simultaneous."

"Are they still pursuing *us?*"

"One team has been engaged by the military. They are immobilized at this point, likely not a threat to us. Another disappeared. We assume they escaped. The one that attacked your group's position followed you as far as the white room. Slim chance they'll make it any farther. They'll end up trapped there."

"Is there another way to get down here?"

"Other than the shafts?"

"Yeah." Sarah the planner was not a pessimist. She was a realist.

"Yes. But...."

"I'm just concerned that...."

"We've given our military everything they need. Michelle has her own army up there too, all the codes, blueprints, schematics of each of our defensive systems." He nervously fingered his chasuble as he spoke. The initial confidence was leaving his voice.

"So a mole in Italy's military would actually make it easier for our pursuers to get to us." Sarah persisted.

Miguel frowned. "Yes," he said. Then, after only a short pause, "I guess we have *another* reason to keep moving."

Michelle had already approached them and now stood by the Pope's side. Sarah looked down at her feet.

Her head cocked to one side as she noticed the Pope's own pair of feet poking out from under his long white simar. Bright red shoes.

"What's with the shoes?" she quietly asked Joshua, as the Pope became engaged in fervent conversation with Michelle.

The professor considered the question with curious eyes. He frowned slightly as he looked down at the shiny pair of ruby leathers peeking out from under the Pope's vestments. He was about to say something to her about clicking heels together to get us all out of here, but Sarah spoke again.

"He said *another* reason."

"Yes."

"I wonder," she continued, "what is the *first* reason we need to keep moving?"

"ACTS 8."

"Like a play?" Via asked.

"Not act. *Acts*," Naomi enunciated.

"Oh."

"So Joseph of Arimathea may have had the burial cloths for some length of time?"

"Why did you say burial *cloths*?" Via asked, as the emptied salad plates disappeared silently from their deuce. "The shroud is a single piece. Isn't it? The Turin shroud is."

"The true shroud had at least two pieces. There was a smaller part that wrapped around Christ's head."

"How do you know that?" Via asked. Then she caught herself. "Never mind. Acts. Right?"

"No. The presbyter. John. One of the gospels."

"Oh. So any Bible student should have known the Shroud of Turin was a fake all along?"

"No. Not at all. The traditional one-piece pall that covered both the front and back of the deceased is entirely consistent with the Scriptural account. The main piece of cloth was large enough to cover the face and head along with the rest of the body. It would have been exactly as is represented by the image on Turin's shroud. Undoubtedly, the head-wrap was wound over the top of the main section."

"So the Shroud of Turin *could have been* authentic," Via considered out loud.

Naomi nodded in agreement. "The Shroud of Turin is actually so perfectly a representation of the real thing, I'm still trying to imagine how it was so quickly a consensus that the one hidden in Istanbul was the real one. Who's to say Turin's isn't the true shroud and the Orthodox Church had the replica?"

"Provenance," Via answered. "I know for sure. And I left proof of my knowledge for the Byzantines. I placed an original parchment at the scene to prompt them to make the disclosure themselves. I figured they would save themselves the embarrassment if they believed that I'd go to the press. My little missive showed them I had plenty of proof that theirs was the real shroud all along. I was banking on them figuring I had a copy and other original documents that would back me up."

"And you were right. Whatever you left there was pretty powerful. The Patriarchate practically ran to the media. You really thought of everything."

Naomi smiled as their waiter materialized once again. He perfectly positioned two steaming entrees on the two-top.

A polite, "Ladies," got their attention. "Will you need anything else at this time?" he asked. "Fresh ground pepper? Perhaps you've decided to complement your meal with a bottle of red Zin?" He motioned ever so slightly to the unopened leather-bound wine list still lying where Via had asked him to leave it earlier.

NAOMI HAD WAITED tables at a high-end eatery in Houston to help pay her way at Rice University – despite her free ride. The full scholarship only covered tuition, books, and on-campus room and board. Her host parents were wealthy Rice alumni. The husband and his wife had both graduated only nine years before they welcomed Naomi into their home. But the young sophomore was determined to earn her own spending money and even to contribute to the pantry and frig at the house. She'd brought home an armload of groceries every Saturday morning until her late-rising hosts finally realized what she'd been up to – walking a mile to the nearest bus stop, shopping and then taking the same route home. They told her not to buy any more food. But her determined response earned her a ride in their Chevy Suburban from then on, leaving at 9am sharp each Saturday.

They had discovered her weekend ritual, but it took them much longer to discover another secret. A full year into her stay with the family, the couple found out that she wasn't spending every weeknight at the library on campus. It was on her fifteenth birthday that they'd gone to the Fondren Library to surprise her, only to find out that she wasn't at the library after all. First, they had frantically searched the stacks, fearing the worse, half expecting to find her light green backpack abandoned at a cubicle desk due to abduction or worse. Finally, one of her classmates spilled, but only because she'd overheard Mrs. Touhy on the phone with the police.

When Naomi tipped out at the bar that night, she'd put the balance in her purse. Not bad, $132 even after giving the bartender his ten percent. She'd rushed out the front door with little time to spare. It was the last bus that she must catch each night if she were to make it back home at all.

The big green SUV was patiently waiting for her just outside the restaurant. Kind words put her into the back seat for the long journey back to the house.

"It's no problem. Our sitter lives two doors down. You know her."

"But you didn't have to come get me."

"We showed up at the school to surprise you."

She was handed a birthday card and a very sweet gift.

"I'm sorry I put you out."

"You didn't inconvenience us at all. We think of you as one of our own kids. Anyone would be proud to have you as their daughter."

"But I lied about my age to get the job. They think I'm 18."

"We figured as much. You know the ABC would shut them down."

"But I *look* old enough." She'd then hung her head. "I don't want them to get in any trouble. They've been very good to me."

"We won't tell you what to do, but we do have a proposal."

And so it was that Naomi became one of the few enterprising teens in the state with an *agricultural* work permit, yet held down a desk job at an oil company. Her new job, on the 32nd floor of the Bank of America building in downtown Houston paid better, but more importantly, it opened a whole new world to her. The world of business.

"PEPPER PLEASE," Naomi replied, impressed with their waiter's grace and skill. He made the huge wooden grinder appear out of nowhere and sprinkled her *asado con cuero* generously.

"Please. I need it." Via smiled at Naomi and handed the wine list to him. "I trust you," she instructed. He understood perfectly.

Via's knife and fork dug into her *empanadas*.

Naomi already had her first bite of barbequed beef entrée between her teeth when she returned to the subject of Istanbul.

"What did you leave in the vault?"

"Huh?" Via responded from amidst a mouthful of beef-filled pastry.

"The Patriarchate. What is it that you left them that would have made them run to the press so quickly?"

*   *   *

"WE'D BETTER GET in the carrier," Joshua said. He reached for Sarah's hand. She was in a daze, staring at his face framed under golden brown hair.

Sarah let him grasp her palm like they were going for a walk in the park. On a date. Hand in hand. He pulled her along as he took long strides back to the metal rat lines that were slung over the side of their transport.

She was in another world. Her palms were sweating, even shaking a little as she felt his heartbeat pulsing from his fingers against the back of her hand. Sarah felt the strength of his entire body leading her to safety. She climbed up into the carrier first. He followed up after her. The rest of them were right behind, the Pope and Michelle in the lead.

Everyone was quickly back inside the vehicle. But this time they had an extra passenger.

The Pope sat down right next to Sarah. Joshua sat on her other side. She didn't know if she wanted to throw up, or jump up and down screaming and singing and shouting and laughing.

"You were right," Innocent said.

"I was?" Sarah turned to face the Pope. Then she thought, about what?

"Michelle reviewed the sensor data that showed the infiltrators had passed several deterrent points much quicker than the best simulation scenarios."

"Oh. So you think there *is* a mole." A tinge of a question in every word. Each syllable came out in staccato. She was thinking that she had only been guessing. Just speaking her mind, that's all.

"We are in your debt," Acamayo announced.

"You are?" The Pope just said that? To me? She was still in a state of star-struck shock, sitting next to a man that she should have only seen in photos and video images. And then, there was Joshua, right next to her. She was letting her emotions go. After all this time.

Her professor grabbed her hand again. She swiveled back around to face him. He held her hand in his own and then pulled it up towards his chest. He clasped his other hand around their embracing palms.

"We are all in your debt," he said.

At that moment, when Sarah was already sure to faint, her heart racing and her emotions surging, the Pope stood up and took off his robe.

Pope Innocent Peter sat back down wearing faded blue jeans and a cotton knit pull-over. His feet were now clad in all-white K-Swiss tennis shoes. Sarah immediately noticed the shoes. How did he…?

At the same time, Joshua was pulling her hand to his mouth. He gently kissed the back of her hand.

Sarah lost consciousness.

The kiss hadn't even been completed when she became limp, fainting onto Joshua's chest.

CHARLIE HAD MANAGED to secure a seat next to Michelle. He started peppering her with questions as soon as they'd buckled in. Bear was up in the cab again as they started moving along the table-top of stone, leading a convoy of the amphibious machines deeper into the artesian abyss. José and Arkesha sat on the other side of Michelle with Arkesha nearer the conversation that interested all three of the students.

"How big *is* this place anyway?" Charlie asked, his hand movements mimicking his question.

"We really don't know the extent of the cave system, but this section's base is 8300 meters below the surface and runs near north-south for over 100 kilometers. It veers east at its southern end and the widest section is just a bit south of here, at almost 9 kilometers in width. We are on the only table-rock that we know of in the system, most of it is much deeper, up to 6.4 kilometers, much of it under water."

"Whoa!" Charlie said, "Stop right there. You're saying this dried up, underground, fresh-water sea runs up to five miles deep?"

"More or less," she offered with a smile. "The edge we just stood at looks over a drop of almost three kilometers."

Arkesha couldn't resist, "So if the guys chasing us burst out through the pillar's base and don't stop right away, they'll plunge down into an abyss almost two miles deep."

"That's the plan."

"Wow!" she responded. "What a way to go!"

Charlie was back at it, "You said *this section* runs about 100 kilometers south of here. There are other branches?"

"Yes. This is the largest that we know of. But there is a charted cavern that runs all the way to the south side of Napoli."

"Where?"

"Naples, as you say."

"Wow! That's quite a long way from here."

"Yes. And there are branches to the Adriatic as well as those that reach up to Milano in the north. It is quite extensive. Actually, they are the largest known system of caves in the world. They are just not public knowledge."

"And it's not completely dry down here?"

"Oh no."

José leaned over and chided his friend. "Why do you think these things are amphibious, doofus?"

"Har, hardy har," Charlie responded with a sardonic laugh.

"I haven't heard that one for … well, since last time I watched Nick at Night." José was cracking a big smile. "Hardy har," he mocked.

"I have a question," Arkesha's soft, intelligent voice hushed the boys' banter.

"Yes?" Michelle seemed relieved.

"How did this artesian well dry up?"

"It's a pretty incredible theory. But our geologists tell us that *Monte Vesuvio* drained it."

"As in Mount Vesuvius? Pompey's Vesuvius?" Arkesha's eyebrows were arched high on her forehead.

"The very one. In fact, when the volcano buried Pompey, the eruption is what caused the southern wall of the basin to rupture. That's what drained away so much of the water."

"Where did all the water go?"

"They don't know."

"Why doesn't it fill up again?"

"They don't know. But they suspect the ground water seeps into another aquifer now. Like a channel being diverted."

Although Charlie was just as fascinated with the answers to Arkesha's line of questions, he had a burning one that refocused the whole conversation.

"Where are we going now?" He was looking at Michelle's eyes, trying to figure out how to describe their color to himself.

"North for a bit," she responded, "at this level, then due west for a while. We will come out near the coast. A ship will be waiting for us at Ostia. We will go to Sicily until the Vatican is safe for our return."

"Sounds elaborate." Charlie twisted his lips a little beneath his undersized Roman nose. He had decided that she had light blue-green eyes with specks of gold in them.

"More so only because we've been compromised. And if our military has been penetrated, then other branches of Italy's government are also likely to be," she searched for the right word, "untrustworthy." Her brow shifted slightly upwards as she finished the sentence, allowing the beauty of her face to become quite pronounced.

Charlie couldn't resist.

"You are very beautiful," he said.

He got a stern glare, but he could have sworn he saw in it a hint of welcome.

She said nothing.

Charlie had absolutely no experience with rejection. Bear called it a character flaw.

"You don't wear a ring," Charlie continued. He wasn't looking down.

That earned him another hard stare, and Michelle held his gaze without expression, letting the statement hang in the air like clothespin-clasped laundry on a windy day.

Finally, she retorted, "I'm working." With that she promptly unharnessed her athletic frame and moved up to the cab.

"Yes!" Charlie whispered loudly, trying to restrain the motion of his right hand clenching into an inward fist and pulling down in a victorious gesture.

"What's that?" Arkesha bent the second word heavily. "You call *that* a successful attempt at charm?"

"She likes me." He wore a goofy smile.

"You've lost your mind."

*   *   *

"I'D FOUND PLENTY of documentation over the years, any of which would serve to establish provenance. Of course, a physical examination of the shroud would have to couple with it. But I picked one of my best parchments and left it on the floor of the vault, right where the case had lain."

"And...?" Naomi was on the edge of her seat, chewing a piece of grilled Argentine *befé*.

"It was an original vellum, a simple letter. But the ink was a rich blue made from pulverized lapis lazuli petals from Afghanistan's mountain ranges. The handwriting would be easily identified along with the signature. It was a perfect match to the other known documents that bear his name: the depressions, pauses, up-strokes ... everything. It referred to the plan to hide the shroud in Constantinople."

"Please don't keep me hanging! Who?" Naomi was leaning into the table with a smile and hands that mocked strangling her friend.

"The letter bore the signature of Prester John."

Naomi paused, leaned back in her chair, and shook her head. "Amazing," she said.

"Why would you say that?"

"Just that so many write him off as if he is fiction."

"Are you fiction?"

"No." Naomi frowned then asked, "So the Byzantines would have known the letter was authentic."

"Undoubtedly, and they don't doubt that Prester John was a real missionary-king. They've always known the truth about the presbyter."

"What did the letter say?" Naomi asked.

"Just that he agreed with the plan. That to safeguard the shroud, it was best to secret it away."

"I'm surprised, though." Naomi put another bite of her meal into her mouth. "Why?"

"That the Orthodox Church didn't call your bluff."

"I wasn't bluffing!" There was anger in Via's retort.

"Okay. You weren't. But how were they to know that? Perhaps I chose the wrong word." She paused to look at the ceiling in thought. "A game of chicken, then? One in which you were dead set never to turn."

"I was prepared to make the disclosure. That's what motivated me in the first place. I just want the true shroud on display, not some fake."

"So why try to force their hand?"

"It was their secret, their lie, thus their responsibility to make it right, to tell the world." She was talking with her mouth full.

"Oh."

"Furthermore," Via stopped chewing and swallowed, "the media would take less time substantiating their claims than my own. And I'd have rather not put a spotlight on me, or...."

"You weren't concerned that the Church would rely on the controversial nature of Prester John's existence and try to keep their secret?"

"What? That none of his contemporaries seemed to have even met him? That even Marco Polo appears to speak of him as if he learned about him second hand? Not the case. I have plenty of documentation. So do they. So does the Vatican. Just because the public doesn't have access to the proof, doesn't mean...." Then another thought hit her. "Besides, I now had the true shroud. And surely they knew I would produce it."

"The thief? You would go to prison for this?" Naomi took another bite of her charbroiled *carne*.

Via took another bite of her pastry-wrapped meat: a petite Delmonico, medium rare, with rich, creamy butter hidden inside the layers of thin dough. It melted inside her mouth as she considered Naomi's suggestion. "I'd thought of that. Yes. And I was prepared to do time for antiquities theft if that is what it took."

Naomi looked at Via, searching her eyes. Leaning back into her chair, she decided that Via was dead serious. She would have given up everything for the truth.

In the ensuing silence, Via poured herself a second glass of red Zin and cut off another piece of her *carne de res con mantequilla*. "You are not drinking with me?" She let some of her French accent flow into her complaint.

Naomi stared at her stemmed glass. It still cradled all of its wine. But she didn't answer the question. Her wine continued to breathe. "Where did the shroud get moved to after Jerusalem?" she asked.

Via shrugged off her unanswered query, "In 69 AD?"

"Yeah. I'm assuming that Joseph spirited it out of the city knowing time was short. He knew that the rebellion would bring all of Rome's fury down on the city. She looked for acknowledgment. Via nodded while chewing. So

Naomi continued. "And he was right. It was just the following year, probably only a few months later, that Rome sacked Jerusalem."

"*Oui*. 70 AD is a pretty important date. By then the shroud was in Caesarea, being safeguarded by the Roman governor. Joseph of Arimathea was not only wealthy, he was on the Jewish Council, and remained in good standing with the Romans despite being a follower of The Way."

"The *Romans* protected the shroud?" Naomi's eyes matched her tone.

"Not officially. It was being kept by Governor Felix's wife, Drusilla. She kept it in her own quarters in the palace. I don't know why. But I've been able to confirm that she is the one who safeguarded it during that time."

"Paul," Naomi said with some confidence.

"The apostle? What are you saying?"

"That Paul had something to do with it. He was jailed in Caesarea for two years and spent a lot of time with Felix and his wife. Drusilla was a Jew. It is very likely that both became followers of The Way during that time," Naomi offered.

"Most of the first Christians *were* Jews," Via conceded.

"Exactly. How did you find out that Drusilla had kept the shroud?" Naomi asked.

"A letter. I just love coming across ancient correspondence. We learn more from them than from the written histories. Think about the New Testament. It is full of a bunch of letters. The letter that clinched it for me was one to Drusilla from a Queen Bernice. I bet Josephus never knew that!" Via's voice was energetic.

"Bernice was King Agrippa's wife." Naomi put her fork down.

"I never looked that far. I just clicked over to read the Facebook messaging of the day." Via frowned.

"Paul must have converted them too." Naomi became excited.

"Why do you say that?" Another mouthful of her meal quickly followed the question.

"For a Jew, who was likely now a follower of Christ, to tell Queen Bernice that she, Drusilla, possessed Jesus' burial cloths? It's likely she'd have only felt safe revealing her secret if Bernice was also a Christian." Naomi spoke quickly, like a child making a new discovery.

"Interesting, the letter was from Bernice. The letter's context indicated that it was in response to a letter from Drusilla that had initially disclosed her crime – that she had the contraband squirreled away." The heavy French accent was back.

"Did your grandfather say anything more about what he knew?" Naomi was cautious with the question.

"Just that he used the word *replica*. It has always stuck with me." Via was just responding to the question at first, but then Naomi could see the resentment flush her friend's face.

"Did you look at it?" Naomi's curiosity was intense.

"What?" Via didn't pick up on the intent of the question.

"The shroud. You haven't checked it out?" Naomi's voice was almost in a whisper.

"Ah, no. I guess I didn't really think about doing that. We haven't even opened the case since we nabbed it in Istanbul." Via's face drained.

"Aren't you curious. I mean. What it looks like?"

"I don't think I can. I mean. Look at it. Of course I am curious…." Via almost said "but." However, the word wouldn't form. She just ended up mumbling indiscernibly in her native tongue.

Naomi just stared. Power building in her chest. Her eyes flamed fire as she made her declaration.

"Let's do it."

"I'm afraid," said by a woman who commanded mercenaries.

Naomi almost retorted but their waiter materialized once again. He silently picked up their plates like an accomplished thaumaturgist and vanished from where he'd come. Naomi paused and took a sip of her Zinfandel. She enjoyed the flavor and savored the aroma before it slid smoothly down the back of her throat. Still holding onto her wine glass, she angled her head to one side. "Then let *me*."

"Okay." That quick.

"Really?" Naomi was surprised.

"*Oui*. Sure. And while you are at it, I'll show you something I picked up in Iraq."

כ כ

HER EYELIDS ROSE slowly as she became aware of several things at the same moment: that her head was resting on Joshua's chest, her blonde-streaked hair twisted into a fussy mess, her hand being held in his strong but gentle grip, and that the leader of the world's largest Christian denomination was dabbing her forehead with a wet cloth. The Pope's face was less than a foot away from her own.

Somewhere deep inside her, amidst the apprehensive, nervous excitement, mingled with her disbelief, a new Sarah emerged – one that chose to embrace her world head-on. Boldly. No regrets.

"I love him," she declared.

Not half-comatose. Not groggily. And she wasn't in a dreamy state of fantastic surrealism. Sarah felt clear-headed and alert, fully cognizant and determined in simple honesty. She felt now more alive than she'd ever felt.

Well, she thought, there it is. It's out there. I just confessed my love for my professor, the chair of my dissertation committee … in front of the Pope.

But with her pronouncement, she became altogether pleased and allowed herself a confident smile.

Miguel seemed nonplussed, like he already knew. His eyes spoke volumes, but he only allowed one word to escape his mouth.

"Good."

The Pope said it with a warm smile and lightly touched her cheek with closed fingers, a sweet gesture of a father. His gentle touch was both his blessing as well as a commission. It was an approval coupled with a gift of love, a gift of strength for her journey. His eyes followed the single word with a simple finale. "My best wishes for the two of you."

Then it was just the two of them.

Miguel had practically melted into the scenery of the inside of the carrier. "Sarah…." Joshua started.

He was using a voice she'd never heard him use before. Not romantic, but not rejecting. Not dismissive in the least, but not encouraging either. Not pedantic, nor erudite. Not patronizing nor condescending … and certainly neither angry nor upset. But curiously, which was of most interest to her, his tone didn't register any surprise. So she'd determined what it was *not*, but she was still unsure of what his tone of voice *was*.

One cannot really know the nature of anything by knowing what it is not. It's like proving a negative. It really can't be done.

Did his tone mean, "I'm interested but it wouldn't be proper"?

Did it mean, "I'm flattered but there's someone else"?

Did it mean, "I would have a chance with him if I were only a bit older"?

Or, " …if he were younger"?

What is it that I detect in that sonorous but reserved sound he chose to form in that first word? He spoke my name in a way that clearly says that he cares about me. But I already know that.

Does he find me attractive? Of course he does. Everyone does. Wow, I never really thought of that before.

But he's seen me at my worst. Mornings I'd show up without showering, having slept in my clothes after a night of research. He's seen me angry. Depressed. Fearful. He's even seen me hateful.

"I want…." Joshua continued.

Me! She screamed deep inside. He was using the same tone. Nothing more revealed yet. What about his eyes? What are they saying? He's looking into mine – that's a good sign. I just love his eyes, the dark brown with specks of green and burnt sienna. He always knows just what to say. He seems forever to be creating solutions to the most mind-boggling problems. And he's patient. Calm. Even-tempered. Sometimes I wonder if he has a pulse!

His eyes are saying….

I don't know what his eyes are saying. What about the rest of his face? He's not smiling. He's not frowning. He doesn't look tense or frustrated or bothered. Is he blushing? No. Touched with any kind of discernible emotion?

Can't tell. Swooning head over heels in love with me?

She smiled inside.

"I want to show you something."

But that was not his voice. Wait. Hold on! Stop! Back up! Voice not belonging to Joshua, rewind and go away! Didn't you see the "Do not disturb" sign? Whoever you are, shoo! Sarah was still transfixed on Joshua's face.

"You too Sarah. Come with me."

Reality. The voice wasn't going to go away. Worse yet, the voice belonged to the interloper, Michelle. And Michelle was inviting her future husband to "see something." The fact that she, too, was invited was surely just an afterthought. Sarah turned to look at the woman. She cut her eyes slightly as she considered the situation.

Joshua hadn't let go of Sarah's hand. Neither of them had noticed that the transport had come to a stop. Everyone else was already piling out of the doorway.

"Sure," Joshua finally said, just as his eyes broke away from Sarah's face and looked up at Michelle. "But we need to finish our conversation first."

"No. I need you now."

Sarah's gut burned. Joshua turned back to her and squeezed her hand with assurance. "Sarah," he said, "we will finish this conversation soon. Okay?"

She looked inside his soul and nodded. He let go of her hand. It was still tingling. Her heart was doing back-flips. The anticipation was going to kill her.

They both stood and Sarah walked across the deck and climbed down Jacob's.... But her feet didn't touch the ground. She continued to walk in the clouds. She was still in heaven.

Michelle led the group to a huge wooden door. Sarah lingered at the rear of the cluster of people. She was still lost in her reverie.

Miguel stood at the entrance that was carved into the solid rock wall. The Pope was holding a huge skeleton key. Peter. He stood addressing the group with his back to the door.

Bear was next to Sarah. He was looking back from where they'd traveled across the table rock. He admired the massive pillars from the other end of the cavern's raised section, following their impressive lines as they reached up into the underground heavens. The table rock surface underneath them appeared to end where they now stood outside the closed wooden door. They were at the northern end of this section of the emptied basin. A great schism fell abruptly to the east below them, just beyond where the carrier was parked by Zelfa. Bear's eyes followed its edge to where it merged into a tapered joint with the endless wall that rose up over the frame of the ancient door.

Bear couldn't help but wonder how such a level surface could have possibly been formed here in the upper quadrant of this huge subterranean cavern. He also noticed that the other amphibious vehicles had left them. Where did they all go? There had been over a hundred of them that had followed them through the forest of steel columns. Zelfa stood to his left. He asked her.

"The tunnel that cuts west from here is a bit off to our left," she said. "See, over there, to the south. They've gone on ahead of us. Didn't you hear me in the cab?"

"No. I wasn't paying attention."

She smiled. "Well you should now. We are in for a real treat here."

He began to wonder why they would risk it. Weren't they in danger? Surely they didn't have time to stop for a sight-seeing tour. But then he put it out of his mind. He turned his head back to watch the Pope.

Miguel spun around and slid the key into the giant brass lock. He turned it a full revolution.

The great wooden door swung open on its ancient hinges.

*   *   *

AS THE TWO FRIENDS left *Emil*'s, they stepped into their waiting cab headed for the *San Nicolas* district near *Plazá de Mayo*. As they did, the last of the dozens of digital photos were being captured through the long telescopic lens only two buildings away. The young man hidden atop the flat roof put his triangular surveillance microphone in its case, its protruding nose folding down into its huge arm. He was confident that his audio recording was clear. The mike had a 100 meter range, and he'd heard the entire conversation quite clearly, even with the background noise of the traffic on the street below. His vantage point was across the street and only about 45 meters from the second floor balcony of *Emil's*. He'd chosen his location well. The abandoned insurance building had given him a clear line of sight while keeping him hidden behind boxy mechanicals on the roof. He packed away the AF-S Nikker 600mm F/4G ED VR zoom lens and stashed his Nikon D3X in its padded satchel. Using the exterior metal fire escape, he made his way to a Renault sedan tucked away in the alley.

Again, a long trip awaited him. But he smiled because when he'd arrived in DC from Istanbul, just a few short days ago, his presentation had earned him a bonus. This would earn him a promotion. He wore a very satisfied smile as he drove back to *Jorge Newberry* to catch a flight back home.

VIA AND NAOMI ONLY had two hours to shop. Their *porteño* didn't know the day's fare would be so short, and he had no idea where they intended on being dropped off, but he didn't seem to care.

Not old enough to be her mother, Via nevertheless treated Naomi as if she were her only child. In store after store she spoiled her, refusing to allow Naomi to use her own AMEX card. Their two hours flew by.

"You know I'm not a kid anymore. I have my own money now. In fact, I got a sizeable wire yesterday from your home office in Chambéry," Naomi chided.

Via smiled. "Sweetie, you'll always be seventeen to me. Just let me have my fun. Okay? This has nothing to do with business."

"All right."

"Besides," Via decided to add her own needling, "you'll get to do the same for your own daughter one day."

"Now you've got me married and with a kid?"

"Girl, you look like Rihanna, have the mind of Condoleezza Rice and possess the charisma of Oprah. You're gonna need more than the word *no* to stay single."

Naomi snorted.

"And just wait until you meet Keyontay," the matchmaker pushed.

Naomi glared at her playfully. "How did I get a pasty-white Frenchwoman as my *other mother*?"

Via smiled wide. "Oh, it's time to go!" She looked at her watch. "We have a hot date with the Admiral."

"Who?"

THE PAKISTANI drove them out of Buenos Aires, following the A002. It took a long time to leave the huge metropolitan sprawl behind them. But eventually, the *estancia* cattle ranches of the Pampas replaced the city's spread that over 13 million people call home. And just as the driver was starting to get nervous that they may be headed all the way to Chile, Via told him to turn off the road.

He swung the small wagon onto a dirt road that crossed over a cattle guard just past the graveled shoulder of the highway. The metal rungs were sunk into the ground between two wooden posts that held the ends of a barbed wire fence that seemed to stretch to eternity on either side.

"Just a kilometer down this road and you've earned your fare," Via promised.

The man gave a relieved smile, but once he'd bridged the requested distance his face twisted up in confusion. He stopped the car and asked. It was the same question burning in Naomi's mind.

"*Aqui?*"

"*Si, señor*. Thank you so much." Via opened her door and stood to suck in the fresh, warm air that came inland from the Atlantic. It was pleasantly mixed with the cold currents that dropped in from the snow-covered Andean peaks. Naomi let herself out as well and stood up next to her open door. She looked over the top of the vehicle at Via, and with her hands raised up in the air, her palms flipped over into *Is this a Joke?* gesture.

"Are you serious?" Naomi followed up with the incredulous query.

The driver was looking at Via as well, wondering what was going on. "*Senorita?*" he spoke, hinting a question.

Via ignored them both and motioned to the back of the cab. "*Lo siento, mi amigo. Pero, nosotros estamos bueno.*" Her Spanish was a bit rusty, but the driver understood and stepped around to the back of the wagon. He opened the hatch and pulled out a Chanel bag and a Ferragomo bag along with the large suitcase and set them gingerly on the grass next to the dusty drive.

White billowy clouds moved quickly across an azure sky as they all just stood there looking at each other. Finally, the cabbie muttered, "*Esa mujer está loca,*" and jumped back behind the wheel, leaving his fare standing on either side of the dirt drive.

He turned the car around and started back slowly and politely to keep the dust to a minimum. But as soon as he was a decent distance from them, he took off like a bat out of hell. The dust kicked up into a big cloud of abandonment until they were both alone in the middle of the ranch.

Naomi looked around her. Then to Via. "Why are we...?"

They were standing in the middle of a hundred square kilometers of open field. It was only a small part of a vast cattle ranching operation run by the Gutierrez conglomerate. The two forlorn-looking figures now stood side by side next to their bags on the ground. A moment later Via walked across the dirt road with a big smile on her face.

"There's nothing out here," Naomi started up again. And there was nothing in sight. No trees. No houses. Nothing. Not in any direction.

It was into this scene that the single occupant of *Jonah's Ark* dove.

From 35,000 feet.

Naomi's smile was priceless. Her eyes sparked with energy. The excitement she felt while watching the pelagic ship swoop down at the incredible speed of a majestic bird of prey was indescribable. Color rose ruddy into her cheeks as the gun-metal belly of the flying submarine abruptly slowed to a stop atop a wide cushion of air.

As if alive, the whale-fin-shaped wing nearest the passengers dipped its leading edge to the Pampas grass. With little more than six inches to ascend onto the handy ramp, Naomi was the first to step up onto the Captain's craft. Via had already grabbed the two shopping bags and the lightly-packed portmanteau and followed behind her. Via enjoyed watching Naomi's hesitant, innocent, child-like walk up the back of the ship to the opening hatch. Naomi was drawn to the allure of the slow rise of the thick disk on the top of the vessel's shoulders. The gradual curvature of the outer deck allowed both women to step easily up to the open portal and disappear down its vertical stairwell.

As Naomi descended the porthole's metal rungs, Via handed the shopping bags and suitcase to her. Before she slipped inside the ship herself, Via looked back outside and surveyed the land. The huge open space made her yearn for something she'd always been missing. "I'm coming back to Argentina," she said aloud before climbing down the ladder.

They were both inside the bridge a few minutes later, with Naomi's luggage neatly tucked away at the foot of one of the berths. "Naomi, meet the Admiral," Via said.

She couldn't see his face. The Captain was intently manning the controls. But Naomi liked the sound of his salty voice. "Nice to meet you, Naomi, dear. Welcome aboard."

After the quick introduction they took the short walk down the center corridor. Turning into the Captain's study, Via led her friend to the table. The first thing Naomi noticed as she sat down at the beautiful wooden table was the two large black cases resting on the thick carpet. Naomi knew what was in one of the cases but not the other. The anticipation was making her sit on the very edge of her seat. She barely noticed the pelorus sitting right in front of her.

Via had walked straight over to the metal containers. The chrome latches of the first case were flipped upwards, and its top half turned 90° on silent hinges. Via bit her bottom lip and gulped back the tears. Naomi wasn't sure why Via hadn't already left the room. She had figured she'd be doing this alone. She watched with awe and wonder.

Inside a heavily padded interior of foam, tucked into a rich gold velvet cloth, lay a purple silk envelope a little larger than a king-sized pillow case. With extra girth sewn into its sides, the embroidered bag was designed to hold a significant mass of fabric inside. A beautiful deep red sheen glossed the flap that covered its opening. It folded over the front in a rounded arch like a large flap on a thick manila envelope. The flap had a silver fastener at its apex that exuded wealth and special care for its precious contents. The sterling silver clasp was surrounded by a satin fan of bunched fabric in a rainbow of every shade of green, all brilliant hues of rich verdant life.

Via's hands trembled as she undid the clasp. Using both hands, she lifted the flap of fabric to reveal the inside of the satchel. Folds of white linen peeked out at the underside of the fold's crease. Via was shaking all over as she slid her forearms under the silk and brought the opened pouch over to the table.

Naomi was intent on Via's face. She knew how important this moment was for her friend. Since they'd first talked about only Naomi looking at the shroud, Via had obviously changed her mind.

Naomi thought back to their conversation in the cab.

"I MIGHT LOOK at the shroud with you."

"Really?"

"I may. I need to. I'm still afraid. But I need to. After my grandfather passed, I didn't tell anyone that I knew the truth. Instead I just harbored bitterness against him and the rest of my family. I didn't talk to my father for a year. My mother and I had fewer and fewer conversations, each more strained than the last. Finally, we stopped talking altogether."

"Are they still alive?"

"How old do you think I am?" Via had allowed a strained laugh. "Of course they are still alive."

"Oh. Do you…?"

"Talk to them now?" She paused and a vacant look settled behind her eyes. "A little, here and there. My father's in Paris now. I think he's remarried again. I've lost count of how many times he's been married. My mother is still in Geneva. That's where she moved right after the divorce. I've not talked with them since Istanbul." Then, "Oh!" She suddenly realized how her parents may be affected by the news. The Savoie name had been kept out of the press so far, but it would still be a trying time for her family. "My father knows. He knew that I knew. He's known for a time now. But I don't think my mother has a clue."

"How did your father find out?"

"He dropped in unannounced one day at the family estate a few years after I had inherited it and moved in. We'd been talking more than usual at the time, but just over the phone. We hadn't seen each other since the *velatorio*. Anyway, I had the table in the main dining hall covered with my research about the shroud. In my shock that he was on my doorstep unannounced, I'd just invited him in without thinking about the stuff all over the table in plain view. How was I to know that he would wander in there and put two and two together?"

"He did?"

"He did. He just walked right back into the kitchen where I was preparing us a simple meal. We were planning on eating out on the veranda. When he came into the kitchen, he didn't have to say a thing. I knew. I could see it all over his face."

"Did he say anything?"

"Yup, just a simple sentence – two words. But the horror that he revealed in his tone, the sheer terror of knowing that I'd found out…. He knew I'd figured out on my own that everyone in our family had been living a lie." She paused. "He said, 'You know.' That was it. It wasn't a question, and he didn't ask for a response."

"What did you do?"

"I didn't even have to think about it. I didn't give him time to say anything else either. I was actually glad he'd seen everything at that point. In a weird way, I was then delighted that he'd dropped in on me. Glad he'd walked into that room. I was truly, morbidly, happy that he'd figured out what I knew and that I was going to do something about it. Of course, he wasn't sure at that point what exactly I had up my sleeve, just that I was working on doing something about it. But he definitely knows now. I'm sure he has no doubt that it was me."

"What'd you say?" Naomi prompted, not sure what else happened in the kitchen with her dad.

"I said, 'You lied to me!'" Via said it as if replaying the event, a re-enactment of the confrontation all over again. "I told him, 'You lied to me!'" As she said it again, she could see it in her memory: her father standing there with blood on his hands, every atavistic generation of Savoie having reached through time to conspire with him. His own daughter was given the fortune that should have been his own. It was meant to be devised to the only child of a dying old man. And now his daughter, his only child, had received the wealth. His father had rejected him. Now his daughter was rejecting him as well. Why? Because he'd shielded her from a falsehood that he didn't even create. He'd had to. It was his obligation. He'd inherited it at birth.

But she'd accused her father with such venom, such hatred. It had seethed out of her as the words spewed out. His eyes had shown restrained pain. The type of pain reserved for the very rich. A practiced formality that buries human emotions under expensive clothes, behind luxury vehicles and the gated estates that lock out the real world. He'd left the kitchen without another word, walking through Via's front door with heavy steps of sorrow. She'd heard his BMW drive away.

AFTER NAOMI HAD heard the entire story, she had hugged her friend. Now, with the shroud folded up inside the silken envelope lying on the table between them, the pain Via had shared with Naomi welled up inside her again. They now shared it symbiotically. It was as if it was an aphoristic duty that Naomi not allow Via to bear her burden alone.

So it was that Naomi was the one who covered her hands with a pair of protective gloves that reached all the way up her forearms to her elbows and withdrew the shroud from its sheath. She cradled it across her forearms and laid it on top of the purple pouch. Both women were engulfed with emotion as Naomi pulled a length of narrow cloth from the top of the piles of pall. They were gazing in awe at the length of linen that had been wrapped around the head of the crucified body of Jesus Christ.

*   *   *

THE POPE LED them into a long hall that pierced the vast bulk of rock jutting upwards for more than a mile overhead. Rough-hewn walls ushered them forward. The arched ceiling of the corridor was faceted with a million chisel marks etched by hand and tool. Stone masons swinging a dozen heavy hammers had worked for decades to bore the tunneled chamber centuries before. José could almost hear their rhythmic sounds clinking against the granite, chewing away the solid rock into gravel bit by bit. He was excited as he walked with the rest of the group through the ancient path. He knew deep down that this event would eclipse the thrill he got when canyon shelling. It would easily best kite surfing. It would effortlessly surpass the exhilaration of mountain climbing. As he walked hand in hand with his fiancée, just behind the new Pontiff, he felt euphoric. Who wouldn't have? And he didn't even know what they were about to see. But he could feel it. The look on Miguel's face had forecast an experience of a lifetime.

The long passageway finally opened into a small chapel. It was constructed of heavy timbers, blackened with age and couched among pillars of rectangular blocks of stone that glittered with flecks of quartz. A warm glow came from the light dancing from a trough of flame that ringed the shoulders of the tiny temple. The orange light fell onto the rough surface of a bricked floor. The baked clay was already tinged with red and amber earthen materials molded near the middle of the Roman Empire. The place of worship's lighting made the brick's coloring resemble the western sky at dusk.

But José didn't see any of the crafted beauty that welcomed the wide-eyed pilgrims. His gaze was transfixed on the central altar. All he noticed was the prominently displayed wooden structure that rose up from the dias. It towered above the spot where the Pope now turned to face the rest.

"Friends," Miguel said, "this is…."

José didn't hear a word of the short speech. Instead, he looked up and beyond Miguel's white skull cap. He was mesmerized by the monument. He marveled over its simplicity: the hand-hewn upright post and its crossbeam, the vertical wooden support thicker than he'd imagined, the horizontal transom an artless addition secured by several iron spikes hastily driven through the crossbeam into the thick post. All this, and his gaze now rested on the words still affixed atop the blood-stained post. He didn't know ancient languages well enough to read it. But it didn't take a linguist to know what it was. He knew.

The Pope was finishing his brief oration, and José now listened intently to every word: first in Greek, then in Latin, then in Hebrew. Miguel quoted each tongue's declaration word for word flawlessly while still facing his audience. The aged parchment was faded and cracked, but the words it bore still spoke clearly through the ages, "This is the King of the Jews."

Silence fell upon the room. It was as if the Lamb of God had just been crucified in their presence. A spirit of reverence graced the chapel filled with children of men. Those already adopted into Christ's family bowed and worshiped the Spirit of the one who'd died. Miguel's jeans were bent at the knee. The hard, uneven floor cut into the fisher of men's skin. Corners of the hand-made, baked brick ground against the bones that supported the weight of the Pope. Everyone felt the same holiness. The event spontaneously evoked such adoration, even among those who had not yet yielded to His plan. The few not praying were likewise awestruck by the symbol of torture and death that changed the face of the planet so dramatically two thousand years before. Not a single soul in the time-worn temple failed to appreciate the significance of the moment. After a while, everyone ended up on their knees.

Time passed as it stood still. The fire kept twirling, spinning to a symphonic rhapsody of quiet serenity. Colors danced off the surfaces of carefully crafted joists and tiles. Cedar boards joined with songs of praise as they hugged the holy walls. A beatific swirl of sweet aromas swept the small crowd. Then, one by one, they each stood in reverent motion still subdued with awe. As each mortal, created in *his* image rose up from the floor, the temporal body flesh and bone turned slowly, hesitant to leave. Almost unable to turn a back to the symbol of love, one after another they quietly stood from bended knee and padded softly out, treading into the long hall with the arched canopy of multitudinously-angled chiseled stone, back to the ancient entryway, softly moving under the lintel of the antiquated oaken door, past the heavy iron straps around the great wooden planks. Each were saying silent prayers as they finally departed this holy of holies, carrying with them the remembrance of a death so poignant that bread and wine just begins to touch of ransom paid by price too high to pay. That blood Divine shed innocent of any slight, perfection sacrificed for vile, redemption freely given. They each left the crucifix as did *he* who hung upon its wood was taken down to rise from rock-bored tomb. To earn our soul's salvation. Life forever ours in love to have.

Two silhouettes still stood before the rough-surfaced Roman t-shaped craft. The holy place was holding every orison that lingered, hanging in the air. Each prayer waited, just as the Father waits … patiently, hopeful … begging for the answer so desperately wanted. Over the ages, countless others who'd stood before the same crucifix had been struck with the same splendor. Shadows cast by so many that had come before moved with the swaying light. The ancient candle line still cast against two present frames, drawing one's attention to the fingers interlaced. Both knelt again as she spoke – it broke the silence – barely. Quiet words so as not to leave behind the Heavenly presence thickly cast throughout the room.

"Is it *real?*" she asked.

Of course she knew the answer. But even those things self-evident we want assurance of.

"Can you believe it?" He squeezed her hand to transfer every ounce of love he felt given from his Father to the one made just for him.

"I think I need to make a few changes in my life," she said.

"As long as they include me," he said.

And they turned to look into each other's eyes.

"Always," she said.

"Marry me," he said.

"I already told you I would. Many times, actually." She smiled, remembering his countless proposals, each one more romantic than the last. "I said *yes* the first time you asked me – but you were *about* to…."

"Yes, I was." He smiled, remembering the view from Africa's highest peak and how she had anticipated his impetuous proposal even then.

"So marry me," he said.

"Always," she said.

"No," he said, "I mean *now – here!*"

*　　　*　　　*

"*TWO* PIECES." Via's voice sounded as full as a Gregorian choir chanting from a holy psaltery as she stared deeply into the space occupied by the long strip of antiquated cloth.

"Then Simon Peter came and went into the tomb and saw the linen cloths lying there, and the handkerchief that had been around his head, not with the linen cloths, but folded in a place by itself," Naomi quoted, with liturgical reverence.

"One of the gospels?"

"John's."

"So there's more than two? That's what St. John appears to be indicating." Via was trying to remember her last read of the passage in her own Roman Catholic Bible at a long vespers service years ago.

"That's what we're about to find out." Naomi smiled as she refolded the wrapping and placed it on the dust-free film spread out across the long counter behind where she stood.

It was the Captain who'd so meticulously prepared the study for their probe. The air had been scrubbed. The former military man had cleaned every surface carefully. He'd set out a vast array of tools to assist their efforts. He had even installed extra lighting overhead, supplementing the usual warm amber with three rows of brilliant white florescent tubes.

Naomi turned back to the shroud's main cloth and found its middle fold. The large piece of woven fabric was creased accordion-style with the center of the shroud laid atop the rest of the folds. She lifted the middle fold with both gloved hands, pulling the burial cloth upwards as high as she could reach. The Captain had also thoughtfully equipped the ceiling with a rod suspended beneath the new lighting. In its slotted run were a dozen soft-end clips that slid inside the track with a release of their brakes. The clips were adjustable with a single hand and Naomi slipped a corner of the shroud's folded center into the first one. As she did, she moved the clip down to the far corner of the track. Repeating this process, she continued to secure the shroud's middle to the fasteners that hung from the ceiling of the study. The hanging cloth started bunching as she finished, but Naomi easily spread it out once all twelve clasps were holding onto the burial cloth.

The ceiling wasn't high enough for the linen-woven cerement to unfold its full length over the top of the table. So, as a nurse would pull a privacy screen between patients sharing a room, Naomi gently moved the shroud out over the floor. This allowed the bottom half of the folded sheet to stretch its full length. The submersible's study was just roomy enough for the cloth to unfold from the clips to the carpet. It fell out of its final folds as if in slow motion while Naomi completed its traverse out from over the table.

While 35,000 feet above Patagonia, the brazen image of the resurrected Messiah revealed itself between them. The scourged back's imprint was confronting Naomi, and the kind face of our crucified Lord looked compassionately at Via. Both women stared as emotions welled inside.

They cried.

The shroud showed much more than the true negative of the tortured body of Jesus of Nazareth. For Naomi it unveiled a reality that matched her unflappable faith. For Via it confronted her pride with forgiveness, a picture of redemption through suffering – God having given all for her.

"It's the *same*," a hoarse whisper crept out of Via's chest.

"My side shows no scar that would indicate the thrust of the spear. For some reason I thought it would have been on both sides of his body." Naomi said it aloud, but she was talking to herself. She didn't even have to look on the other side of the shroud, she knew the scar in his side would be evident on the front of his body.

"A *replica*," her grandfather's word – it spoke from the grave through Via's lips. She had spent many years wondering. She wouldn't anymore.

"I guess it makes sense," Naomi continued in conversation to herself, "the spear was thrust into his side from the ground. So it was at an acute angle as it entered his heart. It pierced his pericardium." Her voice faded into the annuls of history. "Blood and water." Her last three words were spiritual, colored with a misty vapor of the clearing darkness that lifted as *he'd* breathed *his* last.

The Shroud of Turin must have been created from this one," Naomi surmised, "to duplicate the real one, to protect it. Like a Head of State double, as an act of caution, as a hen covers her chick with her wing. The real shroud was concealed – the fake shroud was crafted to *safeguard* the true shroud." Then she suddenly added, "King David."

"What?" Via asked, confused.

"Before his eventual coronation in Hebron, David was pursued by King Saul like a hunted animal. At one point, the anointed shepherd fled to the Philistines. They were mortal enemies of the Hebrews. It was of dead Philistine soldiers that the Israelites sang 'David has slain his ten thousands.' So David feigned insanity before King Achish of Gath."

"Oh. I thought it was a sin to lie."

"On another occasion during his ten years on the lam, David lied to Ahimelech, a *priest* in Nob."

"Does the Bible say it was okay for him to lie like that?" Via sounded skeptical.

"It says nothing one way or the other. Not during that story. But it records that Abraham lied to both Pharaoh and King Abimelech on two different occasions. Not only do the Scriptures not condemn his lies, but God was angry with the rulers both times. Not with Abraham. And, instead of punishing the man of God for his deceit, Abraham was blessed with wealth each time: given to him by the very kings who were rebuked by God for relying on Abraham's lies."

"So it's okay to lie?" Via didn't sound convinced.

"I didn't say that. But the language of the 9th Commandment doesn't say 'Thou Shalt Not Lie.' It says 'Thou shalt not bear false witness against your neighbor.'"

Silence.

Neither could really say they knew fully what the text meant.

Naomi was still staring at the main part of Jesus' grave clothes. The shroud hung like a veil between them.

Naomi couldn't see her friend, but she could hear the muffled sounds of sobbing. She came around to Via's side. The younger woman stepped up to Via and hugged her tightly around her neck.

Via's crying turned into a placid, shallow laugh. Then, as Naomi released her hold around her shoulders, Via let out a deep guttural release. She was still shedding tears, but she was laughing loudly now. The laughter shed the years of tension: the strain that hatred and unforgiveness cause, the stress of being unmerciful, the regret of misunderstanding, the pain of being so wrong.

Naomi shared her joy and wiped her tears. But the reflection in Via's dark eyes came from her stare past Naomi's face. The image of the shroud was mirrored against the pupils of a repentant soul. Via's stare made Naomi turn. She hadn't seen the front of the true shroud. As her body led her head in a quick spin, the sight came into focus and her lips parted. "Wow!" she gasped. Even though the eyes of the Son of God were closed, the hanging white linen pall stared back at her. "It really does," she said. "It looks *exactly* like the Shroud of Turin!"

٢٣

"THUMB TRIBE," Sarah chided.

"Whatever."

"I know you don't have a signal down here." She acted like she was reaching for his phone.

"Stop it!" Bear reacted as she'd hoped. Her goading had him shielding his Apple hand-held and stepping back at the same time.

"How can you possibly text at a time like this?"

"I'm *not* texting." His hand was now stiff-arming her, a running-back keeping a would-be tackler at bay.

"Your thumb's not *surfing*." She tried to get around his block.

"I'm emailing my little brother," Bear said indignantly, "if you must know."

"Can't it wait until later?"

"When we finally burrow out of here, it'll send automatically."

"I know *that* silly," she said, making a quick movement in the direction opposite her last, swiping the iPhone from him clean.

He reached to grab it back and missed.

"Ha!" she said, turning her back towards him to screen him from her perusal. Sidling her body in a motion to keep her slim torso between his desperate hands and her prize, Sarah managed to read Bear's missive.

"Hey! That's personal!" he yelped as he wrapped his arms around her waist and reached with both of his pudgy hands.

"Deep," she said, letting him grasp hold of the mobile.

"You really make me mad sometimes," Bear burst. He was now facing her in close quarters as she spun around to gloat.

"Oh come on you baby. What's the big deal? It's not like it's a love letter or something."

Bear suddenly felt weak. He hung his head and clicked *send later* on his AOL account.

"Bear," Sarah said gently.

She was still practically between his arms. He could feel the warmth of her breath against his hairline.

"Bear." The inflection of genuine concern came through stronger. It begged a response.

And then, "Bear, I'm sorry." She put her hands underneath his ears to lovingly raise his face.

"Bear," the voice of their professor. Joshua had walked up to them and now stood next to their embrace. "Can I borrow her from you for a minute?" Joshua said in an even tone.

"Huh?" Bear turned. He saw the face of a man instead of his professor. He wasn't looking into the eyes of the antiquities genius who was friends with the Pope. Instead, just outside the entrance to the rock-hewn cave that cradled the cross of Christ, Bear saw the face of the man who'd been a boy – a man who, in many ways, was still that wide-eyed inquisitive boy that had driven his mother up the wall so many times with all of his questions, a man with feelings, dreams, plans that always seemed just beyond his reach. Sometimes the plans were just too big. Too grandiose. Although they may not ever be realized, they would still motivate him daily, beyond mere day-dreams, beyond simple visions – a man who loved the world God made and the God who made it. Bear saw the man who loved a woman. The man who knew she loved him too. And this man hadn't ever known this kind of love until now. Perhaps he was seeing it from a distance. Maybe it was unattainable. But if he pursued it, he might obtain it, or he might lose it. He was going to try, regardless.

What Bear saw in Joshua's face was something that he understood at a completely different level, a spiritual level. It prompted a quick response.

"Of course," he responded. Bear took a long stride backwards. "It's okay, Sarah." Then another step and a quarter turn. He caught her eye for an instant. "No biggie," he emphasized. He disappeared, but not before she'd noticed the moisture building in the corners of his dark blue eyes.

She felt guilty.

"Can we talk?" Joshua asked.

"Sure." A familiar wave of emotions flooded back and made her unstable on her feet.

Joshua took over the spot where Bear had been standing. He held both her hands in his. He looked into her soul. And he loved her. Deeply. Forever.

His love was raw. Passionate. Powerful. It was both ethereal and wild. Both holy and unrestrained. Hidden behind his position for every day of two years, it had both rested dormant and had grown from interest to romantic desire. It had blind-sided him. He didn't even know when that moment had come. But come it had, and it had changed everything. Still hiding his feelings for so many reasons and so many long months that turned into a year and then more, he found that he was strangely happier. More at peace. More comfortable in his surroundings in a way that he'd never been. Even though he was not with her, in some respects it didn't matter. He had gradually reached a point where he thought about Sarah all of the time. She had invaded his dreams. She never left them. He didn't want her to. When he'd first admitted to himself that he was in love with her, it scared him. But it wasn't their age difference nor even the fraternization taboo that frowned upon teacher-student relationships. It wasn't even his secret. Yet, it was because of his secret that he couldn't let himself hope that they would ever be able to be together. However, despite his destined past that barred him from pursuing his love for her, that was not what terrified him the most. His greatest fear was not knowing if she could ever love him like he loved her. In fact, he knew that if fate forever kept them apart, he would still be fulfilled, even happy … beaming, every day for the rest of eternity. Greater still, he hoped, there was that chance that they were able to share the same love. Even if at a distance, if they could experience a mutual exchange of true love, he would be content. Even if they were never a couple, never able to touch, never able to marry and have a family together, they would at least share a desire for each other that was pure and real. Deeper than deep. Eternal. A fire so bright it would burn without oxygen on the highest mountain or at the bottom of the deepest sea.

"I want you to look at your Facebook," he said.

"My Facebook?" Sarah gave him a confused look that replaced her hopeful blush.

"Yes. Will you check it?" He pulled her hands closer towards his chest.

A swirl of feelings muddled her thoughts and stirred her down to her toes. They curled under as she fought to find the words to respond. *Wouldn't it just be easier to kiss me?*

She said, "Yeah, but we're deep inside the Earth here – at the bottom of a giant empty water tank made of solid rock. There won't be anything on it since I last checked."

"Since we had coffee together this morning?"

"Well...." She was stuck on his use of the word *together*.

"You don't normally check your private messages."

"No, I don't norm.... How do you know that I...?" And then it hit her. He'd sent her a.... She screamed with excitement. She couldn't pull her phone out fast enough.

"When did you send it?" she asked at the end of her squeal. Her head was down, looking into her phone's screen, already opening her WorldOne App that kept her FB account constantly downloaded while online so it could be checked while offline.

"This morning, right before we shared our coffee." He smiled.

She couldn't respond. Her mind was sifting through so much. *Together. We shared our....* The saved data popped up on her screen. She clicked on the icon and opened his message.

He'd only typed five words.

Seeing but not seeing them.

Reading but not comprehending them.

She was overwhelmed. Her heart was about to burst out of her chest.

Sarah read the words over and over. A thousand times. She was ready to jump up into his arms, but her face was still buried in her phone. Joshua patiently waited.

She read the words again. Slowly this time. Sarah looked up into Joshua's smiling face. She repeated the words now emblazoned into her memory forever. Saying them out loud as she smiled back at him felt right. So right.

"I'm a little bit enamored."

They sounded even more beautiful as she heard them spoken.

He took her phone and slipped it, for now, into the front pocket of his faded 501s. Taking her hands in his once again, his expression changed slightly as he inhaled deeply.

"But you see, Sarah, that's not entirely true. I...."

But he wasn't able to finish. He tried. He even went so far as to push Arkesha's body away from Sarah as she ran up to Sarah. But the Olympian would not be deterred. Arkesha plowed into them, jumping on top of Sarah, hugging and climbing all over her.

"I'm getting married!" She yelled over and over and over, until the echoes coming off the cavern walls joined in a chorus with her jubilance.

Sarah was in shock. She was still hanging on Joshua's every word. The FB message was still repeating itself in her head. The rest of what he'd been saying was bouncing off the inside of her skull. She couldn't think straight. But Arkesha's statement confused her too. Joshua said he didn't mean what he'd said in the private message? Why was Arkesha so excited?

"I know," Sarah responded, as Arkesha finally let go of her friend. "I already know you guys are getting married." Then she focused on Arkesha's face. At that moment, she knew. Sarah's face betrayed her sudden realization.

"That's right!" Arkesha exclaimed. "I'm getting married! Now!"

Sarah gave Joshua a look of longing back over her shoulder as Arkesha dragged her away from him. Her eyes tried to stretch the distance that was growing between them as her friend led her by the hand back to the doorway that led to the chapel. As they disappeared inside the passageway, Joshua remained fixed, unable to move.

José appeared but a moment later.

"Professor," he said with energetic resolve, "you're the best man! Come with me!" And Joshua got pulled in Sarah's wake.

As José took him into the warmly lit space, the first thing Joshua noticed was that everyone was already present. The middle aisle was clear, flanked on either side with standing guests, as the groom led his best man down the center path to the front. They took their places at the right of the altar and turned to face the congregation.

José then nervously turned to his professor. "Oh," he said, "I hope it's okay with you."

He got a big grin in response. "I'm happy to be your best man." Adding a little ribbing, "Thank you for asking."

Miguel materialized from the other side and joined them up front. The Pope took the center spot in front of the altar and turned to face the small gathering. He gave them a slight nod and a hint of a smile.

"You're getting married by the *Pope?*" Joshua's tone matched the question.

"Pretty cool, huh?" José responded.

Then Sarah appeared. She stepped slowly out from behind the wall of a small alcove in the back and started making her way down the aisle in the manner of tradition. Her walk was graceful – a slow, melodic, step and stop motion to the absence of music – which created its own melody. Everyone heard it. The song she created as she moved swayed inside the heads of all those who watched her. Joshua couldn't keep his eyes off her. And she smiled at him, just for him, all of the way down the aisle until she arrived at the altar and turned away from him to take her place on the other side.

Arkesha may as well have worn a $40,000 gown. She was exquisite. Exotic. A pulchritude of elegance. Both glamorous and simple. Beauty radiated from her vogue. Her stride down the aisle was a waltz of confidence and unbridled commitment. Her smile melted the groom where he stood and deeply affected the rest of their witnesses. The bride was unforgettable.

Her smile so perfectly said, "I marry you, for better or for worse. And I will never regret it. Not in the least. Never."

*   *   *

"LOOK!" VIA WIPED tears from her eyes and pointed to the large silken pouch on the table. Deflated with its precious contents withdrawn, it still sustained another stack atop its embroidered sheen – additional layers of the linen cloth. Carefully folded like a fan, Naomi started lifting upwards what took shape to be a narrow strip of fabric. "*Three* pieces!" she declared.

"Well it looks like John got it right," Naomi added.

"Prester John?"

"The apostle John."

"Oh yeah, right, the 'handkerchief and the other cloths.' I'd forgotten. What's this one for?"

"His feet, I'd guess," said Naomi. "See how the large section served as a top and bottom sheet. The two strips must have served to bind it all together."

"Like bandage strips for a mummy."

"Not quite. More like just enough to bind the ends." Then Naomi paused as she thought it through, having not yet lifted the strip entirely off the surface of the table. "Wait!" she said.

And she lifted the strip higher into the air, gathering the bottom and pulling it upwards as well.

It wasn't just one more piece.

"Four?"

Then another.

"Five?"

She found yet another in the stack.

"Six?"

Finally the table was emptied of the stack of linen strips that had so carefully been stored together that they looked to have been only one.

"Six – the number of man," Naomi said. "When he was laid in the tomb the body was indeed the Son of Man. It looks like the strips were spread out along the body to hold the main pall in place."

"However they did it, it's amazing. We are looking at the actual grave clothes of Jesus of Nazareth. Do you really think the image was burnt into the shroud when he was resurrected?"

"I think his natural body was transformed into a spiritual body at some point while it was lying in the tomb, just like Elijah's."

"The prophet?"

"Yes. He went to Heaven without dying. God took him up in a whirlwind." Naomi stopped and smiled. She was folding the six strips of cloth to put them back into the silken sheath. The fan-like folds were taking shape once again when she started making the sound.

Via heard humming. First, just a low murmur of a tune, then barely above a whisper, a beautiful spiritual, a perfect ballad, a song of mercy and redemption.

"Swing low…."

Via smiled.

"Sweet chariot…." Naomi's melody faded and her voice struck a mystical chord as she transformed the vocals into mere words. "You know," she said, "Elijah was with Elisha at the River Jordan when the elder prophet was called home."

Via didn't know. She was hearing the story for the first time.

"A fiery chariot came down from Heaven. It was drawn by horses made of pure flame. It swooped down to the banks of the swollen river and separated the two men. The account of the event is found in the Second Book of Kings. I don't think the fire is incidental."

"You mean…?"

"Yes. I think the fire is related to the image burnt into this shroud." She pointed to the pall still hanging up in the middle of the study. "I think what happened to Elijah that day is the same thing that happened to Jesus' body during the resurrection."

"Really?"

"Really. I think that the natural bodies we live in are mortal, a product of the Fall of Man. You know, Adam and Eve ate the forbidden fruit?"

Via nodded. "I know that story."

"I don't think," Naomi continued as she placed the strips back into the large silk pouch, "Elijah's body would have survived the trip to Heaven without it first transforming."

"That makes sense." Via scratched her head then added, "So you think there is a precedent in the Bible for some type of supernatural fire that was part of Christ's resurrection – one that would help explain the image burned into this burial pall?" Via had narrowed her eyelids as she spoke. Now she bit into her lower lip.

"Yes, I do. But not just any resurrection, the widow of Nain's son, Lazarus, and all of the others recorded in the Bible: They weren't being given immortal bodies as part of the deal. But in the case of Elijah and Jesus, the metamorphosis from mortality to immortality involved fire, intense light, or both. I think of a white hot burst of energy. I think of Jesus' transfiguration in front of Peter, James and John. Elijah and Moses were both there and I imagine their bodies resembled Christ's glorified body that day. I think of Paul's description of it all in his first letter to the church in Corinth. I think of the presbyter's description of it all in chapter one of the book of Revelation."

"Wow. I've never thought of any of that."

"Most people don't. Even Christians talk about eternal life as if it is just some run of the mill theological truth. But you mention 'fountain of youth' or 'immortality' to the same group and they freak out. I believe, just like Enoch, Elijah became one of the sons of God that day by the Jordan, like the sons of God mentioned in Genesis 6 and in Job 1 and 2. I believe they are so classified because they are humans who have already received their glorified bodies. Most of us will have to wait until The Resurrection to get ours," Naomi preached.

"Enoch ... Job ... sons of God ... The Resurrection? I'm afraid you've lost me." Via used her rare French accent. She shook her head slowly from side to side. "You know the Gary Larson cartoon with the guy and his dog?"

"I love Gary Larson. He had a cartoon without cows in it?"

"Ha. Ha."

"No. Which one?"

"The one where the owner is scolding his dog but the dog only hears 'Blah blah blah, Ginger, blah blah blah.'" She smiled.

"Yeah, I remember that one. I love it."

"Well," Via tied it together for her, "all I heard you say just then was 'Genesis.'"

It took Naomi a second to catch on. Then she said, "Very funny." Her response was followed by a sweet smile. She then reached over and reverently folded the bottom of the shroud's two sides together until only the top half was visible and pulled it back over the table.

She reached up to unhook the pall.

"Wait!" Via used an urgent tone. Naomi stopped.

Both women stood with the image of the crucified Christ appearing to look their way while Via stepped over the second black case still standing on the carpet.

It seemed like the Captain's study was suddenly immersed in crystal clear water so pure that you couldn't see it, but its force was still there. It was subduing everything into slow motion. As Via lowered the second case onto its side and lifted its chrome clips, the surreal scene watched itself. She raised the lid to reveal the treasure still berthed in its form. What she'd recovered from the barren lands west of Baghdad, she now unwrapped and held between her fingers. She lifted it out of the case as if it was floating on air.

Naomi's heart was racing in wonder and anticipation. Via stood up and turned around. She stepped back over to the shroud, and as she did, the artifact in her hands became visible to Naomi. She felt the shock of seeing it for the first time and trembled at her knees. Her eyes grew wide as saucers. "Is that what I think it is?" she asked.

"I'm positive it is exactly what you think it is – dead on – 100%." The confidence in her voice was overwhelming. And with that said, Via lifted the artifact above her head and matched it point by point to the blood stains that dripped from around the image of Christ's head on the top of the linen shroud.

The points mirrored the stains perfectly.

Naomi couldn't resist. She reached out and touched the crown of thorns.

*   *   *

IT **WAS A BEAUTIFUL** ceremony – one that neither satin lapels, nor cummerbunds, bridesmaids' dresses nor fresh floral bouquets could have enhanced. Not even cute little ones all gussied up, bearing baskets of rose petals and ring-bearing pillows, would have improved on the simple ritual.

Miguel gave a wonderful message about marriage and family being the quintessential expression of love apart from God's own. The Pope exhorted that God's design for couples mirrors His own relationship with his Church. He stressed that their love for each other should equal the intensity of Christ's own love for each of them.

The exchange of vows was beyond memorable.

"I promise to love and challenge you."

"I promise excitement and adrenaline."

"I promise adventure and your wildest dreams coming true."

And then the bride and groom knelt before the jeans-clad Pope Innocent Peter on the *prie dieu* before the altar and bowed their heads underneath the cross that had borne their Savior. They paid their homage to the symbol of Christ's sacrifice that gave us salvation. His gift of eternal life. Immortality.

Miguel blessed the couple and pronounced them "man and wife."

After the wedding ceremony, Charlie managed to find rice, of all things, and passed it around. No one seemed to care that it came from a storeroom full of emergency food rations. Everyone joined in the tradition of throwing it up into the air as the newlyweds ran, hand in hand, out of the little chapel.

As soon as the couple disappeared down the rough-hewn corridor, Sarah scurried over to Charlie.

"Charlie!" she whispered loudly.

"Yeah?" His eyes were still following the steps that José and Arkesha had just taken as they left.

"I gotta ask you something," still in a hoarse whisper.

"Sure, Sarah." He turned to her with a smile.

She grabbed his hand and pulled him away from the crowd. He thought it somewhat aggressive but it didn't bother him.

"Okay. So you know that I like Joshua."

"A little understated, don't you think?" He grinned.

"Yeah … well, okay. In fact, I told him I loved him. Well, no. Actually, I told the Pope."

"You love the Pope?"

"No. I told the Pope, 'I love him.'"

"You told the Pope that you love him?" Now a goofy grin.

"Stop it!" She hit him. "I told Miguel that I love Joshua."

"I didn't know you guys were that close."

"What?"

"You and the Pope, seems a bit of an intimate conversation … unless were you in a confessional at the time?" Goofier.

"*Charlie*," she warned.

"I wish I could confide my forbidden love to the Pope."

She hauled off and smacked him again. Hard.

"Okay, okay!" He laughed. "Ow! That hurt!"

"It was supposed to hurt. I need your help here!" she insisted.

"Okay," his tone now serious. "You told the Pope, of all people, that you have a crush on your professor and…." She cut him off, "It's not a crush."

"All right!" He held hands up in surrender. "Okay, you have a deep, unrequited love and you…."

She cut him off again, "It was an accident."

"Falling in love with a dude twice your age is accidental?"

"He's not…. No, it wasn't accidental, and it's not unrequited!"

"How old is he?"

"I don't know."

"So he's probably more than twice your age and he…."

She cut him off again, "I didn't mean to tell the Pope. I'm glad I love Joshua. And he loves me."

"You keep cutting me off," he whined.

"Would you rather I hit you again?"

He pursed his lips while trying to suppress another grin.

"I'd fainted, and as I came to, I just said it. The Pope happened to be right there," she explained.

"Oh, just an hour or so ago."

"Yeah, I guess." Sarah's eyes rolled to the upper corners of her lids as she considered the time frame. "Anyway, afterwards Joshua told me that he emailed me…."

"You can't email down here."

"Now *you* cut *me* off," she said matter-of-factly.

He gave her a *coming from you?* stare.

"He emailed, well, it was a private message on my FB. It was sent before we got down here."

"In anticipation of you blurting out your feelings for him to the Pope?"

"Are you going to keep making fun of me?" Her eyes were filling with tears.

"I'm sorry, Sarah. I'm here for you. You know that." His hands rested on her shoulders. "Just ask me. What is it? What's your question?" Then he zipped his mouth with his fingers.

Sarah swallowed the mixture that dripped down the back of her throat, her tears mixed with nasal fluids and saliva, and wiped away the moisture on her cheeks. "Independently," she stressed, "from my declaration to the Pope, Joshua had emailed me earlier, and I want you to tell me what you think it means."

Charlie's lips were pressed white together. Still zipped.

"He said," she continued, "'I'm a little bit enamored.' What does that mean?"

He mumbled through lips firmly shut.

"You can talk now." She rewarded him with a small laugh. Both of his hands had been back on her shoulders. Now he took them off and breathed out like he'd been holding his breath.

"You want to know what *enamored* means?"

"No, silly. I know what it means. It means love – or in this case, *in love, smitten*, or *head over heels*."

"Sounds like you had to look it up in your dictionary," he teased.

He got hit again.

"Hey! I bruise!" he protested.

"I hope so!"

"Okay. Okay. I know what he's saying."

"You do?"

"Yeah."

"Sure?"

"Yes. I'm sure. It's a guy thing."

"So what'd he mean?"

Charlie tried to keep a straight face while he used an even, serious tone. "It means he thinks you're hot!" The grin busted out.

"Charlie!"

"Well, you *are*...."

She hit him again.

They'd been gradually left by everyone until they were the only two near the door of the little chapel. Just as her hard fist pummeled Charlie's shoulder, Joshua walked back from the hallway. He approached them as Charlie grimaced and held his bruised muscle.

"Charlie." The professor had stepped up to them and stood facing him. "Can I borrow her from you for a minute?"

"Of course."

Charlie left still nursing his well-deserved wounds. At that point Joshua stood alone with the maid of honor inside the impromptu wedding chapel. Sarah was beaming as he held her hands and picked up as if they'd never left off.

"What I meant to say was...."

٢٤

THE MAN WHO emerged from the cellar beneath *La Basílica de San Juan* was extremely unhappy. He stomped to the silver Maybach and opened Tobin Legg's door.

"Get out!" he demanded.

She did.

Scrabbling out with a bewildered look in her eyes, the Yale MBA straightened her short navy blue skirt as she stood on wobbly knees, her high heels incongruous on the cobblestone drive.

Roland looked at her briefly to ensure she wasn't holding briefcase or phone, and once satisfied, entered the back of the stretched luxury sedan through Tobin's still open door, and slammed it shut.

"Drive!" he said.

The *mestizo* driver was used to reacting quickly when the big boss came to Lima. He punched it.

The gangly sylph was left standing like a willow in the winds. Her verdancy stripped to barren branches at the onset of winter. She watched the rear of the limo shoot down the drive and take a hard right with tires squealing, the drift of an expert driver sliding the entire vehicle to the left as the turn was executed. And then it was gone, leaving only the smell of its exhaust in her nostrils.

All Tobin could do is wonder if she'd been fired.

Inside the Landaulet, Roland was already on the phone with his office in Heidelberg. The German man on the other end was waiting as well.

"How can you not have heard from them? Mike was supposed to call in to both of us."

"Jacks' last contact was at 0800 local. He was making sure I got the package."

"You did?"

"Yes," with a thick Dutch accent, "but it's worthless."

"I'll make that decision."

"A worn paperback novel, a Chromebook and an iPad?"

"What about the notebook?"

"It wasn't in there. And the Chromebook and iPad only have a bunch of school stuff."

"The notebook wasn't in the room?"

"Mr. Jacks said…."

Enson cut him off. "Send me everything that goes along with that Chromebook. And send the iPad."

"But it's…."

"Now!" He cussed and hung up the phone with anger that he hoped would be felt at the other end of the line.

The driver pulled up at his office on the other side of the *Plaza.* A tall blonde stepped up to Enson's door and pulled it open.

"Who are you?" he asked without moving to get out.

"I'm your new PA."

He studied her, looking her up and down from his leathered seat. He figured her for one of the girls from his Paris office. Or, perhaps she was American. Not another one of those!

"That was quick," he said. "France?" He frowned. "From our office in St. Paul?"

"No."

"Oslo?"

"No. *Yo soy de Lima, Señor Enson. Mi padre es de Lima. Y mi abuelito es de Lima tambien.*" In a fluent, very Peruvian accent. "*Y yo me llamo Peña.*"

Roland decided to climb out of the limo. He stood his full height next to the woman and saw that her heels caused her to be able to look him square in the eye. "Let's see how long you last," he threatened as he started up a brisk walk away from the Maybach, brushing past her towards the front entrance of the building that bore his name.

Enson was already on the phone again as he walked through the glass doors and into the lobby. Peña stayed one step behind him in her conservative suit, her hair a neat practical cut that fell just barely to her shoulders. At the elevator bank they only waited seconds for the doors of the first lift to slide open. Enson jammed his thumb against the desired button and it glowed with life.

"B2?" she asked, looking at the lit circle.

The car's doors had shut and the elevator started down.

"Here." Enson barked, handing her a small slip of yellow paper. "Call this number until you get through." Then he turned to face the front of the lift and acted like he was ignoring her, his briefcase still clutched tightly in his other hand.

She started dialing.

He was back on his call, the earpiece that kept him hands-free glowed an eerie yellow as he resumed his conversation. "Yes, I'm still here. The signal's weak. Hold on."

Peña's hand stopped moving over her keypad just in time for his first insult. "We're in an elevator, *Barbie*, why don't you just resign now before you hurt yourself."

She silently held out her iPhone so he could see the screen.

Enson found himself staring at her WorldOne Dialer App already cycling the number. He shrugged as if not impressed.

Their hazy reflections, in the brushed nickel finish of the panels of the sliding doors, parted to reveal a service tunnel. Roland's bulk rushed out in front, temporarily blocking his assistant's exit. He walked briskly across the bare concrete, and Peña followed into the chill of the damp cellar air. She could hear the distant pulsing of electronic beats reverberating through the underground chamber and clicked her heels hard against the cement to catch up.

Enson was back on his call again. "No, they *weren't* successful. I don't need to wait to hear their opsit. If we haven't heard from Mike by now, they've....

"Yes.

"Okay.

"Send it to me.

"No, likely in the bunker.

"But the thing is a dry artesian well.

"*Ostia.*

"How should I know?" He let out a string of profanities.

"They can't stay down there forever!

"Yes, but they won't. We've given our men the intel they need. They can cut them off. I'm headed back to…." He lost his connection.

Somehow Peña had managed to get in front of her boss and had her iPhone extended.

"You got through already?" He spoke with the tone of utter disbelief.

"Not exactly, but you may want to listen to his message. I've saved it."

"Why would I want to hear his voicemail greeting?" But then the derision in his face quickly faded as he realized…. "Give me that!" he snapped and snatched it from her hand. The pulsating music was closer now, and it made it difficult to hear.

"Roland, you're wrong about this. You'll pursue it to the end, I know. But you will eventually realize that I was right. I'm not going to try to stop you. I couldn't if I tried. But I can make this difficult for you. So if you don't want to rebuild each one of your labs from scratch, leave my people *alone*." The audio file terminated as the message ended. Enson's face was beet red. He may know about my lab in Germany, but there is no way he knows about my lab in Quebec, or the one in Oceana. Those are the only three that matter. Can he know…?

He stood there lost in thought. Not angry. Not worried. He'd listened carefully to every word of the message. The tempered tone. The matter-of-fact delivery. The confidence. The resolve. No, he decided, I'm not going to back off. Let him try. If it's a war you want, you got it.

"Mr. Enson." The second time. Peña was holding a hanger that bore a clean shirt, pressed and unbuttoned, ready for a busy executive's second wind.

He feigned no surprise that she'd anticipated the request and moved so quickly. How did she get it down here so fast? I didn't even see anyone bring it to her.

She turned her face away from him while still extending the shirt, giving him privacy to change. He tore off an expensive dress shirt. It had only been on his body once. Today. He slipped into the new silk and cotton weave and buttoned up while the first shirt floated to the dirty floor. Tucking in the tail, he walked on without a word, leaving Peña to pick up the discarded garment from the cement.

He'd dialed his phone again. As soon as he heard the voice on the other end, he growled, "Turn up the heat. Kill them. Kill them all."

*　　　　*　　　　*

THE SNOW CRUNCHED under her light-green Uggs. She'd pulled them up over the ankles of her jeans and walked out into the white wonderland outside Bariloche. Naomi's thick wool sweater was plenty warm, so she let her soft white ski jacket fall open to her hips. Standing in the carefully landscaped space hidden beneath the last of the winter's blanket outside The Brandenburg resort, she faced the age-ravaged German swallowed up by his woolen trench coat. Via stood close by, like a brooding goose about to tend her nest.

"I plan on covering your unique history as part of the piece." Naomi was in the middle of explaining what the old man should expect at the shoot.

Heinrich's vocal chords were strained. The air was dry and cold, having been swept in from Mt. Tronador's Nordic-like rock and the glacial runs beyond. But it was the old soldier who had insisted that they meet under the barren limbs of the Quebracho trees behind the lodge. Always careful, he didn't feel comfortable with the security sweep he had performed upon his arrival. He'd checked for listening devices inside his suite, but then decided against meeting inside altogether.

Naomi found it comical. They were planning a shoot for Internet tv, not an upcoming air-raid.

But it wasn't until they were beyond the limits of the summer terrace by about sixty meters that he'd allowed any conversation. And, before he would let Naomi start, he had handed Via a mini-disk inside a thin plastic case. Now he was listening intently to Naomi's description of how the interview would go.

"I don't have a problem with that," he said.

"We will go over several documents. I'll want you to read a few of the selections that I'd highlighted in yesterday's email."

"All right."

"I'll ask you to explain how one determines provenance."

He nodded.

"And we'll end the segment with a 'big picture' visionary monologue. I want you to motivate the troops out there."

Heinrich smiled.

Naomi continued, "It'll air over the Internet live. The permanent file will hang in the video portal, so we will be able to continue to promote the taped piece through email, text blasts and banner ads."

"Okay. I'm not sure about your Internet lingo." He offered a weak grin. "But I think I get the gist of it." The man extended a withered hand in agreement. "I just hope I live long enough to see it."

Naomi stifled her laugh. "Herr Stauffenberg, you will be able to watch the video file within minutes after we are done shooting. We've already built the graphics that we will be dropping everything into."

"Amazing," he said.

"It's broadcast quality, digital video. We should reach 300 million viewers within the first three days."

"All by computer?" He looked confused under big bushy eyebrows.

"The Internet's a powerful medium, sir. And the broadcast is free. Our servers in Washington can handle 100 million singles a day, bypassing every spam and phishing filter out there. We have pop-ups that engage within ten hours if the initial email is not opened. If we get a delete or unread, the email will roll back up to the top of the recipient's new mail with a new subject line. A different tease."

"But with the content we've got, it will go viral," Via chipped in.

"That's right," Naomi followed, "we're predicting 41% will view, and 28% of those will pass it along with almost half of those forwarding to multiple parties. Within the first 90 days we will reach the entire planet. It will exceed the 1.4 viral coefficient. And that's not even counting our social network campaigns."

"You kids have really changed my world." He gave them something between a smile and a grimace. "When Via first told me that the famous Naomi Young was going to interview me, I assumed it would be for television."

"I hope you are not disappointed," Via cajoled.

"No. Not at all," he assured. "I'm just flabbergasted."

Naomi kept up the pitch. "Sir, you see, besides broadcast and cable television being so expensive, it really doesn't reach near the number of people they claim. And you can't track actual views, length of the view, or the identity of who has viewed the piece. With the internet we can do all of that and more. Using the viewer's unique IP addresses, a follow-up campaign of additional shows, weblinks, book offerings and a conference calendar will target a specific audience with content tailored to what they've already absorbed. Our campaigns give away plenty of valuable content for free, asking only for their contact information and preferences from a simple multiple choice menu. The drop-down menus cut the response time to under sixty seconds. Even informercials that pull in telemarketing leads with 'loss leaders' lose up to 65% of their incoming calls now because the response time is too long."

"I think I follow you," he said tenuously.

"You two mind if I get this?" Via's phone was ringing.

His face told her he needed a word.

"Hold on," she said into her phone.

"Everything you asked for is on that disk." He pointed to the small clear case that held the digital content.

"Do you mind if I go ahead and get it to our graphics guys?"

"My pleasure."

"Let me call you back." Via hung up the call and turned around. "Heinrich?"

"Yes."

"Before I leave, can you...?" She pondered a bit, choosing her words carefully. "What can you tell me about Jundishapur?"

The bushy grey brows arched high. "It would depend. Are you referring to the ancient Persian metropolitan? Or, *Ibn the Turk*," said with a growl at the end.

*   *   *

HIGH ABOVE BEIRUT in the Lebanese mountains a large patio spread out towards the precipice that overlooked the coastal plains of the Levant. The restaurant was crowded, sunshine spilling out over the olive trees and past the low-slung fig groves down the steep grade. They sat off in the corner, as far away from the other diners as possible. A wrought iron table was placed between them with graceful legs and heavy linen pouring over its edges. A much younger version of the Ibn he'd presented the day before sat across from a beautiful young woman from the states. The striking young lady may have been Egyptian or Moroccan, but her Midwestern American accent was unmistakable.

"My father is staying in Santa Barbara now," she said.

He smiled and leaned back in his seat. Taking in the serenity of the highland setting, he breathed in deeply through his hawkish nose, his eyes laughing. "Glad to know it. Glad to know it." The fresh aroma of the alpine cedar forest above them filled the air.

"He asked about you," she added.

"You know that Camille Shamoon was a good friend of mine."

She smiled, but a puzzled look was seen in her eyes. And it wasn't because his statement was not responsive to hers. It was due to the math. She was already quickly doing the figures in her mind. Her great grandfather's first cousin had been President of Lebanon from '56 to '64. But she decided not to ask. Instead she followed up on her father's request. "Are you able to come out to southern California?"

"I have an invitation?" He seemed pleased.

"My father wants to see you. If you can't make it there within the next couple of months, he said he'd be back out here – or again, where would that be?"

"Armenia."

"I thought you were from Turkey," she said, looking at him from behind her pretty, dark eyes.

"Yes. I lived there some time ago." He flashed her an enigmatic smile. "But that was before…." His voice drifted.

The waiter arrived with their meals. They'd just finished the *maaza*, sharing a large plate between them. Her entree was a petite acorn squash stuffed with rice and beef in tomato sauce. Ibn was set to enjoy the shish kebab of lamb with onions, peppers and Roma tomatoes.

"So, my dear, what is it that I can do for you?" he asked as he launched into his steaming course.

"Well, you know, I'm in the Master's Program at Cornerstone."

"Yes. And I'm proud of you. Your father must be as well. You grew up in Michigan, yes?"

"Yes. But once I got old enough, I hung with my dad and brothers in Virginia whenever I could," spoken with an incredibly beautiful smile.

"Great program there. Carroll does good work. Sure, I'll help you. Anything." He took another mouthful of lamb.

"I'm already well into my thesis. It deals with the supernatural delegation of power." She stopped and let that sink in. "Carroll's in Texas now," she added. "We all miss him."

"He is? Oh. Your paper's on an interesting subject. I have a library full of treatises that can help you. Two volumes I can think of right now that would be brilliant helpers, they are original texts from Edessa's libraries." His voice fell off as he looked out over the horizon, then resumed, "Antioch. I have a couple sermons. St. John, the presbyter was still living in Jerusalem at the time, but he gave the sermons to the church in Antioch. They both deal with the words found at the beginning of his gospel, 'He gave them power to become sons of God.'"

"Wow! Absolutely! Those would be great! My dad told me that this trip would be worth it."

Ibn looked pleased. "If your father were with you, I'd give you full reign in my stacks. You could copy whatever you chose. As it is though, I will select what may help you and upload the scans to a secure site where you can download whatever you deem appropriate. The files are much too large to email."

"Thank you," she said.

He used long thin fingers to pick up a grilled tomato and place it on his outstretched tongue.

"So what do you think?" A strong, inquisitive look as she finally dug into the entree in front of her.

"About what?" spoken through a mouthful.

"Jesus making his powers available to us," she said with her own mouth chewing beef and squash. She gave him an irresistible smile.

Ibn raised one eyebrow as he regarded the question. He swallowed and sipped at his glass of wine before answering. "Like when he laid hands on his disciples and gave them authority to cast out demons and heal the sick?"

"That," she took another bite, "and…." She decided to chew and swallow before finishing.

He didn't wait. "Scorpions, serpents, poison…." He spoke like a wizard stirring the pot.

She offered a sly grin, an almost crooked upturn of one corner of her already unique lips. "Jesus *disappeared* from the midst of the crowd trying to kill him outside Nazareth. He just walked right through them. He *appeared* inside a locked room after his resurrection. He spoke to the wind and controlled the sea. He created bread and fish out of thin air."

"He *is* the Son of God." Ibn's long fingers now fanned out, one by one, like the kicking legs of a chorus line.

"That Jesus was and is God himself, the visible image of the invisible God, the Creator of all things, is not really the point, is it, *Mr. Jundishapur?*"

"Ah, your father has taught you many things. Perhaps he teaches you *dangerous* things. Some things are better not revealed." Both spindly hands now rested on the sides of the table, and the tall man's chest bent ominously over his empty plate.

She was undeterred. "The *presbyter's* gospel," she began, paused and cut her eyes, looking at him with all seriousness, "records Jesus' promise in the fourteenth chapter. He said, 'You will do the same things I have done and even greater things.' And the book of Acts is full of examples that confirm the truth of the statement. Philip was translated after baptizing the guy from Ethiopia. Paul was invulnerable to being killed by stoning. The *elder* ... well, it's not recorded in the Bible, but he...."

Ibn gave her another threatening look.

"Elijah," she changed course, "ran so fast he caught up with and passed a horse and chariot. He sustained the race for quite some distance too. What is it? Fifty miles from *Ha Karmel* to *Jezreel?*"

"Wait a second, slow down." He sat back in his seat and leaned back from the table. His demeanor switched into one now fatherly, taking a few minutes to carefully interlace his fingers. "Elijah's a figure from the Old Testament. I thought we were talking about *Jesus.*" He squinted pedantically and tented his hands.

"He is the same yesterday, today and.... I don't need to tell *you* this. Why are you testing me?"

"Is Jesus' promise in John 14 relevant to Elijah?"

She cut her eyes tight and carefully regarded her host. Another bite of squash remained on her plate. She speared it with her fork and paused before putting it in her mouth. Using her ladened utensil as a prop, she waved it in the air, almost wildly.

"Well," she said, acting out the motions of a magician using a wand, "he did lots of cool stuff *before* he became a son of God." She bored holes into his eyes and allowed herself a small grin. "Didn't he," said without the inflection of a question.

The chunk of *konsa* was then ceremoniously popped into her mouth with a confident smile.

"You didn't answer my question." He folded his hands onto his lap. He let his eyes glare at her, but only slightly.

"You said you'd give me *anything* to help me write a knock-out thesis." She poured on an ethereal charm along with the challenge.

He should have known. Ah, he thought, back to business at the conclusion of the meal. "Yes. I did. Whatever you need," he promised again.

"I want the *original* manuscript of Mark's gospel."

"Impossible," he said.

*　　　*　　　*

"I LOVE YOU."

She just stood there, looking up at him. Her eyes were unflinching. Her body remained still as if nonplussed. But a tinge of worry crept up into her countenance.

"I meant to say that I love you too, Sarah," Joshua repeated, hoping for a different reaction. Then he decided to add something that he wanted her to never forget, no matter what. "The love I have for you does not depend upon whether you love me back. It doesn't depend on circumstances. It will never change. I have made a final, irrevocable commitment, part of it is involuntary, part of it by decision, but it's the kind of love that Jesus himself has for you. I hope you understand what this means."

With her still in shock, he decided to tell her the bad news too. She was the only woman he'd ever truly loved. She will be the only one. Forever. She deserved to know the truth. He would tell her everything.

"But," he began, "we can't be together. I…. I love you so much it's killing me. I had to tell you. But then, before you got my Facebook message, you said what you said to Miguel. I was thrilled. Ecstatic. Overwhelmed. And scared."

Her face showed every bit of confusion that she was feeling inside.

"I guess," he continued, "because I'd finally gotten over … well, not really … the fear that you wouldn't feel the same way. It was still there. But I'd resolved to deal with it. If you didn't, that is. And you did allay some of my fear. The way you acted around me. Some of the things you've said. It was never enough for me to *know*. Hope? Yes. But not to know the way I wanted to know. So, I'd prepared myself for that. Fear. Of rejection, I mean. But not this other kind of fear … that you would actually love me back. I mean, really love me. And then, here we'd be, like star-crossed lovers.

Romeo and Juliet *died*. I don't, for one, think that's all that romantic. But I will...."

She finally cut him off. She'd been listening intently and gathering her wits about her. Courage was rising within her. She heard what he'd said about "bad" news and "we can't be together" and she chose to put those aside entirely and analyze the situation as a whole.

Sarah Byrd was *planning*.

And her planning usually meant that she got what she wanted.

"Nervous?" she asked.

She placed a finger against his lips to stop the rambling even though she found it altogether too cute.

Their other hands were still touching each other. Both were now sweaty and trembling.

"A little," he admitted.

"Like you are a *little* enamored?" she teased.

That earned a small laugh. But it was more a release of tension than anything else. Joshua's nerves started to calm though, enough to take a deep breath.

"You're hurting me," she said.

"Huh?"

She looked at her hand: white with bright red knuckles.

"Augh." He let go. "Sorry, I didn't realize."

A pause.

"Are you going to kiss me now?" she said.

A long romantic exchange – the kind of look that goes way beyond just peering into each other's souls.

"There you are!" Michelle called out.

The commander had burst into the room. "We need to move!"

A slight hesitation ... but Joshua turned to look.

"Now!" Michelle ordered.

Joshua pleaded back with his eyes to Sarah and pulled on her hand. He moved, pulling her along with him. They both started up into a trot, and then a run, as Michelle took off back down the long stone hall.

Sarah didn't have a chance to get mad at the woman this time.

They burst out of the tunnel's doorway, and a soldier shut and locked it behind them. The carrier was already loaded except for the four. Michelle quickly bridged the distance and climbed into the vehicle. Joshua and Sarah moved fast, entering right behind her with the soldier on their heels.

Zelfa took off before the overhead door even started to lower back into place. As Sarah sat, buckling hastily into the three-point belt, Joshua rushed to the front and disappeared into the cab. He found Bear already crouched in his spot between the two drivers. Bear's face mirrored that of a child's first trip to the amusement park.

"What's going on?" the professor asked.

Zelfa answered. "Four LAVs. Thirty degrees off the back port side. Wow, they're coming in fast!" She pushed their heavy machine to its maximum speed.

Joshua put on a look of disorientation. Wasn't thirty degrees back of their port out over the expanse of the canyon? "Who's manning the guns?" he asked.

"One of your people," Zelfa said matter-of-factly.

"One of *mine?*" Confused.

"José's on the big machine gun!" Bear exclaimed. "Isn't it great?"

"Oh no!" Joshua turned to go check it out for himself.

ARKESHA WAS with José at the gun turret at the back of the amphibious transport. She stood in the small space on his right side. His shoulders were both pressed up against the curled braces at the massive gun's controls.

"What's that?" she asked her husband. She was pointing at the much smaller barrel that was suspended underneath the .50 caliber Ma Deuce mounted in the center of the nest.

"An M-60." He smiled.

"Both guns look old."

"They are. But these guys pack quite a punch." José's voice quivered with excitement.

Arkesha looked at the approaching enemy trucks, "Are we gonna make it?" There was fear in her voice.

"Make it?" he started, "Sure! These guys are toast!" Complete confidence.

*　　　*　　　*

"I THOUGHT IBN was *Persian,*" Via said, now obviously not going anywhere. "Well, partly. Let's see, his mother was Egyptian, or half Egyptian. I can't remember."

"He's from Sanliurfa, or Urfa, if you please." Heinrich's breath billowed white in the cold outdoors.

"Edessa?" said Via.

"Yes," Heinrich answered. "Sanliurfa used to be called *Edessa the Blessed*. But today? Not a single Christian. Not one." He cast a corrugated frown and added with a spit of spite, "Not even when *the Turk* lived there."

"I thought Ibn was a Christian?" Via took a step back towards the other two.

Another growl. "*Origenist,*" he said, accented by the wisps of grey hair that seemed to prepare for an attack as he spoke the word.

"Is that like a Creationist?" Via asked in all seriousness.

Naomi found it very funny, but hid her smile. "Origen," she clarified, "was a 3rd century priest who taught that salvation and damnation were temporary to eternity, yielding ultimately to *apokatastasis.*"

"Apoka…?" Via looked truly concerned.

"That everyone will eventually go to Heaven and that the Devil himself will be saved!" A guttural snarl issued from between the cracked lips. "Hitler too! Charles Manson! Dahmer!" His heavily creased cheeks strained to give his jaw enough room. "That these demons would end up in Heaven? It is nothing short of *heresy!*" He finished spouting and ended up in a coughing fit.

Via put her hand on the old man's back as his hacking continued. "We need to get *you* inside."

They all started moving through the snow covered grounds towards the patio doors only barely visible on the other side of the grove of barren tannin trees. Dark clouds moved in and the sun lost its place in the sky.

"We'll talk again later," Via assured the old man. Her thoughts were already on the mini-disk in her coat pocket. There would have to be a change of plans now that she knew more about Ibn.

The women ushered the antiquated German up to his room inside the resort. His coughing calmed as they took him through the lobby. They were pleased that Heinrich seemed to continue to improve the rest of the way to his room.

"I'll be here first thing in the morning to retrieve you." Naomi was standing at the threshold as he opened the door to his suite. "We'll ride together to the shoot after an early breakfast if you'll join me."

"Thank you, dear," he managed and shuffled underneath the header into his hideaway.

"Get some rest, Herr Stauffenberg," Via added, as a wrinkled hand waved a feeble goodbye, and he disappeared behind the closing door.

"Wow!" Via said as they walked back down the heavily carpeted hall. "I guess I shouldn't have brought *that* up." Her voice playfully mocked the old man's. "*Hitler* in Heaven? Blasphemy! Napoleon? Damn you to Hell along with 'em! Teddy Kennedy? God strike you with lightning right here!"

"Hey!" Naomi cautioned.

"How can I possibly keep my deal with Ibn after all of that? I thought *you Christians* had open arms? Am I wrong? 'For God so loved the world that *whosoever*....' All that." Via's accent was thick again. "What happened to forgiving the sinner?" she demanded – their moment with God while in the presence of the Shroud now all but lost.

Naomi just gave Via one of those looks.

"You Christians?" she bit back. "That's not fair, Via." Immediately Naomi's tone was menacing alacrity.

Via was startled by the strong reaction, but quickly her chagrin was cast. "I'm sorry," she said.

A heavy spirit fell between the two. One of the black clouds that had settled into the sky had found its way inside.

"Forgive and you shall be forgiven. God is merciful to those who show mercy. I know. I went to Sunday school too. I don't mean to be rude about it, but why wouldn't Hitler have the same right to redemption as the rest of us? I just thought...."

"Let's just drop it, okay?" Naomi pleaded, "I'm tired."

She turned around. Her pivot put her back to Via's downcast face.

"I'll see you at the shoot," Naomi said quietly as she started for her room.

Naomi left Via as she walked back up the hall and made her way to her door at the far end. Sadness overwhelmed the young woman. Her thoughts turned back to last year in DC.

What is forgiveness? What is salvation? It is nothing if the past cannot be erased. We make mistakes. We feel regret. We want to make it right. Sometimes we can't. Sometimes nothing can make it right. It's often an impossible task.

But we still need to be forgiven. We still need redemption. We can only live with our guilt for so long. But if we are pardoned, can we forgive ourselves? If true salvation is the washing away of every sin, why do I still remember them all? God may remove them as far as the East is from the West and forget them at the bottom of the deepest sea, but I can't forget my own sins. Naomi started to cry.

So redemption is just beyond my reach. How will I ever be free?

In this mind-set she kicked off her Uggs and sat on the edge of her bed. She took out her phone and dialed.

"Warren?

"Hey," she said quietly, "it's me.

"No. Nothing's wrong." Her face said otherwise.

"Yes," she said.

"Tomorrow," she told him.

"No. I'm fine," she lied.

"Yeah.

"Okay.

"Warren?

"I … I just want to be forgiven."

٢٥

ZELFA EXPERTLY raced the huge vehicle along the table rock towards the entrance to the transverse passageway. Bear remained in his cat-bird seat. Joshua was in the rear of the vehicle, climbing the steps to the turret to find José. Michelle was with a group of her soldiers in the back, going over contingencies like a coach waving her play book in the locker room. Charlie was watching Michelle. Sarah was watching Charlie. Her mind was rolling over and over all of the words Joshua had said. She continued making plans. Already Sarah's highly evolved blueprint included a home and little ones running between Joshua's legs in the kitchen.

Miguel was typing with both thumbs into his hand-held.

The professor emerged at the rear of the craft immediately behind José and slipped into the spot opposite the young man's new bride. "Having fun?" he joked.

José answered with a big goofy grin.

Arkesha bent to look around her husband. "What can I do? Can you help me with him?" she teased.

"He's *your* husband!" Joshua raised his voice above the windy din. "You guys be careful out here, okay?" He smiled, waved, and disappeared back down the stairs.

Arkesha yelled as she turned to look behind them again. "They're gaining!" She glanced at the LAVs and quickly ducked as if an incoming bullet was imminent.

"They are in range now!" José yelled back, obviously pleased. "Sweetheart?" he screamed.

"Yes?"

He puckered up.

She smiled wide, leaned up into him and gave him a big kiss.

José took aim. He loved the big M-2. He'd used the Vietnam War era favorite during his basic training.

The Ma Deuce was let loose and its AP round ripped through the dense air of the subterranean well. It plowed into its target. A direct hit!

The lead LAV flipped up over its hood and onto its back before bursting into flames.

"Whoop! Whoop!" Arkesha's fist circled in the air above her head. She pointed at the LAV that moved up to take the place of the fallen leader.

"Get 'em!" she cheered.

He pushed his neck out, vying for another kiss.

She planted another good one on his anxious lips. "I love you!" she yelled.

"I love you too, honey!" he yelled back and leaned into his weapon.

José carefully sighted the new target and depressed the trigger.

The aim missed. It was a little too far to the right.

"Come on darlin'! You can do it!" she screamed.

José aimed again.

This time the sighted LAV's nose raised high up into the air as José's third try detonated into its front bumper and shot jagged pieces of steel into the rock underneath its engine carriage. The truck thrust up into the cavernous expanse, and huge flames shot out either side of the vehicle like dragon's breath. When the front tires made their way back to the smooth stone surface, they bounced several times and the doors flew open. Soldiers scrambled away from the destroyed machine. As the men hurried away from the truck, its gas tank exploded into a great ball of fire.

"Woo hoo!!" Arkesha shouted.

"You wanna try?" he yelled back at her.

"I thought you'd never ask!" she screamed against the wind.

José moved out from under the M-2 and Arkesha ducked under the shoulder braces ready to fire.

Their professor popped in on them again, stepping into the spot that Arkesha had just vacated. "You too?" he asked. He wore an approving smile.

"You staying to watch?" she yelled.

"No, just checking on you guys." He looked back at the force still chasing them and nodded approvingly. They'd already cut the number of their pursuers in half.

Joshua disappeared again as Arkesha lined up the sight of the big gun. She centered the cross-hairs on the LAV to their left, the one that seemed to be trying to race up ahead of the other. She could see weapons poking out of their windows, and she tensed, assuming that lead would be tearing into her body at any second.

She didn't have the military experience that José had gained in ROTC and then the Reserves. Of course, the fact that José had grown up in south Texas hunting large mule deer didn't hurt either. He'd promised her a trip next year to a hunting range near the Frio River. She was an accomplished athlete. Everything was always perfectly executed. Her body was rock hard, her nerves could steady her, and she had excellent eyesight.

She pulled the trigger.

The shells hit the front of the LAV so hard that it seemed to push it backwards across the rock. Metal twisted, and the truck broke up into a brilliant explosion.

"That's my girl!" José cheered.

She sighted the final Light Armored Vehicle as grim determination lit up her face. She bit her lip and put an earnest smile of resolve in her eyes.

But before she could depress the trigger, their own vehicle abruptly swung into a 90° turn and quickly plunged them into blackness. Zelfa had driven them skillfully to the right and headlong into the long tunnel which was the cross-cut between two of the massive cavern sections.

José groped in the darkness for the M-60 tracers that he'd seen earlier lining the adjacent bin of shells.

Bear watched the bank of headlights below his forward perch. The lights washed the rock in front of them with a yellow glow. He ducked.

Yusef laughed. "These tunnel ceilings are pretty low, aren't they?" he called out as they zipped through the shaft like a coaster inside of Disney's Magic Mountain.

"The walls don't look wide enough either!" Bear seemed to narrow his own frame as if to squeeze in between the rock on either side of them. He cautiously raised his head and peered back out the window. "Are we going to get stuck in here?"

Zelfa took her hands off the wheel to answer.

"Augh!" Bear screamed.

She laughed again. "If I were the only one driving at this point, we'd be in big trouble. Stuck? We'd be a tangled wreck. But these transports were built to fit these tunnels perfectly. They have only five centimeters of clearance on each side and seven on the top."

"The transports were built for the tunnels? Not the other way around?"

"No," still laughing. "The tunnels were carved out by the Romans. There are hundreds of them down here."

"Impossible."

"Impossible today. Without slave labor, these kinds of projects just aren't feasible anymore. But that's not an endorsement."

"When?" Bear asked.

"After Pompeii they noticed that their deep wells had suddenly dried up. There was already a network of hand-hewn tunnels and catacombs that they had built networking the upper caves."

"Okay." Bear was curious.

"After the volcano drained their wells, they set out to dig new ones. Titus Flavius Caesar Vespasianus was the emperor who ordered the exploration of the underground rivers and lakes." Yusef continued, "But when the soldiers hiked down into the rock formations with their torches, they found the lakes and rivers down here dried up also. The engineers eventually recommended excavation."

"I thought they used aqueducts to get water from the river?" Bear asked, with a tinge of skepticism.

"The Tiber?" Zelfa laughed. "You're kidding, right?"

"Well, I just figured it wasn't polluted way back then."

"In the 1st century? It was *worse*," Zelfa bemoaned. "Raw sewage was everywhere. The Romans weren't too far behind the Chinese in keeping their streets clean, but the rivers inside and downstream from the larger cities were entirely non potable. Upriver, the Tiber wasn't so bad, but they still depended heavily on their wells to supplement water supply. Besides," she added, "the wealthy preferred the cold, clear waters that came from the deepest wells."

"So," Yusef took over with a smile, "the Romans dug deeper to determine how far the water level had dropped. They started excavating the gravel layers that filled the largest of the basins and then just kept going, putting the traverses in place, escape routes for wars and rebellions … even trade routes from the ports."

"How do you guys know all of this?" Bear challenged.

"Because," Yusef sounded confident, "the historians agree."

"Historians never get it wrong?"

Zelfa felt compelled to interject. "Bear," she said, "before Vesuvius buried Pompeii in 79 AD, this place was under a *mile* of artesian water. There is no way these tunnels were created prior to that."

"Well, what about before the caverns were submerged?" Bear offered. "We don't know how long the artesian basin held all that water. Maybe an *older* civilization dug out these tunnels."

"Why do you say that?" Yusef jumped back in with piqued curiosity.

"Because," Bear surmised, "this tunnel doesn't conform to any known Roman design."

*　　　*　　　*

VIA WALKED BACK to her own suite. Once inside, she left a trail of clothing on the floor as she made her way to her bedroom. She fell face down on top of the down comforter and buried her head into the soft fluffed bedcover.

And she cried.

Naomi had suggested earlier that the Savoies had, perhaps, *noble* reasons for perpetuating their lie. Via hadn't been able to get the idea out of her mind. She'd been thinking about it outside while Naomi talked with Heinrich. It had been on her heart when Ibn had called her to ask if she'd been able to collect the mini-disk yet. It increasingly bothered her. But her discomfort had been more on an intellectual level, at least at first. The hard shell around her heart seemed impenetrable. So it seemed. Somehow the combination of recent events and her conversations with Naomi got all tangled up into the years of anger. Years of searching. Years of unforgiveness. The weight of her spite. Now being pulled down by yet a heavier burden – her own guilt.

Had she got it wrong?

All this time gone? Had she been wrong about her family? Was her rage misplaced? She'd been working so hard to redeem her family's name, working to earn redemption for herself in the process, separating herself from the shame. That's why she'd changed her name. That's why she'd opposed her father. That's why her grandfather had borne the brunt of so many angry prayers. She had built up a solid wall of granite around her heart. Perhaps her angst had clouded her mind too.

Her wall had served her well though. It had its purpose. It had numbed her anguish over the years, allowing her to survive. It gave her a semblance of normalcy that let her press on, day after day. She had relentlessly pursued the truth, but she had already decided what the truth was.

But now? Now, with the shroud in her possession and the Savoie family secret shattered? Now that she had aired her own family's dirty laundry, soiled by the public display of shame in dignity's clothing? The truth was out there. Part of it, anyway. The fake grave clothes had been *designed* to deceive all the way down to the embedded pollens from the Holy Land.

Stunningly, with the real shroud came the revelation that the Savoie linen was in fact *identical* in every respect to the real one. Except for the burn marks and the amount of grime that had gathered inside the weave from years of public display, the Shroud of Turin was a perfect match.

But what Naomi had said about her family's motives…. Possibly. Probably, even. Naomi said she thought that they were honorable. Via was still digesting what that could mean. She'd mulled it over and over again. She could still hear her grandfather's words as clearly as if he were speaking them over to her again. Right now. His choice of terminology was very specific.

"Replica."

He'd almost said it with a proud tone. She'd never realized that aspect of the conversation before. Her subconscious was still piecing it all together. Did her grandfather know of a noble purpose behind the fake shroud? If so, why didn't he tell her? Why hadn't her father told her? Surely, he'd have known about it too?

The only way such a perfect replica could have been fashioned is if it was done side by side with the original in hand.

Somehow, with that light dawning, it shed away the dark of her doubt. She began to see it differently. Her family had to be acting to protect it. It was part of the fabric of who her grandfather was. He'd always been truthful, fiercely loyal to the Church, a man of intense beliefs and great faith.

But she had discarded all of that. Everything she'd known to be true about him had been cast away in favor of believing that he was, instead, the worst kind of charlatan: a Pharisee, a whitewashed tomb, part of an aristocracy that had more closeted skeletons than the commoners ever could. She now realized he was the man of honor she'd always known: a man sworn to secrecy to protect a priceless artifact, using diversion and fraud, just like generations of his fathers before him.

But what really made her cry upon her bed was how she'd been treating her father these past few years.

As she lie there, her father's face burned its way into the blackness behind her closed lids.

Her father, he was the one who had borne the brunt of her hatred. *Grand-pére* was dead. He'd never even seen a minute of her anger, her debilitating sorrow, and embarrassment. He'd not looked into her spiteful eyes. He'd not felt the unending pain when she changed her name.

But her father had.

She'd taken it all out on him. And he likely knew the truth about the whole thing. The Savoie's were not wrong for doing what they did. They were the *protectors* of the true shroud.

Via's pillow was soaked. Could she forgive her father? Could he forgive her? After all, even if Naomi was right, her father could have explained himself. He should have defended the family name. Yet, she should have given him the opportunity.

Would it ever all get fixed?

Via's phone rang. She wiped away her tears and answered. It was Ibn calling back.

NAOMI'S ROOM WAS down one floor at the end of the hall. As she sat in the corner on the floor of her dark room, tucked up against the wall, her phone rang. It was Joshua.

כ ו

PEÑA FOLLOWED him through the heavy industrial door into the club. One of Lima's catacomb-style watering holes confronted them. It had the look and feel of a burrowed crypt. Oppressive. Yet full of manic energy. Most of it was drug induced. The imbibed spirits. The inhaled powders. The pills. The needles. Steam and smoke. But the evil wasn't satisfied. Rebellion. Desperation. Both the empty and the emptied occupied the crowded space.

Peña wove through the dancing mass of bodies – a strong sea of flesh that moved in erratic waves under strobe lights of blue, and white, and red, and green. The shafts of rainbow spots bounced with synchronized blasts of pyrotechnic flame against the rhythmic heads. Underneath each skull, a flailing of arms and legs and bending torsos swayed and lost their form inside the beats.

Peña had already passed Enson's worn shirt off to a subordinate who would launder the garment and donate it to the local mission. It was a silken weave with a Gucci label that her boss would refuse to ever wear again. He used to have them tossed out with the trash. It was well known among his personal staff that he wouldn't even wear his best Canali suits more than a couple times before discarding them.

Peña thought about the position she'd been groomed for and the price of allowing herself to be selected. It was now her turn. No one lasted very long working as a personal assistant for Mr. Roland Enson. Most were fired. A few disappeared, never to be heard from again. She asked herself if it was worth the risk. Of course not. She knew that but took the job anyway.

Peña found herself worrying now about her personal safety, all the while struggling to stay on Enson's heels amidst the fluid crowd. The people packed inside the strange dance club were pressed up against each other in a single mass of heat and sweat. It was still daylight outside. A version of hell, she thought. Decadence. Despair. Degradation. Baring skin. To lure another in. Conspiracy. To join in sin-indulgent flesh, a lair of pain that kills long after the act is done. Cravings vainly pursued in a futile effort to substitute something, anything, for what they owe their Creator. She'd grown up in the Church. Most in Lima did. However, the Roman Catholic tradition in Latin America was not truly Catholic. From the beginning, starting with Pizarro's priests, the mixture of Christian and pagan tenets were used to win converts quicker. And the cultural fusion in the Americas became far worse than that tolerated by Rome elsewhere throughout the world. Incense and icons were misused by the Church everywhere, but no more so than in Lima. Idolatry ran rampant. Peña didn't like it. She had initially shunned the Church because of it. But then, she found her peace in spite of it. The world was bigger than man. Neither science nor any form of religion had any allure for her. She found comfort in the truth. She read the Bible for herself.

Peña followed Enson into a private room tucked away behind a huge wall of glass blocks that ran up the back of one of the many bars. They were manned by a dozen females in black and white uniforms that left little to the imagination. The towered shelving against the blocks displayed the fact that the club stocked only the best of everything. Alcohol was king. The illegal substances running through the veins of every guest as well as most of those clocked in? Queen.

The private room was quiet, soundproofed. Peña was thankful. As soon as the door puffed shut, only the vibrations of the pulsing rhythms could be felt, and only in her bones. Her ears were spared. Peña looked around the lavishly appointed lounge. Enson had already dropped down onto a large leather couch and lifted his phone to his ear again. She picked out a workspace near her boss and moved to get settled. The door swung open letting in the ghastly sounds of impatient beats, and a young barmaid entered and pushed the barrier back into its place. Her syrupy tone showed recognition: a sticky sweet voice that poured out its flattery onto the world's most well-known VIP. Her body was dressed for the streets, a piece of raw meat on display. Was she selling drinks or something else? It was disgusting. Peña just wanted to put some clothes on the kid and send her home to her parents. Was she yet sixteen? It was hard to tell under all of the clowned make-up that made the girl look more like a brothel madame than the school girl she may have been only months before. She was throwing herself at the man, bending over in front of him and whispering into his ear. But Enson appeared to ignore the sad display and just barked his order. When the young pusher lingered, he shouted her out of the room.

Peña wasn't about to order a drink. She simply sat one seat away from Enson. It was a plush, overstuffed chair that sat perpendicular to the couch. She perched herself on the edge of the velvet fabric and pulled out her pad and pen. Her iPhone lay on the low table in front of her, waiting for instructions. Enson dropped the phone down mid-call and started throwing a cascade of tasks at her. They streamed out of a foul mouth for ten minutes straight – rapid succession. Then, without seeing if there were any questions, he picked back up on his call and ignored the fact that most of what he wanted done needed clarification.

Peña had taken copious notes. As Enson jumped back on his phone, she converted the notes quickly into a list that organized and grouped the jobs. And as fast as she could make decisions with regard to how to accomplish the tasks, she typed. Her iPhone received a barrage of information and catalogued her list into appropriate functions. The calendar received scheduling matters. Her Dialer program would handle the various calls that needed to be placed. The emails went into a WorldOne App that scripted outlines of messages and proposed full lines of text in menu format. A "to do" listing of miscellaneous items held the balance of Roland's data dump. She seamlessly closed her calendar and activated each alert as marked. She assigned numbers from her pre-loaded contact list to her outgoing phone work and set up the priorities for the Dialer. The first two calls were already cycling. Her thumb added a couple of thoughts to her list of tasks on the notepad. Before she was finished, she drafted and sent two emails using almost entirely the menu choices prompted by her App. She managed to accomplish all of these things while Enson stayed on his phone. The second email was completed just as her first outgoing call went through.

Peña politely waited during the ensuing greeting. She'd reached Enson's offices in Dubai. "Lima here," she finally was able to say as the man on the other end of the line finished. "Our best assets are needed in Ostia, the Roman coastal port.

"Yes.

"Yes.

"No.

"Mike Jacks?

"No. He's out.

"No. Permanently.

"Right.

"Thanks."

The second number had already gone through. The Dialer had asked the recipient to hold until she was done with her other call. She picked up. "Tokyo? Lima. Mr. Enson wants the beta testing done by 0900 Friday.

"Yes. That's right.

"I understand.

"I'm sorry.

"Okay."

The Dialer was still tasking. It had picked up the next couple of numbers and was already trying to put the calls through in the proper order. She took the opportunity to complete three more emails.

Her third call went through. "Lima," she answered.

Peña asked Sydney to hold. Enson had just got off his first call and was speaking to her without warning: a string of additional commands. Tasks spilling out from between his teeth like water over a broken levy. He used his piercing black eyes to challenge her with every swiftly spoken word and blurred them as much as he cared, slurring the speech to trip her up and rushing through incomplete requests. His last order was cut far short of a complete thought as he got back on his phone and left her hanging.

"I'm back," she said into her own phone.

"Thank you for holding.

"Send Brasher, Collins and Theissen to Tuvalu.

"No.

"Yes. I'd do it yesterday if you value your paycheck.

"Okay.

"Thank you."

The girl finally waltzed back into the lounge with Roland's drink. She was wobbling over to him on impossibly high heels. Is that a swimsuit? Her mother would be so ashamed. If she lives long enough, so will her own children. Unfortunately, she will live with her own shame the rest of her life. Peña wrote another email. She completed another call. More instructions. More intolerable treatment. She tolerated it. What is that saying about a duck's back? *Agua.* The thought made her thirsty. "Bring me an Evian, please," she asked the girl. But the half-naked nymph was too busy contorting in front of Enson to hear her. Peña had to repeat her request as soon as Enson finally shooed her away. This time she got a response as the server stumbled out the door. "Sure," a curt reply from the tart.

Peña put yet another email into the airwaves. Her device sent the signal and it was picked up by the Intranet that Roland had insisted be installed in the underground pub. Lima was famous for it. Enson frequented all of the catacombs. Every club owner owed him something or everything as the case may be: wireless broadband, 3G, 4G, and even higher – available under the streets of the vast metropolis in the heart of Peru. Eight million people call this city home. Peña shuddered to think of what it would look like over the next twenty years. She answered another call that was just put through. "Sir," she said, "Sir!" Her voice got Enson's attention. "It's *him.*" He glowered. "I know it's impossible, but it's him. This time it's not a recording." Enson took the call with a heavy scowl. Within a couple of short minutes he threw the phone back at her. He hadn't said a word.

Peña completed all of her phone and email tasks and started typing the first of two letters. Enson finished his drink and hit the call button. The call brought the girl, but no water. She scurried back out to grab Enson's next drink. Patron Platinum. Chilled. Straight up.

Peña sent the text of the first letter upstairs. Thermographed letterhead and envelopes were already loaded in dedicated trays, and the printer hummed to life. Roland got off another call and was screaming about his drink. He pounded on the call button as if urgently tapping out code during the last world war. The barmaid finally reappeared with Enson's drink. Still no water.

Peña sent the command to print the second letter and fielded two incoming calls. "Thank you, Dubai. I'll let him know.

"Collins can't make it?

"I don't care who died. He's expected on the island by tomorrow noon. He knows what will happen.

"I understand.

"Okay."

Roland's call dragged on. He took his tequila from the tray as soon as the teen could serve it to him. This time the slinky gamine anticipated Enson's scream and ducked right back out the door.

Peña finished her scheduling. There was a knock at the door. She rose to get it. Enson ignored her. Peña found her assistant standing on the other side of the door holding a file folder. She ushered him in and took the folder from his hand – pulled out original letters and placed them along with a heavy Montblanc on the table in front of Enson. They were ready for his signature. He looked down, trying hard to look unimpressed. He frowned and signed the perfect work – then made a snide remark about a problem. He was immediately in a hurry. No time to make copies. He had to have copies. But they had to leave right now.

Peña silently handed him the pre-printed copies of the letters. He looked at them and then stuffed them into his briefcase as Peña folded the originals and stuffed the stamped envelopes. Her assistant sealed them and took off for the post office. Roland decided he'd better stand to go through with his ruse of having to leave right away. He continued his charade by rushing out of the lounge, bowling over the barmaid who was coming in as he was leaving. The tray in her hands held his third drink along with an open bottle of Evian perched precariously to the side. As Enson's bull hit the rodeo clown, the drinks flew up into the air and spilled everywhere. "My water," Peña moaned.

Peña was glad to be out of that club. She could still smell the smoke on her clothes. Tobacco and marijuana and who knows what else. She would need a long hot shower and fresh clothes at the next opportunity. She slipped into her seat in the back of the Maybach. Roland peppered her with questions. He was demanding results from his long list of orders he'd given her only an hour ago. He tried his best to undermine her: to find a command ignored, a task forgotten, a job undone. But Peña had completed everything he'd assigned. He narrowed his eyes and lodged a final complaint.

Peña answered, "Sir. I didn't expect you *would* remember all of these details. That's why everything is set out in the memo." He growled. "The one in your briefcase…. Sir. An electronic copy has been both emailed and texted to your mobile." Enson opened his attaché and saw it. The three page memorandum expertly organized each of the assigned tasks along with the corresponding result.

*　　　*　　　*

"WHERE HAVE YOU been?" she asked with pleading eyes.

"Checking on everyone." He was breathless.

"You've been going back and forth so many times."

"Just nervous, I guess." Joshua sat down next to Sarah.

"Oh." She smiled. "I make you *nervous*." The last word was inflected while slowly moving her chin up and down with a Cheshire smile.

Her tone reminded him of one of Sandra Bullock's characters, but he couldn't place it. It made him relax. "You," he smiled and spoke passionately, "make me *very* nervous." He reached for her hand.

"You want to *kiss* me." There it is again. Bullock. One of her early films? Same smile too.

"We're in an ancient tunnel almost two miles underground that should be submerged by highly-pressured artesian water, *and* we're being chased by a military vehicle full of armed criminals."

"You want to *marry* me." She continued the role.

Miss Congeniality! That's it!

She looked from his eyes down to his exuberant smile. "You do. I can see it on your face."

"I do," he said.

"I do too," she said. "So this like qualifies as common law marriage in seven states, right?"

Too cute.

"Sarah…." His voice got serious. "I can't."

Her smile drooped. He squeezed her hand.

"I *love* you, Sarah."

She saw pain in his eyes. "It can't be that bad," she said.

Joshua exhaled loudly. "I wish it were that easy."

"Look," she said, grabbing his other hand. They were sitting side by side, Sarah still strapped into her three-point belt, their bodies now contorted to face each other. "I don't *care* what it is. Whatever. *Anything.* A long list of who knows what." She was taking control of the conversation. "It won't matter to me. *Nothing* in your past matters to me. In fact, *nothing* in your present matters to me either as long as we get to be together. So, go ahead and tell me. It'll be fine. Or choose never to tell me. That would be fine, too."

His eyes widened.

"Joshua. I *love* you. I've loved you for a long time. *Nothing* can change that."

His eyes relaxed. His love for her was very strong. Genuine. Permanent. But he couldn't figure out how he would ever be able to get around…. He opened his mouth. Slowly. Thinking. He was choosing every word with care. "I've loved you for a long time too, Sarah. But…."

"I'm too young for you?" she guessed.

He paused. A slight smile passed over his face as he considered their age difference. Yes, it was considerable. But, no…. "No. That's not it." He smiled wide.

"I'll resign from the program. I'll transfer to Cornerstone."

He looked confused.

"You are on my committee. I'm one of your students – your GA even. If I go, it will make it easier that you are marr … dating me." Slurred words.

Joshua gave her a crooked grin. "If that were the issue, *I'd* resign," he offered. "We'd stay in Eugene until you finished your PhD, and then we'd go wherever we were called. I have offers all over the world. You will too."

"You've already forgotten?" she needled. "I already have a professorship waiting for me in Rome. And so do you." She made it sound both heady and exotic. Then she added, "But you said *if.*" Not missing anything. "Is there someone else?"

Joshua didn't choose his words carefully this time. It just came out. "Yes," he said, "but it's not what you think."

"You're married."

"No," he laughed and then assured her, "I've never married."

"You're engaged."

"I was, once, but that was a long time ago."

"Girlfriend?"

"Just you." He smiled. She looked *so* cute. His heart was pounding. He felt like the racing off-road tires beneath the transport, spinning over the surface of the tunnel floor. "I didn't say it artfully. I, well…," he resolved to tell her everything, but then he hedged, "I've made a vow to God."

۲۷

MANDY WOKE UP after a long sleep. She didn't feel comfortable. Her leg was still throbbing with pain and her whole body ached. The surroundings were unfamiliar. Perhaps she was still dreaming. Her eyes blinked. She rolled over and looked for a clock by the bed. She found one, but it wasn't hers. Disoriented.

She wasn't in her flat in London overlooking the Thames, that is, her flat where she was barely able to see the river between blocks of buildings. She wasn't in the hotel in Dubai. That crazy, opulent, sailboat-looking thing perched over the water. Via had them staying at *Burj al Arab*. Had she given in? Had she given up? Was she in a cheaper hotel in the UAE waiting to be picked up to be carried back to Chambéry a failure?

Her thoughts turned to Iraq's barren desert. What happened to the Mesopotamian fertile crescent? The pain in her leg further reminded her: the success at the compound, the spectacular escape, the *spaceship*, the strange Armenian, and now, Argentina. Good. I'm not in Dubai. I'm in Bariloche.

Groaning, she rolled out of her bed and stepped carefully onto the floor.

He was here, after all these years of not seeing him.

The curtains were drawn and the clock told her it was 2:59. Was it the middle of the day or the middle of the night? No light came in through the thick drapes. She looked back at the red numerals, squared and separated inside their crouching box. The little round light off to the side was on top. Oh great, 3am! An extremely sardonic intonation inside her head. Is it still called jet lag if your submarine flies you through the outer atmosphere the circumference of the planet's hemispheroid?

Waking up now. Via had said a breakfast meeting was arranged. Early. When again? Not *this* early. Mandy remembered. Her grandfather had to be at the shoot with Naomi. Why couldn't she remember when? Perhaps it was a lunch. Coffee. I need it.

The 4-cup unit was brewing into the carafe. The smell itself woke her enough to start processing thoughts. What will I say when I see him? Jew killer? How 'bout just *Nazi*. Doesn't that say it all? But she had such fond memories of him before moving away. She missed Lima. She missed the mountains. She missed the moonscape sculpted coasts and the Bolivian plateau with its UFO-inspiring rock and trench art. She missed the annual trips to *Machu Picchu*. But most of all, inextricably, she missed him. Even now. Even now that she knew the truth about his past.

It was her grandfather who'd taken her all over South America while she was growing up. He'd loved to carry her along with him while walking the old Incan roads that still traversed much of the Peruvian Andes. *Abuelito* had taken her hiking so many times she didn't try to count them all, just the two of them and a llama. The sure-footed ruminant always carried their lunch along with enough emergency supplies to stay holed up in the mountains for a month. Picnicking on the flax-weave cushions with *Abuelito* remained one of her favorite memories.

It was because of him that she hiked and picnicked throughout the British Isles whenever she had the opportunity. Her last trip had brought her to a mid-day feast sprawled out in the Hebrides, underneath the Callanish Stones. *Abuelito* gave her that. She smiled. She could smell the tobacco and brandy mixed with the musty taint of old books that always lingered about his clothing. He carried the aroma with him as if it were a requirement, a condition precedent to breathing. Even on Sundays. He'd show up early. He'd carry her as he walked with her mother to mass. He'd get them back home in time to head out with father to his Anglican parish.

It was easier once they were in London, just one service on Sunday morning. Her mom didn't seem to miss the basilica. But her eyes held great sadness year after year. Mandy had always known why. Her mother missed *Abuelito* as much as she did. And now, Mandy missed him more than ever.

There was a knock at her door. She looked at the clock again: 3:14am. Her coffee had finished brewing. She'd been lost in thought but now sensed impending danger.

Apprehensively she walked to the door and swung it open hard and fast. Violently.

Abruptly.

Mandy's Glock 17 leveled at the heart of an old man teetering on shaky legs.

NAOMI WAS WEARING pajamas. After waking up in the middle of the night, she'd felt compelled to walk up the stairwell off the end of the hall, then along the hall above until she arrived at Via's door. Naomi was reaching out to knock on the door when it opened.

Via screamed. Not normal for the woman.

"Via! I'm sorry!"

"No. It's okay. I was just coming to see *you*," Via said as she recovered.

"You were?"

"I thought you'd be up," spoken with a thick French accent.

"It's not even 3:30 in the morning."

"*You're* here!" she teased, then looking down at Naomi's hand, "And you brought your phone." More of a sarcastic tinge.

Naomi didn't think anything of it. "I thought you'd be up." She stepped inside the suite as Via moved aside. "Your place is bigger than mine."

Via looked around at her palatial space. "I need more room than you do."

"Ha. Ha. You have coffee?"

Via walked her into a full kitchen with stainless steel appliances and granite tops. Dominating the commercial-grade cooking area, a gorgeous espresso machine with shiny brass fixtures reflected the black marble countertop.

"Pick your poison." Via's accent was thick and sleepy.

"Can I get a non-fat, double latte?" Both curious and doubtful.

"Coming right up." Via pulled a brass single-liter pitcher from the French-door fridge and plunged the machine's long steamer into the fat-free milk. The high pitched scream of the stainless steel arm, frothing hot the white liquid, was a welcome sound.

A series of colorful pendant lights hung off silver chains and insulated wires over the counter that ran perpendicular to the monster barista's dream. Via grabbed a large cylinder from the counter and poured from a film-lined paper bag. A coffee bean grinder of polished walnut and copper trim with a leaded crystal top made quick work of the dark-roasted whole beans. Everything glistened under the warm kitchen lamps, while Naomi smiled and waited as patiently as she could. As the grinder's blades pulverized the espresso beans into a fine powder, the entire suite was filled with a rich fragrance that made both of their mouths water.

"Have you met Keyontay yet?"

"No. Via I...."

"Don't tell me you have a boyfriend. I know better. Keyontay was down in the bar last night hoping you'd show up."

"Via, I...."

The *café moulu* was packed into the brass cup on the end of a soft black handle. The chrome and brass machine squeezed drips into the triple-shot tumbler that Via had placed below. "It's okay," she replied. She stopped the brewing and turned the pitcher slightly to one side to foam the top of the steamed milk. "I just think you'll really like him." She was raising her voice to be heard over the gurgling milk.

"*You* never married," Naomi said as soon as the noise subsided.

Via combined the ingredients into two *café crème* cups as beautiful as the rich beverages themselves. "I've been too busy to marry."

Naomi's eyebrows arched as if to say: *And you're giving me a hard time for being too busy!*

"Actually, I couldn't sleep because of what you said yesterday." Convenient subject change.

Naomi was too afraid to guess. She just silently sipped her coffee and waited.

"You said the Bible says it is okay to lie."

"I didn't say that," Naomi interrupted.

"Hold on. Let me finish." With Via's smile came a more relaxed poise. She leaned back against the counter and completed her sentence with almost no hint that English was not her native tongue. "I was saying that you had said that the Bible says it's okay to lie in certain situations."

"I didn't say that either," Naomi said. "Can we move to the dinette?" She motioned to the kitchenette area and slid off the bar stool.

"Sure."

As Naomi sat across from Via she reminded, "I'd simply given you a couple of examples in the Bible where people with a close relationship with

God lied, and their actions were not condemned by the Lord as best as we know."

"Abraham and David," Via recalled correctly. "Are there others?"

"Plenty. But I don't think any were praised or otherwise received any kind of affirmation from God that their lies were okay."

"Who else?"

"Well," Naomi had to think, "Rahab lied to the king of Jericho to protect the Israelite spies."

"The prostitute?"

"Yes. But not only was she not condemned for lying, the book of Hebrews may imply that her lying was the very expression of faith that she was praised for."

"You mean her lies are what got her into the Hall of Fame of Faith?"

"More or less." Naomi was half-way through with her coffee and the caffeine was doing its work nicely.

"Okay. Give me one more example – this time not a hooker."

"Hey! That's not fair! Rahab ended up married to a wealthy Israelite and mothered a child who ended up becoming King David's great grandfather and an ancestor of Jesus."

"Sorry. Any priests or rabbis?" Hopeful.

"Yes. Actually, now that you mention it."

"A priest lied in the Bible?" Via obviously found it funny.

Naomi ignored her smirk. "The prophet Samuel – he was both High Priest and Judge of Israel. He served in place of a king, like a president or prime minister, until Saul was anointed the first king of Israel. Interesting thing about it – God himself is the one who told Samuel what to do."

"God told a priest to lie?" Via sounded incredulous.

"Not exactly."

"God instructed Samuel to anoint David as king over all Israel while Saul was still their monarch. Needless to say, the prophet objected. So God...."

"A prophet *objected* to what God told him to do?" Via's French accent was quite pronounced.

"Uh ... yup, happens a lot, actually. The Bible is full of examples."

"Wow! If God spoke to me, I'd...."

Naomi stopped her with a stern look.

"Well, okay," Via conceded, "I really don't have much to do with *God*."

She whispered the word as if suddenly forbidden. "I'm not sure what I'd do if *he* actually spoke to me."

"Anyway," a smiling face continued, "Samuel protested that Saul would kill him."

"The Bible speaks of other prophets who told God off?"

Naomi gave her another look. "Are you going to keep interrupting me?"

Via's face showed stubbornness that seemed to be receding. Naomi wasn't sure. There was no verbal response.

"They didn't *tell him off per se*." Naomi's voice betrayed her frustration. "Moses retorted that he couldn't speak well. Jeremiah complained that he was too young. Jonah ran away."

"*L'homme* that got swallowed by a fish?"

"Yes. The man that got swallowed by a fish. Are you gonna let me finish?"

"Please do." As if Naomi was to blame for the interruptions. Via's cup was empty. She stood and strode off back into the kitchen. From the other side of the granite counter top, "Continue, *s'il vous plaît*."

Naomi started, "So Samuel didn't…." The steam started whining. The brewer churned at a high pitch, competing for attention. Naomi yielded to a weak smile and finished her own latte. Patience.

Via waltzed back to the table. "Sorry." A sheepish look. "So Samuel was afraid of Saul."

"Yes. He was afraid of the king." Naomi's mouth dimpled up at the edges. She paused and cut her eyes with a long pause.

Via got the hint. "I won't interrupt. I promise."

"So God," Naomi said and then hesitated with a crinkled smile, "told Samuel to bring a sacrifice with him to Bethlehem. He told him to tell everyone that he was there to offer a sacrifice for David's father."

"But he was *really* there to anoint a new king." Via couldn't stay quiet.

"Uh huh." Like Oprah.

"Subterfuge." A thick French accent again.

"Pretty much."

"God's idea." A light bulb moment.

"To protect Samuel. To protect David. Jesse."

"Who's Jesse?"

"David's dad."

"Oh." Then, "Wow!" She put her cup back down onto the table. "So you think God was okay with the true shroud being hidden away and the fake shroud being used to protect it?"

"I would think so."

Via bit her bottom lip. "What do you think God's reaction will be to what *I have just done?* I mean, I'm the one who has exposed the covert plan. I'm the one who has ruined the whole thing."

"I...." Naomi started not knowing what to say. She'd not thought about the issue.

Her phone rang. Saved by the ringtone.

"Naomi," Joshua said, "I need your help."

SHE LOWERED HER gun.

"*Abuelito!* What are you doing here?" Her voice sounded like the eight year old girl greeting the gift-bearing patriarch at the front door of her parent's home in Vista Alegre.

"I thought you knew I was here, Pumpkin."

A flood of memories made her own knees weak as well. "Come in. Come in!" She was now doing everything to make him feel welcome. "I almost killed you. Yes, I knew you were *here*, but it's, what? Three in the morning? *Über alles!*"

He looked at his watch. "Almost three-thirty." As if it made some difference.

"Why are you here?" She was pulling a robe over her nightclothes.

Heinrich shuffled over to the nearest seat. "I had to talk to you."

"We were supposed to meet for breakfast, or lunch. I'm actually not certain now. *Abuelito.* I would have come," she assured him. Her tone was sweet and remained child-like.

"I didn't think you'd show."

She pulled up a chair and sat across from him. Close.

"I...." She stopped on her own. Doubt had crept into her mind.

"I have things I have to tell you. I'm dying, child. Things I should have told you a long time ago, Pumpkin. Things I told your mother. Then she told your father and … unfortunate things. *Abscheulich.* Worse."

"That's why we left for London?" She leaned forward on her seat.

"I assume so. Your father was very upset when he found out."

"*Abuelito*." Endearing. "I'm so sorry." She reached out to hug him.

He blocked her embrace. "*Nicht wahr?* You surely will be angry when I tell you. Pumpkin, you will hate me too. I'm a dying old man, and I must. You deserve to know the truth."

"*Abuelito.* I will not hate you." A solid statement. She reached again.

"Pumpkin, just hear me out first." He turned from her in sadness.

She moved as close to the feeble old man as he would allow. Their knees were touching. Her face crowded in towards his.

Heinrich looked back into Mandy's eyes, and from behind a vacant stare he said it.

"My name's not Heinrich Stauffenberg."

Silence.

He looked into her eyes.

She looked into his. "I already know."

Heinrich's eyes grew wide.

"*She* told you," he said, stumbling over the words.

"Mum never said. *Papa* neither."

"Then how?" He lowered his head with sad eyes and a wrinkled frown.

"I do research for Via when we're not in the field." Mandy put her hand on top of the large protruding veins coursing over the back of one of his hands. "Your *name*. It came up a lot."

"My *real* name?" Desperate. Weak. "*Feste Gott.*" An orison, not a curse.

"No. Stauffenberg is a famous researcher among students of antiquities. You are respected and quoted world-wide." Mandy beamed. "I'm very proud of you."

"But…," he stammered, with great drops of tears flushing over the rims of two lower lids.

"I'm sorry, *Abuelito.* I found your *real* name buried inside one of Jundishapur's blogs."

"*Ibn*," he snarled. Then the growl vanished. Fear entered his tone. "It's on the Internet?"

"Not enough to come up on any searches. I found one minor mention of it. Like I said, it was buried. The blog was a bit incoherent. Long. Tedious. Probably no one read it." She wrinkled her nose. "I'm not sure, but perhaps he was a bit inebriated at the time. He put a '[sic]' after your name along with an aka disclosing your former name. If anyone had read it, they likely wouldn't have paid any attention to it."

"*Weltbild*," he said, shaking.

"Everyone loves you."

"But not the *real* me." The tears were streaming down his corrugated cheeks.

"*Abuelito*," Mandy said with her child's voice.

"Wait a minute," he gulped and then froze as if suddenly paralyzed. "If the blog revealed my true identity, then...." Furrowed lines pulled at his eyes.

"I'm sorry," she pleaded.

"You checked me out." He saw the admission in her hazel irises and he could no longer look at her. His head hung on the end of a limp neck.

"*Abuelito*. I'm sorry. I shouldn't have." She squeezed his hand.

"You don't owe me an apology. It is I who owe you one, and an explanation. Don't you hate me?"

"No."

"But I was not *Abwehr*. I was not part of the People's Front. I was not *Schwarze Kapelle*. I was *Schutzstaffel*."

She cried, holding onto both of his hands. Her forehead leaned into the wisps of grey that languished on his crown.

"I...." He cringed. "I was SS. So how could you possibly not hate me?"

"That was a long time ago." She was barely able to force it out between sobs.

"I lied to you."

"I've forgiven you for that."

"How could you?" He let his anguish pour out into the hue that colored each word. "I was at *Kraków*. We.... We were murderers."

"You were young."

"I was an adult."

"You were under orders."

"I should have run. I could have left the country."

"You...." She had run out of excuses for him.

"I was *never* punished."

Silence.

He hung his head further over his waddled neck. His salty tears washed down over their clasped hands. Neither was able to speak for some time.

Then he mustered the strength. "As the war was drawing to a close, they put me on a U-boat. I disembarked in Buenos Aires with thousands of men like me. War criminals. They took us *here*. Here, where dozens of plastic surgeons worked around the clock. We were given new papers. New lives. I.... I was sent to Santiago. But I ran. I ran away from who I had been, from what I had done, and from who they had made me to be: from my old life. From my new identity, I ran to *Gott*. I begged him for mercy. I had done terrible things. I have spent the rest of my life trying to make up for what I did back there in Poland. But the guilt has not left me. It invades my thoughts. It controls my dreams. I've had the nightmares now every night for almost seventy years."

"You say you were never punished?" she suggested gently.

He responded by raising watery eyes to look into her face, and here, now, he regarded his only granddaughter. The only child of his own only child. And he sobbed.

"*Abuelito*," she concluded, "you have punished yourself more than they ever could have punished you. What could they possibly have done to you that you haven't already done to yourself? *Lebenswelt*."

"I just ... just want redemption," he wept. "I want to be forgiven," he pleaded. Then, "*Innigkeit*."

"Prison doesn't do that," she urged.

"The end of a rope would have. *Galgen*."

"Really?" She cast him a life line.

He was quiet. The tears dried. "You've really forgiven me. Haven't you?"

"I guess I have. I'd never really thought about it. It still bothers me. What you did. And how you lied to your own family about it. But I've missed you so bad. I regret the years we've been apart. I've thought about you so much. Not a day went by...."

"Has *she* forgiven me?"

"Mum? I don't know. I guess you'll need to come to London with me. We will find out." She gave him an encouraging look.

"My health."

"You must be almost one hundred by now, *Abuelito*. One more plane ride won't kill you." She allowed a small laugh.

He returned a smile and finally relaxed. It seemed he'd just now started to breathe. "Are you hungry?" he asked.

"Yes, actually, I am *starving*," she said, smiling past her tears.

"How 'bout we take some breakfast together, Pumpkin?"

"Sounds wonderful." She stood up with him and gave him a great hug. As they both turned towards the door to see if the kitchen down in the lobby was stirring yet, she stopped him, holding on to a thin arm.

"*Abuelito*. One thing, though. I'm curious."

He nervously braced for the worse.

"When you said they brought you *here* after the war for the plastic surgery and all, did you mean Argentina? Or Bariloche?"

"Pumpkin, everyone came through Bariloche before they disappeared after the war. And, when they arrived, *this* is where they all came."

"*Here*?" She raised her eyebrows high.

"*Here*, in this very hotel. The plastic surgeons worked their magic in this very hotel."

"*This* is where it all happened!" She shuddered.

٢٨

NAOMI WAS ON her phone.

Via decided to make her own phone call. After all, it was already past 8am in Paris.

Naomi got off her call before Via had ended hers. She immediately started drafting a text message and preparing to send it to several numbers at once. Her WorldOne App automatically pasted her text into her email as well, popping out a duplicate that was simultaneously delivered to the same group of people. Her first call was completed by the time Via had hung up her phone.

Naomi stopped dialing her next call.

"What'd he say?" she asked.

"How did you know I'd call *him*?" Via's eyes darkened.

"Remember when we first met."

"How could I forget. You were just a child."

"I was in college."

Via gave her a look.

"Yeah, okay. Right. I was still a child." Then, "When you saved my life at that train station…."

"It was nothing." Via's accent was back.

"You saved many lives that day."

"I just happened to be at the right place at the right time," Via lied.

"The bomb would have killed hundreds of us."

"I got lucky."

"When you took me off that bench and whisked me away…. I could see it in your eyes."

"What?" Indignant.

"The same look. The one you had just before you called your father."

They shared the early morning silence that ensued.

They both heard it.

Coming from the other room. Knocking. Naomi and Via left the kitchen and dinette behind and passed through the living area, wondering who it could be.

Via opened her door. Two figures stood before her hand in hand.

"They won't serve us until 6am," Heinrich said quietly.

Mandy slipped past Via into the large living area past the foyer. "Wow! I could fit *five* of my rooms in here."

Heinrich stood in the hall as if unwelcome.

"Come in, Herr Stauffenberg. Come in." Via took him by the hand.

"*Guten Tag*," he managed. "Do you have eggs?"

"No," she laughed, "just coffee and *croissants*." She thought about the request for a bit. "I have assorted jellies and jams. Real butter."

"Room service is open 24/7," Naomi suggested.

"Of course," Heinrich stammered, "I should have thought of that. Pumpkin, come. We will let these ladies be." He turned toward the door.

"*Pumpkin?*" Via looked at Mandy with a crooked grin.

Naomi jumped in too. "Don't go. I have some questions for you Herr Stauffenberg. We could use the extra time together." Then she saw Mandy's face. "Oh. I'm sorry. If you two need some time alone…."

Mandy's voice squeaked, "We will find the time later. We'll stay. I'll make the call to room service. What shall I order for the rest of you?"

Naomi led Heinrich into the dinette area. After they sat, she showed him a document on her phone.

Via was ordering for herself and Naomi. Mandy was already on the phone with the kitchen staff.

"Dear," Heinrich said, "I'm sorry, but I can't read text this small at my age." He handed her back the glowing screen.

"I'll read it to you," Naomi said. "Mark's gospel." She scrolled down. "The original was kept with the shroud. At least up through Edessa." Then she read the entire document to him.

"My research confirms this," he responded.

"From Jerusalem they took it to Caesarea."

"Yes. But not just Mark's gospel ... Luke's and Matthew's original manuscripts as well. Joseph of Arimathea had the money and connections to protect the gospels along with the shroud." Confident.

"What about John's manuscript?"

"It wasn't with the others at that point. The Elder was in India at the time, on the Kerala Coast planting churches. He took his original manuscript with him. But several copies had already been made. One stayed in Jerusalem and there was one in Antioch. I don't know where the others were at that point – likely strung along Paul's path. He took copies of the gospels with him when he traveled and left them with the churches."

She looked back at him. She'd never thought about that before. It made sense. She scrolled back up to the middle of the document to refresh her memory. "From Caesarea to Cyprus. Mnason's house? Is that how you pronounce his name?"

"Yes. The gospels were there along with the shroud for almost a year."

"Then to Alexandria. Then Antioch."

"It was on display at the university in Egypt for several years before they moved everything to Antioch."

"The original gospels? The shroud?"

"Yes. But the historians ignored the importance of the event."

"Then what?"

"Mark's manuscript eventually got separated from the rest. After Antioch, everything ended up on display at the university in Edessa, but Mark's gospel was taken to Malta for four months. It was then taken to Minorca, on the island *Isla Baleares*. From there it landed in Barcelona and then Cartagena."

"You really tracked it down. I'm impressed." She smiled.

"But then I lost it. It disappeared during the Napoleonic wars."

"It still amazes me that the original manuscript of any of the gospels lasted that long."

He gave her an enigmatic smile.

"All right," she concluded, "we will cover all of this during our shoot. It's planned for the first half. Then, we will turn to the crown of thorns. I will have you examine it while we...."

His face went white. But he didn't waste any time interrupting.

"You have the crown of thorns?"

*　　　*　　　*

THEIR TRANSPORT shot out of the tunnel into a faintly lit cavern. The cave was rough with loose and jagged rocks. Weird lighting made it appear wild and unfriendly. The ceiling was barely one hundred feet above them and was covered with a dense, hanging forest of stalactites. The air was so wet that the front windshield of the transport immediately fogged up with droplets of condensation. An underground river ran a course on the far side of the uneven floor.

José and Arkesha looked above the turret they were in and shuddered at the thought of one of the heavy formations, like inverted unicorn horns, breaking loose and dropping down onto their heads. And there was briny mist that was laced with the smell of sulfur.

"We are near the sea," he announced.

"This place gives me the creeps," she said, shuddering.

The weak fusion of olive-colored illumination mixed incongruously with the dampness of the black air. They couldn't find the source of the light, but Arkesha wasn't about to leave their vehicle to find out.

"I'm going inside."

And she did.

The carrier slowed to a stop. Michelle slid out of the truck and down onto the dewed rock: an uneven surface strewn with puddles of dark liquid. She walked purposely, but carefully across the stone floor of the cave. She slipped a little on the film of water that streamed in rivulets between the small pools. Two of her soldiers followed out after her. Each carried a small metal box along with a spool of insulated copper wire. The trio headed for the entrance of the tunnel from which they'd just emerged. As expected, the LAV was far behind them. It had been unable to keep pace in the cramped confines of the ancient tube.

Michelle listened as she stood in the shadow of the tunnel's exit. She could hear the distant sound of the truck's tires and the motor's chug. The driver must have been doing 10-15 km/h – if he dared that. Without the radar guidance to keep them off the sides of the squared burrow, the LAV couldn't go much faster. Zelfa was an expert driver, but the radar system was necessary as the clearance was simply too narrow for error. Michelle considered their situation for a few minutes. The final LAV pursuing them resembled an H-1 Hummer with an open bed. It carried a mounted cannon on its back. It would be another ten minutes before it arrived here. They had plenty of time.

She turned to look back at their own vehicle. The safety wheels, that had protruded from the sides of the transport as an extra precaution to keep the carrier off the tunnel walls, were retracting into their horizontal berths. They could go on without delay, or take the time to block their enemy from further pursuit. She made the call.

Her ordnance crew strung the wires so that the detonators were connected to one end of each fuse. In turn, they would activate the contacts inside each box. The rectangular containers were slightly larger than an ordinary car battery. One was placed on the left and one on the right against the tunnel walls, about four meters inside the tube. The two soldiers were now walking backwards, unfurling wire from the spools until the lines were stretched out to within a short distance from the transport's open hatch.

Miguel came out to talk with Michelle. He climbed down the dampened ladder and made his way gingerly over the wet rock.

"Oh!" Sarah exhaled. The high-pitched exclamation was not as much a word as a primal gasp. Joshua felt her feral fear but didn't understand it. She let go of his hand and disappeared down the rat-line after the Pope.

Arkesha made it to the bottom of the turret steps and turned to face her husband. "You coming?" she asked.

"Not just yet. I have a bad feeling about this." José gritted his teeth.

Once on the ground, Sarah paused and looked over at Michelle and the Pope, then quickly began closing the distance between them. The two soldiers had already finished their set-up and now stood at the end of their wires waiting for the command. The metal boxes were poised, anxious to unleash their TNT fury.

Sarah rushed up to the Pope, careful not to slip. "There's something wrong," she said.

Bear was the first to see the black shadows that rose up from the inky waters at the far end of the cave. "Hey!" he yelled.

Yusef was looking in the opposite direction. "What?" he asked as he turned his head.

"We need to leave. Now!" Sarah was yanking on the Pope's arm.

Michelle almost tackled her in defense of the Pontiff but stopped short.

Joshua heard Bear's yelp and rushed into the truck's cab to answer the frantic call of distress.

Zelfa immediately disengaged the emergency auxiliary jeep and her foot hit the accelerator.

Arkesha fell. The heavy machine was lurching forward. It's tires dug into the crevices that ran across the stone surface and catapulted the transport forward.

José braced underneath the strong arms of the turret's gun. His eyes searched their dim surroundings, and his hands readied themselves for battle.

In the tornadic confusion that followed, one of the modern wicks got lit. A great explosion rocked the cavern and a brilliant orange light washed out the eerie greenish haze. Half of the tunnel's exit was blocked with falling rock and debris.

Sarah and the Pope were rushing back to the transport as Michelle drew her weapon and spun around. But the carrier was racing off beyond their reach, running for the water's edge, headed for the subterranean river.

"There!" Joshua pointed at a line of heavily-armed divers coming out of the water.

Zelfa saw them. She turned the small steering wheel slightly to her left and headed for the greatest concentration of attackers, like a great bowling ball aiming for the head pin.

José's cannon swung around. He sighted the first of their enemy as the rapid fire of fully-automatic rifles bounced off the many angles of their underground drum of stone. He released the massive shells of his Ma Deuce, spreading them generously among the men that crenulated the shore of the dark river.

Zelfa's quick action had left a lifeboat for the Pope, Sarah, Michelle and her crew. It had appeared from under the back of the carrier like a goose laying a golden egg. Sarah grinned as she ran towards the fully-armored jeep that sat right where the transport had been just moments before.

Behind Sarah and the Pope, Michelle was laying covering fire, moving quickly to catch up to them, searching the shadows for the most direct threats to her charge. One of her soldiers was already flanking her and assisted in the task. Both were using their HK416 assault rifles expertly. The other soldier had stayed behind to activate her dynamite.

Zelfa careened the amphibious carrier into the attacking soldiers. The nearest figures dove out of the way while the others continued to pepper the transport's armor with lead.

Bear's eyes were searching the enemy line from one end of the water's edge to the other. That's when he saw it. "RPG!" he yelled. It was aimed right at them.

The missile was thrust out of the launcher, coming straight for Yusef's side window. The amphibious craft was already at the water's edge, poised to launch off the ledge.

And then it did.

The armored carrier took off, flying through the air like a humpback whale. Like the marine beast's graceful dance that creates an awesome splash as its bulk flops across a wide swath of the water's surface, the amphibious vehicle dove off the bank.

José, with the craft air-bound, was still clearing off the deck, washing away the threat with an awesome spray from the power of his weapon. He found the mark he had been searching for and a massive shelling burst from the M-2 and headed straight for the source of the RPG assault.

Arkesha, hanging on, had made it back up the steps and was now at her husband's side once again. Quickly she grabbed the nearest pistol from a cache of small arms that lined the wall next to the munitions bin and braced herself opposite José's aim. Using a Walther PPK, Arkesha started picking off enemy soldiers, one by one.

Miguel was behind the wheel of the jeep. He backed it up quickly to protect, and then retrieve, the final soldier. Sarah was in the passenger's seat up front with the Pope. Michelle had slid into the back seat with the door propped open and her weapon still peppering bullets, now laying a cover for her still-exposed ordnanceman. One soldier was in the jeep, busy across from his commander, working hard to stop the bleeding in his side. He'd been hit.

The other bomb-specialist was running and ducking, spraying lead from her own HK as she made her way towards Michelle and the jeep. The Pope was handling their escape like a pro. Sarah immediately pictured the lead actor in *The Transporter*. Miguel would make a great action hero, she thought.

The warhead would have hit the amphibious transport but for the drop. The surface of the inky water lay almost a meter below the rocky shelf. If not for the massive displacement of liquid that its weight created, the carrier would have been destroyed. The drop plus the great depression of water allowed the grenade to miss impacting the side of the vehicle. The missile's widest edge, instead, burned the corner of the carrier's roof line. It marked the steel with a tell-tale scorch. Everyone inside the armored amphibian shuddered at the skin-crawling sound of the near miss.

José's flying shells lined up nicely with the end of the bazooka's barrel. The soldier was still aiming for his second shot when he realized his fate. A single AP round blasted into the man's weapon, creating a great ball of flame. The mass of fire and burning matter was forced back across the surface of the murky water. The reflection of the explosion racing through the air traced a line of bright orange all the way to the other side of the underground river and crashed into the wall of stone on the opposing bank. The granite surface from where the RPG had launched a few moments ago was now empty. The enemy never got the second shot off. The only sign that he'd even been attacking from that spot was a grave marker of steam rising up off the wet rock where he had stood.

Michelle's ordnanceman was still running. The young woman had almost made it to the jeep. But she was cut down within a meter of reaching safety – the harboring bulkhead of the B7 armor plating just seconds away.

"Marta!" Michelle cried out as the woman's body ripped apart and fell to the rock floor. Her skull was damaged beyond recognition, her chest a bloody mess. There was no need to wonder if she could be saved. Michelle reacted quickly by closing her door. "Drive!" she ordered. The Pope quickly reversed gears and the jeep squealed as it continued to slide backwards, tires spinning, now forward, vying for purchase on the wet surface, until it lurched forward and off to the left to follow the river's course.

The second blast at the mouth of the tunnel followed.

It was larger than the first. By design, Marta's charge was three times more powerful than the other, and she chose a delay that had only given her 30 seconds to make it to the jeep. The explosion laid waste to the entire scene.

The jeep raced against time to stay ahead of the blast. It did.

Just barely.

The dynamite blocks encased in the brittle alloy of Marta's box were as lethal as they come. The blast tore into the deep recesses of the Earth's crust and great boulders and smaller jagged sections of rock shot out from the center of the destruction. The stone projectiles fanned out in a lethal web of fury. Sharp pieces of ancient rock cut down everything in its path.

José and Arkesha saw the white ball of flame fringed with reds and yellows, and they dove back inside the carrier moments before a thunderstorm of stone rained down on their position. The Ma Deuce was bent to useless as the entire rear section of the boat was tattered and dented. The ship churned up the black water as its prow pointed them downstream, rising into the air with the gathering speed.

Joshua breathed out one frantic word, "Sarah!"

٢٩

"THEY HAVE THE crown of thorns?" Enson was facing her in the back of the Landaulet.

Peña confirmed it, "Yes. The Judean cap. The shroud. They may even have the missing Mark by now."

"There's got to be plenty of DNA on that crown," Enson mumbled to himself. Then his eyes blazed. He flashed a quick burst of anger towards Peña and hit his intercom, yelling at the *mestizo* driver, "Step on it!"

His driver nodded from the other side of the one-way tinted barrier as he feigned acceleration. He was already pushing the limo to the airport as fast as traffic would allow.

"Where are they now?" His saliva garnished the tone of his growl.

"Bariloche," Peña said with confidence, "and *he* is there."

"*The Nazi*," a satisfied snarl of anticipation. Then, switching gears with a seamless shift in tandem with the Maybach as they broke free from the traffic and sped up along *Avendida Oscar R. Benavides*, "Rome?"

"We lost three LAVs before they got to the tunnel. The last one hasn't reported in since they entered it. Our strike force was in place on the other side, last report." The limo turned onto *Avendida Elmer Faucett* and crossed into Callao. They were now only minutes away from LIM. Peña could see the anxiety on Enson's face.

"Sidney?"

"Only two. They'll be there by the time we arrive."

"*Collins*," he seethed.

She nodded.

"Are the labs…?" Enson's face showed a rare glimpse of worry.

"Heidelberg is still putting out the fires."

He swore streams of vulgarity.

"Basil thinks we can be operational again. Three days tops," she relayed the message.

He swore again. "Tuvalu had better be locked down. I want everyone on high alert."

"He doesn't know about Tuvalu," Peña assured her boss.

"You don't know him like I do." Roland's hands twitched nervously. He loosened his Armani silk tie. "Get Lucent on the phone. We have to know."

"I've been redialing constantly." She held up her device, showing him the screen's indicator that displayed the activity.

"Hupft." He kicked out his soles almost punching into her shins. "Soon these computers will do it all. And I won't even *need* a PA." The gruff volley was intended to throw her off balance. His eyes were lined in spiteful red.

Nonplused, she continued to stream continuous updates. "Tokyo is tracking for Friday. They were able to get Drs. Suri and De La Cruz off to Tuvalu already."

"They'll finish Beta by the time we arrive?" Enson was doubtful.

"I already…," Peña attempted.

"Without De La Cruz?" he responded, glaring at her.

"Yes." Definitive.

He seemed satisfied. The driver pulled the silver stretch parallel to the waiting Hawker 900XP. The corporate jet was humming, ready to take off as soon as they were aboard.

"Sir?" Peña took the opportunity, "You said *we*." It was a question.

"Hupft." As he got out of the car.

*   *   *

"THEY'LL BE IN Quebec as scheduled." She was leaving a voicemail message while walking out of the lobby entrance. The ancient scholar was shuffling behind her, trying to catch up. Their waiting car idled under the spacious canopy that was casting a long shadow over the concrete pad in front of The Brandenburg.

Naomi opened the nearest door in the back of the Lexus LX570 and ushered the old man inside. By the time she rounded the back trunk and reached for her own door, she'd dialed her office in Washington again.

"Oh good," she said, "you're in." Almost a question.

"After the text, email and the incessant ringing of your persistent App?" Celeste ribbed.

"Yeah. Sorry about that. Who else is there?"

"Everyone, boo. You know we love you."

"Aren't you an hour behind me?" Naomi asked.

"Two, actually, but it's no problem." Celeste laughed. "Well, except for Percy. He was out all night in Georgetown again." Not a sinister tattle.

"Figures." The boss smiled as she settled into her seat next to Heinrich and closed her door. "Who was the lucky girl this time?"

"Next in line, I'd guess." Her laugh was lighthearted, but there was a substantial weight that oppressed the tone a bit. Celeste had followed Naomi from Houston to their office in DC. She was in her mid-thirties but enjoyed the face of a twenty-one year old. At 110 wpm, Naomi couldn't find a better PA – smart as a whip, highly organized, and above all, incredibly driven.

"Girl, he's going to die young. But me? And you? We're gonna live forever."

As Naomi made her proclamation, she turned her ear to the sound of the raspy, winded breathing of the shriveled body sitting next to her. He was barely still inside that frame, crawling towards the finish line. It made her doubt her own youth: the optimism that assumes immortality, at least the temporary semblance of it. "Or, we will die and *then* live forever," she resigned.

"Enoch didn't." Celeste held on to the initial claim.

"You are *Baptist*."

"The Mt. Zion Baptist Church in Chevy Chase is hardly *Baptist*."

Naomi let that one go. "Boots?" All business now.

"1205 local."

"Wheels?"

"1300," Celeste boasted although she regretted that the vehicles wouldn't already be on the ground by the time the team of soldiers arrived.

"Cool. That works. Thanks. You are a miracle-worker. We are on our way to the shoot now."

"You know I'm upset with you, girlfriend," Celeste interjected before her boss could get off the call.

"*Celeste*." You know the inflection.

"The *Andes* too! You know I've always wanted to go there."

"Celeste, babe. I promise. Bangkok. Me. You. Next month."

"All right." A sigh. "I'm holding you to that."

"Thanks for all your help. Get the next team ready to head out by 1400 local. We're going to need all the help we can get in Tuvalu."

"No prob."

"Thanks again. I owe you."

"I'll cash in, boo. Don't you worry."

Naomi carried a big smile as she hung up and turned to Heinrich. "My best friend," she offered.

"Ah," the old man began, sharing the smile, "And you are able to work together. That is nice … and rare."

"We have our moments," she laughed. Then, thinking ahead to the shoot, "Any idea what happened to the missing Mark in Spain?"

*   *   *

SARAH WATCHED the amphibious carrier disappear into the dark recesses of the cavern's river. The wide band of water wound through the network of caves and underground culverts like a necklace of pearls as it connected with a series of subterranean lakes. Both the chambers of stone and the underlying stream meandered slowly towards the coast, the river emerging not too far inland from the ancient Roman port of *Lido di Ostia*.

"Joshua," she whispered as the jeep slowed at a rough patch of rocky floor.

The Pope was carrying them along the edge of the river but now had to turn off that path as the walls converged at the bank of the slow-moving waters. Their road now ran uphill, leaving the ruined cave behind. The jeep struggled over a rock-strewn surface as they traversed an ancient path that obviously wasn't designed for vehicles. The going became extremely slow as Miguel navigated around great boulders and carefully negotiated climbs up antiquated steps of stone. The caverns that laced their way out of the deep earth were widened in places and leveled out in others. It appeared to Sarah that at least some work had been done in more recent times to make the passageways somewhat navigable.

They kept moving. The escape vehicle was mounted on huge off-road tires. Sarah figured she'd need to upgrade her Bronco after seeing this machine. She twisted around and stared at the M-60 machine gun mounted in the rear such that it could be operated by a gunner in the back seat of the jeep. She smiled. Maybe she could get one of those too. It might come in handy while camping out in the Cascades.

Miguel was amazing. He'd managed to get them out of the cave, even with the massive explosion on their heels. He'd dodged rock after rock, climbing the jeep perfectly over the hardest path she'd ever seen. The CEO of Fiat and Chrysler would eat this up. What an ad campaign, she thought. They were now moving south-southwest, and she could smell the salty sweetness of the sea ... stronger now.

Then, the words all flooded back into the forefront of her mind. "Vow." The word was preeminent among them all. It was an enigma. He wasn't a priest, a monk, or anything of the sort, at least that she could tell. Then, the word "enamored" pushed its way to the front. "Love" shoved to the head of the line. And all along, his name flipped over and over, spinning endless emotions behind her eyes and down into her limbs as her heart grew larger and larger until it filled her entire torso. *Savior*, she thought. She'd looked up the meaning of Joshua's name some time ago. She saw him sitting tall on a white horse, far below the castle's highest tower. She'd been waiting to be rescued. Loneliness was her captor. She needed to be rescued. And he was perfect. He was the one that her soul loved.

"Sarah."

The Pope was saying her name.

"Yes?" she responded as if in the distance, in a place far, far away.

"There's something about Joshua that you should know."

Here it comes, she thought. The jeep had slowed again. They were now climbing a 25° slope that was irregular at every meter of ragged rock that skipped underneath their chassis. Then she heard her response, although she wasn't sure whether or not it was her speaking. "He told me. I...."

She wanted to say that she didn't believe him. That it didn't make any sense. That even a vow to God wouldn't matter under the circumstances. Because their love was.... But none of these statements of bravado could reach her vocal chords. No matter who was listening, she couldn't have formed the words. With the Pope her one-man audience? No chance.

"What did he tell you?" Miguel's voice became mystically flavored. She found it sublime and yet scary at the same time. He was maneuvering the jeep over a three-foot wide boulder that served to block the next impossible section of their climb.

"About his vow," Sarah said innocently.

"His *vow?*" The Pope's voice dove deeper into an alchemy of surreal.

The breath was knocked out of her. Her eyes became heavy, her lids sagged and her chest ached with symptoms that resembled the flu. But she managed to say, "Yes, he…."

Her words merged into a silence that they shared. The entire cabin of the vehicle let it gestate to full-term. But when Sarah's eyes flitted back to Michelle, the commander quickly restarted her hushed conversation with her soldier. The two in the back pretended to be entirely preoccupied with the logistics of their route into Ostia.

Finally, she spoke again, "He's *married*, isn't he?" Not icy. No hint of anger, just severe disappointment.

"That's just it," the Pope replied, "he's not allowed to marry."

"Because he made a vow to God?" She returned to what was now once again plausible.

"No." And then he thought about it. "Well, perhaps in a sense. But I certainly wouldn't put it that way. More like a command. I don't think he really had a say in it."

Although Sarah felt a little better that Joshua's claim wasn't completely off base, she felt an uncontrollable urge. Anger. It rose up from deep in her gut and it was unstoppable. "What's that supposed to mean?" She cut into Miguel with the sharp edges of her words.

Miguel took her response in stride. He looked into her eyes. He showed her as much warmth as he could communicate before he used words. "Perhaps," he said slowly, "the best way to explain it is to tell you about myself." A cauldron of smoky colors swirled over his words.

"Okay…." Hesitant. Understandably so.

"I know what happened to the Cardinal." Ancient magic, deeper than the earliest myth, his tone was full of power and brimming with restrained wisdom.

"The Card…?" She couldn't place it. Not at this moment. What would the Pope's own story have to do with Joshua's inability to marry? What would a Cardinal have to do with the Pope's story? She didn't even know which Cardinal he was referring to.

But then a picture flashed into her mind. Just this morning she'd been sitting in a lavishly decorated conference room at the Vatican. She'd been in the heart of the glorious city of Rome itself. She'd been sitting across from her one true love, enjoying the dawn's early rays that warmed her through the panes of melted sand. José had....

"*Isabella's* ring." Finally putting her thoughts together.

"That's right. *Isabella.*" He said it dreamily and with endearment.

She leaned her head to one side in wonder.

"And, I know that the Cardinal was able to retrieve his trunks."

"You do?" Sarah's confusion transformed into excitement. She'd not been entirely sure of her earlier hypothesis, despite the letters she'd studied. "Were the trunks in England?"

"Yes. He received them in short order. A very honest captain made good on his word. But alas, he was not able to return the contents of the three trunks to the locations where they belonged."

"Really?" Sarah was profoundly affected by the story.

"Sadly," he hung his head and continued, "they were intercepted and carted off to Paris. That's the last the Cardinal saw of them."

Sarah sat dazed and confused. Finally she said, "Do you know if the missing Mark was part of...?"

"Yes," he interrupted.

She felt as if her jaw fell into her lap. A feeling she'd never experienced washed over her, making her skin tingle and her heart feel light as a feather.

He continued, "Three original vellum scrolls in John Mark's own hand, Peter's personal eyewitness account, were safely tucked away in one of the trunks."

Sarah sat stunned. Her mind was a tussle of tangled thoughts now, her emotions overpowering her logic. She just couldn't think straight. After a long pause that would make worlds collide, she asked the only question that made its way to the top of the heap.

"How do *you* know all this?" She cut her eyes at him.

"Because Sarah," he said slowly and deliberately as he regarded her from behind his Mauritanian eyes, "*I am* Cardinal Martín de Aviles."

*   *   *

THEY WERE DROPPED off in front of the quaint stone-faced clock tower in the center of Bariloche. As much as any structure in the mountain town, the tower was reminiscent of Swiss alpine villages like *Bey* and *Villars*. Naomi had chosen the outdoor site for its striking visuals. She and Heinrich sat in canvassed director's chairs, receiving heavy doses of base and rouge. The old man drew the line, however, when his artist tried to cover his cracked, pale lips. The make-up tray got knocked over as he jumped up from his seat. His arms were flailing along with a string of "I never!" A protest of the indignity of it all.

The camera crew was in position. The lighting was bright and mounted at every angle around the small set. Shadows could not hide behind a single surface. The area in front of the clock tower was barricaded from traffic. The road that led up the hill from the corner was entirely blocked off. The street that ran in front of their set was cleared for a half-block in either direction, along with a small part of the sidewalk to the east from the corner.

The set work was done brilliantly. Props, surrounding the two facing chairs, angled out just slightly toward Camera One. A small round table on three wrought iron legs, nestled in between the two chairs, made the semblance of a cute little sidewalk café under the looming Bavarian clock.

Heinrich, now becalmed, shuffled to his spot and collapsed into the small chair. He was handed a real vellum scroll, yet another prop, but it upset him, and he put it down on the table as he lodged his complaint that protective gloves should be used under the circumstances. It took time for him to explain that his hands were dry enough, but the viewers wouldn't understand that they shouldn't do this at home without gloves. Naomi smiled. However, he was assuaged once he was made to understand that the parchment only looked old. It was made to appear so for the camera, and it was a blank scroll. A prop only.

Heinrich profusely apologized and shook his head in disbelief as Naomi took her seat across from him.

"I don't think I'm ready for prime time," he joked.

"You'll do fine," she assured him. "Are you miked up yet?"

"What?"

She laughed. "I need to get you hooked up to your wireless microphone." Naomi waved the audio tech over.

In five, they were ready. The director cued. She looked into the lens underneath the red light hovering over the round glass eye of Camera One.

"Friends," she started, "it is my great personal pleasure to share my time with you today. We are in for a real treat as we get to sit with the world's foremost scholar of Christian antiquities. You know Herr Heinrich Stauffenberg."

Naomi turned to her guest and with one look made him feel like the only man left on the planet. "Welcome, Herr Stauffenberg, we are thrilled to have you with us."

She began by asking about his granddaughter who was spending time with him here in this quaint alpine village deep in the heart of the Patagonian Andes. His face brightened and his voice came alive as he talked about Mandy. She then segued to his many decades of archival research in Lima with Acamayo.

"Did you have a clue, Herr Stauffenberg," she asked, smiling wide, her dark almond gaze sparkling like smoked crystal, "that all those years you were actually working hand-in-hand with the future Pope?"

"Well," he said graciously and with genuine humility, "he wasn't Pope at the time. But it was a great pleasure to work with him. Truly, he has been a good friend to me. He will lead the Church with wisdom and love." He paused with excitement in his eyes.

Naomi let the cameras capture the expressive silence.

The old man spread out his fingers and rotated wrists outward as he said, "It'll be like Solomon ruling the New Jerusalem."

She felt the shivers start on her forearms, race to her shoulders and stream down her back.

Another pause to let the statement sink in … then, "Tell us about your most important discoveries in over 70 years of digging."

He started with the documents he'd found that helped lead Via to the true shroud. Naomi had secured Via's consent to a full disclosure of her role in the research, but not the actual heist. Heinrich gave the viewer an intimate portrait of the history of Jesus' burial cloths all the way to Edessa and then the pre-Ottoman furtive escape into the night. He described the arduous journey on foot, as the brave monks risked all to make it to Constantinople. He put his audience right inside the Hagia Sofia, so they could imagine what it must have been like to stand under its grand basilica and gaze upon the shroud centuries before, when it was on public display in the Orthodox See. He got you to picture walking from the display of the shroud, to the cross, to the original manuscripts of the synoptic gospels, and other early Church writings inside one of the most beautiful of buildings the church of Jesus Christ ever constructed.

Then Heinrich took his listeners to the present day, with a brief description of the heroic efforts of the Savoie family and others, including the Vatican and the Patriarchate, to protect the shroud.

Naomi held up her hand in a prearranged gesture. It was designed to pause Heinrich's presentation and at the same time signal the grand entrance that they'd staged. To fill the small gap in time that had everyone waiting with anticipation, she urged caution. She assured the viewers that by the time most of them viewed the video of this interview, the artifact would be returned back to Istanbul.

A hush fell over every heart. Eyes clouded. An overwhelming Spirit of Holy washed the guilt and pain away as the simple wooden frame was wheeled in and rotated 360° so the viewers could see both sides. The loom-shaped display easel gently stretched the fabric over a thick back-lit section of Plexiglass. It made the ancient linen that held the photographic negative of the crucified Messiah translucent, framed just wide enough to showcase the large cerecloth along with the head wrap and the other strips of fabric. The presentation was spiritual. Beautiful. Powerful.

Heinrich stood. He was shaking. With Naomi's prompting, he explained every detail of the shroud. He was able to verify its authenticity in every respect and gave a point by point analysis of its perfect match with the Shroud of Turin.

"Finally," he said, "the carbon dating has yet to be done, but our team here in Bariloche has been examining the pollens." He smiled at Naomi. The key grip walked ceremoniously up to the pair and handed the host a sealed envelope.

She opened it. The white paper carrier had a short one-page report enclosed within. She withdrew the document and looked down at it briefly before handing it to her guest. Heinrich marveled at its contents. Where Naomi's expression had been reserved, his reaction was one of pure elation.

"Ninety-two varieties of pollen!" he announced as he read. "Fifty-nine of which come from within 50 miles of Jerusalem … twenty-five of which are *exclusive* to the area!"

There was another pause to allow for the significance of the data to be absorbed.

Naomi then drew his attention back to the blood stains that outlined the image of the skull on the cerecloth.

"Ah, yes," he said as his hand outstretched to point to the detail that shone in the middle of the lights on either side, "the blood that soaked into the fabric here," he pointed to another part, straining his compressed frame to its full height, "and here," his gnarled knuckles were pronounced but poetic as if he were moving in a ballet, "are consistent with a crown of thorns." He paused to accentuate the next sentence. "However, not a Greek-style wreath!" Another pause. Naomi looked into Camera Three until the red light answered her cue.

"Wait a second, Herr Stauffenberg," she started, "are you telling us that all of the great masters' oils got it wrong?"

He smiled as Camera Two caught the passion in his eyes. "*Every* religious painting, every sketch, every etching, save only a scant few – they got it wrong. They depicted Christ wearing a circlet of woven thorns. But," he paused, "the Romans in Jerusalem *consistently* used a Judean cap of thorns."

Naomi had donned protective gloves while off screen and now held it in her hands. Her fingertips gingerly placed to cradle the crown and present the true cap of woven brambles to her guest.

"Like this one?" she asked him.

She'd been insistent. He'd begged her. Pleaded even. Indeed, Naomi had refused to let Heinrich see it until this moment … live, on camera.

It worked as she had intended.

The lens captured the look in his eyes, the ethereal change to his complexion, a radiance – shining reminiscent of the Son of Man as he appeared in Patmos, seven stars in clenched fist.

Above her head she lifted the tangled mass of long, sharp talons that had punctured the scalp of our Lord and marked his bone with their razor-sharp points. She held it up to the image of the face of Christ. Matching thorn to stain, she felt immersed in the same worship she'd experienced aboard *The Ark*. The sound of rushing wind swept across the small assemblage of participants and the crowd that had gathered on the other side of the barriers.

Mandy had been standing next to the director's side. But now her tears turned to weeping as she turned to leave. Her head was down. She was praying as she walked. Barely opened eyes kept watch lest her shoes stumble over an obstruction lying on top of the pavement. But as she threaded her way through the entranced people, all still facing the set, she inadvertently bumped into a tall, lanky figure. Her head still down, she mumbled a quick apology and moved on. But as she swept past the man, a darkness shrouded his face and a strange walk ambled towards the set. He reached for his gun.

THE ICE HOTEL in Quebec opened early with the onset of predicted lows that would stay twenty to thirty degrees under the average temperatures for this season. *Hotel de Glace* in the northwest portion of Quebec City on the *rue de la Faure* normally didn't open until January. This was a grand occasion. It was the first time the establishment decided to open months early. And they did it with much fanfare. A huge grand opening party was planned. Tonight it was underway, marked by a thousand snowmobiles and a few hundred SUVs strapped into their chains over studded snows. It was during this lavishly appointed party that they attacked.

Hidden under all-white combat camos, a crack unit of former special-ops soldiers descended upon the frozen lodge. The huge blocks of ice that were artistically stacked, molded, shaped, and suspended made one of the most unique structures in the world. It housed a network of watering holes, a hotel, and dining rooms in a fashionable cave-like design. The huge igloo was packed with connoisseurs of the unusual along with those who love to see and be seen: the social elite, the privileged few who didn't have to work for their wealth and rarely did a good job preserving it.

As the soldiers rushed in, cocktails flew up into the air. Long evening gowns streamed behind scurrying heels. The penguin-dressed men fled for exits without a chivalrous thought. The storming troopers quickly secured the center of the main lounge and dragged in a heavy boring tool.

In seconds the wide-screwed drill was scraping away the icy floor, spiraling down to the hidden lab. The manhole-sized aperture sucked soldiers down into its frosty depth a short ten minutes from the inception of the operation. The test-tube riddled, stainless steel space below received them like a stream of white lotto balls that matched the winning number. In this case, the jackpot's matching ticket was held within the firm grasp of a very satisfied Celeste.

Hundreds of miles separated her from the action, but she was sitting in her Washington office watching the live video-feed like a White House peeping Tom glued to the lead Osama-cam.

"We're in." Her own voice echoed the mike of the unit's commander. Celeste spoke into a phone dialed into a sound file that rode the text message to space and back, until it reached Naomi's mobile device in Bariloche.

"The professor is coming down the chute now. Twelve minutes to extraction. Move!"

The crackled voice delighted Celeste. She passed the news along to her boss in the form of another recording. Then she glanced at her grandfather clock's narrow hands: twenty-five after. They'd be back out in a few short minutes. Their mission completed. Success. Sweet success. She wore a victorious smile.

*   *   *

THE BRIGHT GLARE reflected the puffy cotton clouds far below their 35,000 foot cruising altitude. The pilot scraped his ceiling religiously after leaving Lima. What little turbulence encountered didn't change the plotted path he'd filed. Avoiding radioing any alterations was part of his standing orders. Mr. Enson didn't like unpredictability. A rough ride he would tolerate. But any diversion, any digression, it would drive the CEO nuts. Lost time. Cost fuel. Unnecessary communication with the ground. None of his complaints made any sense to the retired Bolivian Air Force Lieutenant. Arellano maintained a steady throttle and kept the nose of the Hawker 900XP sniffing out the shortest, albeit not the smoothest, route to Bariloche.

"Sir," Peña spoke.

"What?" Dissonant. Not really a question. A demand wrapped in arrogance.

"Quebec is down."

"I moved it." Confidence.

"Sir." Persistence.

He had lowered his eyes back to his iPad. The conversation was over.

"Sir, they penetrated the facility. Everything is...."

He barely looked up. His eyes flashed his anger. "I *said* that it has been relocated. The facility in Quebec City is under...." He turned his attention back to his tasking.

"*Under* the ice hotel," she disclosed.

He looked up. How did she know?

"Melted." She used the imagery.

A frown, a heavy sigh, then he started breathing laboriously. It gradually increased in lengths of breaths and volume of sound until the blood that was rushing to his face deepened his complexion from crimson into a purple rage.

She watched him rise from his seat.

His steps were heavy. A warrior's walk. He could have been straddling a Mongol's stallion or leading a Spartan charge. Peña's eyes followed his frame as it stormed down the aisle and vanished behind the restroom door.

Other than Enson and the pilot, Ricardo, there was no one else on the plane. Peña looked around anyway. She pulled a tiny Nokia from a hidden pocket beneath the seam of her skirt's waistband. Her thumb masterfully danced over the keypad.

The text raced from her hand all the way to the satellite before dropping back to Earth like a bolt of lightning into the selected device at the other end. It was a simple missive. Direct. It would mean certain death to her if her boss ever discovered it.

"Bariloche ETA 1100 local. Enson + 30 boots. Air support."

*   *   *

NAOMI'S STAGE reverted to the outdoor café and they sat back into their seats to tackle the final subject.

"Tell me about the New Testament. We've heard a lot about the Old Testament since the Dead Sea Scrolls were discovered." Naomi spread out the foundation for the finale. "But most of us don't know anything about the origin of the rest of the Bible."

Heinrich gave a thorough overview of the gospels, the Acts of the Apostles and the Pauline Epistles, before touching on the other letters, the Revelation of the presbyter, and lastly the disputed authorship of Hebrews. Then he deftly swung back to the eyewitness accounts of Jesus' ministry.

"The originals got separated early on. John's likely remained in India. However, it is possible that his manuscript made it back to Palestine or into Asia Minor prior to his exile. Matthew's, along with both of Luke's books, eventually made their way to Constantinople along with the shroud and the true cross."

"But the original manuscripts eventually disappeared."

"Yes. But copies were being created as fast as the early disciples could get them written. Remember the printing press was still 1400 years away, so it took a lot of work, many hands, countless followers of The Way toiling long hours. Those who were literate, in their off hours, were hand copying the documents that now make up our New Testament. After time, it was a job that consumed the full-time work of many dedicated monks worldwide. Men as well as some women gave their entire lives to create copies of the Word of God."

"What about the original manuscript penned by John Mark?" she added with flair.

"Ah...." His hands became more animated as his face lit up. "The synoptic gospels were copied with consistent accuracy. There are so many copies with so few mistakes that we have *complete confidence* that the present existing manuscripts perfectly reflect the text of the originals."

"No issues at all?" she challenged.

"That's the extraordinary thing about the Bible. In both the New Testament and the Old Testament, over the span of 1500 years of authorship, over 50 different writers, all of the original manuscripts penned have been either lost or destroyed. But the thing is, we have *conclusive* provenance with regard to the accuracy of the texts: more than any other historical writing, *bar none*. The Bible was accurately transcribed, passing down to generation after generation the inspired Word of God." He let his tone create some tension at the end of his statement.

"Except?" she grabbed hold of his inflection and prompted.

"Except the Gospel of Mark. The last...."

"Lies!" an angry voice interrupted. "Lies! All Lies!" Screaming, a tall dark figure emerged from behind the cameras. He was running headlong for Heinrich.

And he was waving a gun.

*   *   *

NO ONE NOTICED. He had slipped out before Sarah had left the amphibious vehicle. He would call it curiosity. Watching experts set up explosives. What thrill-seeker would pass up such an opportunity? Why weren't José and Arkesha beside him? He wondered. They should have been out there with him. Watching. Experiencing the adrenaline. Facing the danger. But the risk caught up with him this time. At least he was alive. He had been hit. That was a given. He became disconcerted if not afraid. The bodies lying near him could barely even be called corpses, they were in pieces. He couldn't move. He just watched the dusty light settle in around him. It felt like the air had died along with the dozens of men and women in the cave. Already buried. Perhaps, already forgotten.

The light was faint. He figured the explosion had knocked out half of the lighting that had illuminated the cavern before the destruction was unleashed. The sounds had disappeared as well. The residue of a thousand tons of rubble filled his eyes, his nostrils, and seeped down into his lungs. He could taste the film of mud that built up on his tongue.

He tried to move again. At least his eyelids worked. At least both pupils captured images and his optic nerves properly received the data. He couldn't feel his legs. Even numbed limbs would be good news at this point. It would mean they were still attached. Since he was conscious, he assumed they were. He was surely losing blood, but not at a rate fast enough to have put him out. Not yet at least. He started praying desperately.

Ah, there. Good. Searing pain. It was burning in his right hand. He tried to look. Pinned – he gathered. The pile of rocky debris blocked his view.

And his ears worked. At first there would have been no way of knowing. But now he heard something. A grinding noise. The sound of a.... A motor! A motor straining to push weight over the strewn scene.

"Here!" he yelled into the cold, gritty fog, "I'm here!"

But no sound came out.

He tried again, "I'm here! Over here!"

It was weak. But audible enough. Maybe.

At least they hadn't left him here to die.

They must have left, but realizing that he wasn't with them, turned back to retrieve him.

I think I got shot before the second explosion. I fell before the blast. Perhaps that is what saved me. The bullet felt like being hit by a truck. I must have passed out when I hit the granite floor. The flying missiles of stone from the blast must have flown over me while I was out. At least the avalanche of spewed rock didn't completely bury me. His thoughts continued to meander, but the sound of a motor drawing closer brought him back.

"Hey! I'm over here!" He could feel his vocal chords working better now. Surely they'd have heard the call.

Michelle. That's really why he'd slipped out of the transport when he did. Is she the one coming to pull me out from under these rocks? He thought of what it would feel like. Her touching him. Her hands on his arms. Her fingers palpating for broken bones, for fractures and contusions. He'd make his next move then. Just as she had her face close to his own. Her arms would be tucked under his shoulders. Or perhaps one of her palms would be flat on his chest. That's when he'd smile. Tell a joke. Reaganesque. Make her laugh. Confess his feelings for her. Get a commitment. He was dying to have dinner with her. They'd hit the town. Rome. *Above ground.*

The motor idled. It was close. He breathed a sigh of relief. It made his chest hurt. He noticed the pain in his left shoulder now. It was enough to make anyone else faint, but he was used to pain. The skateboard park's half-pipe was his first instructor. The pains of strains and sprains and broken bones. The aches of still-mending skeletal structures as he'd tear into the ramps again.

His hand was throbbing, and now he was able to move his fingers. He rotated his wrist. He tried to lift his arm up out of the pile of rocks. Nope. He stared at his upper arm. It was shiny with dark blood, the red cloak wrapped around his skin like a layer of cellophane. It glistened in the hellish light. As his nerves started recovering from the shock, excruciating pain began to course through his entire body. For all of his injuries over the years, he'd never experienced anything even remotely close to this. His head pounded. His shredded side burned as if lain on hot coals. He started to convulse.

The sound of boots.

She was here.

Here to rescue him.

Jokes. He had to think of some jokes.

He couldn't think of anything.

He'd at least ask for a kiss.

A face. Her head leaning in? He puckered up his lips.

The sodium pentathol took his pain away.

* * *

"BUT THAT'S . . ." Crazy. You are a nut. Certifiable. Instead she chose to tell the Pope, "Impossible."

"Yes. Sarah." Fatherly. Kind. Disarming. Honest. "I know how it sounds."

Delusional, but nice, like a senile great uncle or.... Too bad the Pope is wacky. She would have enjoyed working for him. The orphanage trips were now definitely off.

"Holding that ring again. This morning. Wow! Amazing! I never even saw her face."

"Who?" Lost.

"*Isabella.*" Endearing.

"The ring." Just now registering. She could see his face. Just this morning. Their first meeting. Her photographic memory was a blessing, and a terrible curse. It kept her from focusing at times. From sleeping. Full color. Crisp cinema. What was she seeing in his face as he held the ring up to his eyes and turned it between his fingers in the morning light? Recognition.

She'd seen it then, barely, but through a glass darkly. A sentimental word. He'd spoken of her in a familiar tone then. And then ... a joke. No. A diversion. Sarah stared into his eyes. Who brought up Alex the Lion?

She remembered.

Her gaze flicked away from the Pontiff. She looked out ahead of their jeep. Back into reality. The caves. Their escape. Her love now separated from her by time and space. When she turned back to regard the claim, the Pope was looking away from her, his attention back on his driving. The beams of light that shone out from under the hood were broken by rock and crevice, crack and stone. Were the headlights searching for truth? Or just an escape? Just a path to the outside. A different reality.

"She sang," he said.

Sarah pressed silent lips together.

Miguel's dreamy voice continued, "Sad songs, but they comforted me."

Sarah didn't remember anyone telling the Pope that part of the story.

Joshua hadn't heard it. It was late at night that José spoke of *Isabella* again. José told the story that was passed down through the generations as if he had been on that ship with her.

"*No ser*," Sarah sang. Almost to herself. Her rich voice mimicked the mournful ballad just as José had whispered it in the room at the hotel. "*Yo mismo mi niña, otro día...*"

"*Sin ti, mi pequeño, mi corazón, mi gran amor....*" The Pope picked up the song perfectly and took over. His voice cracked as a heavy tear rolled down his cheek. "Her father," he explained, "sang it to her when he tucked her into bed at night. She.... She sang it for me from the adjacent cell in the ship's hold."

Sarah couldn't move. She was frozen with her own realization now. Fear gripped her. Her hands were shaking and covered with sweat.

"Joshua," she breathed.

They saw the light.

Daylight.

It reached for them. It pushed long arms inside the dark hole and dispersed the blackness.

Beckoning.

Miguel slowed the jeep. He cut off the headlamps.

The backseat's murmur quieted.

"I cannot marry either," the Pope added, "but not because the Roman Catholic church forbids it." He leaned towards her and put a hand on her arm.

"He loves you Sarah. He will always love you." Miguel looked at her squarely as her tears washed her face. "But you have to let him go."

*　　　　*　　　　*

VIA WAS AT the airfield. It was on the other side of the lake from Bariloche. Their reinforcements were scheduled to arrive any minute. Tran and Nena carried Benelli M4 Super 90 semi-automatic shotguns. Nena would have preferred a 12-gauge Smith & Wesson Riot Shotgun with 3″ magnum shells. But Tran got to pick from Via's extensive arsenal before they had left France.

They stood sentry at opposite ends of the long, snow-covered runway. It had been scraped by the plow and the gravel underneath was stirred up enough that Via felt confident the mammoth planes would find their purchase on the ground. The airfield was huge and level, a necessity for their purposes. The commercial airport on the other side of town wouldn't accommodate them in the least.

Keyontay was with them, but still sat behind the wheel. They had rented a burnt orange metallic H2, its reflection now ablaze off the bank of snow at the edge of the runway's end. He stared off through the afternoon sun at the corrugated metal shed that serviced the strip. It was a very small building. Not much for such a long airstrip, he thought.

Via was on her phone, standing several meters away.

"What's wrong?" she asked.

"I just had to leave." Mandy sucked back her tears.

"You left the shoot? Are you going back to the resort?" Via asked.

"No. I'm coming to you."

"That's not...." Via stopped.

"Via?"

"Yes?"

"Back at the set, what were they planning on using the guy in the robe for?"

HIS ROBE SMELLED of freshly sheared fat-tailed sheep. As he lunged past Camera One, he bowled over the director. He was taking great strides as he charged forward – straight for the old man who stared at his attacker, wide-eyed from his seat.

The gun in Ibn's hand assaulted the air, as if borne by a Taliban fighter on his horse rushing across a mountain ridge into the fray.

"Liar!" he screamed again.

The careening body stopped, grinding to a halt right at the foot of the old German's chair, the gun still brandished. It wove around in circles menacing an unspoken threat, as Heinrich mustered his response.

"*The Turk!*" he growled. He rose up from his chair, toe to toe with the attacker. Heinrich reached his full height, coming nose-to-nose with his adversary.

"It is *not* missing!" Spit followed each word, assaulting the Catholic's face. "And you *know* it's not!"

"*Heretic!*" Heinrich boiled over. "What do you care, *Nestorian?* Remember *Ephesus?* 431 AD? You and your kind were excommunicated!"

"*I....*" Ibn retorted with pride, "*I* am a *Jacobite!*"

"Jacobus Baradaeus wouldn't allow *you* to step inside his parish! You, Origen, or the rest of your kind. You are a...." Heinrich was screaming louder than his age should have allowed, just inches from Ibn's face. "A *false prophet!*"

The director was back up off the ground. He was brushing dirty snow off his clothes when he suddenly turned to his lead cameraman. "You getting this?" He pointed at the set.

The cameraman smiled as he trained his lens on the fight. The director was pleased. He checked. All three red lights were pointed in the right direction.

"*Idolater!*" Ibn shouted back.

"*Blasphemer!*"

"Gentlemen!" Naomi's voice rose enough for them to hear her. Professional, her tone was calm and warmly engaging.

Heinrich gave her a pleading look and sat back down with a crackling of brittle bones.

Ibn gave her a sheepish look. He lowered his gun to his side and started looking around for a place to sit as well.

Naomi stood.

Her graceful hand ushered him to sit in her own chair.

He obeyed.

The key grip had a third chair facing the two wrinkled faces in seconds.

Naomi pulled it a little closer to the scolded quarrelers and smiled at each man with twinkling eyes. Her countenance showed them a curious approval, greeting their meeting with respect and gregarious charm.

The stunned old men just stared at her. Bewildered. Hypnotized. Under her spell. They waited for her to tell them what to do next.

"Ibn?" Naomi queried the grey-haired Arab, "You *are* Ibn?"

"Yes. Yes, ma'am. Uh, ... Ibn Bukhtishu Jundishapur," he said it without thinking.

"*Jesus has saved,*" she said with a far-off look that matched her tone.

"You are correct," he beamed, "Jundishapur's meaning." He gave her a warm smile.

"Ibn?" Quietly, with respect and almost a motherly tone, "Ibn, will you put the gun away?"

*   *   *

BEAR WAS BUSY. He was calling out directions to an amused Zelfa.

José was in the middle of an excited conversation with his wife.

Joshua appeared in the cab. His face was bright red and yet drained of color.

"Where's Charlie?" he asked.

"Left!" yelled Bear.

"Port?" she asked with a smile as a wall of rock angled towards them from their starboard side.

"*Charlie*," Joshua reminded.

Bear turned to face the professor. He'd not even noticed him. "What about Charlie?"

"Where is he?"

"We left him?" Bear looked scared.

"He's not here."

"When did you notice?" Bear's eyes fretted.

"Just now. It's been…." Joshua looked at his watch but his mind drifted quickly to Sarah. He could see her. His heart leapt. He saw her eyes, her energy, her courage, her stubborn determination. He was back at the Vatican at sunrise. They were sharing coffee. The aurora of dawn right after he'd sent his confession of love. "Enamored." What an understatement.

"Almost 40 minutes since we left the cave," Yusef finished. "We'll be in Ostia in ten."

Bear was staring at the professor's jacket.

"Is that ice?" he asked.

HE WALKED INTO the lobby of the stately resort, cinching up his tie and kicking the snow from his leather soles onto the slick marble floors. His eyes exuded determination. He stormed past the front desk, cutting his eyes even tighter as he headed straight for the manager's office.

"Can I help you, sir?" the man managed before a bullet entered his skull through the cartilage at the bridge of his nose. The projectile pierced thin skin, quickly finding a brain underneath the ophryon before bouncing around inside the cranial cavity. The lifeless body slumped to the floor.

Enson snatched the key ring that hung like a prison guard's bell from the man's belt loop and slipped his silencer-ladened, Beretta 9mm back into his shoulder holster. His black Canali suit jacket barely bulged with the weapon tucked back inside, and the door puffed quietly behind him as he left the room.

One of the keys on the ring turned the deadbolt that braced up the manager's tomb, and the CEO's hard leather treads slapped against the Italian tile as he made his way to the bank of elevators down the hall.

He took a lift down.

From the lobby, the elevator regularly ran one floor under. But the brass button Enson pushed read LL. Its call had required yet another key. The panels soon parted and he could see the recreation floor. Ping pong. Billiards. Gaming tables in the foreground. Miniature golf and shuffleboard beyond. His feet stayed in place.

He turned the key another quarter turn.

The lift closed up again, and it began *another* descent, this one covert, following a path not taken for many years. Yet only one more floor down, the doors parted once again, and Enson stepped off the lift into a lavish world of ornate European decor. A magical world. Rich medieval tapestries greeted him. Greek busts. Egyptian relics. An original Rembrandt in a solid gold frame. A wall of priceless old books.

His aggressive stride over plush, carpeted flooring ran under an arched ceiling ten meters high. He paused and bent back his neck at the scenery riveting his gaze.

He remembered, but it would never cease to amaze him.

Fresco. Mosaic. Stained glass scattering a natural-looking light.

A mixture of French and Austrian architecture. A merger of the best of Europe's cathedral art.

He'd been away far too long.

He moved. Turned.

He followed a long hall that snaked underneath The Brandenburg resort until he was able to reach out and put his hand on the brass knob. It was the last door on the far left.

"Ah...." As if for the first time, he opened the door. He'd stopped his movements and just stared at the dimly lit room in front of him.

He smiled.

They were still there.

ARELLANO SEAMLESSLY landed Enson's jet on the runway. The terminal of the commercial airport that served Bariloche was busy. He taxied off to the north where there was a waiting luxury sedan.

Peña glanced back at the restroom door. Enson had been holed up in there too long. Was he okay?

*   *   *

IN THE CENTER OF the resort town, Naomi felt relieved to see the Makarov returned to its holster. She admired the wide leather belt that wrapped the thin Arab man in his long eggshell-toned robe. Then she saw the scabbard with the hilt of a short sword sheathed on his other hip. It was a good thing the shiny blade of the yataghan's wavy edges were shrouded inside the hard leather cover. Naomi decided to let it go.

Ibn's teeth clattered as he answered her queries, a series of tough challenges to his vehemence against Herr Stauffenberg only a few moments ago.

"He is wrong about the missing Mark," he concluded.

"*Ottoman*," Heinrich snarled uncontrollably as he unleashed the insult.

Naomi stayed focused.

"How is he wrong?" she politely asked Ibn, ignoring the old German for the moment.

"He's got it!" voiced with an accusing finger like a barren twig pointing out over the freshly fallen snow.

"Well, I *never!*" The Catholic was practically out of his seat again. "I've dedicated my life to…."

"Using the government to force your will?" The Eastern Church spoke from the grave. "On the Syrians. Against Armenia. Georgia. Mesopotamia. Not to mention the Moors and *the Jews*." Ibn's sword may as well have been unsheathed at that point. Naomi could imagine it thrusting itself into the middle of the German's chest.

But Heinrich parried, "I was the one who traced the shroud to Istanbul. I was the one who'd traced the path of the original gospel manuscripts. I found the crucial letters, the evidence of their journeys. I have dedicated my life to this cause, and the Gospel According to St. Mark is gone! Gone without a trace! It disappeared during Napoleon's march into Castile!"

"*Not true*," that's all the Nestorian said in a curt reply.

Heinrich just glared at the Jacobite.

"What makes you so confident, Ibn?" Naomi's steady voice was professionally toned and smooth as soft butter.

"Because…," he said, "because I saw it."

His eyes bored condemning holes into Heinrich's endive blue irises.

"I saw it," he continued, "in Berlin."

*　　　*　　　*

THE SOUND OF the cargo prop bounced off the crystalline surface of *Laguna Nahuel Huapi* as it lumbered towards the long landing strip. The C-130 had made good time, practically catching up with the much smaller transport plane that had landed only minutes before to off-load its soldiers.

Via waited to combine the force of the two deliveries. She never left anything to chance. Having already leased a fleet of Pathfinders, she had three of the Nissan trucks at the airstrip already filled with part of her new crew. They were motoring off to the rental lot to pick up the balance of the

Nissan fleet. Not armored. But boots on the ground, relegated to remaining on foot wouldn't do her any good. Not today, anyway.

She answered her phone, "Via."

"I changed my mind." It was Mandy. "I'm headed back."

"To The Brandenburg?"

"I'm almost there now."

"All right. Stay off that leg. Try to get some rest. I have a feeling things are going to heat up here real quick. The location of the stolen shroud has just been broadcast over the Internet around the world. Surely the authorities…."

"Via?"

"Yes?"

But the connection terminated.

*   *   *

SHE'D BEEN QUIET.

Too quiet.

"Are you okay?" They'd almost arrived. He'd steered their jeep out of the crevice in the Earth and down a narrow back road. Since then, Michelle had directed each turn, from secondary roads to dirt paths and even over the course of a meadow bisected by a pebbled stream. They'd made their way to Ostia's ancient port. Miguel was pulling into a place to park now.

He didn't get an answer.

Sarah sat staring out the window like her life was over.

Life as she knew it.

Or perhaps she was just trying to wrap her head around a radically different reality. Upside down different.

If, that is, *he* were to be believed.

Could the man sitting across the jeep's center console really be hundreds of years old? Could this man, who didn't look a day over 50, really be that old?

Could she have found true love just to lose it?

Or could she have befriended the Pope just to find out that the man had issues? Serious issues.

How does one prove a birth date anyway? What about those who were born prior to the advent of public records that kept track of names and dates of birth? Does a piece of paper "prove" the day of one's birth? Surely, even today, there are many born throughout the world whose birth is not part of an official record. Mid-wives. Rural births. Third World births. Public records are not often checked to verify a claim anyway.

"I'm 25. I'm 43. I'm 72." Who's to know? Or, "I was born in Atlanta. I was born in Michigan. I'm from LA." We just take his or her word for it.

Take his word for it.

How could she take his word? The Pope claims to have been a Cardinal back in the early 1800s. He's claiming to be well over 200 years old. How many centenarians are there alive now? Many. Top age? 120? 125? She couldn't remember. Surely no one over 200. Of course the Chinese have claimed…. The Bible records….

The Bible mentions some amazing life spans. 200. 500. Some over 900 years old. Sarah remembered Arkesha's detailed recollection and shuddered. She turned and looked at the man who had made this amazing claim. Miguel stopped. He turned the key. The motor died. They were parked in Ostia's shadows next to a pier. The harbor's waters were darkened under a shaded sky. The waves lapped up against the old bulkheads. They all disembarked.

Michelle quickly led them from the safety of the armored jeep and rushed them down onto the dock. They sped along splintered planks of rough-milled boards black with pitch and rainbow colored with fish oils and a million dislodged pelagic scales. The HK416 assault rifles of the two soldiers looked out over the rest of the fishing port as they ran the length of the iridescent carpet.

The afternoon sun shone over the aquamarine water in the harbor as the clouds shifted. The shadows that had blanketed this corner of Ostia's coast continued to draw back, revealing a quaint Italian village. Sarah couldn't see the monstrous ship at the mouth of the harbor at first because the sun's rays were peering out from over its shoulder, blinding her eyes. It was about 800 meters out from the end of the pier. A pilot sat in the back of a dinghy, holding an idling outboard that gurgled in the murky water behind him. Michelle was already untethering the small boat as her party, one by one, climbed into the little wooden craft. As Sarah took her seat, she looked back at the ancient stone bulkheads that made up the seawall at the far end of the little harbor. The old Roman port looked like a neat place to spend a weekend.

Instead, she was running for her life.

The shallow watercraft carried them over the dark and dirty portion of the water surrounding the piers. Suddenly, the color shifted underneath them.

Sarah found it a dramatic change. The saline waters that bore their boat had broken into a clear, light blue-green hue. The color of the Tyrrhenian Sea. As they got closer to the great ship, Sarah shaded her eyes and stared.

The ship was massive.

They were heading straight for a gigantic vessel that looked like a cross between an aircraft carrier and a catamaran. Its double-hulled design was connected far above the surface of the sea by another huge hull that carried a deck large enough to launch jets from its two runways. She had no way of knowing that it was modeled after the Joint Venture HSV-XI. This model, however, was built in Tazmania by special order for the Vatican. Its sky-blue tint glistened over the water and made it practically merge into the horizon. It was sleek, powerful, and very beautiful, she thought.

"What do you think of our ship?" the Pope asked her. They were seated opposite each other in the bow section just behind a pointed prow, his voice barely rising above the rushing wind and the slapping of the seawater against the tender's hull.

"Yours?" She had to raise her voice.

"It belongs to the Church ... had it built by the same outfit that did the smaller ones for Uncle Sam." He was smiling and shouting to be heard.

"I like it."

"Named it *The Piper Dolphin*," he announced with pride.

Interesting name, she thought. A piper cat.

Suddenly, the water in front of them bulged into a huge mound of briny blue, blocking the path of their small craft. It bubbled up and churned the beautiful waters into a dark and angry hill. A large black shape rose from underneath the bubble of sea. It boiled the waters and threatened to capsize the little wooden skiff.

The pilot tried to avert catastrophe. Heroically, he swerved and created his own great wake off the starboard side of the dinghy's hull. The wave he formed folded quickly into the water now streaming off the dark mass that was almost alive, towering out of the sea, and casting a great shadow over them.

The bulky craft rose up like Hemingway's great fish, and Sarah grabbed the rail behind her. The little launch cut deep into the water. The port bulwark was furiously taking in the temperate waters of the Mediterranean as their pilot tried to keep them afloat. The small boat lurched off a crest and thumped into the bottom of a great wave. The impact tore hands loose from the rails they were clutching.

Miguel reached out.

Sarah slipped out.

His hands grabbed for her.

She was washed over the side.

When the Pope had tried to get a hold on Sarah to save her, Michelle had jumped into action. She crossed the careening craft's keel and held on to her charge, keeping Miguel in the boat. Sarah had disappeared into the darkened waters. Michelle and the Pope both fell off the starboard side into the open hull, past the keel, and underneath the bench where Sarah had been sitting only moments before, Michelle's arms still clasped around the Pope's waist. Michelle looked up. The old Italian fisherman was clutching his till, holding on for dear life. Her ordnanceman was gone … washed over the side with Sarah. The motored craft swung back up to level and Michelle yelled a command to the pilot. He responded and raced away from the scene. They couldn't afford to search the water. She had to get the Pope to the safety of the ship. "Go!" she commanded. "Go!"

Sarah had seen Miguel lean towards her, reaching for her, trying to save her. She'd seen Michelle rush to grab him. She'd seen Michelle restrain the Pope while his Moorish eyes were pleading. Sarah's body left the aged wood of the tender and was flung out into the sea. The water swallowed her.

Sarah sank. The blackened brine sucked her into its depths and took her breath away.

٣٢

ENSON EXITED THE restroom and returned to his seat to gather his briefcase.

Peña was bewildered, but said, "Our Apaches will be here in ten. We have people on the way. They should be at the shoot within a minute or two." A matter-of-fact report.

"Good," Enson said and they stepped off the Hawker together.

"We have two in custody. Two kills." She chose her words carefully. "But otherwise, the operation in Rome failed." She waited for his tirade.

"Primary targets?" he asked.

"No, secondary. One of the mercenaries is dead, and one is presumed drowned. We have two of the students." No, you didn't succeed in kidnapping the Pope. What kind of business are you running?

A car was waiting. Roland brushed past her to the nearest door and had the driver moving even before both of Peña's feet were inside the opposite door of the sedan.

"Clock tower," he barked at the *mestizo* behind the wheel. Turning then to Peña he asked with a sly grin, "*Which* students?"

*　　　*　　　*

"*THREE TRUNKS.*" Ibn's tone was confident. "They looked like treasure chests. You know, like the pirates had." His eyes were glowing with intrigue. "Wooden. Strapped with iron bands. Rectangular, with rounded lids." His lips curled up into a smile. "I saw them in Hitler's bunker."

"Oh balderdash!" Heinrich burst. "You were nowhere near Hitler. There is no way you were in his bunker!"

"Oh, he wasn't there. He was off in his mountain overlooking Saltzburg."

Heinrich cut his eyes at Ibn. "Haven't we had enough already? Conspiracy theories. Nazi ice bases in the Antarctic. UFO alien technology possessed by the Germans since before Pearl Harbor. When will it end? The *obsession!*"

"But I did see them. I was there. And I looked. I saw. I looked inside the trunks."

Heinrich started cursing in German.

"But I saw them! The scrolls! The missing Mark! They were in one of the trunks!" Ibn seemed convinced, but his anxious tone was creating more doubt that it was allaying.

It was too much for the feeble old German. He boiled over. His thin frame involuntarily jumped up out of his seat like a spider from its hole. Long thin limbs reached out to seize the prey.

Naomi thought he was going for Ibn's throat.

But he didn't

Heinrich got both of his arthritic hands on Ibn's hair.

And yanked off the wig.

*　　　*　　　*

"WE CAN'T TURN back." Zelfa was firm.

"We have to go back." The professor's voice sounded like he thought he was in charge.

"I have my orders." She remained stalwart.

"Doc?" It was Bear. "What are we gonna do?" Bear's voice was imbibed with fear.

The transport shot out of the network of caverns. Borne by the waters that spouted from the caverns, they raced over the surface of the river until they joined up with the Tevere. The great channel led them to the coast and would allow them to travel south to reach *Lido di Ostia* via the sea.

"We'll make it to the Great Sea within the next few minutes." Yusef used a placating tone. "Michelle is in Ostia now. Once we meet up with her and verify that the Pope is safe," emphasizing the relative importance, "we will send a rescue team to retrieve Charlie."

José came up into the cab. "Professor," he said anxiously. "You gotta see this!" He handed Joshua his wife's mobile.

The text message read: "If you want to see your girlfriend alive, be in Bariloche by day's end."

Joshua found himself reading it out loud.

"Arkesha's phone?" Bear was confused.

"How are we going to get to Bariloche by the end of the day?" José asked.

"Who's girlfriend?" Bear twisted his face up into a new contortion.

"We can use the ship." Zelfa posed.

"A spaceship?" Bear picked up on the other conversation.

Joshua wasn't listening to any of it. He was staring into the backlit screen. He'd read the text over and over again. He was trying to figure it out. The message was on Arkesha's phone. But he was sure the missive was meant for him.

He turned to José.

"This text was sent only a couple of minutes ago." A professor's query.

"Yeah."

"The sender is *URWhiteSistah*." Joshua cut his eyes, deep in thought.

"Yeah." Urgency.

"Who's that?" Walker demanded.

"That's Sarah's phone."

*   *   *

"EVERYONE'S HEADED into town."

Via paused. She was on her phone again.

"I'm concerned about Naomi's safety."

"No. I can hear our cargo plane, it should be making its approach now." Another pause.

"Okay. We are picking up the Nissans now.

"No, the last plane should land in a couple of minutes."

Via looked up.

"I don't hear it now. I could have sworn that it.... We'll just have to come back later to retrieve our armored fleet."

She looked back down, her eyes skipping from one to the other of her personal guard, then on towards the group of soldiers waiting near the shack.

"No. Just Tran and Nena. Keyontay is in charge of picking up the Pathfinders."

She looked up again as if willing the plane to appear.

"Okay."

She stared into her Suunto and worried about the operation.

"Okay. We'll be careful. Thanks."

Her hand spun in the air. Tran and Nena came running through the snow.

"We have company in town," she said. "Let's roll."

They piled into the orange H2. Tran and Nena held their weapons as if a target may appear at any second, a threat around any bend. Via drove.

High above the Patagonian highlands a monolithic cargo plane laden with its heavy load chugged along. It had a dozen brand-new Mercedes SUVs in its belly. The trucks were recently customized with large off-road tires, steel-cabled winches, and brush guards. Each shell was armored with B7 grade steel plates.

As the C-130 finally started its descent towards the long strip on the far side of Bariloche's lake, the pilot radioed Celeste to adjust his ETA.

He was late.

*　　　*　　　*

"INTERCEPT THAT PLANE!" Enson barked into his phone. "*Shoot* it down! Is that clear enough for you?" he screamed.

Peña was making calls while standing outside the sedan. Enson was still sitting inside. He had ordered the driver to stop three blocks away from the clock tower. The Maybach 62 idled as Enson growled into his phone and started cursing one of his helicopter pilots. Peña shut her door to give herself a little quiet.

A convoy of black Suburbans pulled up.

The lead vehicle stopped beside Peña's tall frame, and an electric motor lowered a tinted window.

The driver's handsome face stared at her.

He wore an ugly smile.

Almost a full minute of ogling preceded his comment.

"We are going to rip them to shreds," he gloated.

"You're as bad as Jacks. Related?" she retorted.

"Mike is an amateur compared to me." He glared. The smile dipped. "My team is going to make mincemeat out of them all."

"Who?" She cut her eyes at the vaunting soldier. "The women?"

The skin underneath his eyes sagged.

"Or the old men?" She gave him a sardonic smile.

His glare spit back at her.

"He demands that you capture the German alive." A simple threat passed on.

"Special plans for that one, huh?" He relished the thought in his snarl. Peña could see the torture dancing in the flash behind his eyes.

"Just don't screw it up, soldier." Biting words. Peña looked at her watch.

The dark window rose as the platoon leader spun his tires so that the dirty slush kicked up in his wake.

Peña deftly stepped to the side. The brown melting snow stayed airborne just long enough to hit Enson as he opened her door to yell at her.

*   *   *

HE RAN.

Bear watched the Professor rush back through the center of the main cabin and disappear into the inclining corridor that led to the destroyed cannon. Joshua's face was distraught.

Zelfa pushed the craft out of Tevere's mouth and into the sea. "Eight kilometers," she spoke into her throat mike. "No. We're short one. A student." She cursed under her breath not sure if Michelle could hear the raspy expletive through the sensitive comms. "The surfer," she resigned.

The Greek woman endured a string of words. Yelling. Screams. She waited. Finally, she spoke, "We'll be at the ship in under seven. I'll go back myself." But her words were digitally reproduced only to travel into space and back to a dead line.

Bear's stomach churned.

He was heaving great breaths under his leather jacket. He ran after the professor. He was confused. He checked the seats that lined the walls of the personnel hold. He looked in vain in the back and in the turret. Where was Dr. Walker?

Shaking his head he walked back through the carrier once more, checking every place he knew a human could fit. He ended up standing outside in the back, underneath the battered gun.

The salty air was warm and the wind heavy, created by their incredible speed across the water. The sun's great ball hung high. It created a brilliant light against the back of a flock of puffy cumulus clouds that looked like ewes floating in the sky – bright white lined with silver rainbows. The horizon was a translucent light-blue that faded into a deep azure heaven overhead. The air that rushed over the front of the amphibious craft washed the back of Bear's head. It pushed every hair into a wet toweled mess around the edges of his face. He held on to the rail for fear of being swept into the sea at near breakneck speeds.

Where was Joshua? How could he have just disappeared?

*   *   *

HE DIDN'T HAVE to level the accusation.

Heinrich simply carried the evidence back to his seat. He shuffled slowly but his face was exuberant with his trophy in hand – a scalp of sorts – the prize of a battle as old as primeval savagery itself.

Naomi showed no sign of shock or amazement. The consummate professional appeared as if the entire scuffle had been scripted for a daytime tv talk show. She gave Ibn a look of compassionate prompting that said *confess lest we expose you further. I don't want you to suffer even greater embarrassment.*

Ibn got the message. She would attack. No matter how sweet the exterior, the Katie Couric-type ruthlessness that was unleashed on Palin would crush the man with matted hair. He looked naked, stripped of his dignity. His black hair pressed down tightly to his scalp, his eyes dropping in sadness. But he seemed determined: as if he wanted to get over this hurdle so he could return to the subject at hand, as if the truth of the trunks was far more important than the truth about his age that he was masking.

"It's true," he said as he allowed his false teeth to clatter upon the ground at his feet, "I've misrepresented my true identity."

Corrugated flesh peeled off from his forehead, then around ocular cavities such that the dark purple rings of puff melted into a much younger expression. "Living a lie is not easy," he continued.

The rest of his face, all but the same dark crystal eyes and hawkish nose, transformed into the same, but much younger, visage: the one seen by the young lady at the restaurant in the mountains overlooking Beirut. The transformation so transfixed the crowd that no one noticed the noise of the gun battle raging only a couple of blocks away.

"But," Ibn maintained, "I was, albeit hard to believe, in Berlin. It was late '43 and the Fuhrer wasn't around much during that period of time. We all crashed the bunker after Himmler...."

"Before you were born?" an old German's biting words.

The sarcastic remark didn't seem to bother the Arab. "The trunks had been stolen from the vaults below *Musée du Louvre* in Paris. Hitler's stash was full of paintings, busts, books, assorted sculptures, antiques, and jewelry. The treasures came from all over Europe and North Africa, from monasteries and temples, from museums and private collections. Plenty came from the Vatican. And it all disappeared before his alleged suicide. Carted away along with the thousands of...." He turned and looked at his stolen wig and then up to the wizened face above it, "Along with the *war criminals*."

The German exploded, "You would have us believe that you were in Hitler's bunker near the end of World War II! In 1943!" Heinrich narrowed his own aged lids as he regarded the middle-aged man seated across the little round table from him. "You lie! You couldn't have been there!" he stressed, seething.

Ibn felt defeated. His strength ebbed until he could barely stay erect in his chair. Great tears formed in his eyes as he prostrated his tone at the German's feet. "Please," he begged. His cheeks licked at the stream that found its path across the mask-reddened skin. The tears coursed in steady succession down his face and fell to the cobbled walk. "Where did they send the trunks?" he pushed his plea. "Surely you know. Surely, *together*, we can relocate the scrolls."

At that moment, for some reason, Heinrich believed.

He didn't understand it. He didn't know why. Perhaps he never would. But somehow, he knew that Ibn was telling the truth. It was a question he'd never considered before. When he was whisked out of Krakow to Berlin, then north to that cold Baltic port with all of the other officers, what was in all those crates? He would never forget the docks, loaded with huge wooden crates like so many PODS filled with accumulated life treasures destined for perpetual storage. He'd never allowed himself to wonder what his superiors loaded onto the waiting ships. He was busy being corralled into one of the u-boats. He was off to Buenos Aires. He was only in his twenties.

So now, over 7 decades later, he was finally considering the contents of the crates. Why? Because his nemesis, *the Turk*, was imploring him to do so?

No. It was something else. He was about to respond to a much older plea: the one rejected by his beloved Church in 431 AD in Ephesus, the one rejected in Chalcedon in 451 AD. What may have been proper in Nicaea had gone horribly awry. And an entire network of churches, monasteries, Christian universities, and families of believers in Syria, Ethiopia, Persia, India, and China, to name only a few, were abandoned, left to fend off the militant Caliphates alone, naked to ward off the mongol horsemen, excommunicated to a horrible fate as the Ottomans finished off what was left of the Eastern Church. What was once hundreds of millions of Jacobite and Nestorian Christians in the Near East and beyond, were systematically exterminated while the Church in the West watched from its self-righteous throne.

The Church was Heinrich's life. His work for the diocese was his chosen path to his own redemption. Like Bernard Nathanson's penance, Heinrich would try to undo the damage he'd done. He had sinned. It was not just youthful indiscretion. It was more than lack of judgment. Is it not an ancient, primal evil, born in Eden, dark and malevolent, that hides deep inside everyone's soul?

No one worked as hard as he to reach out to the Jews, the Poles, the Ukrainians, the Russians. He'd lobbied the Vatican through Acamayo's office. He'd fought for ecumenical programs. He'd practically forced the Vatican to make reparations to families for turning a blind eye to the concentration camps. He'd even wrested restitution from the Church where it was shown that "donations" were no more than stolen funds paid for "humanitarian" safe passage out of Europe.

But for all his effort, his guilt was not assuaged. He'd eventually resigned himself to death without redemption. He hadn't found the pardon he'd so needed. His work didn't bring him salvation. He'd carry his badge of dishonor to the grave. He would follow so many others throughout history who despite every ounce of will and effort, could not manage to outlive their past. "Buenos Aires," he said. "The crates were bound for Buenos Aires. They followed us there. It was pasted on the sides: 'Slaughterhouse machinery – Gutierrez Ranches.'"

"The trunks?" Ibn raised his eyes, his head still bowed.

"If they were in his bunker...."

Naomi let both men sit in their own separate stunned silence. After a minute of reflection, she chose to ask the old man, "Herr Stauffenberg," she said, raising a brow, "where do you think those crates ended up after they were off-loaded in Buenos Aires?"

The German hung his head now in tandem with the Eastern Christian's own, and spoke amidst his own gush of repentant tears.

"Here," he finally surmised.

"Here?" she prompted.

Nothing.

"Herr Stauffenberg?"

"*Here*," he said. "Here in Bariloche. They brought everything here." He looked up misty eyed and stared into Naomi's face. Then he turned to face Ibn and cast Ibn's wig aside.

As the wig floated down to the pavement, he confessed, the cameras still rolling.

"Stauffenberg's not my real name."

३ ३

THE AMPHIBIOUS carrier having reached *The Piper Dolphin*, Michelle was yelling orders. José and Arkesha scrambled aboard. Bear was lagging behind. There was no time to waste. Charlie was somewhere back in the caverns and they needed to go find him – now.

Arkesha was distraught, wondering why the rescue boat had left without them. She focused on José with accusing eyes.

"Michelle's orders."

"We should be on that boat!" she protested.

"It's not our call. I *tried*," he pleaded.

"We owe it to Charlie!" Arkesha was screaming into her husband's face.

José was bracing himself against a rail inside the upper deck of *The Piper Dolphin*. After Zelfa, Yusef and two medics left in the amphibious craft to search the cavern for their friend, the towering catamaran had churned the waters with its huge propellers. It moved gracefully through the water, gaining momentum with a quiet resolve, quickly reaching a top speed well beyond the Joint Venture fleet's own still classified speed.

"They won't...." José broke off his gaze and turned to look out at the fast retreating land. His voice was weak. He looked defeated.

His wife already felt bad. Now she felt worse. "I'm sorry honey. I guess with Charlie *and* Sarah missing...." She paused and prayed to the God she had still not embraced. Then she added, "At least we know where Charlie is."

*   *   *

HE AWOKE TO PAIN. Every inch of his body throbbed. The piercing, debilitating heat of screaming nerves coursed through his body. His muscles convulsed. He forced his eyes to open.

Charlie saw two IV bags suspended above him.

One bag of clear liquid.

Another of deep red cellular life carried by the plasma that had saved his life.

The roar of jet engines that rattled the deck beneath him made his head hurt even worse.

He closed his eyes again to block out the light, willing that it would also block out the pain.

His tongue was dry and a sour chemical paste lined the inside of his mouth.

Well, at least I'm safe. Rescued in the nick of time. Was it Michelle?

Boots.

The unmistakable walk of a soldier.

Two.

Talking.

As they drew nearer, he could make out their conversation.

"Enson said to keep him alive."

"I still don't know why we just didn't leave him there. A bullet in the brain couldn't have killed him any quicker."

Charlie couldn't help the humorous thought: I guess I'm not saved after all.

"We'll be there by the end of the day."

Cursing. Then quietly, "He's awake."

"How do you know…?"

"Here, give me that."

Charlie couldn't resist. He opened his eyes just as the soaked rag was pushed into his face for the second time in so many hours.

*   *   *

"WHERE ARE THEY?"

"Two blocks out. They've set up a perimeter. Naomi's surrounded."

"How many?"

"We've counted sixteen. We think there's more."

"Enson?"

"Yes. No sign of law enforcement yet. But I'm sure they'll show up soon."

"Okay. Penetrate the net. Get to our people as fast as you can." Via's tone was even-tempered, authoritative and fused with grave concern.

She initiated another call.

Mandy's voice mail answered.

Nena was driving. Via had switched with her as soon as they'd arrived to the edge of town. The burnt-orange Hummer raced over the plowed roads that circled the lake inside the touristy alpine resort town. Tran was strapping so many grenades to his body that he resembled a tumorous armadillo.

Via made another call.

"Where are you?" she asked.

She was puzzled. "No! I'm so sorry.

"How soon?

"Uh…. Okay." The call ended. Her face looked lost.

The H2 bounded into the center of town headed straight for the clock tower. Via tried Mandy again. Voicemail. Texted. Mandy, why aren't you answering?

They hit the final stretch of slushy pavement and slowed. The scene ahead looked like Kabul, instead of a quiet Germanic replica. On each side of the street, the Bavarian architecture sheltered warring groups of heavily armed adversaries. They were taking cover in watchmaker shops, candy stores, toy stores filled with wooden soldiers and coo-coo clocks, and the ubiquitous German pub. Flocks of lead tore down plate glass windows. The fusillade ripped off placards hanging from golden chains, splintering images of Black Forest maidens and Switzerland's bell-laden cows.

Via's eyes were drawn to the clustered Pathfinders on one side of the street. Her eyes narrowed, targeting the opposite curb. She pointed a command. Nena followed it, smashing her foot to the floor.

The Hummer shot up over the curb, raking the lamp posts and trash bins lining the sidewalk. It toppled potted plants leaving broken shards behind. The unsuspecting enemy gunmen were so engaged in their volley that the first soldier's skeleton splintered into surrounding tissues as the crushing force of the H2 connected with the man's frame. Others scattered as the orange truck entered, causing an explosion of craftsmen's clocks. A quick movement of her hands and right foot and Nena had the SUV skidding back onto the street. As it plunged into reverse, it caught the clothing of another combatant and dragged him out onto the pavement into the middle of the street.

As the Hummer continued, rear forward, across the street, Enson's thug was deposited in a crumpled wreck on the grey, tarmacadam surface. Seamlessly, Nena swung the truck into a defensive profile, shielding their own men and women.

Celeste had sent the very best. They quickly attached themselves to the left side of the bulky SUV as Nena started forward at a slow cruise. Together they battered the troops along the opposite side of the street, the moving palisade providing excellent cover for the advancing force.

Two black Suburbans burst onto the scene to even the balance of power. The smug Don Juan drove lead, heading straight for the back of Nena's vehicle. He depressed the control that lowered the dark-tinted glass to his left. This allowed his left-hand to air his light FN P90 automatic weapon at the exposed back of Via's infantry. He squeezed the *Fabrique's* trigger, spraying a lethal dose of lead. Two young soldiers folded onto the slush covered asphalt. The rest of the bullets scarred the metallic paint and the spare on the back of the H2.

Nena's response was lightning-quick. She shoved the H2 into reverse and spun the tires while cutting hard on the wheel. The truck carved an arc in the pavement and kicked up enough wet snow to blind the enemy for several seconds. The movement was perfectly executed and put Via's lethal mind into the perfect position to strike back.

She performed.

From the front passenger's seat, Via showed the world how to use an FN FS2000. The barrage of lead it unleashed was aimed so precisely that it unzipped the cocky soldier's hand from his wrist. Enson's lead man dropped the P90 still wrapped by the dismembered grip. The gun clanked onto the road and rolled up onto its human appendage, still firing as it settled on the ground. Via continued to unleash her fury through the FS2000 *bullpup,* taking out the front tires of both Suburbans.

With her window still down, Via reloaded as Nena continued the tight circle of tail-first spinning until the nose of the orange SUV stopped in a stare facing the disabled GMCs. Two warriors stepped out of Nena's small tank.

Via and Tran both walked with purpose, almost in slow motion. Via had the *bullpup* stretched out in front of her and Nena's Benelli slung over her shoulder. Tran lobbed a series of grenades aimed for the undercarriages of the enemy's vehicles and the remaining combatants still holed up in the shops on the far side of the street. He had his own M4 Super 90 strapped to his back ready to use.

Heavy return fire forced both of them to retreat behind their still open doors. In perfect tandem, like a well-choreographed dance, Via and Tran switched to their shotguns and blasted shell after shell in return. The Suburbans became charred remains and the landscape increasingly shattered, the returning volleys gradually lessening. Via shouted.

"In!" she yelled.

There were three soldiers left standing of the group Celeste had sent. They quickly ran and jumped into the back of the H2 as Via's eyes searched the carnage for Keyontay. Where is he?

"Keyontay!" she screamed into the remains of the shops on their side of the street.

"Via!" Nena's voice rose up above Via's.

She responded. It was time to go. They had to get to Naomi and make sure she was safe.

Via slipped into her seat and slammed the door firmly shut.

Tran saw movement out of the corner of his eye, the glint of black steel underneath the awning of a candy shop. An outdoor display. No, the front window was gone. But the flash of light came from....

A medium caliber carbine behind a bank of *marzipan* figurines sent a single shot into his side. The well-aimed bullet entered just over his left kidney and lodged into his disc atop his second lumbar vertebrae. His Kevlar ballistics vest should have stopped the shot from penetrating his flesh. Was it a kink in his armor? A vest piercing round? Via heard his gasp and turned. Her face went ghost white as she saw Tran's body jerk backwards and begin to crumble. A vacant look in his eyes sent shivers up her spine. As Tran went limp on his feet, strong arms pulled him into the back seat, and Nena pressed the gas pedal to the floor.

The motion closed the door behind Tran, and Nena spun them back around to her left so the grille bore down on the confectioner's store. She gunned it and jumped the sidewalk such that the H2 picked up some air as it flew into the face of the almond-paste molded candies. The display rack splintered into a hundred shards and the shooter was crushed underneath the wreckage.

"Medics!" Via ordered.

Nena shot the Hummer into reverse and pulled them back and around, off the sidewalk, into the street now quiet, their enemy all down or scattered. The gears shifted once more and they were off spinning away from the clock tower.

Three blocks lay between them and the station where two medics waited. Via was anxious. Perhaps Keyontay was there. They raced over wet asphalt and screeched around corners while Tran's involuntary moans egged them on. In two minutes they found the medical tent and unloaded Tran's broken frame.

"Tran, you hang in there." Via had her hand on his chest as they placed him on the back boarded stretcher.

"I'll be okay," he said, wincing with pain as he opened his eyes to her surprise.

She bent to his ear and whispered, "Don't die. If you do, I'll...."

He smiled weakly, "I won't let you down."

"Naomi," Via breathed.

Nena heard, "Let's go."

Via rushed for her door and started dialing her phone as she climbed into the truck. Her thoughts screamed inside her head. Naomi, you better be okay. Mandy, where are you?

SHE BENT OVER the dead body.

The Brandenburg's former manager had no pulse but the corpse was still warm.

Mandy had heard a woman's scream just as she walked into the lobby. Her leg was acting up, but she forgot the limp and rushed down the hall beyond the front counter and into the manager's office. Now, with the body at her feet, she turned to the frightened woman cowering in the corner of the office.

"Money?" she asked in Spanish.

The whimpering desk attendant pointed to a tightly closed safe behind the desk.

"Enemies?"

The blonde head swiveled back and forth. Tears fell from bloodshot blue eyes.

"Keys?"

The woman's stare darted to the waist of her fallen boss. She opened her mouth and let out a startled burst of only air.

"Tell me where he had exclusive access." The Brit was a well-trained intelligence expert. She would do well as a trial lawyer or a police detective. MI6 had instilled into her the analytical skills necessary to fully evaluate a situation and focus on the most important issues without delay.

A blank look.

Mandy turned her attention back to the body. Flipping the face-down frame to supine position she studied his features. She looked back to the woman's frozen face.

"*Sprechen sie Deutsche?*" Mandy's German was impeccable.

"*Ya.*"

Mandy was hoping for more. She asked a series of questions in the woman's native tongue. No answers came.

"This place." Mandy stood up and looked around, still speaking in German. "It has a secret level where the plastic surgeons did their work." Not formed as a question.

The woman's mouth remained tightly shut.

"He didn't have the only key."

The desk clerk started for the door.

Mandy's Glock 17 pistol politely asked the woman to reconsider.

She did.

IBN FIRED HIS Makarov.

He squeezed off three shots from his old Russian handgun, each in rapid succession.

Heinrich just squeezed his eyelids shut as the rusty bullets pierced the air in front of his head. He said a final prayer.

The old German had stopped praying to saints years ago. Ultimately, his Marion devotion waned as well. There came a time that he discovered why. His work had kept him steeped in the study of the Scriptures. The actual texts. Not commentaries and sermonaries. Not prayer books and lexicons. Not devotionals and Christian inspirationals. Just the Bible itself. Since his focus was generally historical and archival in nature, his hands pouring over the millions of pages of antiquity buried in Lima's vaults, he was constantly opening his own Holy Bible to compare its historical record with the other documents as he deciphered them. He would compare everything against it. Its sixty-six books boasted a provenance far superior to any ancient civilization's stone tables, or monoliths, or parchments, or temple ruins. If the documents were consistent with the record established in the Scriptures, he would presume them authentic until proven otherwise. It was the basis of his research, the foundation of his work.

At first, however, he had viewed the Bible as only a tool that would help him test the authenticity of the documents he was examining. Historical. Accurate. Authoritative. More reliable than any other ancient of texts ... partly because of the unique span of various authors over so many centuries that produced an uncanny consistency so complex, yet so perfect. Was it also a religious text? Of course. Was it the inspired Word of God? After time, he finally realized that it was.

So with his eyes tightly pressed together, he made his final peace with God.

The bullets entered living flesh and stopped the electrical charges in the brain, the beating of the heart, the flow of life to limbs. All ceased.

And all three bodies crumpled to the ground beyond Heinrich's trembling face.

Plus two more of Enson's mercenaries were forced to leave their bodies within a few seconds. But the smoking barrel that unleashed the .45 caliber slugs that took out the pair was clenched tightly in both of Naomi's steady hands. Holding her semi-automatic firmly, she was down on one knee already leveling her sight at other black-clad figures piling out of large SUVs.

Behind her, everyone scattered.

The sound of gunfire and squealing tires filled the alpine air. The ground shook with pounding feet running this way and that, not knowing where to go ... looking for cover. Everyone was in a panic.

Except for the director.

The director saw that his cameras were unmanned and jumped up to take hold of the controls behind Camera One. He captured the action. Still broadcasting live over the broadband connection, he didn't think twice about his own safety. He just kept asking himself, "Did you get that? That? Over there? Back over here?"

Ibn advanced.

He swept quickly to a protective position at the old Catholic's side.

After dropping two more of their attackers, Naomi was still kneeling as she panned a wide angle to her right.

Ibn and Naomi ended up fanning out several shots at the same time. Simultaneously, their bullets found additional targets. They released a barrage of fire that further reduced the threat. Both were skilled marksmen and their shots boasted deadly accuracy.

Ibn's weapon jammed.

He took one more look at it and gave up on the old Russian gun.

He flung the pistol. His Makarov found one final mark as it advanced in the air, as if on its own, to crack bone in the center of a menacing smile that was moving in for the kill. Blood cascaded down the face of the enemy soldier as he raised his AK-47, leveling it at Ibn's chest.

But the words didn't leave him. His commander had barked them into their comms. Through the pain of the broken nose and bone under his ocular cavity, he heard the words loudly. "He stays alive or you don't." So he changed his angle. Stepping to his own left just slightly, making sure that when he mowed down the unarmed Arab his bullets wouldn't pass through the man and hit the old German next to him and somewhat behind him.

It was the slight delay more than the better angle, but both helped. Seeing the busted Russian firearm fly, Naomi knew she only had seconds to intervene if she could. As Naomi tried to help, another henchman emerged from the back of one of the Suburbans with his assault rifle already blazing. She would try to take care of them both if she could.

As Naomi swung her gun around to the nearest threat, Ibn reacted as well. He took advantage of the couple of seconds reprieve by reaching for the *yataghan* still sheathed on his belt. He pulled it out and in one quick motion sent it flying right after the Makarov as if chasing it down. It flipped end over end and spun into a deadly plunge that stopped only after its entire blade was buried inside the enemy's chest. The *yataghan*'s unique squiggly razor-sharp edges had pierced through the man's bullet-proof vest.

Naomi stopped her movement to her left and switched gears in a seamless motion to squeeze off several rounds at the soldier who'd just jumped out of his truck. The guy got off a spray of shots that wildly scattered above her. His head snapped back as she found her own mark.

Just then three more Suburbans made their way over the top of the hill. They careened around the corner in a rush of power, a formidable armored array that repelled Naomi's bullets as she peppered their windshields in vain. She lowered her aim and sparks flew off of grilles that had plating behind the polished GMC chrome guards. She stopped to reload.

"Come!" Ibn grabbed Heinrich. "Come with me!"

He pulled on the old German's arm and looked over his shoulder at Naomi, still perched firmly on one knee on the cold pavement.

"Come!" he screamed. "Come!"

"THEY HAD TO LEAVE."

"Go ahead and land. Unload the trucks. They'll be back.

"No. Just wait with the vehicles.

"I know. I'll make sure the additional wire goes out today.

"As soon as you radio back that you are in the air again.

"Yes.

"The contract calls for….

"I know. And the rates for any ground delay….

"Okay. I'll call your home office.

"Okay.

"Huh?

"What?

"Karl? What's going on?"

Celeste lost the connection. Her phone was already reaching out to Tim Dodge. She depended heavily on the logistics wizard. And this time he'd really come through for her. On short notice he'd been able to get a dozen armored Mercedes G-class jeeps onto the US Air Force cargo plane in Germany. Within ten short hours he had them in the air. Of course, the *Al Saud* prince would be upset that his order had been pulled to supply another, but Tim would tackle that challenge next.

"Tim. I lost Karl.

"You too? What's going on?

"Oh no!"

She hung up and dialed Via.

The line opened up to the sound of gunfire and screeching tires. "Via! Via!

"Oh, thank God you're okay. I can't reach Naomi. What's going on?

"You can see her?

"She's doing what?

"Naomi doesn't know how to fire a gun!

"Hey! Hey!"

Celeste was hysterical when the connection was lost.

She dialed Naomi again.

Celeste's phone signaled an incoming call, interrupting her dial out. "Unknown number" was blowing up her Blackberry.

She picked up.

"Who?

"Your name is Mandy?

"Okay.

"Via's with Naomi. They…." She hesitated.

"You're where?

"Secret what?

"Sub-basement. Got it.

"Okay.

"Mandy? What about…."

The call was over.

"My oh my oh my!" Celeste had already been out of her seat when she lost Karl. Now she was circling her office. Call after call she couldn't reach anyone. How would she send Mandy help if no one would answer the phone?

THE HERCULES BEING piloted by Karl Grüten was already nosing back up. It aborted its approach quickly. Evasive maneuvers are always difficult with any large aircraft. With the C-130 they were practically impossible, especially now. The nimble little machines that threatened his airspace would not be outrun. His giant craft was one of the largest that rubbed up against the clouds. He felt helpless, but he wasn't going to give up. He swung out over the lake and pointed straight for Bariloche on the other side of the glistening water.

The old cargo plane creaked through the turn. Its huge mass of straining bolts and rivets struggled. Its fuselage was aching to give in to forces long patient but now eroding its strength quickly. A deterioration that had progressed over many thousands of engine hours was about to reach its apex.

With two Apache attack helicopters bearing down on him, the pilot felt the great weight of the load in his hold. So he pushed forward on the yoke and dipped back down towards the mountain lake.

He had to gain some speed.

Karl adjusted his flaps and opened the tail's wide cargo bay door.

"Soledar!" he yelled. "The central release!"

The cargo specialist was in a jumpseat just outside the cockpit. He was carefully watching every shift in his precious inventory. It was his job to tie it all down, to wrap it all up, and to avoid the slightest dent, ding, or scratch. The German-engineered trucks would arrive at their destination without the slightest mar to clear-coating or black-walled rubber. Not if he had anything to do with it. Tim chose only the very best. And he was it.

"What?" Soledar protested. He couldn't believe his ears.

"Just do it! Release the load!" the pilot ordered.

Hesitation.

"Now!"

The desperation was fused with anger and the alloy of riled despair pushed him past his resistance. He knew the Apaches were on top of them. He allowed his mind to override his overwhelming instinct to protect his valuable cargo at all costs. So he rose – but as one from the grave. Disoriented. Bewildered. Acting as would any other zombie, he followed the order. He released the master connector. It held every chain, every sheepskin-covered strap.

The champagne-colored fleet of Mercedes jeeps had been destined for Riyadh. Now, they shifted and rolled within the slack to the limits allowed. One more control. The trucks just hung on until....

"Let 'em loose!" Karl's voice shouted from behind the standing man's still vacant stare.

But the trucks will roll into the front of the cargo bay. They will crush me. They will break through the thin metal barrier and pancake the pilots. The plane was still nose down and Soledar thought Karl must be out of his mind. He stretched his neck around to see if the co-pilot might take over and bring some sanity back into the helm.

"Now!" Karl barked.

We will all be killed thought Soledar. His thoughts were muddled, but his catatonic mind was already responding to the command. His dazed countenance was used to following orders. He reached for the lever. Every truck was in neutral to protect the transmissions. Once he pulled the lever, they would be free of any constraint.

He pushed the long metal handle forward. Loosed! He screamed inside his head as the deed was done. Like demons from hell unleashed ... he closed his eyes and waited for the metal to crush him.

As Soledar breathed out a long, last exhale before his lungs collapsed under the weight of a hundred tons of steel, Karl pulled back on the yoke.

Hard.

The yoke was all the way out to its fully extended position. The co-pilot was busy adjusting the ailerons and flaps as Karl strained against the forces that resisted the lurch back towards the sky.

They were already half-way out over the lake when the C-130 cupped in mid-air and found an uphill path once again.

The nose of the Hercules strained skyward. The interior of the plane had allowed the trucks to start rolling towards the front just barely, and then they stopped. Soledar opened his eyes. The fleet of jeeps just stood still for a few seconds, suspended in space, until they started to roll in the other direction toward the open cargo bay at the rear.

Soledar wished he were dead.

No! They couldn't just dump these beauties! Each one was customized and worth at least $250,000. He reached for them as if to stop the small army of skydivers' retreat out the tail.

The first of Prince Abdullah's diverted order plunged out the open cargo door.

A steely paratrooper without his chute.

Hurling its heavy mass down towards the shining water a thousand feet below.

MANDY LET THE elevator doors close out the world behind her and just stood invisibly indented on the lush piles of expensive textiles beneath her boots.

Listening.

Not just with sharp ears, but with every one of her senses. Both with her physical five and those beyond this dimension. She could feel it. Before the rustling finally became distinct against her eardrums, she could sense it. Her skin vibrated microscopically, sending electric signals to inside her head, reacting to the faint waves that reached her from the end of a very long hall.

Her Glock led the way. As she crept along, even her breathing stopped creating any sound. Her heart's normal rhythm changed. It was reduced to a barely discernible thump. Every cell that made up her frame was now coordinating a practiced hush that caused her to vanish into the dimly lit corridor.

She sensed his movements. She could see him on the other side of the wall. The sound of crisp edges of antiquated parchments stopped their brush against the ancient salted wood.

Tensed but fluid, she continued down the ornate sub-basement's wide lane. Although it was lined with priceless value, her mind remained uncluttered. Even so, the hall wooed her. She passed an oil by Rogier van der Weyden that hadn't been seen since it was painted for the Cross Bowmen's Guild, shortly after its matching altarpiece. She stepped alongside the beveled edge of a Grecian pedestal bearing the carefully sculpted bust of Aristotle by an unknown artisan. Her eyeballs couldn't help glancing at a brightly colored papal scene painted in brilliant hues by Pinturicchio: the ornately framed, pigment covered canvass easily six feet across.

Mandy forced herself to continue in measured stealth. Her face sternly set to the end of the long hall. Her jaw flexed as she neared the open doorway.

She knew the intruder was just inside.

The semi-automatic pistol entered the room first. She effortlessly aimed its dull-finished barrel at a man's head. He appeared unarmed, but she didn't relax. Not in the least. Her gaze fixed itself on his face and mid-section simultaneously. He stood facing her with an open scroll in his hand. The man had been examining the scripted parchment, but now his gaze rose to meet her own.

He didn't appear either threatened or threatening. Speaking only from a staid stare, he asked what she wanted, like he was a grocer behind a counter.

Her mouth remained closed as she tried to figure out how he spoke without moving his own mouth. His lips didn't move. But her ears heard his words.

She responded, using a look that bored a hole in the space between them as they stood in repose. Her stare of grim determination and resolve went beyond the power of her firearm. Meant to force a response to the *Who are you?* and the *What are you doing here?* – she was demanding answers.

It was as if he could read her mind. But rather than give her what she expected, the silent figure stepped out of the shadows. He moved into a swath of muted light from the hall that now fell across him to reveal, for an instant, his appearance.

Mandy tensed.

Her finger almost released a bullet into the stranger's head.

The scroll practically rolled itself back into shape. Then the silhouette of the man blended its borders with the shaft of thin light, and the trunk received the vellum. The ancient wooden chest abruptly clamped shut its jaw once again.

She blinked.

Again.

She shifted her angle.

Fear gripped her. In a panic, she scurried back out of the room and breathed heavy brush-with-death breaths. Weak knees collapsed her against the baseboard, the blood having all but left her face, her legs, and everywhere in between.

Now she couldn't breathe at all.

How could she?

For the intruder had just disappeared before her very eyes.

٣٤

BEAR COULDN'T FIND José and Arkesha. They'd left the amphibious carrier before he'd had the strength to climb back down from the turret. By the time he had stumbled into the belly of the amphibious craft, Zelfa was shouting at him to disembark into *The Piper Dolphin* so that she could leave. The two medics had already boarded and were strapped into their seats. Yusef had been talking into his throat mike with a security team. Bear gathered the other team was moving from a safe house half a mile underneath Vatican City to meet them in the cave where Charlie was last seen.

He blindly looked back around again for Joshua, to no avail, and reluctantly stepped onto a steel gangway that bridged the two strange watercraft. And he walked into another world.

Bear had seen the towering twin hulls from a distance. He'd been up in the cab before he had started his search for the professor. From his vantage point between Zelfa and Yusef, the ship had looked gigantic. Now that he was walking inside of it, he felt like he was being swallowed by the Earth itself.

Outside, the catamaran had looked like a military ship. So it was natural for Bear to assume that the inside would resemble one as well. But, instead of steel walls of plain Navy grey, he walked off the clanging metal ramp onto dark polished teak flooring. Graceful paneling greeted him such that he had the feeling of entering a high-end hotel in Manhattan or Chicago. However, this was a ship the size of an aircraft carrier. He was dumbfounded.

His eyes moved from skylights high overhead to antique tables that lined the walls under beautiful paintings and lavish tapestries. He turned in circles to admire the art and the grandeur of it all. Bear breathed in deeply and smelled the comfort before padding off to the elevators at the far end of the wide corridor.

He pressed the only brass button between two elevator doorways with their kissing panels in an elegant gold veneer. The doors to his left parted, and he stepped aboard. He rode up as far as the lift would take him and walked off the platform into sunshine on a level high above the runways on the outer deck. The wind rushed over him almost knocking him over.

Beyond the rails that kept him grounded, he could see Zelfa speeding back north along the coast. He said another prayer for Charlie and then for Sarah. He said one for Joshua. Who else? Was another going to be lost? Would they all disappear?

The huge ship was moving fast beneath his feet. He could feel the weight of its mass displacing thousands of tons of the Mediterranean as it shot away from the Italian peninsula. He hung his head, leaning his hairline all the way down to the back of his hands where they wrapped around the top bar of the railing. He didn't have the strength to deal with this kind of thing.

The wind picked him up and pushed him back. His hands loosened their grip. But he gathered his resolve. He focused on what he was able to do. The others may be gone, but José and Arkesha were on this ship, and he was going to find them. They would regroup. They would come up with a plan.

Searching the massive catamaran was time-consuming to say the least. A few sections were indeed relegated to the sparse military decor he had expected. It was in these parts of the ship that cautious eyes regarded him skeptically. He passed workstations of engineers and radiomen. He watched sailors doing things that he would never understand. And there was a lot of painting going on. Always someone painting something. As he sidled up to one of the crewmen in a narrow passage, he was stared down like he didn't belong. He didn't.

He searched for hours. Bear was determined to find them, and he knew that eventually he would run across them in the mess hall, or on the galley, or on the bridge. As he passed a large round porthole, he froze in his tracks. Was that the Rock of Gibraltar? He pressed his face up against the heavy glass and looked out.

The monolithic, white-faced landmark blurred by like the countryside from a speeding train.

Impossible.

They couldn't be going that fast. He ran to the next porthole only a dozen meters aft. The sea-encircled mount was gone. He found the nearest stair. He rushed up the steps. Several flights took him to a final steep stairway of narrow metal steps open to the flight deck above. He grabbed the rail and pushed his way up to the top.

Bear entered the wind force of a hurricane. He couldn't get off the top step even if he crawled on hands and knees. The worn leather coat that hung from his shoulders almost ripped from his torso. He would have lost it had he not ducked back into the well. Peeking up above the barricade that held off the force of wind, he peered down the length of the main deck's runway that led off the edge of the stern. He saw a tiny version of Gibraltar's stony protrusion disappearing from view.

Could they have already passed between the Pillars of Hercules? He looked at his watch. He could have sworn that they had just left Ostia a little less than four hours before. He turned and looked ahead into the rushing wind. It made the slits between his eyelids water, but he stared off into the bright distance of nothing but blue skies and blue-green ocean as far as he could see in every direction.

They were already in the Atlantic!

He ducked back inside the stairwell and cautiously made his way back down the metal treads. We've just crossed half the Med ... half of the entire European subcontinent. Bear refused to call Europe a separate continent. He saw the map in his head. Ostia is almost due south from Munich, right in the heart of Central Europe. Gibraltar marks Europe's southernmost point, and as far west as the Eurasian continent reaches into the Atlantic.

How fast does this thing go?

*　　　*　　　*

SHE COULDN'T SEE Ibn or Heinrich.

Somewhere off in the distance, perhaps in her dreams the night before, she'd heard Ibn's urgent cry.

"Come!" he had said.

She hadn't even looked to see the two tall figures melt into the battered scene. Like wisps of smoke that stretch into tall spires before the wind disperses their cumulative gathering that forms their appearance but for a momentary glance. Like life cast against the backdrop of eternity – they were gone.

She was focused on the new group of black Suburbans crammed full of black-clad soldiers all heavily armed and now barreling down the small hill right for her.

Naomi was alone.

Except for the producer – he'd managed to stay alive behind his camera still framing the action.

She was outnumbered. She peered through the windshields and pushed another clip into her semi-automatic pistol. The Suburban windows came down and no less than half a dozen weapons poked out.

She was definitely out-gunned.

Not seeing any other option, Naomi decided to stay put on one knee and make her last stand. Surely she wouldn't be able to outrun these guys on foot. They definitely meant to kill her for some unknown reason. But she was more concerned with the shroud and the crown than for her life at this point. Did the artifacts make their way back to *The Ark?* But no time to think about it. She aimed and fired at exposed arms that were bearing weapons. She braced herself for the death that is always certain but never real until it's upon you.

She said her last prayer.

Two Uzi-bearing arms were the first to drop their Israeli-made weapons. She'd hit the shooters in the wrists or forearms; she couldn't tell. They were still about a half a block away. But they'd be upon her in another few seconds.

She tried aiming at the grilles again, then the tires. But the ground leading up to her position was fast being torn up. The Bariloche pavement was riddled by bullets headed her way. The snow-slushed asphalt was ricocheting lead that traced a path straight for her heart.

Yet, she was undeterred. She kept on shooting. She knew this was her last clip and only a few bullets remained. She would make them count.

Naomi managed to fell three more attackers firing submachine guns. But there were too many of them. One of the Uzis finally launched a spray that found its way to her body. She was hit.

At a thousand rounds per minute, it was a miracle that only one piece of lead penetrated her skin. But the power of the single projectile knocked her backwards. She fell hard, twisting to her side as she fell, her knee bending back beneath her body. The rest of the barrage of bullets ripped through the air over the top of her fallen frame.

As the gun that dropped her ran out of bullets and the man reloaded, another soldier was jumping out of the lead Suburban. Training his weapon on the ground where she lay, he squeezed the trigger.

The pain was fire. It was blinding. It was red. Black. Heated white. Screaming.

It took her breath away. But Naomi gritted her teeth. She locked her eyes as she stared up through the clouds. She knew she had at least one shot left. She turned back with her cheek against the frozen pavement and aimed one last time.

But the new flock of bullets from Enson's minion was already racing towards her struggling figure that writhed on the ground. In less than a second a hundred killers would rip her body to shreds. She wouldn't get another shot off. She didn't have the time.

Naomi became frozen in time. Too fast for the naked eye. She could see the army of leaden missiles splitting the invisible particles that floated inside the space between the gun's muzzle and the body that had carried her since birth. Her very best prayer died before it had a chance to be sent off to Heaven. She didn't even have time to scream.

They struck.

In rapid succession. Each bullet only nanoseconds behind the other. Plowing into matter. Destroying what was in their path.

The sound of death. A body riddled with streaks of terror.

But she didn't feel the terror – any of it.

Because the body wasn't hers. It belonged to a Pathfinder. Factory assembled in Tokyo. Shipped to Buenos Aires. Rented by Via and driven by a dreaded knight. The white clear-coated armor branded by Nissan.

Keyontay.

He'd driven hard. And at the last possible second he'd slammed on the brakes, skidding the last twenty meters, stopping just where he needed to stop. The Pathfinder shield took the full brunt of the flying lead from the Uzi. The rear door just behind the driver opened and a small hand reached out to pull her inside.

Naomi's hand wouldn't release her weapon. And although the pain was disabling, she managed to get up with the assistance of two eager hands. Her body clambered into the rear of the SUV. Keyontay's skinny dreads spun like a washing machine's clothes-wringing cycle as he swiveled his head around and shifted the vehicle into reverse just as fast as the seconds it took for Naomi to make it into her seat. A petite body leaned over her and pulled the door shut just as they shot back from their stop at a speed that made everyone inside the truck lurch forward.

As the Nissan screamed backwards away from the battle, the lithe young woman next to Naomi said as loud as she could with her small voice, "My name is Pei-chin. Are you okay?"

"Yeah," Naomi managed to say through a weak voice. "I'll be fine."

NENA YELLED AND POINTED, "Look!"

Via looked out over the lake. She could see the massive belly of the C-130 swanning upwards as the first luxury SUV tumbled out of the back of the plane.

Nena's foot lifted up from the accelerator and the Hummer drifted to a stop as her mouth gaped open and she stared, mesmerized at the sight. The flying behemoth had dropped a huge bomb. The two Apaches behind the aircraft fell back and stopped shooting.

The champagne glazed Mercedes flipped over onto its back as it fell. Its rear wheels had rolled down the ramp first and then the weight of its engine under the hood coupled by the plane's motion had created a spin of slow but destructive grace. As the German-built machine shot like a meteor towards the lake's surface, it continued its forward motion. The SUV's rooftop hit the water at its spoiler. It was still in a slow rotation when it made contact with the body of water right at the tip of the top of its rear hatch. It swung into a curve at the surface like a smoothed stone as it pushed down on the unbroken film of glass.

It was skipping over the surface headed right for them.

Nena punched the accelerator to the floor. Just in time.

The Mercedes reached the shore within seconds – like a giant skipping stone.

It kicked up over the lip of the shoreline and smashed into the street. The truck traveled the pavement on its back over the spot where the H2 had been stopped only moments before.

A doctor's office across the street faced the lake. It was beautiful. Built in 1939, it was fully restored to pristine condition: a building reminiscent of Bohemian storefronts in quaint mountain towns. The Mercedes scraped over the macadam and tar and slammed into the perfect visage of handcrafted architecture. Into the front of the office. Into the lobby. Taking out supports that bore a full three stories from the curb into the Andean sky. The truck burst through the narrow building, its weight hitting the structure like a Kansas tornado. The force toppled the building. As it did, the jeep shot out the back wall and into an alley before lodging itself into a wall of stone that backed a Bavarian brewery.

The second-generation doctor's signage read in German and Spanish. A proud shingle now dashed with its hanger, crushed in destruction. The sign lay on top of the pile of rubble. *Hans Schönberg, plastic surgeon.*

"HE DIDN'T LOOK GOOD." Nena had shaken her head with a frown.

"It'll take a miracle just for him to live." Via's chagrin dressed her face. It dragged her whole body down with its unbearable weight.

Tran's muscular frame was in the medics' hands. They'd left him at the tent on *E. B. Morales*. Only a short pause separated their race back to *Costanera Avenida 12 de Octubre*. Nena had taken Via to the water's edge to try to provide support to Keyontay. He'd radioed his position after ducking into the alley. He was a block north of *Libertad*. The Nissan was pointed west out of the center of town. He was headed for The Brandenburg.

And so were they.

Via was back on the phone. "Mandy, pick up. Mandy, come on!" she had said out loud, as the phone kept ringing but to no avail.

The H2 now buzzed westerly down the waterfront. Via was relieved that Naomi had been saved, but stressed over Ibn and Heinrich and that she couldn't reach Mandy.

She started thinking about Tran again and speaking to herself. "Come on Tran. Don't leave us now."

PEI-CHIN CRADLED the fainting body as Naomi's consciousness slipped away. She was losing blood and her body was in shock.

The young woman from Beijing was already tearing at Naomi's clothes and pulling out her first aid kit. She needed to clean the wound and stop the bleeding.

"What's wrong? Is she going to be okay?" Keyontay exclaimed, as he continued to catapult their vehicle away from the clock tower's intersection. He turned his head forward, spinning his dreads, as the

Pathfinder pirouetted before disappearing down a narrow lane that wrapped behind a *laiterie*. On the other side was a French bakery bearing a Spanish name.

"She's been shot," Pei-chin answered with raised eyebrows.

"Is it serious?" His voice found itself personally vested.

"I don't think so," she said, shaking her head while holding Naomi's limp frame against her chest and putting pressure on the cleaned wound, "but I'm not a medic, so I don't really know for sure."

"You're not one of the medics?" he asked, with a confused look on his face as he peered at her reflection in the rear-view mirror. She was so small, so fragile. She couldn't be one of the special-ops soldiers Celeste had commissioned. He'd figured her right off as one of the paramedics that....

"No," she answered. "I'm a paleographer."

*   *   *

SARAH'S FACE WAS bruised where Enson's naval diver had hit her. Her first swim in the Med and she had been rendered unconscious. But her eyes had opened for only a few seconds, and in those fleeting moments she had seen a strange world of swirling colors that left a submarine's sick bay. Aware that they were moving her, she had closed her eyes again and kept them closed in fear.

Enson's submersible had been sleek and fast, typhoon-class, privatized, and his men had their catch for the day promptly delivered – to the boss.

ENSON WAS BACK on the sleek corporate jet. He had changed out of his slush-drenched suit and wore more casual attire. The Hawker 900XP reached 35,000 feet quickly and passed over the highest peak of *Monte Tronador* spiking up over the Andes' southern stretch.

Peña was typing 120 wpm on her laptop. Roland Enson was on his iPad. He had the newest generation and was wearing a boyish grin on his face as he manipulated through the latest applications.

Across the aisle from both of them, Sarah now struggled in a wide leather seat. She wore plastic tie-cuffs, wet clothing and an awesome scowl. The hard plastic that bound her wrists and ankles chaffed at her salt-crusted skin.

"De La Cruz and Suri are already there," Peña reported, almost nonchalant.

"Our ETA is six hours," Enson shot back.

"You need a faster jet," she retorted.

Enson growled. He didn't care how efficient she was at this job. He was still going to get rid of her. Soon.

"Do we have enough?" Peña continued in another vein.

"DNA? Plenty. Those fools led us to the best relic imaginable. I've been trying to find that (expletive) cross for centuries, and…." He laughed diabolically. "The Pope. *The Pope himself!* He led us straight to it!"

He continued, "I've had them clone the samples. They've managed to create quite a bank of plasma." Then his face became masked in a far-off look. "I looked at the manuscript again. Maybe it is the real thing. I'd always believed otherwise. I don't trust carbon dating. The followers of The Way have always been tricky. Like that Shroud of Turin fake. No wonder we couldn't do anything with the DNA off of it! But this cross, it's the real deal!" Then his face revealed a sudden jerk of doubt. He paused and then seemed to recover. "Surely my scientists have been successful this time. Immortality. It will work." His tone became increasingly confident. Peña figured he'd really been talking to himself the whole time, trying to convince himself of the truth of his own assertions.

"Immortality?" Peña used a skeptical inflection.

"The Fountain of Youth." His face chameleonic, transforming back to intrepidity from the hint of doubt that still hadn't left it. "And so much more. *Divine* blood, my child," said derisively and in a way that made Peña feel like she needed to take a shower and change into clean clothes.

"The world will drink it," he continued. "They will need it. And they will pay me. They will crown me. They will worship me for giving them eternal life."

"Doesn't Christ offer that for free?" the Catholic Peruvian responded.

He cut his eyes at her and snarled, "But I will offer them *eternal life without rules*. To live forever but not have to be moral. No ten commandments. No God. No resisting temptation. Just immortality without strings. All I want is money," he said with an innocent smile. "Christ's cloned blood won't come cheap."

Peña looked at the crazy man with compassion.

"Hedonism," he bragged, "it will be encouraged."

"Epicureans," he continued with bravado, "they will be lauded."

She thought, Lord save us. Save us all. A sad fear fell behind her eyes.

"Eat, drink and be merry, do *whatever* you want and still *live forever!*"

A dark shadow fell over him and he stood from his seat. Stepping jubilantly into the aisle, to the music in his head he danced on a black river of blood towards the back of the aircraft. With another devilish laugh, he disappeared into the bathroom once again.

"How can you work for such a monster?" Sarah had stopped wiggling.

Peña swiveled her neck, regarding the captive with a cryptic grimace. She let her eyes turn dark while deciding how to respond.

But she said nothing and returned to her work.

*   *   *

"TUVALU?"

"That's right."

"What is that?"

"*Where.*"

"Where?" Bear asked, still a bit off kilter since he'd seen Gibraltar disappear in the distance and he'd stumbled upon the Pope's office. Still unable to find José or Arkesha, he'd sought an audience with the Prince of the Apostles and Miguel had ushered him right in.

"The proper question," Miguel explained, now dressed in his informal papal attire, while sitting behind his desk. Bear was on the other side of the massive piece of office furniture that had an uncanny resemblance to their ship. Two thin legs ran the width of the monstrous desktop and cross-triangulated to the floor. The tiles beneath were an Italian marble of ice cream swirls. Purples and reds on a creamy white that made Bear hungry. "... is, '*Where* is Tuvalu?'"

"Oh. It's a place?"

"It's a nation."

"A country?" Bear thought he knew them all. Geography was one of his passions.

"An island. Well a group of islands."

"I've never heard of it." Bear shook his head in disbelief.

"Fongafale used to be the capital of the former British...."

"Elice Island." Bear interrupted the Pope, consumed with showcasing his knowledge of the globe. "*Islands,*" he quickly clarified. "It's called Tuvalu now?"

Miguel smiled sympathetically. "It is one of the world's newer nations, by some definitions." He offered as if he were an *amicus curiae* in the international court of the Hague.

"Ah, so that explains it," Bear said smugly, crossing over a line he should have left alone. "I've been *so* busy this year helping Dr. Walker with this antiquities project, I must have missed it."

The Pope couldn't just let it go, lest the young man later embarrass himself in front of a less understanding audience. "1978," he said with apologetic eyebrows raised.

"What?" Bear's face was dripping with disbelief.

"Tuvalu. It became independent from Great Britain in 1978."

Bear lost his normal color. Instantly.

"And, we'll be there by morning. So, get some rest if you want to be ready."

"Yeah," Bear replied, "I'm going in."

"It'll be dangerous," spoken with a strong, warning-hued tone.

"I'm not scared." He puffed out his chest from under the beaten jacket.

"All right. I'll put you with Michelle's insertion team. But if the professor objects, I'm keeping you on the ship."

"You know where he is?"

"No."

Bear had to think about that for a second. "But you know Sarah's being held in Tuvalu?"

"She will be." Confident.

Bear gave the Pope a quizzical look. "Like a *prophesy?* Or a revelation? Does God," he lyrically stressed, "like – really *talk* to you? I mean, you *are* the Pope and all." Bear's tone had dipped into the cabalistic. "So, I guess Jesus hangs out with you, huh? Daily chats? Garden walks?"

Miguel gave Bear an affirming but amused look.

Bear got the point.

"By traditional means, actually." Miguel slowly resumed the conversation. "I communicate with God by traditional means. Through prayer. He usually speaks in a still, small voice. Dreams. A vision from time to time."

Bear's jaw dropped and his eyes became like saucers.

"As for Sarah being on her way to Tuvalu now," he said, smiling with the sudden humor of it all, "our information comes to us by *traditional* means."

*   *   *

TIME WAS LOST, faded out to specks of sand, disappearing through the narrow waist of an hourglass.

How long she'd been folded against the wall of the lowest level of The Brandenburg, she'd never know. But Mandy finally recovered enough strength to pull herself up off the floor of the corridor outside of the room with the trunks. She stood on her feeble legs and forced herself to step cautiously around the corner and look.

She had just spent an eternity in lifeless animation, suspended inside time itself. Somewhere in ethereal space. She gazed back upon the three treasure trunks. As if deaf, she heard nothing, and stepped inside the darkened room.

The triad of ancient wooden chests occupied a crescent of the floor that was barely lit by the muted light coming from the hall. She instinctively reached up to the inside wall, feeling for a switch. It was there, a standard placement. But flipping it upwards didn't release a standard current of power to a light fixture. Instead, the lighting array was a golden candelabra standing sentry behind the trio of trunks. It glowed with a warm tangerine yellow that immediately chased the shadows into crevice-like corners hidden behind the countless other crates and boxes that filled the room.

Drawn by Heinrich's life-long quests, her feet crept forward. She walked up to the same chest that had swallowed the floating scroll; like a privateer unearthing Blackbeard's nest, she knelt. Both knees drew up to the base of the iron-bound trunk. She raised the arched roof of the weathered archive. Ancient hinges creaked loudly as the top of the repository revealed its cache. Inside, a library of parchments … a bevy of scrolls … a pile of rolled skins wound into neat little cylinders of history. The vellum that the apparition of a man had held was still slightly unrolled where he'd dropped it. Its volumetric curve still tailed and marked with faded prints.

Mandy reached for the perused script and trembled. As she touched the tubular shape, an innate sense that Ibn would dance and her grandfather would cry engulfed her. She started unrolling the lamb's sacrificial hide.

Water stained.

Ink was heavily smeared.

The tusche-quilled medium was a stained mess, barely even characters now, destroyed where words once spoke. Her eyes scanned the page, reading slowly upwards from the end of the manuscript as she unrolled the former text.

Mandy froze as she found the simple calligraphy above the washed-out ending.

She read the last legible words to survive the damage. They were written in ancient Greek. Then she said them in English. She said them in reverence. She heard her own gentle voice sounding them out as the words slipped past her trembling lips.

"They said nothing to anyone, for they were afraid."

۳۵

THE PILOT WAS straining against a shuddering yoke. Its vibrations reflected the stress on the entire air-borne leviathan as it continued to pull away from the surface of *Laguna Nahuel Huapi*.

Soledar could have been suicidal. But it was just his sorrow exacerbated into an expression that aged his face all the way into his twilight. A second G-class jeep slipped out of the back of the C-130 as he screamed a silent scream.

The SUV somersaulted. The Mercedes acrobatically aimed itself for the shoreline. The edge of town. The Bariloche beach. As it tumbled down towards Earth, the first truck had already done its damage and another was rolling down the tail's open ramp.

Karl continued the pull that pushed the nose skyward. Eight more wooden wedges let their tires go. Two more SUVs chased the last to fall. Block after block failed to keep the fleet at bay. Tires rolled over them, kicked away the woods and otherwise skirted the final keepers of place, yielding to a rush for the door. The loose chains released their wards and the entire balance of the group of chaulked vehicles began to roll towards the back of the Hercules, peppering the air with their tonnage.

The turboprop played the bombardier as it continued its futile flight from the Apaches, their pilots having dropped back in wonder at the sight of the dropping jeeps. The flying luxury trucks were catapulting towards the resort town below in rapid succession. As the second SUV hit, an entire rooftop caved in, a Rhineland clothier demolished with the blast. The next bomb, with fine leather interior, destroyed another store. And the next, another. A bistro was leveled. A micro-brewery was trashed. A pub boasting Bavaria's best *sauerkraut* was shelled by a missile equipped with a DVD and a rear camera back-up display. Another German-engineered warhead plastered an entire row of chalet-looking condos. Time-shares loaded with wooden flower boxes of yellow and lavender Crocus became engulfed, as if with napalm, in a fire spread by a full tank of unleaded fuel. Cruise-controlled incendiaries swathed a wide line of ruin. Fire consumed what the heavy boxes of metal didn't pulverize on impact. A tornado's path couldn't have looked worse than the broad strip of blackened annihilation cut through the center of town. Hungry flames remained to lick up the debris.

Keyontay had seen the falling trucks careening towards the picturesque waterfront and was already racing away from town and towards the resort. Nena sped the H2 along the lake's shore until she caught up with the white Nissan. The medics and other soldiers employed by Celeste had hastily packed patients and gear and left the scene of the air raid as well.

But the black Suburbans that remained intact were still searching the grid of the town for the elusive Pathfinder. Their focus made them oblivious to the raining barrage of Benz-branded bombs. Blind. Until.... An armored Mercedes demolished a quaint façade housing accordions, wooden flutes and a wall of hickory clogs right in front of the small fleet of surviving Suburbans. A wooden shoe shot out at the lead GMC and cracked its front windshield.

The inferno that followed tore into the street as premium gasoline ignited the tinker's wares. An eclectic mix of organ-grinders and polka traditional that shared display space with the dancing shoes and dozens of wooden piccolos exploded into the street.

Backing up after being kicked in the face, the lead Suburban crashed into the truck behind it and tried to spin around to escape. The other trucks were squirming all over the street in a jumbled chaos. Climbing all over each other for the exit, they stampeded into a mad crush as the billowing combustion fulminated over them.

*   *   *

SARAH SHIFTED uncomfortably in her seat. The soft leather under her body did nothing to relieve her situation. Under other circumstances, she would have enjoyed her first flight inside a plush corporate jet. Unfortunately, she wasn't even able to savor the gourmet cuisine the steward had served. Having recovered from swallowing and inhaling the saline water, she had begun to recall the struggle in the sea with the neoprene-clad man. The flailing. The kicking. His heavy fist having hit her head. And that groggy, spinning sensation. Once on board the jet, she'd been paying attention to her surroundings and had only counted three of her kidnappers, but she'd figured there were two pilots up front. The door to the forward cabin remained tightly shut. When a meal was served to Enson and Peña, the same food was placed in front of Sarah. She felt guilty that she didn't have an ounce of gratitude.

With raw wrists and numbed hands, she managed to lift her fork to her mouth while cuffed. Each piece of lobster thermidor was swallowed whole, the saturnalia lost as she gulped each piece, one after the other, as quickly as she could. But even so, Sarah's rush didn't allow her to complete her meal. The steward was also her jailer, and he took the half-eaten meal away from her even while the others were still picking away at the beginning of theirs.

Sarah then tried to sleep, but her body ached. Rest escaped her. Her lungs still burned from inhaling the water when the skiff was nearly capsized by the sub.

Now what made her body hurt the most was the fact that she couldn't move. The restriction of motion, not being able to use her hands and feet normally created a strange loss of freedom that changed who she was. Ankles tethered while seated for a long ride would drive anyone nuts. It made her cramp up. Pain. Lots of it.

Her wrists were bound so tightly that she bled. Both feet and hands were not getting the needed circulation. She kept moving as much as possible to improve the flow of blood beneath the constriction. She was shifting and squirming to relieve the pain and making constant adjustments to try to open arteries and veins to keep circulation going. Back and forth. The stress of being tied up in captivity. The stress of the unknown. The tension of constant fear. Sarah was exhausted.

Now, with the meals finished, Enson and Peña were back to work. Peña practically ignored Sarah, either working quietly or updating Enson. She was an incessant machine of efficiency. Enson continued to feign disinterest in her reports. But then the big man's square shoulders disappeared down the center aisle and he was out of sight behind the bathroom door again – for what seemed an eternity.

Sarah hoped he'd had a heart attack. Then she believed she needed to repent. "Pray for your enemies," she whispered to herself.

The chaffing on her wrists was worse because of the encrusted film of seawater on her skin. Her clothes were still wet. She was cold and shaking in the air-conditioned cabin of the jet, muscles increasingly tight and stiffening, and skin feeling scratchy over her whole body.

She finally fell into a fitful sleep. In her nightmares she heard a strange voice ... no, a familiar voice which had said horrible things when she had first regained consciousness ... terrorizing her. The nightmare repeated itself over and over. Each time the scene lasted a bit longer and became more and more real. The melting scenery between the sub and the plane became an existential rush of what was more hallucination than dream. More memory than vision.

*   *   *

"YOU HAVE A SPY?" Bear was excited. He jumped up from his seat. Now, standing over the far edge of Miguel's plateau of a desk, he leaned as much as he could towards the Pope, with both hands on the wooden top. "I want to be one of your spies," he said with determination.

"Why would you want to be a spy?" Miguel asked – glad to not have to answer the previous question.

"Excitement. Intrigue." He sat back down figuring he'd stumbled onto the perfect career choice. After all, the man behind the desk had already offered him a *sweet* job in Rome. He smiled, nodding his head up and down slowly as he regarded the luxuriously appointed office on the high seas. Bear's initial nervousness was dissipated. And he began to consider the possibilities. The Pope's got to be the richest man in the world if you consider him as CEO of a personal playground with an enormous amount of assets at his disposal. Of course he deploys spies. He likely has more of them then the CIA, MI5 and the secret police of Russia, Israel ... who else? Combined. I could become one of his top agents. Or? What would I have to do to become the Pope? Is there a lot involved? Would I have to become Catholic? No. I'd be precluded from marrying. Would I be able to change that rule once I got the job? But he said, "If I was good at it, would you hire me?"

"As a spy? I've already hired you as an assistant professor."

"What if I'd rather be a spy?"

"You'd have to lie."

"I'm really good at that," he responded to the Pope.

Miguel raised both of his eyebrows and frowned. "You'd end up killing someone. Either directly or indirectly. It's inevitable."

Bear gulped. His mouth suddenly dry.

The Pontiff continued. "And eventually, someone would kill you."

He tried to respond, but his throat was too dry.

"And it's very lonely. Extremely boring. Some stakeouts take months. Some undercover operations take years."

Bear thought, I don't like boring. Who does?

The Pope continued, "Being alone gets monotonous. You can't really have any friends. If you have any family, you must sever all ties, at least while you are active."

"Active?"

"Actively spying." Miguel said, looking humored by the exchange.

"When are you inactive?"

"When you quit or get killed. Whichever comes first."

"So no wife?"

"No."

"No kids?"

"Never."

"Not really a nine-to-fiver, huh?" Bear resigned.

"Not really." The Pope grimaced with pursed lips.

"Tell me more about the teaching position." Bear smiled.

"Before I do," Miguel said, returning the smile with relief, "I want Michelle to brief you regarding Tuvalu. You still want to go in?"

"Yes." And then he was reminded, "Any word about Charlie?"

Michelle materialized in time to answer, "Not yet, at least not definitive." She had been addressing the Pope, but now she looked at Bear. Her eyes revealed both her empathy at his predictable sense of loss and her own ineffable realization of the unexpected. She couldn't place it. But she'd felt something for the blonde-haired student. "We think he was ... *removed*."

"Removed?" Bear hadn't planned on actually verbalizing the question.

Miguel had. "What do you mean?" speaking quickly over the top of the young man's slow uptake.

"Timon's detachment arrived before Zelfa. They think they located the spot where he had … fallen." She had hesitated, choosing words with caution, for herself as much as for the others.

"Is he alive?" Bear blurted.

Michelle's face spoke well before her lips moved and vocal chords vibrated a response. "We don't know," she finally said. "We just don't know."

She fixed her eyes on Bear's.

"But I doubt it."

*   *   *

A STUDENT OF BOTH Greek and Hebrew, encouraged from an early age by both her father and her grandfather, Mandy knew what she held in her hands. Heinrich's research had often dealt with this very issue – the missing Mark.

Mark 16's ending. Long. Short. None. Many different endings considering all of the different manuscripts. All copies. A similar problem exists with John chapter 8, but not as great a problem as the ending of Mark's gospel. There are many inconsistencies among the various copies of the many books of the Bible from Genesis to Revelation, but it is fairly easy to figure out which are correct, except – the missing Mark.

With regard to the Gospel of Mark, she knew the controversy involved the last section of the final chapter. She knew it well. Since the Bible was divided into verses in 1560 AD, Mark 16:9-20 had become the way of labeling the longer ending of Mark. It was missing from the *Codex Sinaiticus* and the *Codex Vaticanus*. However, the vast majority of other manuscripts included the longer ending.

The ancient scroll in her hand ended with legible words that ran to the end of what is now known as verse 8. What appeared to be enough text to be several more verses, possibly another twelve, of Greek text below it were washed out. Smeared. Erased by water, chemicals, or some other liquid. Perhaps the manuscript was dropped into a tub, or a barrel and retrieved within a panicked split second, quickly dried but still ruined. Many inks used in the first century were soluble, unlike modern chemically fused mixtures. Crushed bugs, plants, flowers, even selected parts of animals were used to create inks that John Mark may have used to write Peter's gospel. Tree bards, grasses, seeds, bloods, soils, minerals found inside granite repositories, the choices were almost as endless as God's creation of colors and types of matter.

Mandy was acutely aware that she was cradling the final scroll of the original manuscript. An *original* Bible manuscript. The scroll felt immediately heavy in hand. A weight of ages. Antiquity's own Divinely inspired text. One of the four chosen to describe Christ's ministry here on Earth. Of all the gospels, she understood the significance of holding this one.

Cephas.

The Rock.

Simon bar Jonah.

Peter.

The leader of the twelve. One of the elders and pastors of the Church in Jerusalem. Mark described Peter's eyewitness testimony of Jesus' ministry. *Peter's* own version of what he saw over a period of three and a half years of daily contact with the Messiah, the Christ, the Son of the Living God.

John Mark had faithfully written down every word.

Peter had seen the miracles. He'd heard the parables. He'd experienced first hand, the compassion, the humility, and the forgiveness. No one more than Peter understood the Lamb voluntarily walking to the slaughter. No one better understood the betrayal of denying Jesus. No one better appreciated the risen Christ's so swiftly granted pardon. No one better felt the immediacy of full restoration to position and reputation.

Mandy's grandfather had been obsessed with finding *this* missing manuscript. For all of his decades of digging, this was the one he wanted to locate. This was the mystery he'd wanted to solve more than any other. He'd self-imprisoned his body in that cellar beneath the basilica in Lima. Buried under mounds of archives. Killing himself daily in his attempt to earn a salvation for his own betrayal. Did he know it was already offered on different terms? *Abuelito* was trying to find out what Peter had already learned.

Unconditional love.

"Peter?

"Peter? Do you love me?"

*   *   *

MIGUEL CLOSED HIS eyes tightly. The Pope appeared to be elsewhere.

Praying? Bear watched the priest petition. He saw an oracle's orison. A pontification? No. A conversation. But the physical had melded into a slow fade. It left the true reality of the spiritual plane in place, like choosing the most effective medium for the desired look. In art. In fashion. In landscapes. Architecture. Music. And even in sermons. "My sheep hear my voice."

Bear heard the quote. Words in red. Jesus said.

He gave the Pope a curious look. Miguel's eyes were still clamped shut. His body was still barely present. His soul may have not been there. His very spirit within him departed for fellowship with the Almighty much like the Presbyter's trip in the vision that wrote Revelation. But Miguel's mouth had not moved.

Bear had heard the statement though. And he answered.

"What?" Bear asked.

Michelle had left the room. The Pope was the only one who could have spoken the phrase. He rolled it around in his head. "My sheep hear my voice." Young Samuel running to Eli in the middle of the night. Bear stared at the Pontiff and waited for his reply.

Miguel's lids lifted to reveal pupils widened by the shutters. It made his eyes look primal. A character from a fairy tale. A figure of myth or of magic. But clearly a patron saint, a follower of the only begotten Son of the Father. He answered with an ethereal melodic tone.

"You were wondering how I pray?" Barely a question.

"I was?" He most certainly had been.

Miguel pulled a small, dark-blue hardback from his top drawer. He flipped worn pages. He read from page 52 of the thin book. "The intrusive ubiquity of visible things tends to draw a contrast between the spiritual and the real...."

"Ubiquity?" Bear knew the word, just couldn't put its use in context.

"Our five senses actually limit us," he responded, "but actually no such contrast exists."

"Limit?"

"They act as a barrier, blinding us to the true reality of the spiritual world that surrounds us all of the time. It is *more real* than," Miguel spread his hands out in a sweeping gesture indicating the tangible representations of mass they could see and touch, "this," he concluded.

"You are saying my physical senses keep me from God?"

"And so much more." Miguel slid the small book across the top of the desk. It's journey accented his point as the friction between the canvassed cover enveloping spiritual thought noisily skidded over the polished mahogany of wealth and power. The movement of the heavenly things over those of the Earth.

Bear's small hand reached out and grabbed Tozer's little book. Thin and yet lengthy. Words packed with years of meditative contemplation. A product of much prayer and countless hours of pouring over verse after endless verse of scripture. The written Word. It was the spiritual unlocked with a string of interconnected characters lined into subjects and vowels and modifiers and conjunctives. Letters. Poems. History. Narratives. Tozer's book sums up his reason for reading the Bible over, and over, and over, and over, again.

Bear looked at the title. It gently told him why the author dedicated his life to the Bible.

"The Pursuit of God."

*　　　*　　　*

SO THAT'S WHY *Codex Sinaiticus* and *Codex Vaticanus* didn't include the last part of Mark, she thought. Her eyes were drawn again to the smudges. The faded ink. Like a muted watercolor that barely cast the hue upon the medium.

But the vast majority of codices, the meticulous work of early disciples and monastery scribes, more and more, *included* verses 9-20. But how? The last section of the original ruined!

Of course, she answered the question. At least one copy was created *before* the bottom of the scroll was damaged. Or Mark or Peter could have been consulted after the damage was done so as to fill in the blanks? Either way, it made sense now. A simple answer would resolve a centuries old debate.

Mandy remembered that some copies of Mark's last chapter have an alternative conclusion that modern publishers usually call the "shorter ending." Still other manuscripts use different endings. Again, answering her own question, "Monks tried to fill in the blanks." Her voice spoke into the surreal stillness of the room. She hadn't intended to speak. It just came out. The physical manifestation of her mental machinations.

Her grandfather would always turn red in anger when he'd said something about it. "What were they thinking? You can't just make it up!" he'd scream. He'd stomp around the house during his Sunday afternoon visits. Her father would join in the tirades. Heated theological debates of exegesis and applicable lexicons. Soteriology. Eschatology. Ecclesiology. Christology. She hadn't understood most of it at the time, but in retrospect she'd always been amazed at how much they agreed upon. Their doctrines were so similar. The apologetics so alike. She'd wondered what caused Rome and the Church of England to split. Surely not theology. Another physical manifestation of the spiritual? Isn't that the truth about all action? Our decisions are not physical, not really. So our acting upon those decisions are just an outward reflection of a spiritual reality.

Did I really see a man disappear?

She thought about that for several minutes as she stood holding the scroll penned by John Mark. She frowned and carefully laid the parchment to rest on top of the mound of forgotten scripts. From her kneeling position, she reached up and lowered the lid down to the lip of the chest.

The treasure trunk puffed its stale air back at her chest as it clamped back down on itself.

Rising from her knees, she asked herself another, perhaps more esoteric question.

Was the man holding the scroll ever really here in the first place?

*   *   *

"YOU CAN KNOW GOD."

Bear held the devotional against his chest. He heard the Pope's words but didn't appreciate their significance.

"I do."

"You do what?" Friendly *and* austere.

"Know God." Bear choked on the words.

"Like you know Charlie?" A poignant choice.

"No."

"Why not?"

"That would be impossible."

Miguel widened the lids over his left eye and reached for his top desk drawer again.

Anticipating, Bear continued, "How can I possibly *know* an invisible God? A Supreme Being? The Creator of the entire universe? How can I know God in the same way that I know my best friend?"

The second book in so many minutes slid across the mesa of hardwood. This volume's physical state marked by a leather-bound cover almost didn't reach Bear.

"A Bible?"

"You read one?"

"I have one."

"It's not the same thing, you know," delivered by the Pope.

Bear sucked air in through his teeth.

"Turn to Matthew," Miguel suggested.

He did.

"Look at 17:20."

He did.

"But...." Bear tried to protest.

"Mark 11:22-24," the Pope persisted.

Bear turned the gold leafed edges and read.

"But...."

"Do you want me to have you read the same theme in Genesis 18, Exodus 3, Deuteronomy 28, I Samuel 2, then in Kings and Chronicles, in Job, Psalms and Isaiah? In Jeremiah, Daniel, Joel and Zechariah? In Mathew 18? Luke 18 and John 12-16? In Acts, Romans 4, I Corinthians 12-14? Do you want me to go on? There are plenty more."

The recitation of so many passages moved so quickly that Bear's head spun.

"No." He was already exhausted. "I get the point."

"Do you?"

"Yes."

"So is it possible to truly know God?"

Bear diverted. "I read Psalms a lot," he dodged.

Miguel began speaking from memory, "Oh Lord, you have searched me and know me.

"Marvelous are your works, and that my soul knows very well.

"How precious also are your thoughts to me, O God!

"When I awake, I am still with you."

"Psalms?" Bear guessed.

"139."

"Ah. I read them. Maybe once a … every couple … few … okay, not a lot." Bear felt like he was sitting in a confessional.

"I'm going to show you something."

Another book? Bear looked at the months of reading material in his lap. Doesn't it take a whole year to read through the entire Bible?

The Pope stood. A graceful walk. In the steps of the Good Samaritan. Elijah at the Jordan reaching out to hand his cloak to Elisha. Paul laid his hands on....

Bear watched the dream unfold. Melting walls. Rose-colored glass. The vision turned into a face. First the flesh and blood that burst into light underneath temporal linens. Grave clothes only gently used. A brief trip to Abaddon. Then to Paradise and back again in less than 48 hours. That same face whose shadow bore resemblance on the three to one herringbone twill weave that had hid in Istanbul for so long, that same face in the flesh now resumed its spiritual form.

Radiance.

Brilliance.

Warmth.

Joy and Peace.

Overwhelming love. The kind that gently puts you prone upon the gold-like glass.

Prostrate before the King of Kings.

Music.

Angels' dance.

A million vocals harmonized in choral psaltery.

Aroma's incense.

Every color. Every hue and every shade in between.

A taste of Heaven's Throne.

"When you awake, I am still with you."

Bear heard himself repeat the words to eyes like flames of fire blazing underneath a head of hair as white as whitest wool.

And then he awoke.

*   *   *

"THEY ARE SHOOTING at us again!"

"Have they all dropped?"

"No. There are a few that got stuck in the cargo doorway."

"We need to drop the weight!" Karl screamed.

"I'm trying!" Soledar continued yelling over the sounds of rushing wind and the scraping of metal. The tail's bay was still wide open waiting to usher out the final trio of trucks.

"Oh, wait. Okay. Whoa! There they go!"

VIA SAW THEM COMING – a cloud of jeeps dropping – a cluster of bombs swinging through the air towards their destination.

They had just arrived at the entrance of the resort. The long drive up to the front of The Brandenburg was ready to receive them. Its open gate before them. The exclusive resort was sprawled over the gentle rise of the hill with the mountain's face behind it. Nena stopped the H2 on the skirt of the drive. The white Nissan pulled up behind them having been passed on the way.

"Back up!" Via yelled, with her neck stretched out of her open window.

Nena slammed into reverse and swerved, narrowly missing Keyontay's Pathfinder.

A Mercedes-bomb cratered the drive in front of them. Nena punched the floorboard as she shifted and rushed away. Keyontay was reacting just as fast. He wheeled the Pathfinder around to his left and spun in behind the Hummer as it took off in the direction they had just come. The pair of trucks barely avoided the ball of fire that erupted exactly where they'd been stopped on the pea-stone drive.

Like rapid-fire shelling that stitched from the drive to the building, the 4x4 missiles cut the hotel in two.

The H2 was shooting off down the road back towards town with Via cursing in French. She used words that called into question whether she was indeed using one of the Romance tongues. She bit her lip and stared out her window in disbelief at the carnage. The mayhem. The resort now burning like Nero's Rome. Mandy, she thought. Where are you?

Keyontay followed but was more concerned than ever that Naomi's unconscious frame needed medical attention. And soon.

"How is she doing?" he asked.

"Fine I think," Pei-chin answered. "Her breathing seems better."

Still driving fast, they were hurling the trucks back down the path that led back into town. Via was planning on heading to the long airstrip on the other side of the lake. They'd have to take the back roads around the center of the city.

Suddenly, Nena hit the brakes and the H2 came to a screeching halt. Up ahead, in the snow that was bunched up on the side of the road, a woman stood smiling, her thumb extended to bum a ride.

Behind the hitchhiking hand stood Mandy. She widened her grin as Via and the others got out of the SUVs. Via ran up to her, relieved, and gave her a big hug. It was then that she first noticed the display behind her soldier.

A few feet back, sitting atop a trio of trunks like two Caribbean pirates, sat the strangest sight.

Herr Heinrich Stauffenberg and Ibn Zeyedi Jundishapur.

* * *

YOU KNOW WHEN you are too tired to sleep? When your body feels almost sick, but you know you're not? Flu-like. *That* kind of aching. That's how Sarah felt during the flight from Bariloche to a small island in the middle of the Pacific. She did finally sleep. Fitful. Weird. She fought against the strange dreams. When she became aware of reality once again, she was so exhausted her first thought was whether or not she'd fallen asleep at all. And being that tired, she couldn't quite seem to fully wake.

The Hawker 900XP landed on the main airstrip. Fongafale International airport. Almost an oxymoron.

As the customized corporate jet taxied, Sarah noticed pain in her wrists. Her fingers were numb. And there was a throbbing feeling in her jaw where she'd been slugged. The fatigue was crushing. Lids so heavy they wouldn't lift. She felt twice subjugated, first by her captors and now by this sleepy submersion of oblivion. Not knowing quite yet which is real, the dream or the inability to wake.

The slap across her face made it clear.

Sarah's mood, which was already sour, got worse. Curdled.

As she opened her eyes, she remembered her wild dreams: divers climbing a cross … Jesus' DNA test results introduced as Exhibit A in a court proceeding … a giant lobster strangling Joshua before he could propose marriage.

Joshua. Where are you?

The bulky flight attendant was standing over her. He'd slapped her hard with his calloused hands. His bulging muscles spoke of steroids and too many hours lifting weights. Pulling at the plastic tie-cuffs around her wrists, he was trying to get her in position to herd her up the aisle.

"Hey!" Sarah protested.

"Come on, now." He was quite condescending. "Easy. Don't try anything stupid."

Sarah gave him a disapproving look. One that said he was not that bright for asking a woman bound both at hands and legs to refrain from resisting. What was it that she would do if she were to *try anything?* But he ignored her non-verbal retort and used his bulging muscles to lift the lissome woman up off her seat and place her in the aisle. She was thankful her feet were still working.

Her knees shook a little, but when he let go, she remained standing. That's a good thing. He reached down and removed her lower cuffs.

She was marshalled up the aisle to the front of the plane. The front hatch was open on the port side, allowing the sun to stream into the forward cabin. The flight attendant squinted as if he couldn't handle the sunlight because of too many hours cloistered in the gym, his place of worship, too bad. God's gymnasium is so much more beautiful.

Herded out, she behaved.

Inside she felt uncontrollable. Hatred. Anger. Of the worst kind. And the cynicism had been building. She didn't like it. It wasn't who she was. Against her nature. Nevertheless, this was the hand she was dealt by the Lord of Lords.

And she had blown it.

Sarah found herself standing at the top of the lowered stairs. She turned back to look at her jailer. He had short cropped hair of nondescript muddy brown. It was receding in panic from beady eyes that were a little too closely set. He appeared to be chewing on something. She found him repulsive and was directing her anger at him.

He practically shoved Sarah out the door. At the top of the steps, she was looking down at the molten-hot, lava-like asphalt strewn all over the tarmac below. She resisted. Stayed put. Looked back at him and gave him another curt look. I've swum in the Med, and now I'm on an island in the South Pacific, some trip, Sarah mused sarcastically.

He pushed again.

The sweet, big-hearted soul trapped in a young blond's body snapped. "Okay already!" She glared and turned to make her way down the steps. Still kind and honest. Still genuine to the point that the real person inside is somehow always inexorably visible. Her heart permanently tattooed on her arm as sure as the inked scallop that rises at the base of her back.

But circumstances have a powerful effect on the best of us.

We can only take so much before we break down. The best parts of us get buried under the rubble of the pain and despair … the regrets and the guilt … the madness of life's downs … its twists and turns. The evil that is inside our hearts sometimes rises up to the surface and takes over.

That's when we need God the most.

And Sarah needed God badly.

Now.

But He didn't respond to her need at that moment. He withdrew. He abandoned her to test her, and He let her know one thing in parting, the Spirit reminding her of a verse – a promise. "The Lord does not abandon anyone forever."

But she wasn't listening. The most sugar-filled soul Joshua had ever known fermented and turned into a sour, biting pool of vinegar.

Half of her was locked up and it made her angry.

Her feet freed for the moment to make it down the stairs, Sarah walked slowly and deliberately. She was mad at the man following her. At Enson. At herself. And at God.

It was hot.

Dreadfully hot.

Thus Sarah arrived in Tuvalu.

*   *   *

BEAR FOUND HIMSELF rubbing his eyes as if he'd slept for years: a deep, peaceful, powerful slumber. He wasn't in the Pope's pelagic office anymore, and he didn't remember leaving it. Perhaps he'd never been there at all.

Was it all a dream?

"Like *The Matrix*," José's voice.

"What?"

José laughed.

Arkesha, trying to shush her husband, said, "You were talking."

"I was?" Bear yawned. "Was I asleep?"

"Your eyes were open. You walked through the door speaking about seeing Jesus face to face, and about spiritual dimensions, and temporal shadows of reality." Arkesha used a motherly tone.

"You know, *Matrix* stuff," José said without looking up from his work. "Hey! Neo! Come and give me a hand," he joked.

Bear dragged his feet as he walked over to where José was bent over a jumble of tools, and metal, and cables, and straps, and wooden strips, and little shiny balls. "What's all this?" Bear asked. Then his eyes fell on what looked like a finished product hiding among the supplies.

Arkesha was using a huge crescent-shaped needle to sew the front straps of a harness. José was welding a final metal single-arc spring to the rolling casing, a bearing at the end of two wings. The harness was a full-torso wrap like a professional skydiver's acrobatic net. Where the nylon ropes would normally string out into a fan, there were long arching metal wings. They looked like they could have been made from a semi-truck's chassis springs.

She answered the question. "We will use a molded graphite alloy for the ones that go into production. It will be significantly lighter than these." She pointed. "José calls it the Shaft Descender."

"Huh?" Bear was holding a metal piece in place where José had indicated.

"I, on the other hand, prefer Crevice Climber."

"But it's designed for *going down* a narrow space," José objected.

"And with some minor changes, it will allow for a quick and safe passage up, as well," Arkesha retorted.

"So it's a belay?" Bear's mind was buzzing.

"No. It's a tension control. It regulates your speed of descent with gears in the casters. You manipulate your rate of fall with this control mechanism on your belt." He pointed.

"So it's a belay." Arkesha's voice. "And, it can be used to go down *and* back up again."

José finished welding. "Okay. It's finished."

His wife gave him a look.

Bear got an apology.

Arkesha got a kiss. "Compromise?" he asked.

So Bear suggested, "Bear Belay."

"Or Bearing Belay?" Arkesha modified.

"The Shaft Belay," José concluded.

ל ו

VIA WAS TRYING to figure out how to fit everyone into the vehicles along with the Cardinal's trunks. Pei-chin was still in the back of the Nissan holding Naomi as Mandy slipped in beside them. Heinrich squeezed next to her and was practically on her lap. The trunks were being loaded, two into the back of the Hummer and the other one into the back of the Pathfinder, when a much larger vehicle presented itself in the middle of the road in front of them! As it rested on its cushion of air, the main hatch rose up slowly like a deep sea lantern's fish lure, beckoning them inside.

Heinrich looked terrified.

Ibn clapped his long slender hands. He was sitting in the front seat of the Nissan. He interlaced his bulbous knuckles and turned around to face Heinrich. "Cool submarine, huh?"

Everyone left the trucks in the middle of the road and climbed aboard *The Ark,* hoisting their cargo up to the hatch. Aviles' trunks just barely fit through.

Nena manned the sick bay, attending to Naomi. Keyontay called their counterparts on the other side of town to tell them to leave without them and meet them in Fongafale.

Via walked onto the bridge. In sylphic stride she walked up to the Captain, wrapped her arms around his neck and kissed the top of his white-graced head. "Thank you, Admiral," she said sweetly.

He chuckled, "I know you told me that we," he patted the instrument panel lovingly, "were no longer needed. But as I was heading back home to Norfolk my radar picked up those nasty bugs. So I turned around."

"Karl!" Via had let it slip her mind. "Oh no!"

"Via, it's okay. We've dispensed with the Apache gun-ships." He patted the dash once again and smiled.

"Is Karl okay?"

"If he's the pilot of the elephant that flew off towards Chile...."

"*Oui*. He is." He got a kiss on the cheek. "Thank you! *Merci Beaucoup*."

Pei-chin flew into the bridge. "Via! Via!"

She was breathless.

"Come. Come! You've got to see this!"

*   *   *

PRODDED BY THE man in the tented shirt, Sarah was directed to the edge of a crowd of people. Her rubber Reebok soles started sticking to hot, tar-soaked gravel beneath her feet. The steward used a Colt .45 to make his point. She wished she was carrying her own Second Amendment version of persuasion. Alas, her Browning was back in Eugene.

Sarah felt the bile rise in the back of her throat as she saw the many other bound souls standing in bunches waiting for the buses, like those whom Hitler relocated with his trains. She was now at the station, on the landing. The vinegar inside of her was stewing like radiation inside Chernobyl's melted walls. She was feeling horrible about her situation. The mass of human flesh that pressed up and around her reminded her of a picnic on a hot summer day that should have been cancelled. Too much heat. Too little food. But this barbeque spelled their demise. Perhaps she was the centerpiece of this gathering – to be laid out on a table with an apple in her mouth – North Carolina style.

The chattel started moving. The buses had arrived. Sarah worried instead of praying. She thought of all of the worst things that could happen next. What was Enson up to? Where were they all headed? Would she live through this? If she died, would it be painful?

And Jesus watching. Waiting. Hoping for Sarah's prayer of faith.

The juxtaposed backdrop of tropical palms. The ocean breeze. The beaches. The crystalline waters of the South Pacific. Not a bad place to be. Just not today. A salty zephyr blew in from over a turquoise lagoon. The atoll wrapped itself around in a huge circle. The lagoon was filled with millions of colorful corals and brightly hued fish.

Sarah panicked and froze.

"What's wrong?" A kind voice.

Sarah couldn't bring herself to respond.

Peña stood near her left side but behind just slightly. She faced forward so as not to telegraph that she was conversing with Sarah.

"Dr. Suri," Peña continued, "he is the madness behind the experiments." The deep intake of breath behind her left ear caused Sarah to remain motionless and concentrate on the words of the speaker. "He has developed a method of cloning." There was a long pause. "And the blood he has been duplicating is – Divine."

"What?" Sarah had heard Joshua's explanation of Enson's plan. But she hadn't really thought it through until now. "Jesus' blood? Cloned? Why?" Her whisper was hoarse. She already knew the answer, on a theoretical level. It is one thing to be hearing such a story in the finery of the Vatican. It is quite another to know you are imprisoned by the man responsible for the scheme. The fraud. The insidious quest to make life eternal through the physical instead of the spiritual. "Why are you telling me this?" she asked, almost turning her head around.

"Dr. De La Cruz specializes in ribonucleics and plasmas. Suri in adenines and thymines. They were able to sequence the DNA into a working model on the computer over a year ago. They just needed enough raw material. A sample with enough undamaged cells. Guanines and cytosines. They have it now. They've done it. And you will receive the serum."

"Me?" This time Sarah did turn and look into the Peruvian's blue eyes.

"Pray that it works," she urged and broke her gaze. Stepped away. Slipped into the back of a black Bentley Mulsanne sedan with custom rims.

Joshua.

In a quiet whisper to herself. "If I ever need to be rescued – now would be good."

*   *   *

"WE'VE LOCATED CHARLIE."

"Where? How is he? Let's go get him!" Bear had left José and Arkesha to again find the Pope.

"Bear, calm down." Miguel was standing in the large library that filled much of the starboard lower hull above the forward berthing area. "We're already headed that way. We should be there within the next few hours."

"There? I thought we were headed to Tuvalu?"

"Yes. We are. Charlie's there."

"That is impossible. We just left the Mediterranean an hour or so ago."

"It's been a few hours."

"But it should take a day or more. Shouldn't it?"

"There's a porthole behind me. Take a look." The Pope was holding a book, standing next to a floor-to-ceiling case which was part of rows and rows of stacks nestled in walnut shelving carefully crafted in neo-classical styling. It was a sizeable library, and the carpets were plush, soft and the colors warm. The large book was in his left hand as he slowly turned the page with his right.

Bear walked past him to look through the thick round glass. Miguel's head didn't turn as he spoke. "He's still alive. We'll do our best to rescue him when we get there. Keep praying."

Bear felt better already and said a quick prayer while looking out. The large window framed a circle of sea with smudges of green far in the distance, moving fast out of view. "All I see are islands."

"The Falkland's windward side."

"So we're almost to the Strait of Magellan!" And as he said it, he realized they'd crossed the Atlantic from North Africa to Tierra del Fuego at the southern tip of South America in less time than it took commercial jets.

"Yes. But we won't use the Strait. It's too slow. We will pass through *El Estredo de Le Maire*, with Tierra del Fuego on our starboard and Staten Island to port."

"New York?"

"No." Smiling. "Argentina's Staten Island is a bit less populated."

*   *   *

"HE'S DEAD."

Via cried. Tran had been with her on every mission since he'd joined her unique private army.

Nena had caught her in the corridor with Pei-chin, to tell her the news.

Then Nena cried. Nena never cried.

"I didn't know him." Pei-chin spoke out of obligation with her slight Far East accent. She hung her head in respect. "He is a good man." Her intonation evoked Great Pandas and bamboo, dragons and silk-robed warriors, treasure fleets of globe-trotting junks and a Forbidden City still hiding itself from the rest of the world. A spiritual people, an advanced civilization since the ancients left the Fertile Crescent stepping on the unspoiled soil of a Silk Road not yet traversed. A people who'd always understood life in its parallel dimensions, such that the message of The Way has always spread quickly among its chosen people, those hungry for truth, willing to live selflessly, intelligent and humble. It was from this heritage of the oldest continuous culture still intact that Pei-chin properly chose the present tense.

"Is?" Nena looked up.

"The Sadducees." Pei-chin's voice stayed steeped in a thousand generations of Christianity in what is now the Fujian region. She continued, "They asked Jesus to solve a riddle. Because they do not believe in life after death, they devised a hypothetical juxtaposition."

Nena was already following. She'd been a prodigal for her entire adult life, but her parish in Boston had instilled in her the basic truths. "Like whether God can create a stone so large he can't lift it?" She wiped the tears from her cheeks.

"Precisely," said with exotic Asian flair. "Ancient Jewish law required the brother of a deceased man to marry his widow. It protected the family name while avoiding state welfare problems or temple charity needs. They asked Jesus if seven brothers in succession all marry the same woman after each former brother dies, in Heaven whose wife is she? Of course, they were hoping to create a problematic situation. Men had been allowed more than one wife under the law, but a woman was not allowed more than one husband. The Sadducees thought it quite the quandary that a woman may end up with seven of them in Heaven. Plus, Jesus had already publicly condemned divorce except for unfaithfulness."

Both women were now entranced.

"Solomon says to answer a fool according to his folly. Then he says, back to back, *do not* answer a fool according to his folly. The two proverbs are each facing opposite hemispheres of wisdom, apparently incongruous.

"In his answer, Jesus demonstrated what the ancient king of Israel meant by those apparently conflicting axioms. First, he took their question at face value, as if it was delivered with integrity, an honest inquiry. He simply explained to them that there is no marriage in Heaven. But then," Pei-chin's voice now wafted over the surface of the Yellow Sea, "Jesus *also* answered their pretextual question, the one hidden within their ill-contrived trap. Knowing their thoughts, he reminded them that they accepted as truth that Moses spoke to God at the burning bush that said, 'I AM the God of Abraham, Isaac, and Jacob.' Jesus pointed out God's careful choice of words. Then he concluded powerfully, 'God is the Lord not of the dead, but of the living.'"

Pei-chin slipped into the study to leave them alone in their thoughts. That Tran was alive … with God.

"Is she a preacher?" Nena asked.

"No," Via answered, "she's a paleographer."

*   *   *

SARAH BOARDED A waiting bus. There were several.

Along with the rest of the imprisoned.

Drivers drove.

The buses had bars on the windows as if men and women with shackled wrists could bust through glass and escape from a moving vehicle. And the driver had a cage to separate him from his "dangerous" passengers. The armed guard up front with the driver was a bit much as well. Sarah furled her brow and settled into her vinyl seat. She thought about praying, but didn't.

Her need to use a bathroom was growing.

Painfully.

But the lengthy ride on the bus from one end of the atoll to the other came with no bathroom. No stops. Just lunch.

Their final meal?

Before the tests. To serve as guinea pigs. Test subjects. Human experimentation. Her clothing, stiff with Mediterranean Sea minerals, scratched at her fair skin. And she was hungry. The half meal she gobbled up earlier had passed through her small stomach and it grumbled now in discontent.

A thin box of green cardboard was unceremoniously tossed onto her lap. At least she wasn't bored. It took the rest of the trip to figure out how to open the packaging and eat the sandwich and chips with cuffed hands. Three chips.

Sarah finished eating and looked longingly at the small bottle of water. She was thirsty. Parched. But didn't dare add any liquid to her already suffering body. Her bladder was protesting loudly already. Her disapprobation of the buses moving so slowly, like snails with all the time in the world, made her even more uncomfortable.

Time.

She felt different about it now.

Time.

God sees it so much differently than we do.

Time.

Had she been praying, she'd have been reminded of all the Scriptures that tell her God's unique perspective about it. Like John's chapter seven. And Job's patience while testing was done. And Peter's proclamation that Jesus would have already returned if not for *his* patience with us, *his* desire that we all come to repentance.

But Sarah was not ready to repent. She was angry. And miserable. And ready to recant her faith if God didn't reverse course. This time she'd had enough.

The buses slowed to a stop. She looked out the window at the tropical paradise. Had they arrived at the fun side of the island? Marty? No. She frowned. Saw Enson's Bentley pull up. Peña's long legs appeared out of the back of the huge sedan. The executive criminal emerged from the other side. A sizable contingent of soldiers armed to the teeth materialized out of nowhere. And bathrooms were within sight!

A wave of hope, almost relief, passed over her body. She broke out into a sweat.

Time.

Forced to wait another forty-five minutes until allowed to use the facilities.

Sarah was ready to fight.

Looking for a means of escape.

But still, she didn't have the mind to seek the face of God.

En mass, the groups that were now separated, men from women, were headed into two huge service elevators. The freight lifts carried fifty or more of each group. Sarah couldn't help thinking of Tom Cruise, and she heard Kenny Loggins singing Danger Zone inside her head. That's how large the elevator was. But it was crowded full of people. Shoulders pressed up against the backs and chests and arms of other women just like herself. Shackled. Doomed. Condemned. Lost. As if she'd died already. And the world forgot her.

She would normally have thought about loving her enemies. But not now. Not today.

She nursed anger. As the lift dropped away from the sandy soils of the surface of the island, she encouraged the rage. Sarah became someone she had sworn she would never be.

They continued to drop.

Down.

Way, way down.

To the root of the island. The Pacific is 8000 feet deep in this part of the world and the islands go all the way down.

The freight elevator finally came to rest so far down inside the rock that her ears had popped for the third time. They were ordered off. Stumbling and tripping over each other trying to comply, they finally managed to disembark.

Everyone entered a huge lab. All Sarah could see beyond the victims was stainless steel, concrete, equipment, cabinets, and white coated laboratory personnel – scurrying in between a long row of hospital beds. And off to the left, down the hall, more beds.

Sarah was feeling sick.

Then she saw the blood.

She cringed.

Not because she was still detained by a megalomaniac. Buried alive at the bottom of his South Pacific base. Inside an evil lair. About to be used as a simian for drug testing. About to ingest intravenously the cloned blood of an ancient body. The DNA of a man killed close to 2000 years before. And not just any man. The Son of God. And not just any son of God. His only Begotten. God made flesh. God Himself.

Sarah instinctively cringed because the underground lab was drab. Dreary. Bland. No color. No warmth. No texture contrasts. The interior designer inside of her wanted to change a few things. She figured Target. Home Depot or Lowes. Just a few things. Lots of paint. And hang a few pictures. The woman in her. Like a hen building her nest.

Which made her think of Prometheus.

The painting used to hang over her mantle in Eugene.

The titan was painted imprisoned and tortured by Zeus for stealing fire and giving it to man. And this made her think of God.

So Sarah prayed.

She poured out her heart to her Creator. Her Redeemer. Her friend. And the God of all creation, Jesus, forgave her for being so bitter. He turned her vinegar into the sweetest Cana wine.

*   *   *

"HE'S DEAD."

"But you said we'd try to rescue him." Not logical, but Bear said it.

Only an hour had passed since Bear had watched *Isla de los Estados*, one of del Fuego's Staten Island group, float by their port side porthole. The Pope was still standing. Still reading. It made Bear think of the animals that sleep while standing. It made him tired just looking at the Pontiff. Bear stared out the window at the South Atlantic and thought of Magellan. He'd viewed the same scenes. The Portuguese explorer had set out for South America's southern tip carrying a copy of the Piri Reis map in his hand, the same map that the Turkish cartographer had assembled from the maps stolen from China's Zheng He collection. Bear thought about how forty-five centuries had passed from the time the continents had first divided, and the globe had to be remapped. Was Zheng He really the first to do so? Likely not. The Earth had changed since the Great Flood. When there was but a single super-continent, mapping had been so much easier. And the months are now longer, the years slightly too. Orbits are off. Tides skewed. Our shifting poles are now on a tilted axis where before Noah's Flood they were not. Bear considered all this along with the simple math that would have been used to determine both latitude and longitude on a single land mass before all of the anomalies that followed Noah's great escape. But then Miguel had dropped this bomb on him. Charlie's dead? How could that be?

A rainbow shifted in the late afternoon mist. It rose from the frigid brine that flowed beneath the catamaran. Bear was staring off into the wide blue expanse of the South Pacific now. Fiji lay many, many miles away, past his horizon.

"We are," the Pope answered.

"But how are we to rescue him?" Bear's eyes now resembling those socketed in Charlie's corpse.

The Pope reached for a book on the nearest library shelf.

He handed it to Bear.

"Another Bible?" Bear was not pleased.

"Turn to John 11."

He did. Reluctantly. But he hid his resistance. It *was* the Pope who'd asked him to do so.

Miguel watched Bear speed through the text. "So?" The Pope spoke as Bear's eyes lifted from the page.

"But Jesus is God," Bear protested.

"Well said," Miguel continued, "now look at Mark 16:18."

A quick turn and another quick read later. "It says *sick.* Dead is different."

"Acts 9."

Speed reading again. "Peter was touched by Christ," Bear argued, still resisting.

"20."

Twenty-two seconds later. "Paul was...." Bear was beginning to experience an enlightenment that only comes from reading the Scriptures in context with each other. Interpret the Word by the Word. It won't come from sermons, commentaries, or best-selling Christian books. Not even this one. Not like it comes from the pure and powerful Word of God.

"You are going to raise Charlie from the dead?" Bear hopefully asked.

"No."

The Pope smiled.

"You are."

* * *

SHE WAS ASSIGNED a bed and strapped in with large leather straps. Then Sarah was cuffed to the metal rails with silver circlets of steel. A nurse walked up to her bedside, the first beneficiary of her Spirit-induced inebriation.

The nurse received Sarah's sweetest smile.

But the graceful curve of warmth didn't have the intended effect. In fact, it had the opposite, yet Biblical, result of piling coals of fire in an apical pile on top of the nurse's head.

Sarah tried to help, gave some suggestions regarding the IV as the nurse tried anxiously to find a vein. Five tries with the big bore needle. But Sarah was now experiencing the same Spirit inside of her that had raised Christ from the dead. So she waited patiently for the stint and then watched as the catheter delivered clear fluids dripping from the bag hooked over her head. The drugs made her feel woozy. She looked up at the top of the pole that held the bag of chemicals being pumped into her body: a large, clear plastic bag with a clear but tinted fluid. Behind it was a blood-red piggyback, then another smaller bag piggybacked … the last one full of yellow death.

The saline bag had antibiotics. The middle bag was undoubtedly the one with the Suri-made clone of cells copied from the body of the Incarnate One. The third label was hard to read, but Sarah did finally make it out – poison.

Enson's Jesus drug. His Fountain of Youth. His serum for hedonistic immortality. DNA stolen. Another age-old perversion of the Holy into the vile. The detestable. Part of our selfishness and cruelty towards a loving God. Each of the human test subjects would first get infused with the antibiotics, then the blood – the fake blood of the Redeemer. Another counterfeit. After the ancient DNA infuses the lab rats, each would receive the lethal injections – to see if the serum of cloned blood accomplished the goal of immortality. Sarah was thinking. Figuring it all out. She looked across the room and saw Roland Enson among the white-coated scientists, doctors, nurses, and Peña – talking with the evil, main man.

The Holy Spirit prompted Sarah. Looking again at Enson she realized she had love for him. Enson. Yes, not the sin, but the sinner. Her brows pushed up into her forehead as she considered the matter. Enson was walking over. Coming straight for Sarah's bed.

"Hello, Mr. Enson. I like your tie. Boyd's?" she asked.

"I don't shop in Philly, Ms. Byrd," he snarled. "But I'll tell your boyfriend that you were in a good mood before you died."

"Not a lot of confidence in your product, huh?" stated with a smile.

"To the contrary," he responded and gave her a devilish grin, "you will survive the first round of poisoning, maybe the second. You will have the same blood coursing through your veins as God gave His Only Begotten Son. They tried to kill Him but couldn't. There is power in the blood, Ms. Byrd."

The old hymn started singing inside her head as she considered his mistaken interpretation of scripture.

He gave her a sardonic glare. "But I have special plans for you. If the Amaryllis doesn't produced a fatal delirium. If the hydrocyanic acid doesn't do you in. If the strychnine doesn't put you into deadly convulsions, I am prepared to have you shot. Drawn and quartered. Hung from the rafters. I'll put you under an executioner's axe if I have to." He paused. "Unless, of course, the serum is powerful enough to prevent any manner of death. Jesus did receive a lethal dose of lashes with a lead tipped whip. His flesh was in shreds when they nailed him to that cross. And he walked away from it."

As Enson finished his monologue, his voice trailed off so that Sarah could barely catch the last few words. But then he added, "That would be interesting. I will keep trying to kill you, of course. But don't you worry your pretty little head about it, I will eventually find a way. And when I do, I will harvest your indestructible organs. I can see the headlines now – 'MIRACLE HEART TRANSPLANT PATIENT LIVES FOREVER!'"

"You just used finger quotes in the air like Dr. Evil."

"No I didn't," Enson insisted.

"All right. Maybe I was just seeing things. Anyway, that still leaves you with a huge consumer confidence problem. You are going to be selling eternal life, right?"

He nodded. Enson found himself curiously drawn into the conversation.

Sarah remained cheery. Confident. Aware. Spirit-filled.

"So," she continued, "I get it – the whole idea of immortality without responsibility? Big seller, I'm sure. But sales will take a nose dive once you succeed in killing me."

He stood silent for a few minutes. Regarding the words. Looking at his prisoner and wondering.

Sarah just laid there. Head propped on a pillow. Draining the saline. Slowly waiting. Waiting to be rescued. Hoping she'd not be subjected to die a thousand deaths before she died.

Enson spoke, "When they smeared the text that described the map to the hidden cache of Jesus' blood, they replaced it with a section at the end of St. Mark's gospel, final chapter, Jesus' own words as recorded by Nicodemus, found among his letters upon his death. He recorded that Jesus said, 'If you drink anything deadly, it will by no means hurt you.' This poison's not going to hurt you. Jesus' heart was pierced with a Roman spear. And yet he walked around and was seen by over 500 witnesses afterwards. Jesus also said, 'By my blood you shall be saved.' Paul was infused with it. He was stoned to death. Several times. They couldn't kill him either. Before St. John was exiled to Patmos, he was boiled in oil and he survived."

Sarah didn't respond. But she was praying for him. She was asking Jesus to forgive him. She was asking Jesus to reveal the truth to him, to draw him to repentance, to save him.

Enson continued, "You may not be able to be killed, darlin', and if so, Jesus was indeed telling the truth. But since you are who you are to my greatest nemesis, you will get to live through every bit of torture. Thank your boyfriend for that. Blame him. Hate him. Every time you live through painful loss of life."

She heard Jesus speaking to her in a still small voice. "Even the demons believe in God and shudder." But knowing the truth is not enough, is it? Finally, she said to Enson, "You have issues."

He smiled a black smile.

She continued, "And your last statement is antithetical. Incongruous. Nonsensical."

"What?" He looked dazed.

"You can't live through loss of life. There can be life *after* death, but...."

He interrupted her. "I can't see what he sees in you. You'd drive me nuts."

She had a retort. "Do you really think that the Apostles went through some sort of blood-brothers ritual with Jesus?"

"Absolutely. What else would explain their powers? They kept the vials of Christ's blood along with their own. First in Jerusalem. Then at Jundishapur. Antioch. Edessa. And then...."

She cut him off. "3940 ccs is a lot of belladonna."

"What?" He looked confused.

Sarah pointed to the smaller piggyback. "It must have taken a long time to secure it all."

"How did you know how much I...." But he stopped.

"I counted. 102 of us. I did the math."

"You *are* nuts," he confirmed.

But Sarah gave him another warm smile. "He's going to save me, you know." Complete confidence.

"Joshua? I seriously doubt it."

"No," she said, "Jesus."

٣٧

SHE STEPPED INTO the study aboard *The Ark*. If she wasn't already walking inside the glory of another dimension, Via was now.

All three of the Cardinal's trunks were on the floor, lids open – gaping maws exposing rich rosewood linings. Pei-chin, Mandy, Heinrich, and Ibn crowded the small room's carpeted floor awash with cartouch pyramids. Half-spread whorls of parchments full of brittled history lay on the desk next to the pelorus.

Donning protective gloves, Pei-chin picked up a small scrap of vellum. Her porcelain face was graced with a beautiful smile. The others stayed lost in their discoveries, still cross-legged on the Berber piles. Pei-chin had been sitting on her heels. As she rose, two small prints showed where she'd been kneeling after coming into the study. "I thought you might want to see this." She was holding the broken shard gently for the bare-handed Via to examine.

Via stared into the aged skin. "What is it?"

"A letter."

"I can't read it."

"It's Mauretanian."

"Morocco?"

"The Moor who wrote it was a skilled linguist."

"It's a scrap of parchment."

Pei-chin gave Via a *pay attention to the expert* look.

Via's face said *go on*.

"He's using a 7th century dialect to converse in the 19th."

Via remained silent but showed her lack of understanding.

"Significant," Pei-chin responded, "because Donatism died out by then."

"All I know is that these trunks were in Spain during the Napoleonic Wars."

"Exactly. What's a Spanish Cardinal doing using ancient Berber to correspond in the 19th century?"

Via could tell Pei-chin already knew the answer to that question. But that's not what interested her.

"What's this got to do with me?" Prompting. Reminding. "You didn't drag me in here to talk about a Catholic Moor's cryptic choice of language."

"Right here!" Pei-chin's exclamation was muted, as if restrained by the library's walls or the contents of Aviles' chests, or both. She was pointing at a word.

Via's eyebrows were getting significantly higher over helpless eyes.

"*Savoie.*" Practically said in Mandarin.

Pei-chin had her full attention.

"This letter defends your family. That what they did was for," said with the voice of all of China, the full-weight of its past, present and future, billions of souls now nodding with respect, repeating the single word over and over, as if synonymous with Via's family name, "honor."

* * *

"THERE," HE SAID. "Happy?"

"Yes. I am," she said.

He held up the Shaft Belay, heavy, but manageable. "Me too." He used his eyes to ask for help.

She held the stitched X-back while he slipped into the harness.

"We make a good team," he said.

"You don't think I'm nagging?"

"Isn't that what a wife is for?"

He got hit.

"We offer classes."

It was the voice of the Pope.

They both blushed as much as their dark complexions would reveal.

"Counseling … therapy even," Miguel continued to joke.

"What are you doing down here?" José sputtered.

"Checking on my Archangel."

Arkesha burst out with a relieved laugh. "You do kinda look like a...." She let herself continue to cackle as she stared at José wearing their invention.

"Arched wings of steel! At your service!" José beamed back to the Pope.

"When I'd asked you two if you could help us plan how we'd penetrate the lab, I had no idea what I was getting myself into." Miguel was laughing.

"You wanna hear it?" Arkesha asked with a sparkle.

"Shoot," said the Pope, in jeans, pulling up a chair.

Michelle, the consummate bodyguard, appeared.

Arkesha moved in front of a large rolling whiteboard.

She began enthusiastically swinging a dry erase sword between artful sweeping movements of a coach's fluid Xs and Os and countless arrows until she even lost Michelle. She finished.

"Pretty cool, huh?" José's chipper conclusion laid atop the mound that Arkesha built.

"Convincing," the Pope ruled. "Michelle?"

"Ah...." Considering the various lies popping into her head, and then the truth, "She lost me."

"Truth," Miguel surmised, "… underrated, isn't it?" He gave her a thankful and approving nod. "Lost me too," he laughed. "That's why I like it!"

José exuberantly turned to his wife. "Who's your daddy?"

"Wayne Rink!"

The married couple exchanged gleeful chuckles while the Pope and his bodyguard looked on with confused expressions. They'd not seen the movie.

"It avoids *Ecclesiastical Atrophy*." The Pontiff further explained, now serious in tone. "Or in your case," he was facing Michelle, "*Bureaucratic Atrophy*." Then he added, "No offense, but aren't all military and paramilitary organizations run like bureaucracies?"

"I prefer a dictatorship model." Almost icy.

"What's the difference?" suggested by the Pope.

"I have a question," José interrupted.

"Shoot," from the Pope.

"How did you know about the hidden lab in Tuvalu? Its design. Its layout. Its security."

"Simple." His frown was an expression of shrugged nonchalance. "Your ring."

"Isabella's ring?" José pulled it out.

My ring, thought the Moor in jeans. "Can I see it?"

"Sure." An extremely accommodating inflection.

Miguel held the ring in his hand, feeling its weight. "Do you mind?" A humble request.

"Not at all." Same inflection.

The Pope slipped it onto his finger and held up the hand so the light reflected off the Donatistic cross.

*   *   *

THE SINGLE TEAR that found its way down her cheek didn't begin to express the range of emotions that Via experienced at that moment. She started laughing and crying as she hugged the diminutive ancient scripts expert.

Via broke into a string of beautiful French. Everyone in the room stopped what they were doing to listen to the musical cadence of linguistic artistry. Via's gamine hairline framed the face of a woman reborn. Ibn saw Eve in the Garden of Eden.

"There are other documents that concern the shroud." Pei-chin didn't have to ask if Via wanted to look through them.

Her dark blue eyes said *show me.*

"Over here." Pei-chin pointed to a stack of parchments next to the pelorus. "They are all in Castilian."

Via nodded. She had a working knowledge of the language from her years of tracing the grave clothes of Jesus. She stepped over, sitting down to pour herself into more of her family's story.

His eyes now back on the small illustrated book in his gloved hand, Ibn turned to the frail figure crouched on the carpet next to him. "The Cardinal was a Donatist."

"*That,* I can see for myself." The testy German grumbled as he perused the original manuscript of the once missing Mark.

"Have you always been this grumpy?" Ibn smiled.

"No!" Mandy answered from her corner of the triangle of bodies grouped together on the carpet. She felt like she needed to pass around a peace pipe. "He's a sweet man. Kind. Generous. Selfless."

But Heinrich had his own response ready, only biting his tongue long enough for his granddaughter to effuse the praise. "Are you going to tell us about the wig?"

"Ouch!" Ibn held his heart mimicking an injury by dagger.

"*Please,*" Mandy begged.

"Roman puppet!" said under his breath.

"Gnostic!" Heinrich shot back.

"Inquisitor!"

"Mystic!"

"Babylonian!" Snarling.

"Cathar!" the German accused.

"Boys!"

Hands reaching for necks.

"Boys!" Naomi's voice finally rose above the fray.

*   *   *

"WHAT'S WRONG?!" Arkesha's worried look.

Bear had burst into the room. He was heaving. Deep breaths. Excited. Hyper. Uncontrolled. "I did it!" he proclaimed. "I did it!"

"Charlie?" Miguel wore a huge surprise. "Already?"

Bear's head angled to one side, his ear trying to kiss his shoulder. Eyes of a puppy three houses down but a thousand miles from home. Then, "Oh, not yet."

"Charlie?" Arkesha.

"Charlie?" José just a split second behind and speaking on top of her.

They hadn't heard.

"He's dead!" Bear announced like it was great news.

Arkesha started to cry.

José almost lunged to attack the harbinger's face. Bear was practically smiling, breathless between his great gulps of air.

"And I'm raising him!" Bear boasted within the next oxygen-sucking break.

Arkesha's tears turned to a trickle.

José's anger stayed unabated, but he restrained himself.

The Pope had to intervene. He stood on white K-Swiss soles and held his hands, palms up between the young men. "It's my fault," he confessed.

Just then Bear noticed that the Pope had changed his attire once again.

The need for Bear to explain himself evaporated as well. Miguel lowered his arms and moved his mouth. "Bear." He turned his back towards José and Arkesha. Then, quieter, "What are you talking about?"

"It's that passage in Mark, the week before the crucifixion...." Still breathing hard and looking at the tennis shoes and jeans. "I did it. It works!" Now at Miguel's face. "I've already done it!" His voice sounded like weathered stone.

The Pope regarded the young man carefully for a few minutes. Silence. José got his wife to help him slip out of the Shaft Belay. A Galilean fragrance from bygone days filtered into the nitrous space.

Bear bent over with palms on slightly folded knees, like a marathon runner at the other side of the tape. He almost threw up. His faltering feet failed. Ankles weak, he tumbled. Miguel reached out and caught yet another fainting man.

*　　　*　　　*

HER SILK BLOUSE was titanium white. Her skirt was a beautiful shade of light green, of course. And her left arm was in a sling, tell-tale of Mandy's efficient work after Pei-chin's temporary bandaging. Naomi stood in the doorway, straddled over the threshold with one hand on her hip and a playful scowl above her eyes. There was residual pain from her gunshot wound radiating in her tone. *"Déjà vu?"* she asked.

Four palms turned to the ceiling, rotating outward over bent elbows.

"I thought they'd become friends," Mandy said.

"I thought they'd gotten lost, or killed," Naomi addressed her boys, "but instead, while I'm worrying about what happened to the two of you, here you are, still arguing with each other."

"They were chummy when they showed up in The Brandenburg's sub-basement," Mandy continued.

The two women conversed as if the squabblers weren't present.

"Last I saw them, before they ran off on me, they were fighting like children."

"They abandoned you?" Mandy gasped.

"Left me in the middle of a gun fight," Naomi replied, nodding.

"Abuelito! How could you!" Mandy turned to scold him.

"I was worried about them. Guess I shouldn't have been." Naomi smiled.

"If it makes you feel any better, when they snuck up to me, I almost shot them both," Mandy joked.

"Oh good."

"Hey! That's not fair!" Ibn responded.

"I still might shoot them myself," Naomi retorted with a sly grin aimed at the Arab.

"They knew about the trunks," Mandy ratted.

"How did they get to The Brandenburg, anyway?" Naomi asked, now puzzled.

"Drove?" Mandy suggested.

"Impossible," Naomi insisted, "Nena told me how quickly everything happened. There's no way they had time to get out of the center of town any quicker than Keyontay got me out. There's no way they had time to get the trunks out of the resort to the side of the road."

Ibn and Heinrich were staring holes into the Berber-wrapped floor.

"Heinrich?" Naomi pushed.

"*The Turk* drugged me!" he accused.

Naomi looked at Mandy. She offered a slight frown with raised eyebrows. The stern look on her face commanded that *Mandy had better tell her what happened!*

"I don't remember." Mandy's tone dropped. "I must have passed out."

Now Naomi felt like she was trying to interrogate the three monkeys, each of them blocking their cranial sensories with their hands. "Oh come on!" You know the inflection. "Heinrich was drugged and you passed out?"

"No, really!" Mandy whined. "When I came to, we were on the side of the road."

Naomi pressed one side of her cheek in towards the corner of her mouth and narrowed her eyes at the ridiculous story. She turned to Ibn. "Tell me." Like from the other side of the elementary school principal's desk.

"I didn't do it." Almost a question by Ibn, more sheepish than ever.

Naomi turned the vice with each word stressed, almost halting, "I want to know how you and Heinrich made it from the clock tower all the way to the resort so quickly."

"And how," Via had been silent but she couldn't resist double teaming, "did you end up hitchhiking at the very spot we'd just passed only seconds before. It doesn't make any sense. You guys weren't there when we drove up to the resort. Then, all of a sudden, you were there as we rushed back."

Naomi turned back to Mandy. "Please, just tell me."

Mandy showed her resolve briefly and then turned to Ibn. Her voice whispered, "I told you they wouldn't believe us."

*   *   *

"DO YOU HAVE any idea what he was talking about?" Arkesha stared at José after they were left alone again.

"No. But we need to go to the library."

"Great idea." She was already exiting their make-shift inventor's shop.

"Which subject do you want to tackle?" José asked, following.

"What a sweet *husband* I have. I'll take Donatism." She smiled. "You are so considerate."

"I'll read the last few chapters in Mark," he concluded.

An hour later she found José staring out of the same huge round piece of clear fused sand that had Bear captivated earlier. He was watching the South Pacific rush by at unbelievable speed.

"You'll never believe what I found," Arkesha whispered, wrapping her arms around his neck from behind.

"Perpetual daylight," he said.

"Huh?"

"If you travel west fast enough," he continued.

"Honey, I love you, but you are not making any sense. You need to get some rest," she spoke softly into his ear and kissed him. "The Earth spins at almost 25,000 miles per hour. No one can travel that fast."

"Yeah, I've already calculated it though, my sweet buttercup. We *could* travel at a little over 1000 miles per hour at the equator, right at the Earth's widest place, and the sun would stay overhead forever. Of course, it would seemingly fluctuate back and forth in the sky as the Earth acquired its seasonal positions due to the obliquity of the spherical elliptic." José was excited.

"I love it when you talk to me that way," she breathed heavily into his ear.

"The tilt of the Earth's axis would make the sun appear to move back and forth, but since the planet is a sphere, we could cut our speed down considerably, say, deep in the Southern Hemisphere, and still achieve lasting daylight."

"Are you trying to say that this day seems like it will never end?" Her joking aside, they were both beat. They'd been up since early this morning in

Rome and their day was nowhere near over. The sun was still high in the sky.

"God made it stand still for Joshua once."

"The professor?" Her head cocked to one side.

"No, Moses' successor," José laughed.

"Oh. So, you think we're going fast enough for the sun to stand still?"

"Considering how far south we are now on the globe, and how fast we appear to be traveling. Considering the sun's position in the sky, which hasn't changed at all since we left the southern tip of South America. Yes."

"How fast do you think we are going?"

"Well, we got married in four months. Six kids by this time next year?"

He got hit.

"Ow!" He laughed. "Sorry, babe. Since we skated out of the Med like Apollo...."

She had to interrupt him. "Interesting analogy for tropical waters."

"Europe used to be under a glacier."

"You have this on video? Witnessed by a hundred nuns?"

"No video. No nuns. Besides, witnesses aren't all they've been cracked up to be, considering all of the cases where witnesses convicted the accused only to find out that DNA proved otherwise."

"Good point. So you aren't sticking with that glacier theory?"

"Makes you think," he ignored her, "that if the judge and jury got it wrong in so many of those cases where DNA proves their error, what about all the cases where DNA is not a factor? How many innocent people are falsely imprisoned?"

"Glacier, honey. Drop the Europe-wide glacier."

His face was glued to the porthole again. He became silent. She joined him. "Mesmerizing, isn't it," she finally said.

"Yeah. I don't think it was the sirens."

"What?"

"Odysseus," he said, his eyes still fixed on the Pacific expanse of blue. "The sea itself will do it to you. Bad mermaids are just unnecessary."

‏ל״ח

"SPILL."

It was Via's command that Mandy obeyed without hesitation.

"I was in this room where a man, holding one of the scrolls, disappeared. I heard voices in the hall. Suddenly, the bloke in the robe waltzes into the room like he owned the place. I almost put a cap in him. But then *Abuelito* steps in and starts telling me that Ibn's got magical powers and that we had better do what he says."

"He *drugged* me," Heinrich mumbled.

"You were lucid, *Abuelito*, please don't." She was forceful. "So I put my gun away," she shot Ibn a teasing look, "temporarily." Then back to Naomi, "And then Ibn here tells me that there's a holocaust of SUVs raining down overhead outside, and that we'd better get out of the resort, that the plane is headed our way. So we grabbed the trunks."

"I'm the one who figured out where they were," Heinrich boasted. "After Ibn said he'd seen them in the bunker in Berlin, I...."

Ibn talked over him, "The young lady was nice enough to follow my instructions, and we were able to save the trunks." He smiled wide. "And here we are!" His long fingers stretched out from outspread hands.

"Okay," Via started slowly, trying to piece it all together and put some rational thought into the air. "How did you get to the resort? How did you get to the side of the road?"

"Uh...." Ibn. Timid.

"Did you just beam everybody up?" Sarcastic Star Trek reference.

"Scotty is a Turk."

Everyone just looked at Heinrich.

"What? You don't think that's funny?" The old man cackled at his own joke.

"Scotty?" Naomi decided to use the moniker to address Ibn and press him further. Her eyes were scalding, implying *confess or else....*

Another lamb-eyed look.

"Ibn?" Via joined back in. "What did you do?"

"Ah ... yes, well ... sorta like that. Maybe. Yes." The Turk.

"That's all you're gonna get out of him." Heinrich.

Mandy gave Ibn an apologetic look. Then she turned to Via with an answer. "I promised him I wouldn't tell, but ... Ibn's an angel," she blurted.

"No!" The Persian. "I'm not!"

All eyes were on the son of Zebedaeus.

"No. He's not." Pei-chin.

The Chinese scholar had been quietly listening. Thinking. Ancient texts swirling through her mind. Now, with confidence, she spoke. "He's not an angel." Then, looking at Mandy, she added, "He's *like* an angel."

Mandy nodded. "That's right. That's what he said."

Pei-chin continued. "Jesus made it clear that we will be *like* the angels in Heaven. He demonstrated for us a taste of what life will be like for us once we receive our resurrected bodies, the spiritual body that Saint Paul describes in the second to last chapter of his first letter to the church in Corinth, the same body worn by Moses and Elijah on the mount of transfiguration, a glorified body like Jesus wore when he showed us his nail-scarred hands."

"He ate fish." Ibn.

"And wore clothes, and spoke audibly," Naomi added, "and walked through walls."

Pei-chin didn't wait, talking over Naomi's final words, "He showed us both the physical and the spiritual *united*. Not an angel, but *like* the angels."

"So, Ibn's a *ghost*," Mandy concluded, "a dead guy who gets a brand new body and permission to come back to Earth?"

"No." Pei-chin looked at Ibn with resolve. "He never died. He never will."

A long period of silence filled the room. Ibn stared at the floor again as if willing himself invisible as a child with his eyes closed. Finally, Naomi asked Mandy. "What about the man who disappeared?"

* * *

"500 MILES PER HOUR."

"Nautical?"

"I've not calculated it that far," José admitted. "Anyway, it's just a rough guess using an astrolabe in my head. I've figured the sun's rate of descent at a little more than half of normal since we left the Med." He looked at his watch. "Of course, a reliable chronometer goes a long way. I cheated."

"No! My baby cheated?" She kissed his cheek.

"There's an Oxford's Atlas over there." He pointed behind a cream colored leather couch. "I plotted our course and figured the miles we've covered."

"Well, that's too bad that you felt you had to cheat." She began to feign a pout. "I thought I'd married a Mexican Einstein."

"Why are nautical miles longer than a mile?" he asked her.

"6080 feet instead of 5280 feet," she considered.

"Yeah. Weird, huh? The *statute mile* was originally measured out at a thousand paces. Do you think it was because they couldn't walk on water?"

"Probably, hun." She squeezed his hand and smiled at his humor. "Or because they didn't have reliable chronometers like my hubby's, so their longitudes at sea were always getting screwed up by the ocean's currents."

"Oh." Finally remembering, "What did you find out?"

"The Donatists were Christian Moors. Wild, huh?"

"I thought all Moors were Muslim."

"Before Mohammed was born?"

"Oh, yeah, right."

"Okay. So back in the first through the seventh centuries AD," Arkesha said, her hands around his waist now and pinching him playfully, "North Africa was predominately *Christian*."

"Wow! It's just like what we were talking about back in Eugene, just a few days ago. Sarah was all excited about it after her meeting at that coffee shop. What's it called?"

"Dutch Brothers."

"Yeah, that's right. Egypt and Libya were Christian too?"

"Mostly. And Nubia, Ethiopia, Carthage ... *all* of North Africa. So, the Roman Catholics had churches and monasteries everywhere. And so did the Syriac Christians."

"North Africa." José was still dumbfounded.

"Yes, honey. And Central Africa. The Jacobites and Nestorians were everywhere, including the Near East, Middle East, India and throughout Asia, even the Far East."

"Wow. Just like Sarah said."

"Just listen, sweetie pie."

He did.

"They were rigorists. The Donatists. Upset with the *traditores*. Those who didn't withstand the persecution of the Church under Emperor Diocletian in the early 4th century."

"Diocletian." He was recalling the words of the Pope.

She smiled and moved to where she was standing right in front of him and looked deep into his eyes. "Diocletian only reigned from Rome for three years. But in that time he demanded that all Christians turn in their copies of the Scriptures to be burned."

"Book burning!"

"Yes. And the Donatists employed spies to help them hide Scriptures from the authorities. Later their spies helped them compile a list of *traditores* – traitors who'd gone so far as to recant their faith in Christ under persecution. After Christianity became legal under Constantine, *traditores* were put back into leadership positions in the Church. Even the Bishop of Carthage was one of the turncoats. Although the Donatists believed in forgiveness, they also respected the requirements in Timothy and Titus regarding Church leaders. So Rome severed its ties with the sect. That's why the Donatist ring reminded Miguel of spies in Tuvalu!"

"Astounding!" José blinked. "The Donatists were orthodox conservatives that were excommunicated by The Vatican," he added, more interested in the history.

"Pretty much. But it was the Roman Emperor who had them excommunicated, and then slaughtered. Pope Miltiades never dreamed of taking it that far. But that's what happens when the government takes over the church. Even Saint Augustine sided with the Donatists, but it was the Roman civil authorities who had the last say. Tell me what you found out."

"Oh. My reading of Mark's gospel?"

"Yes."

"Well," he said, "interesting that you should ask."

She smiled as he paused for effect.

"I learned that Bear is going to raise Charlie from the dead."

* * *

"WE'RE HERE!"

Keyontay pushed his way into *The Ark's* study. His yell made Naomi bend her head away from the noise.

"Oh, sorry," he said. "Oh, it's you! Wow!" He smiled big. "You are even more beautiful awake."

"You said that out loud." Naomi smiled.

His dark chocolate face turned into a strawberry.

Naomi wasn't blushing. She looked at the thin-dreaded, shoulder-length strands that framed a handsome, rugged face. Her look became one of admiration. "Thank you for the compliment," she replied.

"We're here?" Mandy welcomed Keyontay's interruption. She was still getting used to the idea of Ibn being a resurrected human, angel-like anomaly, since his miraculous, ah, *activities* back in Bariloche. But a man who has never died? Now that freaked her out all over again. She popped up off the floor and left the invisible teepee behind. The two old Christians were exchanging barbs again.

"So you are a *dead* Turk," the Catholic grumbled.

"Well, you're so old you look like you're dead," Ibn retorted.

"Zombie!"

"Transubstantiationist geriatric!"

That got the Arab weird looks all around.

Heinrich started laughing. He slapped the Armenian on the back. "Good one." He chuckled.

Via had been pondering it all as well, so it took a minute for it to sink in that they'd made it to Tuvalu already. How fast is this spaceship? She jumped up and followed Mandy out of the study. Pei-chin quickly followed. Keyontay took another look at Naomi and grinned, but then took off after them.

With only the three of them left in the hovercraft's study, Naomi took full advantage of the opportunity. "Okay," she said, "*now*, spill."

Heinrich obediently started, "He didn't drug me."

"And so all of this fighting has been just *acting?*" Naomi narrowed her eyes to a cut.

"Uh, not under the clock tower – that was real. But … uh … yeah, since then."

Ibn gave her a pleading look as if to say: *Please don't be mad at me.*

"We were trying to protect his identity," the German defended.

"After yanking off his wig on live international web-tv?"

"That was live?" Ibn paled.

"Yeah!" You know the inflection. "And it's already hanging on YouTube. The video's already been viewed," she consulted her iPhone, "1.375 billion times."

"I'm gonna need a new disguise," Ibn moaned.

"Why the disguise in the first place?" she asked.

"Just to conceal my … uh … ageless appearance." He squirmed.

"What the heck does that mean?" She tapped her foot.

"That he's *old*." Heinrich laughed.

Ibn turned to the German and grinned.

"Older than me," the Catholic said with glee.

Naomi grimaced. Her eyebrows arched high as she braced herself for the answer. "How much older?"

Heinrich couldn't resist being the one to tell. "Lots older," he said. "*Centuries* older."

*　　　*　　　*

"WE'RE HERE!"

It was Michelle, she was in the lobby of the library yelling over the top of the center stacks. José and Arkesha came running.

"Hey!" José finally noticed as he ran. "My ring!"

Feeling the absence of its weight as he ran, he had checked his neck and slowed, pulling the empty chain out of his pocket.

"*Isabella's* ring!" Arkesha stopped with him.

"Where…? Oh, the Pope." His voice became lost in the realization that Miguel had unwittingly kept his ring. "It's okay." He reached for Arkesha's arm to pull her along and stepped back into his run. She joined easily with his stride as they made for the exit just in time to see Michelle's combat boots disappear around a corner at the end of the narrow corridor that led away from the library's entrance.

Arkesha became excited. "Do you think our plan will work?"

"You bet it will!" he said. "Darlin' your plans always work." They rushed to catch up with Michelle.

Back behind his massive desk again, Miguel was praying for the success of the mission. He knew that they had almost one thousand men and women aboard who were combat ready: special training for just such an operation, prior military experience gained from almost a dozen different countries around the world. But he also knew how risky it would be and how dangerous Enson and his people were. His eyes opened and he stared off across the flat plain that served as his work station on *The Piper*. He was thinking of Bear's new found faith. Amazing, he thought, to have so much faith so soon after reading the Scriptures. He chuckled to himself. "I already raised Charlie from the dead!" But that's what Jesus says for us to believe in Mark 11. The waning sunlight reflected off the golden treasure on his finger. "Oh no!" he said it out loud. "My ring!"

"I figured it was yours," a voice from the past.

"Where'd you go off to?" Miguel asked him as he moved up to the other side of the grand desk.

"I had some work to do." Joshua put a book down on the outer edge of the immense structure that the Pope called a desk. "The labs in Germany and Quebec have been destroyed."

"So I heard." Miguel smiled with satisfaction. "Did you reach Naomi?"

"Once, then she was down. Shot. But she's okay now. I did get through to her office. Celeste filled me in." His deep breaths betrayed a busy day.

"Where is she now?"

"Here. Naomi. Via. Heinrich. Ibn. We're all here." Joshua smiled.

۳۹

"YOU ARE ONE of them." Naomi's face radiated as she drew the conclusion. She stared into his face.

Ibn nodded slowly, not exactly sure yet what label she had stamped on him.

"May I?" She reached for one of his hands.

He stood and offered them both.

Heinrich felt compelled to stand up as well. But his wobbly knees caused him to quickly move to one of the chairs that now sat empty at the desk. He was muttering something about how he needed a glorified body too.

She touched Ibn's fingertips. Then she reached for the center of his palms.

"Human," she said with surreal clarity.

"Since birth," an uncomfortable Ibn quipped.

"What's your *real* name?" Intrigued.

"I'd rather not say." The Armenian stiffened.

The old Catholic chuckled. "Should have known. Nestorians are notorious for...."

"Maronite," the Arab corrected, "I've converted."

"Where were you born?" Naomi asked, as her hand reached up as if not connected to her body anymore. She touched his face.

"I'd rather not say." The Arab pursed his lips.

Naomi's fingers traced the contour of his cheeks. His hawkish nose. Then the curve across his forehead. "Amazing," she said. Ibn was very uncomfortable but realized Naomi was filled with wonder that needed to be expressed.

"The worst thing about finally meeting one, you find out he's not even Catholic. A heretic. What was God thinking?" Light-hearted delivery from the other old man.

"Funny guy." Ibn's sardonic tone moved to Naomi, his hands motioning while he talked. "Where'd you find him?"

Naomi was in no mood for their jokes. She was still completely immersed in the experience. "Incredible!" she breathed as she felt his hair and touched each ear before withdrawing her hands and stepping back to get a better view of his entire frame. "You know, three years ago I took a homeless man off the street. He'd been living on a sidewalk for at least thirty years according to the local police. I bought him a townhouse and moved him in. He'd lived out his final couple of years out of the weather, with food and medical care. Hot showers, a toilet, a sink. Things we take for granted. His bedsores cleared up within the first two months. He'd suffered in wet clothes for so long, his skin had been covered with lesions. He said he was a drunk, but I never saw him drinking. He knew things he shouldn't have known."

She paused and then looked over at Heinrich. "I've always wondered if I'd been entertaining an angel unaware, like the Bible talks about."

Heinrich nodded as if he knew what she meant.

Naomi let her lips part once again to finish. "But this? This is different. This is something … this is like … meeting Enoch. Like having interviewed Elijah!"

"Elijah was a good Roman Catholic," the old wrinkled face offered with a gentle grin.

She ignored Heinrich's jest and kept staring into Ibn's face. The Persian shifted uncomfortably on his feet.

"You," she declared. "You're one of the sons of God."

*　　　　*　　　　*

"SIR."

Enson turned in response.

"Sir. They've penetrated elevator Number Two." Peña stood next to him. They were both facing Sarah's bound body still strapped to the medical bed.

He didn't turn his head. "So, they've found us," he said.

Peña continued to stare off into the space above Sarah's head. "And they are already *here*."

"They'll get eaten alive."

"It does appear that the first intruder is in a free-fall down one of the elevator shafts."

"Nylon ropes are so easily cut," a snide flavor emitting along with his snarl.

"The others are still engaged on the surface."

His face carried a smug look. Focusing his attention back on Sarah, his eyes were sharp flashes of black midnight. "Into a trap, darlin'. Your boyfriend has stepped into my...."

But he stopped his words as soon as it registered.

He blinked.

His body automatically recoiled.

Enson stared at the empty straps dangling from the bed in front of him. They were still moving back and forth as if swaying in the afternoon breeze.

Sarah was gone!

Disappeared.

Escaped. Right before his eyes. And yet he'd not seen it.

She'd been singing. "Hear My Cry" had been playing over and over inside her head. And then, just like Peter ... "Sarah." She heard the audible voice.

"Yes," a natural response.

"It's time to go," the angel spoke with urgency.

"They can't see me, can they?" Sarah was within reach of Enson's massive paws.

"No," replied the angel.

"They can't see you either?"

Although in human form, the angel was visible to her alone. And his appearance was *not quite physical*. Later she would describe it as if looking through a really thick colored glass. His hair was a curly plume of black that shone in blue, spiraled streaks of light that bounced back as he walked. His gait was strong and purposeful like his face. A kind warrior. One that would be weathered were he not a supernatural breed. Large shoulders over muscular features, just short of a body-builder, but somehow bigger and better proportioned. A deeply tanned skin, both smooth and rugged. And yet, she could see right through him, barely, like peering at the other end of a faintly lit, smoke-filled room.

He reached for her hand.

"Sarah. We need to go."

He led her away from Enson and Peña who apparently stayed frozen in time gawking at the empty confinement straps. Walking past the rows and rows of Enson's other victims, Sarah felt drawn to each one. She wanted to rescue them. She wanted to save them all.

"We have to help them."

"Others will." Confidence.

"Where are we going?"

"You. It's – 'Where are *you* going?'" Twenty yards from the cattle-car lifts, they reached one of the much smaller passenger elevator doors. A large letter hung above it on the cement wall: "A." Next to it, the matching shaft's doorway: "B."

"Real creative." Sarah couldn't help the sarcasm. As the angel pushed the button, Sarah asked, "What's your name?"

"Appelgelic."

"Cool name." She looked back towards where she'd been held hostage. "You blinded their eyes?"

"Yes."

"Like in the Bible?"

"Like in the Bible," the angel answered with a warm smile.

Her head nodded slowly, a tight smile below sparkling eyes. The word was spoken with melodic inflection. "Cool." Two notes. One high. Then one low.

"Do angels take elevators often?" she asked as the doors parted and they stepped aboard.

"Define often."

She smiled.

"I've taken a ladder before."

"Jacob's?"

He smiled.

"Appelgelic?" she asked.

"Yes?"

"No wings?" She pointed.

"Sarah, do you want to *know* God?"

Immediately, Sarah felt a strong chill start between her shoulder blades, radiate down her arms, up her neck and into her lower back. Then the warm oil, yes, warm oil she was sure must be flowing down from the top of her head, over her ears, her face, onto her neck and shoulders. Looking up as if she could see Heaven right through the ceiling she said, "Yes," almost breathlessly.

They went up.

As they rose up towards the surface, José passed them, falling down one of the larger shafts. The total distance from the surface of Tuvalu to the bottom of the shaft was "unreal," the word José whispered as he fell.

Gravity's pull kept him falling fast. All the way down. Well, almost all of the way. He found the smooth interior of the shaft fascinating. Just as Miguel had described it.

No cables.

No wires.

Nothing.

Except … a small seam every so often such that the casters on his shaft belay, strapped to his body, ran over them making a sound reminiscent of a train over railroad tracks, or radial tires over those big concrete sections on the interstates and toll roads.

The tiny lights that arced out from his shoulders, covering the length of his metallic wings, let him see just a bit in the darkness. The bottom of the shaft was a dark pit of nothingness below him. The expanse well above now was equally lost in his fall like a black hole in space. Unseen. Like he'd never been there. Like space never passed through. Like he'd always been falling and would never stop.

But he knew. He'd reviewed the stolen schematics and had figured his rate of descent. The depth of the shaft was exactly as he'd memorized.

1.0867 miles.

He kept falling.

Sarah kept rising.

Finally, staring at the stopwatch that glowed on his wrist, José hit the magic number and dialed the tension control on his belt. He started slowing at much the same rate as a paratrooper until the little lights on his wings illuminated the top of the elevator car appearing now slowly beneath him. The landing on its roof was perfectly executed. Perfectly controlled.

He didn't make a sound as his feet came into contact with the metal surface that now supported his weight.

*   *   *

"WHERE ELSE did you go?" Bear's voice. But richer, stronger. More mature. Almost formidable. Certainly it no longer belonged to the young man who'd left Eugene just three days ago.

His voice came through the air from the alcove off the back corner of Miguel's office.

"Oh." Miguel showed surprise on his face. "You're awake."

Bear crawled off the small sofa that was hidden behind an antique sideboard covered with candles. He lumbered over to the continental piece of furniture that occupied the considerable space between the Pope and the professor. He looked at Joshua. "You left us three times." He tightened his lips before speaking again. "So, if you went to Germany the first time, and Canada the second time, where did you go the last time?"

"Observant little weasel," Joshua teased. "What else do you know?"

"I know that you have great faith."

Joshua didn't expect that response, especially from Bear.

But Bear continued, "Because I read about faith and about calling on the power of God." His hands were raised up like he was leading his own tent revival. He turned back from his congregation of two and gave Joshua a knowing look. "And I know about *Philip*."

Joshua discerned an accusatory tone in Bear's voice. "What happened to *him?*" The professor turned to the Pope while pointing at Bear.

"He *fainted*." A Pontiff's weak smile.

"No. I mean, what did you do to him?" Joshua prodded although he had a good guess already.

"Me?" An Innocent face. "I just gave him a Bible."

Bear seemed to be enjoying the exchange.

Joshua actually frowned in acceptance of Miguel's half-hearted defense. "Oh." He shrugged. A short high note.

Turning to his student, "Yes, Bear. Translated. Like Philip in the book of Acts."

"I knew it!" Bear jumped up in a cheer. "So, where'd you go?"

"Which time?"

"I'm right about the first two?"

"Yes."

"You had ice on your jacket the second time."

"All right Sherlock."

"What about the third time?" Even Sir Doyle couldn't have deduced this one on his own.

"Ashland."

"Virginia?"

"No."

"Kentucky?"

"No."

"Ohio? Pennsylvania? Kansas?"

"No. No. And no. Very funny." Joshua shook his head. "You know Sarah's folks live in Oregon."

"You went to destroy two pharmaceutical labs being used by a powerful villain for human experimentation, and then you supernaturally translated your body to a third location ... for a *social call?*"

"How did you know about Enson's experiments?" asked Joshua, dodging the issue.

"I read the book."

Joshua cocked his head to one side and tried to wrap his brain around that one. But he answered the hanging question. "It was important."

"To meet her folks?"

Joshua nodded.

"In the middle of all of this?" Bear waved his pudgy hands around in the air like he was orchestrating the battle plan to win Armageddon.

Joshua just nodded in the affirmative. But his face glowed in reflection.

Bear saw it. "Oh. I see." And he pulled up a chair and sat down. His theatrics over, now Joshua was the one prying.

"You see? You see what?" the professor demanded.

Bear grinned with confidence. "You asked permission to marry their daughter."

*   *   *

"THERE." SHE POINTED.

"I don't see it."

"You ignored the memo."

"I ignore whatever I choose to ignore."

"Last year," Peña explained, "I was the one responsible for compiling the report on security upgrades."

"You've worked here that long?" Enson frowned.

"I don't work *here*. I work in Lima. I've worked for you for over three years now, surveillance and defense systems. We're based in your Peru office. I was on the task force you created to evaluate penetration risks."

His frown drooped further.

"Our findings included the need to update your cameras, lighting, or in the case of this dreary place," she motioned to their immediate surroundings, "*both*." Derisively.

"I thought you were a PA."

She let out a deep sigh.

Enson's face appeared elastic with a frown so pronounced it seemed to have been painted on him.

She held her phone's display up so he could see it again. "That's why it's so hard to see, sir. Your video surveillance system is," borrowing a word from her written report, "*substandard*."

"It looks like an angel."

"I'm sure it's not." Peña shook her head again. "We've been over this before, sir. I know the picture is grainy. The grey on grey decor doesn't help any. There is not a lot of contrast to help the lens pick up what…."

"You've been with me for three years? I thought you just started."

She was getting impatient. "Mr. Enson," Peña raised her voice, "I just started as your new PA *today*. I've been with your company for over three years. Will you focus on the issue at hand, please?"

He stared into the screen. The video clip looped twice in her hand as he studied it. "He has *wings*."

She rolled her eyes.

"Maybe that's how the girl got away."

She rolled her eyes further back into her head. The corners of her mouth tightened. She wondered how such a driven, selfish man could become so easily defused. His trademark self-confidence, self-indulgence, and self-reliance were gone. It had left along with that girl that had just disappeared. Sarah. She was a unique one. And so profoundly had Enson been affected, Peña now looked at him with idle curiosity. He'd been frozen with her as they stared at the empty bed. Her response, however, had been a freeze-frame of wonder and awe. His? His was of fear, a fear that was rooted in something far deeper than fear itself, like he had a *connection* to something, or *someone*, but not to Sarah. It was bigger than that, spanning out over the normal concepts of time and space, beyond the limitations of our senses – out past the boundaries of the world that we dwell and often hide within. But with our eyes and ears, and barely the other three physical senses, we choose to define all of our own reality. We define eternity with them. But why? Why choose to define an eternal physical universe made up of billions of solar systems with the finite observational abilities on our person? Or, better yet, why try to understand the much larger spiritual universe using solely our five senses?

"Who is she?" she asked.

"What?" obviously faking the lack of comprehension, knowing full well the import of the query, but not trying to mask his surprise.

"The girl. Who is she?"

Impossibly, the frown stretched downward even more.

"The one you flew off to Italy to *personally* investigate while we were airborne in the Hawker over South America." She'd just now figured out that part.

"I didn't *fly* anywhere." Uneasy. Now staring at his assistant with a high level of scrutiny.

"Whatever."

He just stood there. The computer between his ears humming. Processing. Calculating. Filing. Algorithms spinning. Finally, after staring fire through her eyes, he warned. "You know too much." The tone used could not have been more threatening.

"You're going to kill me too?" Obstinate but still a professional quality about her poise. The cadence of the string of words measured, almost melodic.

"Everyone dies."

*   *   *

IBN STEPPED OFF the submarine that had flown onto the beach. Only one person remained inside *The Ark* and he was still in the pilot's seat, sitting behind the helm in order to activate some "special" defensive features that he was hush-hush about. The Captain had only said, "The ship will be available when it's needed." Their escape pod will be waiting. Promise.

The Persian walked off a whale-wing onto the sand and joined the rest of the group who'd already disembarked. They all stood in a tight circle on a tiny atoll and stared off across the massive Tuvaluvian lagoon, over the water that separated them from their goal. Hot sand. Baked by the day's South Pacific sun. Burning underneath their feet. Warm salty water all around them. The little strip of gleaming beach barely held its guests.

"Wrong island?" Ibn said, trying humor.

"Kinda empty, huh?" Heinrich stood next to Ibn wearing high black boots that made him look kind of silly. But they matched his new belt and holster. His Mauser sidearm poking out of the right-handed sling on his hip could only have been better complemented with a short riding crop and a more appropriate cap.

"Where'd you get the hat?"

The old German turned his head toward the Arab. He looked him up and down. Long robe that was supposed to be white, but it needed to be laundered quite badly. Thick leather belt. "I see you found another sword."

"It's not a sword. It's too short to be a sword. And you didn't answer my question."

"Got it from the Admiral," Heinrich said, beaming.

"You look silly," Ibn accused.

"And you don't?" The old German let out a hard laugh.

"Boys." Naomi stepped in between them. She paused, noticing Heinrich for the first time. "What do you think you're doing?"

"I'm going to die soon anyway. I thought I'd go out in a blaze of glory."

Mandy piped up, "I tried to tell him. He won't listen. He's too stubborn."

Via looked at the two old men standing side by side and wondered if they wouldn't fair better without them both.

Heinrich took off the sea captain's cap and placed it atop the Armenian's head. "I assumed you snuck off to Vedi to pick up another Yataghan. If you translated back home, did you at least grab a decent pistol this time?"

Ibn held up another Makarov with a grin and then placed it back in its pouch. "You know, you're not so bad ... for a Catholic."

The German regarded the speaker, the one he'd so hated, the one he'd so misunderstood, the heretic who was now his friend. The excommunicated church, discarded, abandoned, lost. Left to others to be destroyed. But it was this blasphemer, this false teacher, this Origenist, whom God had chosen to give the same status as Elijah and Enoch. He reached out and hugged the man. A warmer embrace could not have been described. Naomi teared up.

She listened to the aged Roman Catholic confess. "You know it was years ago that I ran across words penned by our Church father, Eusebius. He quoted from Origen with approval. It had shocked me then. Now, I think I understand. And, my friend, it will be my pleasure to die fighting by your side."

Naomi felt the grip of her own Ruger P345 tucked in a nylon holster clipped to her hip, and then she turned to respond. She couldn't help herself.

She said it with resolve. With conviction. With prophetic power.

"Not everyone dies."

*   *   *

"TUVALU'S MAIN ISLAND," Miguel explained while seated behind his desk still aboard *The Piper*, "Funafuti...."

Bear laughed.

The professor and the Pope both stared him down.

"Sorry," he responded meekly. "It just sounds funny. One of the best things about the British, when *they* ruled the world? Well, their colonies had *normal* names. We have really let them go crazy with the local dialects, customs, and weird names."

"We?" The Pope.

"You know. The United States. The new English Empire. We just don't call them colonies." He shrugged. "But it's the same thing."

"Or worse," Joshua added, "the U.S. has a permanent presence in over 174 countries now."

"Can I continue?" The Pope wanted to get back on subject.

Two faces immediately attentive.

"Fongafale, built on Funafuti, is Tuvalu's capital city." He looked at Bear to make sure no quip would come. "As it was during British rule." Then looking back at both of them.... "And its surroundings consist of the small islands and atolls that form a large ring around a huge lagoon. The spits of sand that form the circle are separated by strands of water, but underneath, a reef connects them all. It can be quite shallow between the atolls, often as little as six inches of the South Pacific cover the top of the coral."

"You promised I could *go in* with the soldiers. Of course, they are already seeing all the action that I'm missing," Bear whined in complaint.

"You can't do both," Miguel reminded. "Do you want to pray over Charlie or not?"

The reprimanded Bear retreated back to his little couch to wait.

Miguel took the opportunity and lowered his voice to Joshua, "What are you thinking." An accusation, not really a question. "You *can't* get married!" he scolded.

Joshua, from the far end of the expansive polished mahogany between them, cupped his hand over his ear. "Huh?"

"You heard me." A Cephas-stone face.

"You are right." An admission.

Miguel caught the potential sidestep. "About which statement?"

Joshua smiled, then conceded, to himself as well as to the Pontiff, "Both this and what you asked earlier."

"Then, you have a reasonable explanation?"

Silence.

"A rational defense of why you would ask permission to marry a woman when you are not allowed to marry?" the Pope persisted.

"No – no I don't," Joshua conceded.

Another big question mark faced Joshua. But it wasn't just Miguel's face still staring him down like a disapproving mother. It was his own accusing finger. Inside, he was kicking himself for falling in love in the first place. He'd allowed it to grow on him. He'd begun to accommodate it. Then he'd actually nurtured it. He'd welcomed it. His will to control it, to reverse it, subsided exponentially with each passing day. And then, he'd really screwed up. It was bad enough that his own lack of self-control had tortured his emotions and toyed with his needs and desires. Most never know the wonder of perfect companionship. What Adam needed. What *only* Eve, no other woman, could have or will possibly fulfill. Joshua had lived alone in his self-created misery until…. Until he'd screwed it up even worse by blurting out his love for her, to her. Impulsive. He wished the computer hadn't emboldened him so. He kicked himself again. Love unleashed. Utter failure of self-control. How else could he say it? Describe the worst thing you've ever done. Then put it in the context of the best thing you've ever had. We've all done it. He did it. She was the only woman he'd ever loved.

The only one he'd ever love for all eternity. And, in one FB message, he'd proclaimed his love for her. He'd fulfilled both of their hopes and dreams. He'd opened up a dam, flooding their souls with euphoric joy that cannot be expressed with mere words. But at the same time, he'd plunged a dagger deep into her chest, as well as into his own. No Shakespearean tragedy could ever act it out sufficiently.

"Romeo," the Pope provoked.

Joshua looked across the top of the desk. The professor's eyes were misty and forlorn, but they also burned with passion, anger, regret, and forbidden love, all in a dalliance of interlocking intensity.

So it was, from this place he'd put them in, forever condemning himself and his true love, that he answered. "I don't know what I was thinking," Joshua said. "I was just blindly following my heart."

٤ ٠

IT HAD BEEN a simple plan. He just didn't follow it.

Captured on Enson's poor quality analog tape, Peña watched José disconnect his shaft belay and drop in through the access panel of the freight elevator's ceiling. He'd moved to the glowing isosceles button to open the double doors. His crouching approach to the buttons barely showed up on Peña's phone. As the closures parted to open, he'd slipped out through the aperture and floated to the other massive freight lift and hit the call button which instantaneously lit at his touch. Moving inside he'd hit the top square button. Then the alternating current started to push the huge metal barriers back into place to close him in. The skyward-pointing pyramid outside of the lift now glowed with its message, and José was supposed to be heading to the surface aboard the huge elevator to gather a group of soldiers.

But what he'd done next was not part of the plan.

The plan that he'd designed with his wife.

The plan that had been blessed by the Pope.

Approved by the Pontiff.

No. On impulse, remembering what Arkesha had said about his invention, José had changed the plan. He'd quickly stepped back off the huge lift and let the barn-door-size panels slide to a close without him aboard as he raced back to the elevator he had come from and up into the shaft he'd just descended. He'd reattached the harness and began his ascent. But partway up there was a dramatic change.

Such was José's reflection as he now found himself stuck.

Stuck about half-way back up the shaft he had descended.

Suddenly, José was acutely aware of the purpose of the seams that had clattered at him all the way down. For the razor-sharp blades of the large horizontal guillotines were now preventing any movement. They'd effectively closed the shaft all the way up or down.

"We can't use ropes." Those were the words spoken by Miguel when he'd first commissioned the pair to design the shaft *descender*. Now the words held new meaning, the difference between being told by your mother that the stove is hot and actually experiencing the pain when you reach out to touch it anyway.

His initial inclination was to blame his wife.

At first, that's exactly what he did.

"It can go *up* the shaft too," he mocked out loud in his confined space deep underground.

With his exit back up or down the elevator shaft now barricaded by guillotine blades, he suddenly shivered and then thanked God he'd not been cut in half. He'd heard them clanging, thundering, echoing. It was a miracle that they'd all closed while he was in between two of them, climbing back up the shaft.

He kicked himself.

"José!" he yelled into the small space of his shaft prison cell. "You couldn't just leave it alone!" You just had to try it out!"

At least he wasn't still blaming his wife.

ON THE SURFACE of Tuvalu's main island, the freight elevator's stone rolled away to receive an army ordained by the Pope to storm the compound still buried deep beneath the atoll. The Vatican's heavily armed emissaries disappeared into the big transporter. Michelle led the charge. As the huge panels slipped back into place to cover the entrance, everyone braced for the long ride down. The lift started to move. They dropped – the beginning of their dramatic rescue.

Danger Zone was playing in the minds and hearts of the rescue team as the massive elevator rushed the good guys into the heart of the evil lair, while reminders, filed away in their brains, came forth by the way of the pictures of illicit human experimentations. Photos and movies of captives being held against their wills. Victims strapped into hundreds of beds. Blood. Nurses holding big IV needles.

Arkesha noticed it first. On the ride down, she felt it. The mist of another time. A memory that wasn't her own. Rails. Trains. Cattle cars. A stench.

The smell of death. Undoubtedly similar to what millions of innocent men, women and children experienced on the European rails in the years before Hitler was finally defeated. The odor lingered in the moving tomb as they rushed for the bottom of the wide shaft. Human test subjects had been on this lift not long ago, along with their fear, their despair, their utter confusion. They'd left behind their desperate prayers to God. Pleadings, really. Of hearts despondent. Broken. Wondering when God would ... *if he* would ... save them. Begging. Was being saved even in *his* plan? If so, when? How soon, Lord? Come quickly, rescue me! Echoes of the anointed King's Addulam psalms. Orisons of pain. Loss. Separation. Danger. As Saul pursued David's life for ten long years, David's prayers persisted until a Divine deliverance crowned the perceived threat as successor king.

The 101 souls still buried deep beneath the Pacific sand continued their heavenward wails, surrounded by bags of blood. Was the blood of Christ about to be pumped into their veins? Or was it just a cheap imitation? A different Jesus.

Down inside of Tuvalu's bowels, they waited.

As they did, an army of God descended into the Earth.

Arkesha, sensing the significance of the event, momentarily forgot about José. Instead, she thought of the moments after Jesus gave up his spirit on the cross. It was the first place he went: to deliver the souls from hell. To preach. To save. Now she was following in his footsteps ... they all were ... sent by Rome to deliver the prisoners from their hell ... commissioned by the Church to redeem those held hostage by evil. But more so, perhaps, the Vatican was seeking its own redemption, to deliver its own soul through works of repentance. The massive elevator arrived. The huge metal doors slid back into the wall and swarms of rescuers flooded out into the lab.

THE ECLECTIC BAND stood on the sandy rim of the tiny atoll. Via was ready to lead them. Nena and Mandy were heavily armed, flanking each side of their commander. On the far left of the group on the beach, Pei-chin faced the wide lagoon of Tuvalu's main circle of land, dressed in her own unique battle regalia. To Mandy's right, Naomi perched her toes along the outer edge of their islet and turned to look back at *Jonah's Ark*. The pelagic spacecraft rested on the top of the spit like a beached whale. On her far side, two old men stood bickering and pointing at the blue expanse of tropical water that stretched between them and their goal.

Enson's rear entrance, once a secret known only to his own security detachment stationed inside the bunker, was betrayed. The Pope's intelligence had been passed on.

"I see it," Heinrich claimed, his hand a visor over his eyes as he peered under the sun at the thick grove of palms across the channel.

"That's impossible," Ibn challenged as he strained to look. His large nose wrinkled up at its bridge as he focused on the dense jungle just up from a small beach on the other side of the saltwater barrier. "I don't see anything," he persisted.

"Doesn't say much for having a glorified body," Heinrich mumbled, just loud enough for his new friend to hear.

"They don't come with x-ray vision," Ibn snorted.

"Well, your *immortal* eyes should at least be as clear as Moses' at 120. I can see the bunker plain as day," Heinrich boasted.

"Boys," Naomi scolded. "Herr Stauffenberg, that's a *boat* pulled up on shore."

Heinrich squinted and twisted up his mouth.

Ibn chuckled and patted his friend on the back. "My friend, I will storm the bad guy's castle with these other fine soldiers while you go attack that *boat*." He pointed with a huge grin.

"WHY DIDN'T WE just land on the other side?" Mandy asked Via. Her boss was statuesque, still staring across the water as if willing it to recede, leaving them a path over dry ground.

"Egypt," she said dreamily.

"What?" from Mandy, with raised British brows.

"The Israelites had to cross the Red Sea when they escaped. The Pharoah chased them. His entire army trapped over a million unarmed men, women, and children between a narrow pass through the cliffs and the long stretch of saltwater separating Egypt from Sinai." Via spoke as if trapped in a dream. Her eyes remained fixed on their watery path leading to the fortress they must penetrate. They were there to rescue God's children, to release the prisoners, to free those in bondage inside Enson's island, enslaved to the beds in a lab filled with blood. Via's tone was solemn and purposeful. She knew exactly what she was doing.

"I don't get it." Mandy pursed her lips.

"God will make a way for us." Via's confidence was radiant and her thick French accent made its way into her declaration. Then the commander of mercenaries, Via Savoie, led the way, stepping out onto the water with her AK-74 held high over her head.

Without hesitation or question, Mandy and Nena followed. Their own march of feet so quickly aligned with their Chambéry CO that their own boots entered the water but a half-step behind the lead. Pei-chin mimicked the movement and motioned for Keyontay to come with her, fast. He'd been behind the line, lost in thought, Naomi's smile still cast into a digital still in his mind.

On the opposite end of their group, there was considerable anxiety but only a slightly appreciable delay. Naomi froze for a moment as she caught sight of her friend leading their companions into the sea, turned her head, and almost voiced an objection to Via. Heinrich, on the other hand, drew his sidearm and lifted it, as if a great weight, over his head and plunged into Tuvalu's waters.

Within moments, Naomi stood alone on the beach next to Ibn. He was almost close enough to reach out and touch once again. She knew his body was real, as real as the risen Christ's. Jesus our Messiah, alive though crucified, living though having died, the Lamb demonstrated his deity with outstretched hands marred with scars at each wrist, a bloody wound still fresh in his side. Thomas touched the holes and watched his Teacher eat fish after blessing the bread, after *walking through solid walls* to enter a fully-locked room. Naomi's reverie stopped. Looking at Ibn she shuddered. A strange fear engulfed her.

As the rest of the crew took their first steps into the channel that separated the great lagoon from the Pacific, the highly educated young woman spun around and faced the anomaly draped in his Bedouin robe. "Can you walk on water?" she asked. Her Baptist experience in worship was charismatic, raised among those Black American believers who believed in expression and embraced emotion, a product of their past and deliverance: raided, captured, enslaved, shipped, bound, forced, owned, worked, then finally freed to face generations of subhuman treatment by others whose arrogance and spite were rooted in divergence of skin pigments. The Baptists of the black churches Naomi knew so well knew how to praise their redeemer. But theology seeps into every type of pulpit in place of the Bible's own words and Naomi had been taught that the overtly Divine was "not for today." Good people. Strong Christians. Loving pastors. Learned educators. Students of the scriptures with pure hearts. But they maintained that God no longer displayed his miraculous powers as he once did. She'd accepted it. Not because she believed that the Bible taught such a doctrine – just simply that she'd not *seen* it. Reading her Bible took her to fantastic places and allowed her to experience *supernatural* events. But today? When was the last time anyone had seen a dead body tossed into a tomb with the bones of a prophet, just to jump out alive? When did she experience first-hand, Christians thrown to the lions or into a fiery furnace just to escape unscathed? She certainly couldn't multiply bread or fish to feed hungry crowds. She hadn't given sight to the blind or allowed the lame to walk. Jesus did. But he is God. His disciples followed suit, in the gospels, and after Christ ascended to Heaven. Acts records miraculous healings, even dead people brought back to life. However, she'd not seen anything of the sort during her lifetime. Perhaps the preachers who taught that miracles had ceased were correct. Prayer still works, after all, and God still heals people. He still does miraculous things, but he does it differently now. He works behind the scenes. He heals many through doctors and drugs. He saves us from death through circumstances and happenstances directed by his invisible hand. But not like in the Bible?

But Ibn.

Ibn's existence. His *abilities*. This changes everything. Naomi let her head bow. Her eyes fell upon the sand between them as the Arab answered her question.

"You can too," he said.

And Ibn lifted a leather sandal-bound foot and placed its sole squarely on top of the ocean's inlet. His weight thus borne, he moved his other set of toes and started his stride only a slight distance behind the rest of their team.

Naomi looked up, closed her eyes and took a step forward, spinning her body back toward the water to take her first step onto the sea. She thought of Peter, when he climbed out of the boat onto Galilee's waves. Jesus had simply walked over the surface of the great lake and granted Peter's awesome request. The disciple's first few steps carried him on top of the surface of the inland sea. Naomi could now imagine how Cephas felt when he took his first few steps – as she took hers, with the water beneath her willing frame, her semi-automatic handgun still holstered at her waist, one arm outstretched for balance, the other still in a sling.

Then she opened her eyes.

Looked down.

"Oh!" Staring down at her feet, she blushed and then looked up at Ibn, who hearing her startled expression, had stopped to turn and look.

"You did it," he said with a slight smile.

"There's a reef here!" Naomi grinned and looked back down.

"That there is," Ibn responded, now with a wide grin.

The atoll was built atop a ring of coral. Here the reef stood only inches below the water's sparkling surface.

"Shall we?" he invited with a gesture laced with long spindly fingers.

Naomi's combat boots moved once more. She bridged the distance between herself and the immortal man. Walking up to his outstretched hand, together they turned to catch up with the rest of the group. Naomi touched Ibn's hand, clasped it and let both hands latch together as they started a stride side-by-side, while laughing to herself. Ha, she thought, what a fool I've been. Here I thought we were going to be like Peter. What a riot. She looked down again to view the brightly colored coral through the ripples of saline waves. The coral was cast with the ever moving shadows and changing reflections of sunlight. But wait. What is this? No, it can't be!

For her eyes clearly saw, and she undoubtedly knew, that she and Ibn were now walking a meter off the side of the reef, with nothing under their feet but the sea.

AS MICHELLE LED the rush into the deep of the compound, the old German stepped out of the water onto a Tuvalu beach, the shores of his own Normandy. As the sand felt the weight of his boots, his heart bulged. This was the moment he'd been waiting for. Finally, he thought, I will do something worthy of pardon. God will finally forgive me. He yelled a primal cry and ran on elderly legs over the course of the sand towards the bunker hidden in the trees.

AT THE SAME TIME, Charlie's lifeless body lay waiting. It stretched out supine on a cold slab of concrete inside Enson's underground make-shift morgue: a stone table. His spirit was hoping for his own redemption, but of a different kind. He didn't want to die. But he had. Now he wanted to turn back time, to have another chance. To be able to gain a new lease on life that would allow him to try again. To do it right this time. He didn't have any selfish design for this pardon he was seeking. He thought of all the things that he could have done with his life that he didn't ... all of the time he had spent pursuing worthless pursuits ... things that didn't matter. Now, his regrets were balled up in a deep realization that some must die to finally get it right. Die to ourselves in order to be raised to true life. A seed cannot grow into the plant's design that is buried within it unless it first dies to itself so it can become a new life in the ground, sprouting to a new creation. A man cannot experience the life designed for him unless he first crucifies his old man and is born again. Charlie's spirit watched his body as it began to decompose and wondered if God would put him back in that shell and let him have the second chance he hoped for.

Will you, Lord?

"HE'S HERE.

"Bear!

"Bear! He's here!"

A sleepy face poked up over the back of the couch where he'd returned after confronting his professor: a bear looking out from his little cave over the top of the sideboard, peering through stalks of candelabrum. He didn't look like he was even awake yet.

"I told you to pray. Not sleep," the Pope scolded.

Bear stumbled out from his Gethsemane over to the desktop now converted. Except for the missing toe tag, the Pope's great desk now resembled an embalming table in a funeral home's basement. A slab bearing body broken without breath. The frame lying lifeless in life gone with its death. Instead of stone or stainless steel ... a polished hardwood desk.

Charlie's corpse had traded up.

"How'd he...?" Bear started as he noticed the dead body of his friend. Then, "Ohhhh," with musical inflection, drawn out recognition, a choir singing while accompanied by orchestral strains.

He looked over at his professor. Joshua was giving him a harmonic look. "*You* did this." Bear surmised.

"Perhaps," Joshua conceded, then refocused his student, "but can we talk about how Charlie's body was brought up from its grave later? Right now I want you to focus on the fact that the body is here. It has been brought here for you to have a more tangible object on which to direct your prayers."

"Okay," Bear said as if still dreaming.

"Now," Joshua reminded. "Now is the time to pray."

And they did.

VIA'S TEAM DUCKED into the secret entrance. The bunker had been hidden in the dense jungle, but Miguel's intelligence was flawless.

Naomi was still uneasy about Ibn.

It's one thing to *read* about Peter's walk on the water. It's an entirely different matter to have walked right next to a Turk slogging over the top of the sea.

She had been told that Ibn was ... *different*, but water-walking had her examining the whole issue all over again. What else might happen?

The man, after all, had lived through *both* world wars in the last century *and* the Napoleonic wars, the rise and fall of the Ottoman Empire, the fall of the Roman empire....

Unique.

On an intellectual level, she had accepted the reality that Ibn, like Enoch and Elijah, had never died.

Aren't people supposed to die?

It is part of the life cycle, right?

Even Adam died. After 930 years of life, but he *did* die.

How old was Ibn? Crazy when you think about it. He'd only admitted having been around since the second century AD, but how much more of human history had he experienced?

She still had a hard time with the whole concept.

Still, she had always believed in the Biblical account of Adam's age at death. And Noah's.

And Methuselah's. Wow, 969 years! Amazing!

So how old is Ibn, anyway? Why is it so hard to accept?

Naomi believed what the Bible said about the sons of God. She read it in Genesis and Job and figured out what it meant after reading the New Testament references in context with the Old. But Ibn?

He's not a ghost.
He's flesh and blood.
He's real.

VIA'S TEAM FOUND resistance inside the bunker … startled guards in ugly green fought back, armed with the same AK-74s Via, Nena and Mandy bore. Still as reliable as the AK-47s, just better. Punchy. Deadly.

The small company from *The Ark* was outnumbered but not outgunned.

Keyontay, for one, was amazing. He defied gravity as he flew into the compound, leaping up the sides of the walls, dodging bullets and ducking into one room and then the next, dispatching the enemy one by one using only a single sidearm.

Pei-chin was incredible.

She followed in Keyontay's wake, rushing down the center of the long hall. One would never be able to know how the streams of lead filling the hall didn't hurt her. The enemy's assault rifles all seemed to be aimed straight for her as she stormed into the fray. She launched her lithe frame up into the air, spinning … like a spear spiraling through the air, a diver shooting off the high-dive into a layout full twist, a gymnast using her momentum to launch off the vault. And she landed sliding on her back over the smooth tiled floor's slick surface with a *Skorpion* vz.61 submachine gun in each hand. Her weapons spit out their bullets into the open doorways on either side of the hall while the enemies' bullets continued ripping through the air just above her determined face.

Pei-chin's guns spent their last rounds as the bullets coming from the end of the hall started angling down towards the crown of her head. Still on her back, she slid to a stop, let go of the *Skorpions* and they clattered to the imported tile. Her quick hands then nimbly assembled a crossbow whose composite pieces were strapped to each of her small thighs, and she became immersed in deep time as the ancient weapon of her ancestors readied itself and the first arrow found its place inside of its groove.

Her Tartar ouabain-tipped quarrels, unleashed in rapid succession, found their marks and pierced skin, delivering the poison. Men dropped to the floor as Pei-chin effortlessly whirled herself into a crouching position, readying another series of shots. She was interrupted by an enemy bullet that dug into her shirt, lodging underneath the cotton twill into the China doll's impenetrable rhino hide vest. Fashioned long ago in the dusty mountains of northern Mongolia, her leather shield warded off death, despite the impact that pushed her back onto her heels. Recovering, she quickly sent another volley of arrows that would have been unmatched by a dozen expert archers.

The trigger release mechanism of Pei-chin's ultra-modern version of the medieval crossbow clicked in quick succession as she fed it with feathered shafts bearing lethal fluid-dipped heads. One after the other, each found their target with deadly precision. Not one arrow spent without dropping its prey, her marksmanship perfect, her eyes narrowed into a sharp piercing gaze. The fluid movements of the nimble soldier from ancient China's mystique continued her dance with death. Her adversaries didn't stand a chance. There was a certain beauty to her ballet as she dodged and moved and rolled, advancing down the hall.

Pei-chin flew.

Running on a cloud that rose up from the Earth. An island mist. An oceanic fog. A Polynesian steam of salty air that lifted her tiny frame above the fray.

Arrows whispered, cutting through air.

The oriental arbalester ran on silken slippers, threading shafts stripped from strong bamboo. Zhangjiajie. Hunan's rocky spires. They grew the sinewy stalks that Great Panda's chewed. She used their strength to make the compact spears. The feathered vanes aft each arrow finned of angled filigree for perfect shots. Her aim was deadly. The projectiles dropped each enemy soldier as efficiently as a member of a Mongol horde at the point of a horseback surge.

Such a small figure. A lissome waif. Hardly the body-type for a fearsome warrior. Naomi was awestruck.

It was inspiring.

The rest continued to secure the building, doing their respective parts. Naomi let off a shot that dropped a man who'd jumped out from hiding. She ducked into an open doorway and dropped to the floor. Peering back out, she saw Pei-chin still advancing: the choreography of the paleographer. Like artful strokes of poetry. A swirl of mandarin characters running down a page of pressed rice. Paintbrush marks of black in the foreground, serene blue waterfalls and pale mauve bamboo in the back. Pei-chin's martial arts-inspired waltz down the hall loading and releasing her Mongoloid darts eventually neutralized Roland's force.

While the ancient languages expert raced to the end of the hall with her bow leveled and her eyes shining black, Via's small force made it to the elevator bank and pressed the call button.

ENSON PUSHED BACK hard to foil the plan of salvation.

Silently, an army of angels came to lend assistance.

For freedom.

Former victims would be plucked from their hell, taken back above ground, destined for the safety of *The Piper Dolphin*.

The South Pacific sun brightened. A deep but translucent yellow and hot white flame. Then a brilliant orange with hints of red along the circumference. Brilliant light bouncing off a clean blue sky.

AS VIA'S TEAM boarded elevators to head down to the lab to help Michelle's force, Naomi made sure to head for the elevator sans Ibn. Not that she didn't like him, or trust him, for she had a newfound respect for him. Ibn had been portraying himself as some kind of father figure, but now that image was transformed into one of a forefather of sorts, like a founding father, way too old to be.... Naomi's respect had been for the scholar. Now, her respect was more of ... like that which she had for a wild beast.

After all, who's to say what might happen on the way down inside the same elevator with Ibn? Ibn had obviously *translated* himself and Heinrich to The Brandenburg, then added Mandy and the trunks to translate back out, appearing on Bariloche's Gaza road. Add walking on water all in one day, and she just didn't trust being with him in a confined space for a one mile trip into the heart of Tuvalu's depths.

They were almost a mile down the shaft when Naomi laughed.

"What's so funny?" from a World War II veteran standing next to her. Heinrich looked near death, yet nearly a centenarian, was *so much younger* than Ibn. That's what had struck her as so funny, but she didn't mean to laugh out loud.

"Did you hear that?" she asked him about her unintended laugh.

"*Si,*" in a thick German accent.

Then he laughed.

"What's so funny?" she now wondered.

"Just the name of this Island."

"It is a funny name."

"We were going to call it *Gröberland*."

"The Germans had their eyes on Tuvalu?"

"Ellice."

"Why? Whatever for? It's too small for a military base. Maybe a bigger airstrip?"

"Copra."

"Coconuts? Hitler was planning an invasion of nine remote Pacific atolls for *coconuts?*"

"And silicon."

"Tuvalu's a computer chip manufacturing center?"

"No."

Then she gave him a confused look.

"Great beaches," Heinrich explained. "Germans have always preferred the South Pacific to the Med."

Uncontrollably, she wondered where Stalin sunbathed. Then came the image of Kim Jong-il in a bathing suit in the tropics. "Actually, Heinrich, I've been thinking about Ibn and the Bible."

"Yes?"

"Philip *was translated*. He didn't *choose* to translate himself," Naomi posed.

"The scriptures are silent on that point," said the old scholar.

"I never thought about it that way. What about the doctrine of Apostolic Signs?" spoken by the Baptist.

"That the miracles performed by the early Church were limited for that time?" responded the Catholic.

"The belief that only the Apostles were given the miraculous gifts," returned the Baptist, always a student.

"And that the laying on of hands by Jesus and the Twelve was the only way to pass the gifts along ... stringent limits to apostolic succession? There is *nothing* in the Bible that supports any doctrine that God has stopped doing miracles through his people. The God who sent the animals into Noah's Ark, confused the folk at Babel, parted the Red Sea, fed the 5000 with a single school lunch, raised people from the dead, and supernaturally reversed Babel at Pentecost ... that *he* would, all of a sudden, *stop* doing what *he's* always done?" responded the Catholic scholar and willing teacher.

"The same yesterday, today and…." Naomi mused.

Heinrich interrupted her, "Are you familiar with Reinhard Bonnke?

"Yes." She was.

"He takes the Scriptures at face value. Like a child."

"The faith of a little child," Naomi whispered.

"You *cannot* enter the Kingdom of God unless you come as a little child." Wisdom.

"In Matthew, Jesus complained to his disciples right after the Transfiguration that they still had *little* faith. He said that *if* we have faith, we can say to a mountain, '… be removed and cast into the sea,' and it shall be done," Naomi recalled.

"*Nothing* shall be impossible for you," Heinrich added.

"In the last chapter of Mark it says we will drink poison and it will not harm us," she agreed.

"St. Paul was bitten by a deadly snake. Lethal. The folk on the island of Malta stared in wonder that he didn't just drop dead," he complemented.

"Acts 28," she said.

"Right." Unity.

She thought about the *reality* of the Scriptures. What they *really* meant. Then she thought about what she knew of Ibn. "I'm glad I'm not on Ibn's lift," she said.

A PROBLEM, something was wrong. Ibn sensed it immediately as his elevator began to drop. Ibn felt fear but he knew what he must do and do it quickly.

IN HIS MIND he saw his great grandfather. A king in his own right. An explorer. A valiant man. Rugged, yet refined. Climbing ancient peaks with Ibn's grandfather. Surveying the great white North. Hiking to the top of the globe. His grandfather had returned from their last trip downcast and ill. He'd breathed his last by the end of the following day.

Ibn had been there. At his grandfather's bed. Listened to his final words. They'd stuck with him now for so many years it was part of his history. Part of his make-up. Part of who he had become. Ibn's father had been bedside as well. Praying. Holding the dying man's hand. Rebecca boiling water.

"He needs to turn back" Ibn's grandfather had said.

"Granddad will be okay. He knows what he's doing," Ibn's father had replied.

"It's not that. He has good men with him. The best. I don't mean his expedition." His speech halted. His breathing faltered. His face paled ever further. Rebecca came back with a steaming wet cloth and laid it across her father-in-law's forehead.

Ibn cried.

"No," his grandfather croaked. "I mean ... to God. Papa needs to return to God."

"He will." Ibn's father spoke with confidence.

"If he doesn't...." The dying frame coughed and shook. Foamed bubbles of blood. Mucous seeped out of the corners of his cracked lips. "He will drown."

"The world...." Ibn had started to interject. But his father's strong hand upon his chest held him back.

Ibn loved his grandfather. He loved their talks. This was their last.

Ibn never forgot it. He had witnessed every word. He'd been there.

AND NOW, INSIDE the elevator, he couldn't breathe.

Without anyone noticing, he disappeared.

*   *   *

BEAR WAS LEFT alone with Charlie's lifeless body.

Joshua and Miguel left the office in a hurry, and Bear stood facing the corpse all alone. He felt like he was at the edge of a new Narnia. But the deceased was not a Christ-type beast with shaven mane. The dead body belonged to his dear friend.

An internal eulogy erupted in his heart.

Charlie had been a budding philologist. If one could attain to such a lofty title, Charlie certainly would. His studies of literature took him into the ancients – from Cervantes to Plato to Homer to Moses: the fiction, the non-fiction, the poetry, the prose, the lyrical, the mythical, the fanciful, and the true. His studies had led him into the antiquities and then back again.

When Charlie had called Cornerstone to enroll in Dr. Carroll's program he'd found out the Christian Indiana Jones had moved to Texas. Why do all of the cool Christians end up in Texas?

With Carroll having left Grand Rapids, the surfer decided upon U of O. He'd already made plans to go from there to Oxford. He'd been trying to find C. S. Lewis' mantel left on the banks of the Jordan. Hoping to pick up Tolkien's ring. Digging for Joyce's brilliance and learning from P. D. James and the Brontë sisters. Bear's friend had been immersed in the best.

And now Charlie was gone. But Miguel had shown him hope: the way of faith, of taking the Bible literally, believing the promises of Christ for what they are – promises kept.

He says I'm supposed to raise him from the dead, Bear thought.

How in the world am I supposed to do that?

"*You* don't."

I didn't say anything out loud. I don't talk to *corpses*. Even if they are my best friend.

"You were praying."

"I was?" startled, he spoke.

"Yes."

"Oh."

"Bear. I've heard your prayer."

Suddenly Bear became overwhelmed with the presence of God. Like Moses who spoke to God face to face. Like Ezekiel who fell on his face before the Lord in his tent. Like the Elder on the Island of Patmos.

First he felt it in his heart ... an overwhelming love that washed over him. Then he was lifted up from the physical. A new world opened up to him. His eyes were denied any participation and his ears weren't picking up the audible. But he heard every word clearly. Pronounced. Powerful. Perfect.

Faith blossomed. The mustard seed had borne fruit. Hope was fulfilled. Trust was rewarded. Bear had truly believed what Miguel had asked him to read. He'd read each Biblical passage on miracles, especially Jesus' promise that we would do even greater things. He accepted the truth of it. He approached the Word as would a child – with complete trust.

That's what made all of the difference.

"Jesus?" Bear breathed.

"That's right."

"I don't see you."

"My sheep know my voice."

"From the Gospel of John," Bear breathed.

"The disciple whom I loved."

"Papias, Bishop of Hieropolis, called him The Presbyter."

"I love you just as much as I love John."

"What about Charlie?" In a tone reminiscent of the persistent Syrophoenician woman.

* * *

"MUSIC IS THE silence between the notes."

"What?

"Claude Debussy. He said it."

The doors to the lift parted. Armed daughters and sons rushed into a heated battle already underway. But Naomi and Heinrich stayed put. The doors slid back, shielding them from the danger and blocking off the sounds of the fight.

"What do you mean?" she asked.

"When *he* created music...."

"Jesus."

"Yes. When he created it, he was teaching us about his nature. The fusion of perfect math with perfect art. Doubling frequencies at each octave. Twelve chromatic tones within each. Seven and five in harmonic sequencing like a DNA strand spiraling up the circle of fifths in sharps and back down again, counterclockwise, in flats. But if Debussy, the master composer and pianist, was right, it reveals a lot about our Creator."

"Like Romans One."

"Right."

"So when I read my Bible, it's just as important what it doesn't say as what it does say."

"Exactly." The old German bowed his head and pulled his Mauser from its holster. He stiffened and straightened his back and lifted his chin. With great resolve he pushed the button to reopen the doors. "Doctrines of men," he concluded, "are based on the twisting of verses. Like I Corinthians 13:10. They need to pay more attention to the silence between the notes."

And with that the doors reopened, and he rushed out into the fray.

His pistol leading the way.

Within seconds, his tall, thin frame disappeared into the action. His crenulated visage transformed – jumping into the battle was the young SS officer trying to undo his past.

Naomi rushed out too, her left arm still in a sling. Inspired and now invigorated, she too resolved to try to undo her own past. We all have one. Our regret, guilt, and shame are supposed to be temporary – important and helpful – to bring us to repentance and to teach us and others valuable lessons. But the feelings aren't supposed to depress us for the rest of our lives. No sin, no crime, deserves a lifetime of punishment. Revenge seeks it, but only hate owns revenge, it doesn't own justice.

We all need to be forgiven. We need to experience redemption. We need to learn how to forgive others and we need to learn how to receive forgiveness. That's part of what makes us human.

IT WAS EXTREMELY bloody.

Especially in light of the plethora of red balloons.

A lab of bags filled with plasma.

It seemed every airborne projectile passed through a bag of O-positive.

Blood was everywhere.

The cloned DNA washed the place.

Then the lab started to fill with seawater. There had been a breach somewhere that had let in the sea.

Cold.

From the black underside of the ocean.

From the muddy murk of the Pacific's floor.

A putrid smell. Sulfuric from nearby volcanic vents.

Mud mixed with the decayed flesh of giant tube worms.

Everyone scattered.

WALKER APPEARED.

Joshua stood in the center of the oncoming flood.

He grabbed an IV tree: the metal tube like a coat rack, bearing bags of penicillin, plasma, and poison in clear plastic bladders, all with tendrils of lines that appeared like jellyfish frantically flung aside. The professor struck the foot-high rise of the cold saltwater. The head of his staff sunk into the wash. The thud muddled its muted clank under the heavy waters as the staff hit hard cement under the blanket of the black and angry surge.

They gathered around the tip of his pole as if a cyclone started spinning great waves. Trying to expose Davy's Locker. Skeletons of great ships no longer grand. Junked on the bottom. Dead. Even their remains still dying, unseen and forgotten.

The blood that had spilled mixed into the saline slide of oncoming pour from the breach. A broken wall? A valve intentionally opened? A floodgate that wouldn't close as designed? The onslaught of seawater continued to rush into the lab's vast cavern. Walker's eyes were pressed shut as he held the makeshift staff against the concrete floor. His voice whispering petitions of grace. Mercy for the saved. An exit for the people freed from their bondage. Still pursued by Enson's chariots. Weapons still firing. A volley still being exchanged inside the under-island cave. Filling the lab like a sunken treasure chest whose airtight seal had finally given up the ghost.

And the sea turned red.

The water level reached the professor's thighs. Quickly rising. Chilling. But Joshua continued to hold his ground. His eyes shuttered open to see. His staff touching the floor in front of him. His rear guard unguarded. He said a single word. A name. He spoke it loudly, "Jesus."

And the angry waters churning around his legs receded. Retreated. Ran. For the power of the Name Above All Names binds on Earth as effectively as in Heaven.

If you believe.

Christ's own promise to His followers.

Exercised now by Dr. Joshua Walker in the way intended by the Lord.

He stood his dry ground and fended off more of the water's rush. Made a channel, an escape route.

Naomi watched the awesome sight from her crouching perch atop a countertop, unavoidably picturing Moses leading the children of Israel out of Egypt into Sinai … the parting of the Red sea.

This Red Sea was colored by the blood of a hundred broken bags. A crimson tide. Bags busted by bullets. For some reason, Naomi figured that the blood red sea now carried life. A small part of God. Though a counterfeit of red and white cells cloned from the DNA of Immanuel God, it was as if life came from it anyway. She thought about Paul's admonition that though some preach Christ spurred by improper motives, it is still good because the gospel is being preached. She thought about how God works good from those things man intends for evil. And Naomi started to cry. Tears of joy. She sang.

There is power, power
Wonder working power
In the blood of the Lamb

There is power, power
Wonder working power
In the precious blood of the Lamb

JOSHUA HEARD HER beautiful voice. Rich. Deep. Negro. Spiritual. Not Baltimore's inner city. Not D.C. nor Houston. What he heard was the voices of over two thousand faithful souls crowding into the Pee Dee Baptist Church, South Carolina soul. Naomi's creamy tones rose up above the malaise. Her song moved the room. The melody. The rhythm. The lyrics. Combined they gave strength to the prophet. The apostle with the IV pole. The man who would teach and then demonstrate the truth of the lecture. Search history and dig into the dirt to uncover the reality of our past. The instructor who had learned patience through long years of toil on the Earth.

Her voiced comforted him, made him stronger. His muscles flexed. He took in a deep breath. His chest rose under his squared jaw. He clenched his teeth, letting the corners of his lips curve up into a crooked smile.

Suddenly the rest of the water burst into a cloud of steam. Evaporated in less than ten seconds after the liquid turned to gas. The flood simply disappeared. The blood, however, stayed.

The room was covered in blood. Stained. Cleansed. The entire place awash in *God's* color – his robe stained red with God's own life-giving force again given away so that we could have life.

Eternal life – Naomi was just now beginning to understand what had happened to Ibn so many years ago. It was a type of things to come. Spiritual bodies. Promised by God Himself. Enoch received his long ago. She didn't have hers yet. But she would. Someday.

Drowning once. No more. The empty beds a testimony of God's undying grace. Men and women who'd been destined to die. Now saved. Life given back. Another chance. Redemption. Pardoned by the Master. The freed captives moved with joy of freedom toward the elevator doors.

The lifts were ready to move.

Gaped with open arms.

Metal panels slid back.

Those saved by the real Blood entered.

The lifts lifted them up.

To freedom and safety and to a new life.

This time Pharaoh wouldn't follow.

The walls of water now broke back into the lab. The parted sea no longer held back by God. The pocket of oxygen mixed inside nitrogen's realm strained to keep back a new and much more powerful flood. Rushing back in over the path of dry ground that had been created for God's people to escape.

Lights sparked.

Power failed.

Shorted out. Flickering.

And the entire lab was plunged into darkness.

Black.

Like the bottom of the sea.

* * * * *

THE MISSING MARK, now a misnomer, was safely tucked away. Miguel saw to it that it was placed deep under Vatican City: sort of on display inside a little chapel under the cross – both recovered and now safe.

The Shroud? The real one, and the Turin body-double, were put on *public* display in two different places. Via is happy, her heavy burden now gone.

Bear? He had *barely* prayed. But his mustard seed of faith continued to grow in exponential proportions. He, along with a *very alive* Dr. Charlie Farris, *raised* by Jesus, both earned their PhDs and are now full professors in Rome. Just like the Pope promised.

Curious thing about Bear – right after he started teaching in Rome, he started claiming that Prester John was *real!* He reported that he'd received a phone call from the medieval priest-king. Can you believe that? Bear claimed that the presbyter had gone by Yuhanna for some time but now missed his more Western title … said something about having discarded his obcaecation. John had been blind?

Ibn, by the way, when he had sensed a problem ... that something was wrong, was the one who got José out of the elevator shaft. Ibn brought Heaven's Throne to a very humbled José. Indeed, it was a funny sight when they both appeared on the beach, Ibn in his robe and José wearing those funny metal wings.

Heinrich traveled to London with Mandy. Nena stayed by Via's side. Charlie started dating Michelle. Pei-chin returned to Beijing. And Joshua and Sarah? What happened to them is another whole story. A book in itself.

José and Arkesha, still very much in love, teamed up with the Admiral and have experienced some success with their inventions. The Admiral was up to old tricks still playing around with new inventions.

"For Pete's sake, Admiral, what are you up to now, with all of the tricks you already have aboard?" Via asked on her last visit inside *The Ark*.

"A board? Games won't work without a better engine."

"What?"

"Duplication," he said. "If I can build a better engine, I can change the game. Design *The Ark* so it can be reproduced." He smiled.

Epilogue

Dad,

With my own hand, I write of these things, having seen them with my own eyes and heard of them with my own ears. I wrote these things, to borrow the Presbyter's own words, that we should know this testimony is true. There are so many other things that happened to me that I want to share with you. If I were to write all of them one by one, I suppose that even the universe itself could not contain the books that would be written.

It's been another 6000 years since these events first happened. To write you, dad, and tell you my story has been my dream for a very, very long time. After Tuvalu, I saw many more things that I want to share with you, and in my next letter, I will. I want to strengthen your faith. To encourage you if you are still locked up when you get this. And I assume I've left a lot of unanswered questions. I really don't mean to leave you hanging, but my letter had to end at some point in the story. It is quite a long letter already, you will have to admit.

I promise you that I will address them when I write again.

If you choose to publish this letter, please don't use my real name. Oh, and you can pick any title you want. I was thinking about *Missing the Mark*, as a working title, at least. The manuscript was missing, of course, and its final conclusion was missing because of the water stain. But mostly because of Enson so badly missing the mark in his own misguided quest. Then, of course, there is also the fact that I miss you so much. But also, I like it because we've all missed God's mark of perfection. We all need redemption. Some of us just recognize it sooner than others.

I do have a specific title in mind already for the second book. If you choose to publish my letters, of course. It's *969*. When you read my next letter you will quickly understand why I like it so much. It reveals secrets, including the fate of Sander the Macedonian.

Only God knows how to get these letters to you back through time.

Appelgelic came by one day while I was writing.

He told me you'd been seen in the West. He'd heard your mansion was on a beach, and that you'd even called your palatial home "Santa Barbara."

It is so amazing being here with Jesus of Nazareth on the New Earth in Year 12,295, that is if you count from Genesis One. I've seen angels and sons of God swaying and singing the most glorious of psalms inside the beauty of the New Jerusalem. One thousand four hundred vertical miles of walls of layered precious stones and still not enough to contain the glory of our Savior.

I'm sorry I disappeared on you. I've never stopped wanting desperately to make it up to you. My own quest for redemption has been my unending search for you. I know you are here. Somewhere. I even checked the Lamb's Book of Life. Just to make sure. And, of course, your wonderful name was there. Inscribed in the purest gold.

This New Earth is huge. They say it's a hundred times the size of the last one. No Great Sea, but lots of beaches. But I will find you, dad. Writing this letter, telling my story, this is the first step. You will get my letter, years ago, and then you will know, back then, that I am looking for you now. Still, even now.

So, dad, as you read this, know that I love you dearly. And take heart in knowing this —
that like Enoch, like Elijah, like Ibn, Miguel, Joshua and all the rest,
from the day you first held me on your knee,
from then, until now, over six thousand years later....
Just like the other sons of God who'd passed from life to life,
I never died.

Love,
Your daughter

P.S. Dad, I forgot to mention ... writing my story could not have been possible without the selfless help of so many of my friends and family. First, and foremost, I have to acknowledge that Sarah is the one who gave me much of the factual information that I was not personally privy to. She spent hours with me on the banks of the River of Life while I typed into my MacBook Millennial.

I must also extend my thanks back through the countless ages to Ibn, Heinrich, Miguel, the Admiral, José, Arkesha, Cyril, Bear and Charlie. For through them I learned certain facets of the story that I could have no other way of knowing. The Admiral's help was invaluable and the books he gave me were wonderfully helpful. Jolly was my resident weaponry expert, thank you Jolly. Ray was of great assistance in prayer and encouragement. And, of course, José and Arkesha were incredible. Bear and Charlie both helped me fill in the blanks, and Cyril gave me his detailed recollection of those endless meetings in Istanbul right after the shroud was stolen. I could not have begun to write down all of what he'd shared, but I did my best to give you a flavor of what those meetings were like. Ibn was actually here with me too. He would pace up and down and stare off into the healing leaves of the Tree of Life. He was actually the first one to read my letter to you and give me some feedback on the story I shared. So, if I've made any errors, they are all — Ibn's. Ha ha!

Then there is Rachel, Prester John's daughter. She was amazing. I'd not really known the history of the medieval priest king until she found me writing my story. She is so sweet. Skipping up to me, her lithe and athletic frame so carefree, her face always smiling with youthful enthusiasm. Her first question was that of a young child. "What are you doing?"

I shared the story with her, at least as far as I had written as of that time. I think I had just finished the scene at Dutch Bros. in Eugene. When she heard about the discussion my friends were having about her father, she sat down next to me and told me the most amazing story I have ever heard. But I have only been able to hint at it in this letter. It is so incredible, dad, that I had to save most of it for my next letter. You are going to love it.

Finally, I must thank Lawrence, Mark, Jeff, Nick, Tony, Ricardo, Ambir, Vaughn, Herb, Studivant, Alex, Marilyn, Wyngate, Tozer, Stephen, Stan, Warren, John, Eric, Lewis, Tolkien and all of the rest who gave me their insight and wisdom as I worked on writing all of this down for you. Oh, and James. He gave me copies of the pictures he took in Buenos Aires and Istanbul. But most of all, above all of those mentioned and even those I've unintentionally omitted, the Spirit of Christ helped move my pencil, my heart and my mind to remember all the little details that I'd forgotten so long ago.

I will start working on my next letter to you now, dad. I should be able to post it back in time to you supernaturally, soon.

I love you!!!

AUTHOR'S NOTES

THE USE OF the phrase "sons of God" appears in Genesis 6, Job 1 and 2 and Job 38. Within the same context, the phrase appears nowhere else in all of Scripture. That is, the phrase appears in the New Testament but within a different context. In the Old Testament, the phrase is clearly used to refer to a class of beings who have both the ability to appear in Heaven before God and have physical, sexual intercourse with female human beings. The Joshua Walker novels propose through their fictional characters, that it is possible that the phrase "sons of God" as used in the Old Testament applies to individuals such as Enoch and Elijah. The Joshua Walker series utilizes fiction to suggest that it is possible that these two men became "sons of God" when they ascended to Heaven without first dying. The theory includes the logical assumption that a mortal, physical, fallen man cannot ascend to Heaven without first being transformed into a spiritual body as described in I Corinthians 15. Further down this road of rationale is the possibility that Christ's body, following his Resurrection, is an example of a spiritual body like those promised to us in I Corinthians 15. Thus, it is possible that his demonstration of being able to both eat food and walk through walls is applicable to us as well once we are clothed in the immortal body promised at our own resurrection from the dead. Certainly, Jesus had already promised much in terms of supernatural miracles available to us through the power of prayer and his Holy Spirit (for example Mark 11:22-24 and John 14: 12-14).

I have always been intrigued by the stories in the Old Testament that mention, ever so briefly, this enigmatic group called "sons of God." Who were these individuals who married "daughters of men" and produced "heroes of old"? Learned theologians do not know, and they do not agree on any one theory. There is a majority that argues that "sons of God" refers to fallen angels. Another group of Bible scholars hold to the view that the phrase describes the male descendants of Seth, Adam's third son. Finally, there is a smaller sect that adheres to the opinion that "sons of God" is meant to classify a group of angels still in right standing with God. I am not convinced.

That the "sons of God" may be angels, fallen or otherwise, does not make any sense to me. This is because in Genesis 6 the "sons of God" married and had children with "daughters of men." Jesus made it clear in Matthew 22 that angels do not marry nor are given in marriage. The implication is that angels do not procreate as well. The Bible certainly nowhere implies that angels are equipped with reproductive organs. And even if they were, would that allow angels or demons the ability to procreate with humans any more than animals can cross outside their species? Furthermore, if Genesis 6 intends a reference to either angels or demons, why not use the actual terms, or one of the other common words or phrases used to denote "angel" or "fallen angel" that are used throughout the Bible? This point is not only true to the passage in Genesis 6, but equally so to the references to "sons of God" in Job chapters 1 and 2. Interestingly, the only Old Testament reference to "sons of God" that appears to make sense that it would refer to angels (and not to demons) is the one in Job 38. However, again, the most poignant query that should be made is the same: If the passage intends to convey that angels are the actors, why is not a common word or phrase utilized that is used to describe angels elsewhere in the Bible? Why use the phrase "sons of God" *only* in these four, very unique passages in Scripture?

The group that argues that "sons of God" are the male descendants of Seth usually try to make the case that Genesis 6 is relaying a historical account of the "godly line of humans" in contrast with the "ungodly line of the descendants of Cain." In response, I posit that if God intended to convey this, surely he would have used a reference to Seth or otherwise made such a clear connection. Likewise, if a godly line of descendants is being described, why would the males be "of God" and the females "of men"? But the most telling reason that "sons of God" can't refer to "descendants of Seth" is the use of the phrase in Job 1, 2 and 38. Clearly, the use of "sons of God" in Job does not denote a "godly line of mortal humans descendent from Adam."

With all of this said, please know that I don't think it truly matters which of the theories are correct. Whether "sons of God" is meant to classify a group of angels, demons, Sethites, or individuals in their glorified bodies is not central to the Gospel of Jesus Christ nor even important to the Kingdom of God and our responsibilities to our Creator. But it is interesting. And fiction is a fun venue for postulating my own theories and their implications. For example, if Enoch and Elijah are both "sons of God," who were the "sons of God" mentioned in Job 38? Where did they come from? When did God create them? And if one can become a "son of God" without dying, is it possible for one to become a "son of God" with a glorified body following a physical death and prior to the resurrection? Like, perhaps, Moses? The transfiguration interestingly casts the figure of Moses in the exact same manner as a glorified body of Christ and an ascended body of Elijah.

The implications are certainly fun to think about. And fiction is supposed to be fun. The Joshua Walker series is entertainment, but it is more than just a group of novels designed for your enjoyment. They are meant to intrigue you … to challenge you … to help you find new truths in the Word of God. And not necessarily the truths that the novels suggest are there. I am not a theologian. And I am not preaching or teaching doctrine. I am simply trying to bring issues to your attention that God addresses in the Bible. And my sincere hope is that you pick up your Bible. Read it. Study it. Enjoy it. And pray. Ask God to reveal the Truth of His Word to you. He is an expert at doing just that.

So I have used the mystery of the "sons of God" as a backdrop for the Joshua Walker novels and hope my own theory regarding the meaning of the phrase is refreshing and challenging and interesting and fun. I hope that avid fiction readers as well as serious students of the Bible find the enigma worthy of study and contemplation. Discussion. Perhaps a long walk and accompanying talk with God. He likes it when we ask questions.

But I have not stopped there. "Sons of God" is not the only mystery in the Bible that I find entirely engaging. I have had an intense interest in the Holy Scriptures since I heard my first Sunday school lesson. For example, *The Missing Mark*, the title of the first book in the series, in part, refers to the fact that Mark's Gospel has several different endings. When I first read a Bible that published a "shorter ending" and "longer ending" of Mark, I was amazed and my curiosity was piqued. As a result, I studied the issue in depth and found that no one really knew which ending, if any of them, is the original ending (or if it was ever completed at all, for that matter). Thus, my central theme of Book One. In the second book, *969*, I am exploring, among other Biblical mysteries, another big one for me: What happened during the 1500 years of history chronicled in Genesis 5? Did not the Great Deluge erase or completely bury what we could have learned through archeology? Adam lived for 930 years. If Euclid, Leonardo de Vinci, Newton, or Einstein had 930 years to explore their world, what would they have accomplished?

I have also brought a few soteriological and eschatological matters into the mix, in *The Missing Mark*, in *969*, in *Sons of God*, and especially in the fourth book in the Series, *Heroes of Old*. In the first book, for example, there is a little known doctrine called *apokastasis* which was promoted by Father Origen and then his followers, the Origenists. Interestingly, this doctrine is fundamentally the same as that which is espoused by Rob Bell in his recent book, *Love Wins*. My treatment of the issue is both part of an entertaining exchange between Heinrich and Ibn, and an attempt to look at the Biblical issue of redemption from a fresh perspective. The Bible clearly disagrees with Rob Bell's modern Origenism, but it is possible that it doesn't support the common perception of salvation either. Most of the soteriological issues are addressed in *The Missing Mark* and most of the eschatological questions are covered in *Sons of God*. In *969* one of my favorite Bible mysteries I attempt to solve is the route Noah and/or his descendants took from Ararat to Babel. Not that it has any spiritual significance, but that it is fun to figure out the history of mankind through the revelations contained within the Word of God.

Obviously, some of what my characters discuss is highly controversial. For example, I have placed fictional characters in hell who are then raised from the dead. Jesus addressed one of the issues surrounding a soul in hell by telling a parable of the beggar Lazarus and the rich man. But his parable doesn't address every issue one might ask. For example, if the body of one who is not a believer is raised from the dead (let's say, by way of example, that the widow of Nain's son that Jesus raised from the dead had already gone to hell), would not that individual still have an opportunity to accept Christ? And, if that is the case, why would being raised from the dead have any spiritual significance? Or, to put it another way, why would one's physical death have any spiritual significance? That is, where does the Bible teach that our ability to accept Christ ends upon our physical death?

Surely, the Bible does teach that there is a moment in time when it will be too late to accept Jesus' gift of salvation. For some, it appears that moment may precede a physical death (e.g. the unforgiveable sin), and for all of us, the Bible is clear that the Great White Throne of Judgment is a final deadline. But does the scripture teach that physical death is an important date in whether or not the gift of eternal life is still available to us? I don't know. But I think it is important for us to study the Bible to find out.

Then, of course, there is the mystery of Revelation 22:15. The Old Earth has passed away. The New Earth has been created by our Loving Creator. The New Jerusalem has descended from the New Heaven and stretches for 1400 miles east to west and 1400 miles north to south in a single walled metropolis that would run diagonally from America's coast to coast. And Christ himself resides among us, lighting the city without need for a sun. Yet, we read that there are horribly evil people who reside "outside the city." Mind you, this is following the Great White Throne of Judgment where all of those who have rejected God's plan for salvation are thrown into the Lake of Fire with the Devil and his angels. So where did these evil people come from? Is it possible that we return to the state Adam and Eve found themselves in prior to the fall of Eden? Does that state involve real choice ... free will ... along with the choice to reject God once again? If not, then what of love? How can love exist without free will?

So, suffice it to say, I try to raise some interesting issues in the novels. And The Joshua Walker series is meant to raise important spiritual issues. It is designed to get you to read your Bible ... to ask crucial questions about the Scriptures and our relationship with God, and to ask yourself some not so crucial questions as well, and to see what the Bible has to say about those too. Although many of the issues I raise can be very controversial, I do not wish to stir up trouble. Debate can be healthy, but it can be divisive and destructive too. I learned a while back that many of our doctrinal differences do not have to divide us as they do. In fact, the vast majority of the time, our differences in beliefs don't even affect our actions. And with our actions, that is, our duty to God in our daily walk, in concert, why argue over beliefs that do not color our behavior? They do not change how we view our responsibilities to God or to each other. Do we not all agree on the core of the Gospel of Jesus? Do we not all agree on the import of the greatest commandment? And the second?

CPSIA information can be obtained at www.ICGtesting.com
Printed in the USA
BVOW04s1941260314

348734BV00001B/1/P